PRA

Morgan Is My Name

"With equal attention to politics and witchcraft, Keetch's exploration of Morgan's growth shows how the perspective of men has warped the character over the years. Fans of Arthurian legends retold will not want to miss this." —*Publishers Weekly*

"A breath of fresh air . . . The sort of reinvention that every woman in Arthurian lore deserves." —*Paste Magazine*

"A very real, passionate retelling of Morgan le Fay's story, with detail about political and magical lives, and the women who are such a vital part of the tale." —Tamora Pierce, #1 *New York Times* bestselling author

"This is the powerfully feminist, intricately woven, and realistically enchanting Arthurian tale you've been waiting for. Morgan is her name, and I love her." —Kiersten White, #1 *New York Times* bestselling author of the Camelot Rising trilogy

"Compelling and poignant, Sophie Keetch's prose is as mesmerizing as the ocean's tides, illuminating Morgan's life with a deft and attentive hand. Built on the bones of exquisite longing and unsung power, *Morgan Is My Name* portrays a woman forging her own path and reclaiming her story. A stunning delight." —Rebecca Ross, #1 *New York Times* bestselling author of *Divine Rivals* and *Ruthless Vows*

LE FAY

SOPHIE KEETCH

RANDOM HOUSE CANADA

Library and Archives Canada Cataloguing in Publication

Title: Le Fay / Sophie Keetch.
Names: Keetch, Sophie, author.
Description: Series statement: The Morgan le Fay series ; 2
Identifiers: Canadiana (print) 20240305825 | Canadiana (ebook) 2024030585X
    | ISBN 9781039011953 (softcover) | ISBN 9781039011960 (EPUB)
Subjects: LCGFT: Fantasy fiction. | LCGFT: Novels.
Classification: LCC PR6111.E33 L44 2024 | DDC 823/.92—dc23

Cover design: © Andrew Davis
Text design: Emma Dolan
Typesetting: Erin Cooper

Printed in Canada

10 9 8 7 6 5 4 3 2 1

Penguin
Random House
RANDOM HOUSE CANADA

For Jason and Milo.
You are my home.

For thy sweet love remembered such wealth brings
That then I scorn to change my state with kings.

—Sonnet 29, William Shakespeare

UNLIKE TINTAGEL AND her insistent, roaring sea, there was little to wake a person in Camelot. The castle stood proud and encircled in glittering pale gold, rings of high battlements protecting all within from the slightest disturbance.

Silence reigned throughout the chambers, gardens and air, songbirds chased away by falconers on the orders of a Queen who preferred to rest undisturbed. Even the earliest bells rang softer through the cathedral's spires, confined to church cloisters and servants' halls, sounding at a distance for most castle sleepers. Beyond the walls, rolling hills dense with woodland cocooned the city in a warm embrace beneath a canopy of sky that rarely strayed from peace.

But in the distance, if I listened carefully enough, my ear would catch it, amid the flowering meadows and in the forest's swaying boughs; among the tall reeds beside the rivers, shimmering across the surface of the water: a chorus of wild birdsong, crystalline, defiant and free.

I

FOR A WHILE I had risen with the dawn.

Despite Camelot's cultivated peace, my sleep had never been easy, but in the weeks since May Day I had been driven from my bed ever earlier as the pleasant warmth of early summer built dramatically into heat, gaining day upon day until the air hung thick and breezeless within castle walls.

One morning on the cusp of Pentecost, I awoke in the grip of a feverish dream that slipped away the moment my eyes flew open. Stirred and restless, I kicked off the cloying sheets and pulled on a robe, walking through my reception chamber and out onto my terrace to greet the cloudless morning, sun already climbing towards another blazing day.

The flagstones were warm underfoot as I made my way to the balconied edge and sat on the wide balustrade, taking in the view of Camelot's high walls and the green faraway hills. Below, a secluded grove of castle gardens descended in stepped layers, cropped grass and flowered borders shaded by quince and plum trees, beginning to fruit with midsummer's sudden advance. All around me, only quiet and heat.

A close, whispering flutter cut into the stillness, and a lone magpie alighted beside me in a whir of light and dark.

"Good morning," I greeted it. "Aren't you a rare sight?"

The bird hopped closer, flight feathers iridescent in the sun—shades of blue-black and green edged with flashes of violet, like a dancing night sky. It regarded me with a keen inquisitiveness, and I looked down to see the gold coin I wore, glinting with my movements on its long, slim chain.

I laughed and lifted the pendant aloft, the magpie following its gleam. "Of course, the shining thing. No doubt you would steal it away, if you could."

"The Prioress at St. Brigid's used to say magpies were unholy."

I looked up as Alys appeared on the terrace, dressed in cornflower linen, her hair freshly braided in her usual fishtail plait. In her hand she held a pair of gardening shears.

The bird cawed in protest and flew off, landing a few feet away on a wooden arbour. Alys cast critical eyes over the terrace, along the potted rows of herb shrubs, fruiting bushes and medicinal flowers she had planted and nurtured, before taking her shears to a crowd of stiff blue irises.

I slipped off the balustrade and went to her. "I remember. She used to refuse to look the Abbess's pet magpie in the eye. She and our Queen would have rather got along."

Alys smiled, snipping with care. "Speaking of which—our day. The Queen's ladies are due in St. Stephen's to hear Mass with Her Highness at halfway Terce, then this afternoon in attendance. Hopefully she will allow us to sit outdoors, lest we melt."

"Fascinating as that sounds," I said, "I will not be there. I have a meeting with Sir Kay about the tournament."

"You've been little in her presence these past few weeks," Alys said. "It's been commented upon. She's not pleased."

"Guinevere will take any excuse to disapprove of me," I said. "If she still chooses to hold a grudge for what happened a year ago, so be it, but I'll not beg for her approval. The Pentecost tournament is Camelot's first, and of huge importance. I can hardly deny meetings with the Seneschal."

Not that I was inclined to try; I held a particular amity with Sir Kay, Arthur's prickly brother, who ran the Royal Household, an alliance I valued and trusted more than most.

"Besides," I went on, "how does the Queen think things get done? Given Arthur has seen fit to dash out of Camelot during his busiest court of the year."

"The King's absence *has* unsettled the solar," Alys said. "There's been nothing but speculation. The ladies claim even Her Highness doesn't know where he's gone."

I shrugged. "This court's gossip could fuel the winter fires in every royal palace from Cornwall to Orkney. Though it's a relief not to be the subject for once."

"Here you both are." A fair-headed figure in a striped surcoat emerged from the nearby doorway: Tressa, smiling and distracted by a disruption at the back of her skirts. "Lady Morgan, I have someone to see you. Now where did—ah!"

A small body sprung out, slipping expertly past Tressa and barrelling towards me.

"Mama!" Yvain cried.

I swooped down and captured my son of almost two years in my arms, swinging his ever-growing frame up onto my hip. He was pleasantly hot, like a spring sunbeam, and smelled of fresh dried linen and honeyed milk. As he laughed, I inhaled deeply of him, the sweet musk of baby sleep clinging to his dark-gold curls.

Impatient of my caresses, Yvain pushed himself back and studied me. "Mama," he said, serious this time, "I love you. I love *horses*."

"I know, dearest one," I said. "Uncle Arthur has promised to take you to the stables to meet his bravest steeds. But tonight, Mama will tell you a story about a flying horse, and I love *you* more than all the stars in the sky."

My son offered me a charming grin. In many ways, he favoured his father—the facial symmetry that would one day be handsome, his burnished colouring, the easy cheer he was already harnessing into confidence—but his eyes were all mine, the deep blue I shared with my own father before me. Yvain was all of us, and entirely himself.

"What will you do today, my precious eyas?" I asked him. "Riding, archery, slaying dragons?"

"Yes," he said enthusiastically.

"I'm sure he wishes as much," Tressa said. "He's determined to sit a pony by himself this summer. Today yields nothing so demanding. The day nurse says breakfast, then a walk to see the swans and, if he's willing, a midday nap."

Yvain looked unimpressed at the notion, twisting to get down. He ran to Alys, who offered him a cut iris, but he demurred, attempting instead to grab her shears. She put the blades out of reach and pulled her fierce leopard face at him, and he roared back.

Tressa laughed, tousling his curls as he ran off. "Bright as gold in a stream. Just like his lady mother."

Alys slipped an arm about Tressa's waist and kissed her, placing the bunch of irises in her hands. They shared a loving smile that filled me with happiness, and played a note of yearning that I tried to ignore. The magpie, still watching us, gave an impatient rasp.

Alys regarded it in consideration. "Where I'm from, a magpie signals the arrival of an unexpected guest. I don't suppose there's any word from the *invitation*?"

I glanced at my son, busy chasing an elusive butterfly. "No word yet, but between the offer to ride in the joust and Yvain's second birthday, we have to assume he will come."

"Encouraging his presence feels all wrong, given the circumstances."

"Arthur had to invite him, one King to another," I said. "But you may speak his name freely—he doesn't deserve so much power."

"You know what they say, my lady," Tressa said. "Dare not mention the Devil, lest he appear."

*

IT HAD BEEN twenty months since I had last seen my husband.

Two years, almost, since I had left King Urien of Gore, taking my son and what little I could carry and escaping his kingdom in the far northeast, of which I had been the fettered and frustrated Queen. Two years since I had reached my limit in enduring his lies, betrayals and flashes of violence, his presumption that my mind and body were his to control. Two years since I had set him alight with the fire of my rage, conjured in my own palm.

At first, inexplicably, Urien had wanted me back. Messenger after messenger arrived, bearing notes of demand, of exhortation, even charming persuasion. He *forgave me*, he claimed; he *understood*. My "accident" was an irrational act, the likes of which all women fall prey to. He missed me by his throne-side, at court banquets, in his bed. A queen should be in her country, he said; a wife with her husband—presumably whether he was faithful and loving or not. A son, he argued, should not grow up without the influence of his father.

I ignored his missives, having nothing further to say than when I left him in Castle Chariot's entrance hall, the mark of my burning on his face, and the curse on my lips that I would only ever return to Gore to kill him. Back then, I had meant every word of it; now, I preferred to pretend he didn't exist.

Then the threats began, promising all the punishments that the laws of marriage permitted, unless I obeyed him completely. In response, I burned every one of his letters and returned the ashes to him until he stopped sending them.

After that, Urien fell silent, which began as a relief but soon grew into something darker: a tactic, a threat, a way to hold my life in suspension.

When I arrived at Camelot in my flight for freedom, Arthur and I had decided that the simplest excuse for my long-term presence was for me to enter the service of Queen Guinevere as lady-in-waiting. I had long proved unsuited to such a life, but Urien could not insist upon my return if I was required to attend Her Highness. Therefore, I was safe so long as I lived to serve, but I could not step outside the Royal Household's edges, risk being seen breaking marital law, or make plans for any other sort of future.

Then there was Yvain, my son and Urien's heir, who I had carried off to Camelot.

"The rights of the father are God-given and absolute," Arthur's legal men said when I asked the futile question of my position. "Indisputable, and carved into the founding laws of this land." Mothers were mere vessels, if they were mentioned at all.

Urien could demand Yvain's return any time, yet he hadn't, and I assumed it was fear of my brother that was stopping him. I had told Arthur as much as I could bear about my marriage, excepting Urien's acts of violence and my one incendiary incident. He knew of the lies, the other women, the illegitimate child Urien had fathered and given the same name as our own son. But a husband could not commit adultery in the eyes of the law, whereas if I had been caught doing the same, a trial and the stake would have been my fate.

So Urien's supremacy as a father remained, enshrined in law and by God, whereas my presence in Yvain's life ultimately depended on my brother's influence. None of it could last, I knew that. One day soon, it was inevitable Urien and I would have to face one another again.

Meanwhile, I continued to live a twilight life, desperate to rule my own existence, but shackled by the unknowable cost of entering into battle.

My sister Morgause was right, in more ways than one, when she told me that only women burn.

*

"KING URIEN WILL not be attending the Pentecost tournament."

I had barely entered the Seneschal's Great Chamber when Sir Kay called out the news. He stood at his desk, quill in one hand and a ruler in the other, curly brown head bent to an open ledger. Rows of shelves lined the walls behind him, bearing bound volumes and copious correspondence stowed in fastidious piles. A pair of Arthur's banners hung on either side of the unlit hearth, red dragons rippling sinuously in the draft.

"Are you sure?" I asked, before I indulged any relief.

"It's all there." Kay waved to a letter on his desk; Gore's boar-headed seal stared blankly at me, upside-down and broken. "He sends apologies but regrets he has pressing royal business." He looked up in interest. "Did you expect otherwise?"

"It's a surprise," I said. "Though I can't say I'm sorry for it."

"I am," he said drily. "His late refusal plays havoc with my seating chart."

He gestured us towards a long table at the back of the room. Upon it lay a huge piece of parchment covered in Sir Kay's impeccable black script, mapping detailed seating arrangements for the first tournament banquet. He had already redrafted it dozens of times.

Kay glanced at me sidelong. "I shouldn't make light, my lady, nor compare your life's concerns to my trivialities."

"My husband is a trivial man, Sir Kay. He inconveniences us all." I nodded to a pot of quills beside an inkwell. "May I?"

He smirked. "But of course."

Dipping the swan feather nib, I leaned over and struck out *King Urien of Gore.*

"Much better," I said, putting the quill down decisively. We stood before the plan in contemplation. "What troubles you here?"

Sir Kay sighed. "I've been staring at these tables since our last meeting. There are too many feuds and limited proximity to the King. I cannot placate everyone."

"Then don't move anyone," I replied. "Orkney and Listenoise have the most vicious feud. Both are competitive for favour and are already seated as far apart as possible. There's your advantage—distance. Give each of their lords a private meeting with Arthur, tell them it's a secret, and let them assume they are the only faction that has the privilege."

The Seneschal put a hand to his chin. "Risky, if either party finds out, and the High King's schedule is very busy."

"Arthur will agree if it helps ease the tensions," I said. "Nor will they break confidence if they are made to feel chosen and therefore superior. Such enemies will hardly strike up conversation."

Sir Kay regarded me with a sly smile. "You joust like a master, Lady Morgan, but with no need for a lance. I know every connection and grudge in this realm yet I am not half so astute. How do you do it?"

"You don't play chess, do you, Sir Kay?" I said.

"I do not, my lady."

"You should learn. Court, realm, feuds, favour—it's nothing but a game of chess. All you must do is see the moves ahead and plan accordingly. And know the opponent you are dealing with."

"Wise advice," he said. "I'll take your clever suggestion to our royal brother later."

"Arthur is back?" I exclaimed. "I hadn't heard. When?"

"Last night, in truth, though be thankful for his grace. By protocol, the whole castle should have been awakened, but he wanted to rest."

"How is he?" I asked.

Kay shrugged. "He returned as he left us—alone, unscathed and without explanation. I didn't hear from him until this morning. He said he was tired and needed some time before appearing to the court."

A faint unease settled across me, which Kay must have read on my face.

"Don't worry for him," he said. "Once, when we were boys, I poked Arthur awake every hour of the night from Maundy Thursday to Easter Saturday so he would fall asleep during Holy Sunday's dawn Mass. On the day, the little saint never even yawned, and saved *me* from being caught dozing by stamping on my toes. He is made of stubborn fortitude."

His fond, sardonic tone cut through my cloud of concern. He handed the swan feather back to me. "Let's get on, shall we?"

Before I could cast my eyes back to the seating plan, a sudden cacophony made me jump, the bells of Camelot's cathedral and the household's ringing all at once in a clanging, wall-shaking din.

"My God," I said, covering my ears. "What is that?"

Kay looked up, unperturbed. "Don't you know?" he said with a wry smile. "It means our little brother still prefers to make an entrance. King Arthur has officially returned."

2

CAMELOT'S GREAT HALL was a cathedral to its King: vaulting arches above huge pillars carved from glittering pale-gold stone; gilded frescoes of saints and holy scenes adorning the walls; rainbows of light drifting through rows of stained-glass windows. Dragon banners swayed from brightly painted rafters, hanging between iron chandeliers bearing enough candles to light any banquet until dawn.

Alys and I arrived late, and most guests were no longer seated. Behind High Table, a great glazed alcove stretched back like a church apse, casting a pyramid of evening sun upon a pair of gold chairs. Between the thrones, a tall, proud figure stood illuminated like an altarpiece, gilded and surrounded by worshippers.

No eye could miss him: Arthur, High King of All Britain, crowned and formidable in red and gold, as blazing in presence as his absence had been stark. He had returned.

"It's true, then," Alys said. "The King is back in Camelot. I wonder where he went."

"If the realm needs to know, then Arthur will tell us," I said, though my internal curiosity was far less dignified.

We moved through the thronging room, past long tables decorated with red-and-white runners, silver plate and vases filled with lilies and poppies. Pages in royal livery milled about, bearing salvers of spiced suckling pig, honeyed fruits and large-bellied jugs of imported wine.

With High Table risen, the room had been given over to informality, noisy with talk and laughter, minstrels tuning their instruments in preparation for dancing. Richly draped lords sat conversing on land and taxes, while raucous young knights gathered in knots, competing over various affiliations. A few heads turned as we passed, offering bold glances and smiles of appreciation.

We arrived at the ladies' table, where Alys kept her seat. A page trotted past with a platter of bread rolls shaped into small, fat songbirds. Her eyes followed it with longing.

"Sit and eat," I told her. "I'll pay our respects to the King."

I made my way up onto the dais, Merlin's wall of life candles burning alongside me. No one, including Arthur, had seen or heard from the sorcerer in almost two years, but the enchanted candles that burned as long as Merlin drew breath served their purpose, declaring him alive and scheming somewhere.

"Morgan, at last!" Arthur ushered his companion knights away and came to me, arms outstretched. "How happy I am to see you. It feels like an age."

"Such hyperbole," I jested. "It's only been a week."

"Dear sister, any time without the pleasure of your company is far too long."

We laughed, and he planted a kiss of greeting on my cheek. His normality, his easy cheer, seemed to defy the strangeness of his recent absence: the sudden departure without knights or guards; the fervent talk it had caused among the court; the vision of a High King cantering away from his city alone, no explanation given even to his Queen.

"You've been missed, brother," I said. "Where—?"

"Pray tell, what is so amusing?" a sweet, feminine voice cut in.

Arthur turned to the sound at once, like a moth to sudden torch-light. Queen Guinevere of All Britain smiled and took his arm, her fair hand glittering with emeralds.

"Darling!" Arthur beamed boyishly back at his wife. "Morgan and I were just catching up."

"Queen Morgan, how good of you to join us," she said. "You were so late we feared you would not come."

They were a well-matched pair, tall and golden, Guinevere's stature enough to declare her superior to other women, but not dominant of her husband. Like Arthur, a regal confidence masked her great youth-fulness, and her beauty was spoken of with reverence: the large, curled-lash eyes and apple-cheeked face, impudent chin beneath lips like a rose in bloom. In the flesh, she sprung forth to life like a painted Venus, but held herself with the haughty grace of a Madonna—a combination as beguiling as it was daunting, and fascinating to most men.

"My lady," I said, dipping my head. "I commend you to God on this pleasant evening. I was delayed by my charming son, who caught me in a trap of bedtime storytelling."

Her bland expression did not waver. "I have also lacked your atten-dance in my solar. Lady Alys said you have been detained elsewhere."

"The tournament has demanded it," I replied. "Sir Kay and I have had regular meetings to discuss plans and our more complicated diplomatic matters. We have made great strides."

"Dearest Morgan, always busy." Arthur smiled with deep affec-tion. "Sir Kay says your insight has been of incalculable value. High praise, coming from him. Indeed, sometimes I think you could run the kingdom well enough without me."

"If my lord requires a rest, then I will certainly try," I rejoined.

"The Seneschal should know he can call upon me likewise," Guinevere said. "As Queen, no one knows the diplomatic needs of the realm better."

Arthur put his arm about her waist. "This tournament is *for* you, my darling, to commemorate our wedding. My only wish is that you enjoy its surprises."

"Will you compete in the joust?" I asked him.

"I am yet to decide, though Guinevere prefers it if I do not." The Queen opened her mouth to protest, but Arthur shook his head. "I am lucky to have found a wife of such beauty, goodness and consideration. I would never wish to displease you."

She accepted his praise with a hand on his chest, and they smiled dreamily at one another. They had been rapt, it was said, since the moment they met, and not to everyone's approval; Arthur once admitted to me that Merlin himself had been against the union.

I glanced away and spotted two figures gesticulating for attention— Lady Clarisse and Sir Ector, Arthur's adoptive parents, and overseers of his and Sir Kay's quiet forest upbringing.

"Brother, I believe you're being summoned," I said.

Arthur looked up and smiled. "Excuse me a moment," he said, and left us.

The Queen watched him go. "They are the only people he doesn't make come to him," she remarked.

"He loves them," I replied. "He wants to honour everything they've done for him."

Guinevere's eyes, pale green like hellebore, returned to me, sliding down my body in assessment. "What a *striking* gown," she said. "So close-fitting, quite dramatic. Indeed, the eyes of the entire room have been upon you."

So it might have been; I knew how well I wore the gown, though it was little suited to the stifling air. Bronze silk, narrow in sleeve and body above sweeping skirts, the fabric came alive as I moved, artful stitching across the bodice holding me in a fierce embrace like a Trojan cuirass.

"You flatter me, my lady," I said cautiously. Once upon a time, such words would have been genuine, no thought given to insincerity or a swipe at one's character. Not so long ago, she and I had spent many afternoons just the two of us, speaking freely and laughing often; I had discovered she was adept at chess and taught her how to be even better. Once upon a time, we had been friends.

"Your Highness, too, is radiant," I added. "Would that I could wear white with such success."

That, at least, was true: Guinevere was resplendent as usual in flowing white damask, ermine-trimmed despite the heat, yellow-gold hair strung with pearls beneath a delicate, pointed crown.

Unexpectedly, my compliment seemed to mollify her, eliciting a faint smile. "Arthur should not say it's my influence that stops him from jousting," she said in a rare confidential tone. "I could not truly make him *do* anything."

"No more could any of us," I agreed. "In that, he is altogether a king. But you care for your husband's health, as good wives do. It pleases him."

Her pretty face brightened, as if I had raised her spirits. Arthur would have been happy; he did not understand our rift and so wanted for us to be good sisters again.

Our brief accord was interrupted by a flash of yellow silk as a male figure rushed up and grabbed the Queen's hand, spinning her towards him. Guinevere gasped in outrage, but at the sound of his laughter she realized who it was and broke into a girlish smile.

"Guiomar!" she exclaimed.

"My sweet Gwen! How fares my beloved High Queen?"

No man on God's earth besides Arthur could have addressed her in such a way, but Sir Guiomar of Cameliard was Guinevere's favourite cousin. The knight swept her fingers to his lips and kissed them irreverently.

"I am well, dear one," she said. "I didn't think you would come."

"And miss Camelot's first tournament? No indeed. I am a man who belongs at court." His eyes flicked to me, the same green as his royal cousin's but livelier, appraising. "Lady Morgan, you look beautiful as ever. Like a Roman empress."

There he was, blond and brazen. Sir Guiomar—handsome, good-humoured, and the reason Guinevere could neither bear me to be in her sight, nor straying too far from it.

He and I were not strangers: in my first year at Camelot, soul-weary and filled with an undefined hunger, what began with dancing and flirtation became an affair when the Queen's favourite cousin invited me to his bed and I went.

For a few weeks, we were covert lovers, Sir Guiomar a carefree reminder that I could still want and feel and take pleasure in my distractions. All was well until the Queen suspected he had a par-amour and, worried for his place in court, he decided to confess all. Scandalized and outraged, Guinevere forbade any contact between us, and her weak-willed cousin complied like a lamb. She kept our transgression from Arthur to save Guiomar's reputation, and chose to blame me wholly for leading him into temptation.

Of course, I was furious: at his cowardice; at her meddling in my private life; at the freedom I had fought for being curbed yet again— and the Queen could not see beyond my carnal sins. So our friend-ship burned to the ground, bare civility the best we could muster from the ashes of our former sisterliness.

Now, under Guinevere's severe gaze, I let him kiss my hand. "It's good to see you, Sir Guiomar."

"The pleasure is all mine, my lady, without a doubt."

His honey talk meant nothing to me. For want of a spine Sir Guiomar had squandered his appeal, but Guinevere would not force me to act out shame I didn't feel.

I looked away and Arthur caught my eye, alone again, beckoning. "I must go," I said, and without taking leave of the Queen, I escaped, joining my brother farther into the large recess.

It was quieter there, sequestered, and as Arthur drew me under his steel-grey gaze, the noisy room faded into insignificance. Bold evening sun sliced through the leaded glass, crisscrossing us with yellow diamonds.

"I have missed you, Morgan," he said. "You've managed things so well during my absence. I cannot express enough gratitude."

"It's my duty," I replied. "Any way I can help you or the realm is an honour."

"You go far beyond duty. Kay and I were discussing your suggestion to cool the temperature of the Orkney blood feud. Even my unyielding brother was impressed."

"Sir Kay shares the credit," I said. "He and I are good partners in strategy. The tournament is set to be a marvellous success."

"Good," he said. "Now that the wars in Benoic and Gaul are almost over, it is imperative my Crown is seen as an arbiter of stability and peace. Camelot's first tournament marks the beginning of how I wish my reign to be."

He paused, raising a hand to his modest coronet, thumb rubbing the gold ridge at his temple. When pensive, he looked like our mother, but less than before due to the spun-gold beard he now wore, clipped close to the jaw. His hair, too, was shorter, cut above the collar; men were barbering themselves like him all over the Continent now, foreign knights swearing fealty and adopting Camelot's fashions as its influence continued to grow.

"Where did you go, Arthur?" I said quietly.

He looked away. "A meeting, 'tis all."

"Sir Kay said you came back last night."

"I needed to rest, and Guinevere insisted on tending to me. This afternoon, I went to St. Stephen's and knelt awhile in private prayer. It was restorative to speak to God undisturbed."

"Was your head troubling you? Because you should have called for me."

He smiled and placed a hand, unadorned aside from the gold ring given to him by his wife, on my shoulder. "Your concern moves me, sister. If nothing else, I hope you know how happy I am you are here. It pleases me beyond measure that I can trust you with my kingdom, and my life."

Gratitude swelled in me, the warm triumph that came with being elevated in Arthur's regard. "And I trust you, with mine."

"I'm glad," he said. "Unfortunately, until the tournament and Royal Summer Hunt have concluded, there will be no time for our daily meetings. But we must discuss all I've missed. Come to me tomorrow—shall we say midday? Give me a chance to conquer the pile of correspondence Kay insists requires my attention."

"I look forward to it," I replied. "It's good to have you back, brother. Wherever you were."

He paused, silvery eyes searching my face, as if he thought to speak but didn't know how to begin. At some sound, his head snapped up, leaving me wondering what he wanted to say.

"Arthur?" I said, but he stepped back, suddenly watchful.

"The heat is unusual." Sir Kay's voice sounded behind me. "We are used to more of a breeze."

"It's hotter here than high summer in Rome," came an unseen reply. "Across the Channel, heavy storms conspired to keep me away. *Alors*, I am grateful you accepted me into the joust lists."

The voice—deep, musical, French—stopped my heart.

"It's an honour to have a knight of your reputation ride our tilt field," Kay said. "Though I know many of your fellow competitors will have been praying for you to be detained."

The quiet laugh thrummed through my chest like the low registers of a harp. "You flatter me, Sir Kay. Now I am here, I'll do my best to ride for the glory of the High King."

No, I thought, *it cannot be.*

"You may tell him so yourself." Kay appeared, opening one arm towards Arthur and the other at a tall, dark figure lingering where I dared not look. "My lord, if I may make an introduction?"

"Of course," my brother replied. "Come forth."

I considered turning away, even leaving, but too quickly he came, stepping into the evening sun, his shadow sliding across my body like the touch of a ghost. His hair was cut shorter, though it still fell long across his forehead, and like all the others he had a beard. But his face, his bones, those angles once so dear to me, remained, every line and curve a prayer to my younger heart.

In all that time, he had never truly gone from me: his hands, his face, the hard grace of his body against mine and the unbearable pleasure we found there. I had transformed the memory enough to keep living, burying it deep until it was nothing but a bittersweet lesson, an ancient myth I had read too many times.

But he was real, and there he stood, alive, edged with sun; beautiful and profane. And for the first time in almost a decade, I took in Sir Accolon of Gaul.

3

"MORGAN," HE SAID, with the end of his breath.

Just like that—*Morr-ganne*—my name from his mouth, as if he had never stopped saying it, had never forgotten what we were, or could have been, nine years, hundreds of miles and a thousand unanswered questions ago. As if he had never loved me until I was blind to everything but him, just to abandon me in the greatest act of betrayal I have ever known.

I was the only one who heard him say it. Sir Kay was busy explaining his guest to Arthur, unaware of our locked gaze holding us motionless like statues. Then, abruptly, Accolon stole his eyes away as if I had vanished, not a hint on his face that seeing me again had caused him an ounce of pleasure or pain.

"My lord, this is Sir Accolon of Gaul," Kay said. "One of our most pre-eminent knights and captains, recently arrived from fighting your cause across the Channel."

"I commend you to God, good Sir Knight," Arthur said. "Welcome to Camelot."

Accolon bowed, shaking my brother's outstretched hand with a slow reverence. "King Arthur, it is the greatest of honours to meet you."

Sir Kay reeled off a long list of Accolon's achievements while I stood staring into nothing, with my existence shattering in ways I could not yet discern. The Gaulish coin felt like a droplet of fire hidden within my gown. I plucked at the fine gold chain at my collarbone and hoped to God my careering pulse wasn't visible on my body.

Knowledge is control, I told myself. *Look at him.*

Forcing my eyes to focus, I studied Accolon piece by piece. His lithe, broad-shouldered figure was still made for expensive cloth, and he wore a thigh-length tunic of dark-grey silk, precisely tailored and cinched with a black belt. Infuriatingly, he had refined rather than aged, his sculptural features well-inhabited and effortlessly striking, ash-dark hair shining as he pushed it off his brow. He looked loose and rested, as if he had lain for a long time in a warm bath.

The only significant difference in his appearance was the beard obscuring his face—contrived, too fashionable. I decided it didn't suit him and felt a strange sense of satisfaction.

"I've entered Sir Accolon into the tournament lists," Sir Kay was saying. "Perhaps luck in the jousting arena will make up for your difficult journey."

"I'm happy to have reason to stay awhile," The Gaul replied. "Regain my courage before sailing again."

"You do not like the sea?" Arthur asked.

"I do, my lord. Unfortunately, the seas have seldom been a friend of mine. I spent my early knighthood in Cornwall, so it's not the first time your wild waves have tried to . . . drown me."

Accolon's eyes met mine almost by accident, as if the thought could lead nowhere else. His gaze rested briefly on my face, then flickered across the bronze gown that fitted me so well, and in that quick, nerve-sparking moment, I was glad my women had clad me in armour.

He looked away and cleared his throat. "Regardless, I am glad to be here. My sincere thanks for allowing me to enter the joust at short notice."

"I'm sure we will be well entertained," Arthur said. "Your reputation with lance and sword goes before you."

"That my lord has heard my name at all is an honour." A flush appeared on Accolon's cheekbones, and his modesty struck a small chord within me, before I remembered his ways were often pretty but meant little. "Due to my time fighting in Benoic, it's a while since I have tourneyed. I fear my skills might carry a little rust."

"You are too modest, good sir," Kay piped up. "Jousting aside, your duelling record alone is a thing of legend."

"Indeed!" Arthur agreed. "Hand to God, I have had more defeated knights sent to kneel at my throne with Sir Accolon of Gaul's name on their lips than any other man in my service. Your endeavours in Benoic ensured us a far swifter victory. Clearly you are a great knight of pure and noble heart."

I resisted the urge to scoff.

"I am proud to serve Your Highness's Crown," Accolon replied. "Though I could not succeed without the valiant men who fight alongside me. One worthy knight in particular, if my lord will permit me an introduction?"

Arthur assented, and at Accolon's beckon, a tall, slim knight stepped into our circle. He had serious hazel eyes and hair the colour of alder bark, and wore a stern, set-jawed expression.

"My lords, this is Sir Manassen of Gaul," Accolon said. "My close cousin, long-time travelling companion and most trusted brother-in-arms. He has fought courageously for Your Highness under my command."

"My liege," the knight said with a deep bow. "It is a great, *great* honour to meet you." His voice reflected the accent of his cousin, but his manner differed entirely, his phrasing studied and precise, without humour.

Arthur smiled and ushered him up. "You are most welcome, Sir Manassen. Any man so high in Sir Accolon's esteem is doubtless a boon to this court."

"My lord King is indeed gracious. May I say, your city is a place of wonder. My cousin and I have travelled a great deal, and nowhere is as impressive as Camelot."

So this was the cousin Accolon had spoken of, whom he planned to seek his fortune with beyond Tintagel, back when all I wished was to take that journey with him. I looked at Sir Manassen in interest, and he met my gaze with eyes so devoid of warmth it made me shiver, like catching an ill wind.

"My sincere thanks, good sir," Arthur said. "Camelot is beautiful, and I am immensely proud of it. Are you staying inside castle walls?"

"They are," Sir Kay put in. "I arranged beds in the barracks on the northwest courtyard, with many of the highest-listed knights."

My heart gave a kick; lodging within castle walls meant The Gaul was free to dine in the Great Hall and walk through Camelot at will, an unwelcome memory lurking around every corner.

"It pleases me you are nearby, Sir Accolon. I feel there is much for us to speak on." Arthur gestured at High Table. "Sit with me awhile, would you both? Tell me of your experiences in battle."

Accolon bowed. "We serve at Your Highness's pleasure."

Kay hurried off to arrange seats, and a heavy silence fell upon our quartet. I hadn't spoken for so long it felt glaringly significant, but soon I could escape, have time to think, or curse the skies.

Never tolerant of lulls, Arthur said, "I hope you enjoy good wine, Sir Accolon. It will be a joy to converse with a knight of such great skill and unassailable honour."

That time, the scoff escaped me, drawing my brother's attention.

"Forgive my manners!" Arthur exclaimed. "All the while we have stood here and I have failed to introduce one of the most important people in this court—and indeed my life. Gentlemen, meet Lady Morgan, Queen of Gore and my own dear sister. Morgan, this is Sir

Accolon of Gaul, honourable knight, famed jousting champion, and one of my most respected captains in our battles overseas."

There was no choice; we had to look at one another. Accolon's eyes were flat, cast through me as if I were glass. Neither one of us seemed willing to break cover.

My brother frowned. "Unless . . . you've met?"

"No, my lord," Accolon said quickly.

"Didn't you say you spent time in Cornwall?" Arthur said. "Lady Morgan hails from there."

"I did, Your Highness," came the unruffled reply. "We must have missed one another." He paused, and I felt the brush of his eyes. "Of course, I've *heard* of Lady Morgan of Cornwall," he added.

He said it so casually it took my breath away. In one cruel swoop, he had both acknowledged and dismissed me, his killing blow my long-ago title, which he had once called me in affection.

Fury flared within me. Who did he think he was, to believe I would conspire with his lie? Perhaps I would *not* pretend, and make him look a liar and a fool, though I was loath to risk drawing the light of suspicion upon us. Still, he should not assume my compliance. Accolon of Gaul had no authority here.

"You must excuse me, my good knight," I said pleasantly. "For all your accolades, I have never heard of you." I thrust out my hand. "Pleased to make your acquaintance, Sir . . . what was it?"

He hesitated, struck wordless. Beside him, Sir Manassen stiffened, wearing a face that could have turned milk sour. Then, with a sweeping arm, Accolon's cool hand was beneath mine, lifting my knuckles to his lips, the contact no more than a whisper from his ill-advised beard.

"Sir Accolon of Gaul," he said. "*Enchantée.* I am my lady's loyal servant."

He fixed his eyes on mine, stormy and alive for the first time, challenging me to shake him free. I let my fingers remain in his firm grip and held his stare, blood drumming in my veins, nothing left of Camelot's Great Hall but the two of us, refusing to pull away first.

"Loyal?" I said acidly. "Are you indeed?"

Accolon dropped my hand as if bitten, leaving victory thrilling over my skin.

Arthur gave a youthful laugh. "Ah, Morgan! My sister is known for her wits and fiery spirit, gentlemen. It takes time to earn her regard—good judgment I am grateful for."

The Gaul made an unsteady bow and I smiled, all sweetness and teeth. Let him think I was a threat; let him note the close bond I shared with my brother and understand that his peaceful passage through Camelot would depend on my grace, and not his choice to pretend the past had never happened.

"If you will excuse me, brother," I said, "I'll leave you to your knightly talk."

Arthur bid me a genial good evening, accompanied by muted Gaulish courtesies.

"Good luck, Sir Accolon," I said as I passed, letting my bronzed arm brush against his dark steel. "Though I'm sure you know *exactly* what you're doing."

Head held high, I swept along the dais, set my sights on the nearest side door, and didn't draw breath until I had left the Great Hall altogether.

4

I BURST OUT into the night, gasping for the warm, still air. Behind me, the Great Hall's babble of chatter and jaunty music carried on regardless, mocking my disbelief, my shock, the fact I could barely catch my breath. I shoved the door shut and staggered farther into what I realized was a charming, little-used courtyard, built to resemble the style of the country villas of Ancient Rome, smooth arches leaping over a tiled pathway, lined with pale colonnades. I leaned against a smooth white pillar, letting it bear me up, calmed by the sweet scent of climbing jasmine.

In the centre of the courtyard stood a large fountain, the glassy music of falling water cutting through the breezeless air. I pushed myself upright, drawn towards the sound, and sat on the fountain's edge. Marble horses glistened white-gold under the warm moonlight beside carousing nymphs and spouting sea deities, throwing droplets into the air like jewels.

A vision of Accolon rose up, lucid and unwelcome. How dare he come here, to my own brother's court! I had defied the fate he handed me and was contented for the first time in years. He could not simply glide back into my vicinity and disrupt everything, with his face and his voice and his deep, unholy knowledge of me. I was unbreachable, immune; never mind that my heart still beat like the quick wings of a wren.

I sighed and focused on the water, imagining myself far beneath the cool depths. One hand reached down into the shimmering pool until it was submerged, followed by my wrist, my forearm, the edge of my sleeve trailing a bronze streak along the surface. Above, a stream of water sprung from a horse's mouth, arcing across the wheel of stars. I leaned over, up to my elbow, sinking deeper.

"*Nefoedd wen!* What are you doing?"

A hand grabbed my dry arm and pulled me upright: Alys, her face pink with heat and hurry. We looked at my dripping sleeve, then at one another.

"I saw you, up on the dais," she said breathlessly. "Was that . . . ?"

"Yes," I said. "Accolon is back."

To acknowledge it aloud brought a shudder of reality, my watery calm seeping away.

"But . . . *why?*"

"For the tournament, of course," I said. "What better reason to saunter into Camelot and disrupt my life than for *sport?*"

Alys sagged onto the fountain sill. That she knew the enormity of it gave me succour, an assurance that I was not wrong to feel stunned, jilted anew.

"That *knave*," she said.

I managed a morbid smile. "So your magpie told it true. Unexpected guests."

"One could hardly have imagined this. Do you think he knew you were here?"

I recalled Accolon's sudden motionlessness, his half smile faltering as our eyes locked. His quick, unguarded exhalation of my name.

"No," I replied. "He didn't."

"How did he seem?"

"Indifferent, full of himself, without a care. Apparently he's been off jousting all these years to great acclaim, before becoming the star knight-captain of duels and battle in Arthur's wars."

I looked down at my hands, wishing I held something, anything, so I could throw it at the wall.

"Morgan?" Alys said. "What happened?"

I closed my eyes against the memory, the feeling, all of it.

"He snubbed me," I said.

She gasped. *"What?"*

A wave of gall rose up, and I saw it all over again in my mind's eye: Accolon's dismissal spoken so matter-of-factly, as if it were an amusing coincidence we had never crossed paths. The sheer sharp-edged boldness of him. *Of course, I've* heard *of Lady Morgan of Cornwall.*

"He mentioned time in Cornwall, and Arthur asked if we'd met. Before I could even *think*, Accolon looked right through me and said no. And God help me, I accepted it! I stood there, threw some toothless barbs, then fled." I stabbed a finger towards the Great Hall. "Now *he's* sitting at High Table with my brother and it's too late for me to do anything."

"What else could you have done?" Alys said. "You couldn't have confronted him outright, though he deserves it. Perhaps he'll think again and leave."

"I wouldn't waste wishes on that. He's been added to the tournament lists, to ride in the joust. The men are giddy with anticipation."

She tutted. "The *nerve* of him, coming here at all."

This time, her venom only left me weary. I sighed and looked back at the water, once more imagining a blue abyss, giving myself over to cool, dark rest.

At length, she said, "What will you do?"

I considered it; seeing Accolon was unavoidable, maybe, but the tournament wasn't real life, nor was it infinite.

"Nothing," I said. "Proceed as if everything is the same."

Alys regarded me sceptically.

"I mean it," I insisted. "There are the tournament arrangements, Yvain, Arthur has requested a meeting tomorrow—I'm far too busy to think of Accolon. He's only here for two weeks, and that's if he lasts the entire tournament. If it's indifference he wants, he can have it back tenfold. And you shouldn't give him any thought either."

Alys smiled, her youthful mischief flashing through. "I suppose you're right. Though if I see him in close quarters, I can't promise my reaction will be one of grace."

I laughed and pulled her close, feeling my bones lighten a little. A sudden burst of cheering echoed from the Great Hall, along with the opening bars of a popular reel.

"Let's retire," I said. "You and Tressa can spring me from this cage of a gown, then spend the rest of your evening together. You are kept too much apart as it is."

Later, as I stood at my bedchamber window before the heat-blurred stars, I thought back to that morning and the errant magpie, my internal calm that seemed so distant now. All at once, it felt impossible that Accolon and I had never crossed paths in nine years, or that I had not sensed him on the air the moment his ship touched the coast.

"*Cariad?*" Alys appeared in her night robe, silhouetted in the doorway. Her eyes went to my fingertips, plucking at the Gaulish coin's gold chain at my collarbone. "Are you sure you're all right?"

She waited for my confession, but I had none.

"Yes, dear heart," I replied. "Blow the candles out as you leave."

She extinguished all but one light, then with a last look of doubt closed the door between our chambers.

I had not lied to her, I decided. There were simply no words to explain what I could not articulate within myself: why I wasn't quick enough to make a fool of Accolon before he made one of me; that since him, in many ways, I had never been fully all right; of the supernova of blazing fury and remembered love that disarmed me when I first saw him again, racing through my body like a flash flood.

That when our eyes locked like lodestones, for a heartbeat it had stopped time.

5

OF ALL HIS castles and meeting rooms, Arthur's Great Chamber at Camelot was my favourite, both grand and comfortable, with blue-and-gold-painted rafters, an enormous hearth flanked by stone lions and an array of chairs suited to every type of meeting. A series of tapestries adorned the walls, depicting Jason's pursuit of the Golden Fleece.

I entered without knocking, and found my brother before a long window, hands clasped behind him. He wore a blood-red tunic and the same understated coronet, his only movement the grinding swing of his jaw.

"Morgan," he said without stirring. "Come in."

I joined him in the embrasure, sharing the view of Camelot's vast and busy entrance courtyard. A red steel dragon the size of a warhorse reared over the enormous main doorway, drawing stares from arriving guests. In the sky, a rare cloud drifted across the sun, darkening then re-illuminating Arthur's modest crown. He raised a hand and rubbed his thumb against its golden edge.

"Brother," I said, "what's wrong?"

He gestured to the window seat. "Let's sit."

I perched on the cushioned sill and he sat opposite. Seriousness lay across him like a mantle of steel, and I wanted to chase it away, return us to the cheer of the night before. At length, he cleared his throat and regarded me with the direct grey gaze that was entirely our mother's.

"This morning," he began, "I was catching up on my private correspondence when I opened a letter from your husband. It seems King Urien wants to see his son."

My stomach turned over. "He will attend the tournament after all?"

It was possible, I supposed; if Urien had taken to the road not long after his original refusal, Gore's retinue could arrive within—

"No." Arthur's solemn voice cut through my racing thoughts. "He's not coming to Camelot."

"Then how does he expect to see Yvain?"

My brother said nothing. A cold creeping dread began to rise up my body. "Arthur?" I urged.

He sighed. "A royal escort is on its way to accompany Yvain to Gore. King Urien has called him home."

A flash of fire fought with the chill. "*This* is Yvain's home," I said forcefully. "He's not going."

"You cannot refuse," he replied. "And by law I cannot prevent it. The rights of the father are inviolable and absolute."

Air caught in my lungs, eyes swimming in the unrelenting sunlight. I pushed myself out of the window seat, visions of my son rising in the shade: as I had seen him that morning, clambering across my bed to touch my nose with his and laughing as if there was no greater joy.

"He'll be afraid," I said. "Without me, my women. He doesn't know anyone in Gore."

"He won't be afraid, I promise you. Yvain is confident, cheerful— I've never seen a more sociable child. *You* raised him that way."

Arthur stood, a wavering tension in his stance, torn between loving brother and righteous, law-abiding king.

"He has two nurses, yes?" he continued. "They will go with him, of course, for familiarity and comfort, and report back. One word that he's being cared for beneath the standard you set, and his father will have me to answer to."

"*His father* didn't even come to retrieve him in person," I protested. "Yvain is my son and your nephew, not a cart of wine barrels. I don't know Urien's escort from the Devil."

"You won't have to," Arthur said. "However many come, I will send double my own men to match them—the best in the land, loyal to me, to *us*. Yvain will be safe anywhere under my banner."

"God's wounds! Are you saying that I should accept this?"

"I'm saying your husband could have called for Yvain at any time." He spread his hands in a calming gesture. "You knew this moment had to come, but it's not forever. I am dedicated to my nephew's knightly education at Camelot, and the importance of time spent with his mother. When we ride north for Michaelmas, I will call Gore to court and we will negotiate an arrangement fair to all. King Urien will be convinced."

"Convinced!" I exclaimed. "He should have to *beg me* for clemency, and still it wouldn't be enough."

"You are distraught and rightfully so, but would you not want fairness if the situation was reversed? Despite your differences, your son is also his. Surely you cannot deny Yvain and his father deserve to know one another?"

I stared at him, wordless, defiant—maybe because I did not know the answer, or because I knew that he would not like it.

Arthur sighed. "Do not think this pleases me. It's abrupt and uncivil, and I will tell King Urien in no uncertain terms. What we have gained in bargaining power due to his behaviour is immeasurable. But for now, you must be calm and rational—it is not as hopeless as you think."

"I see. You think because this was bound to happen, I should not react so strongly." My voice was sharp, turning bitter. "Perhaps if you had your own son, you would not believe it so simple."

His eyes flashed like a drawn blade. "I know you do not mean that, sister. Indeed, I *hope* you do not."

His entire being had hardened, while my form felt hot and liquid. I knew Arthur's anger well: occasionally the same wildfire as mine; at other times, an instant, impenetrable coldness, deepening into ice. But we had never flung our fury at one another, and I felt a swift resentfulness that it was Urien who had broken our peace.

"No," I conceded. "I don't know what I mean."

I sank back onto the window seat, letting my head loll against the sun-warmed wall. Arthur remained where I left him, his gaze fixed beyond me, the room, beyond us all.

Suddenly, his shoulders loosened, like snow falling from a thawing branch. With startling speed he came to me, dropping to his haunches and clasping my hands as if kneeling at prayer.

"Do you want me to go to war for this, Morgan?" he said. "Because if this is the difference between keeping our bond or losing it, then know that I will. It's against my principles, almost certainly illegal, but if it's the only way to retain your love and the trust we share, I will gather an army and march tomorrow."

An image arose: Arthur's men at Urien's door, delivering a stark, severe message instead of my son. Gore didn't have the men, nor its King the stomach for such a confrontation—Urien would quail and concede without opening Castle Chariot's gates. It was the most satisfying thought I had encountered in a long time.

I looked down at my brother's beseeching face. He would do such a thing, I believed it, but then what would he be? Just like his father, Uther Pendragon, the man I had hated more than anyone; a High King violent and unreasonable, destroying everything in his path. I had suffered it, seen first-hand what such tyrannical power could do. It was not a world I cared to live in again.

"No, brother," I said. "Your vision for the realm is one we share, your ideals what set you apart. I would never ask you to compromise yourself for the sake of lesser men. I just wish there was a better way."

"I know." Arthur squeezed my hands tighter, a slight tension creasing his brow. "It's little consolation, but . . . you must want things from this—from life—and . . . I swear if I can give them to you, then it will . . . be done."

He grimaced again, the cords of his neck flexing.

"Are you all right?" I asked. "Does your head trouble you?"

"No," he said. "I just . . . need to know that you trust me."

"I do."

"I mean it, Morgan. We are bound by blood, regard . . . mutual affinity. Sometimes it feels like we share one mind." He sucked in another sharp breath. "There's . . . nothing more important to me than keeping us that way. But you . . . have to . . . *trust me.*"

A sudden guttural cry cut him off. He tore away, cradling his face in his hands.

"It *is* your head." I leapt from my seat, prising the crown from around his temples. "Damn it all, Arthur. I've told you not to pretend with me."

His savage headaches, which I had often healed when I arrived at Camelot, had become a rarity in the past year or so, but I knew what to do. I knelt beside him on the floor, steepling my fingers along the top of his skull, feeling for the wall of pain that I had dismantled over and again. Unusually, the source was obscured, lost within a thick, ashen fog. How he had managed to form coherent thought was a mystery, but Arthur was young and stubborn, and stronger than anyone ought to be. Still, he needed me now.

Drawing him closer, my hands held firm, pushing light through the billowing dark until I found the headache's rocky surface, hard as a sandstone barbican. I braced the golden force against it, pulling heavy breaths and chipping at the damage until the pain gave way, stones splitting to shards, shards into dust.

Arthur's eyes snapped open and he released a transcendent sigh. "Thank you," he said.

I let my hands fall from his head and studied him. "This bout is extremely developed. It must have made you sick."

"The night of my return," he confessed. "Then again, the following morning."

"You should have called for me," I said.

"I know."

He smiled wearily and I sat back, enjoying the healing's golden warmth through my body. However, the greater my rush of success, the worse the affliction had been, and it had been so long since he'd suffered an attack. Why this; why now?

"What happened, Arthur?" I asked. "I trust you, but you have to trust me. Why did you leave?"

Arthur eased upright, rotating his neck. "Merlin," he said. "He summoned me."

I knew it, I thought. Who else but Merlin would Arthur run to, alone and at the slightest demand? Who else would absorb him for days, then send my brother back fogged and exhausted, with vicious headaches scraping around his skull?

I swallowed my unease. "To what end?"

He looked up, eyes sudden and silver, regarding me with the same searching scrutiny as in the Great Hall.

"Yes," he murmured. "You are the right one . . . the only one."

Before I could question him, he helped me to my feet and guided us across the room to a shadowy side table, upon which was a long rectangular object in red-and-white cloth folded thick as a tomb lid. With great care, Arthur picked it up and turned to face me.

"Please, remove the casings," he said, and I obeyed, unwinding the layered fabric. My fingers brushed the edge of something both hard and soft, and a rush of pleasure surged up my arms, glittering into my head like a shooting star.

I gasped, but Arthur didn't notice, his attention fixed upon the uncovered object. Across his palms lay a sleek longsword, sheathed in a jewelled scabbard. The hilt was pure gold and so bright it illuminated our darkened corner, as if sunlight had been forged into the metal. The pommel bore an inlaid image of a crown, the arcing golden crossguard carved with bold lettering that looked ancient as the land itself, but no language I had ever learned.

In one flashing movement, Arthur wrapped his hand around the grip and unsheathed the sword, revealing a shining silver blade, double edges singing of their fineness. It too seemed to contain its own light, only cooler, sharper, like the moon cutting across a lake. He tilted the weapon back and forth, its chill radiance shimmering across his face. It could not have been a new sight to him, yet he seemed transfixed by the starry steel's sheer presence.

"Last week," he said, "I met Merlin beyond the city gate. We travelled far and long, until he brought me to a lake crowded by trees and engulfed in mist, so large I could not see beyond it. So deep, he said, that no man could enter it without meeting certain death. We waited awhile, then the most remarkable thing happened. A woman's arm rose from the water, brandishing a sword—*this* sword."

He sighed and lowered the blade. "It sounds too fantastical, I know."

"Not to me," I assured him. "Go on."

"The mist obscured the sight, but when it cleared again, a young woman stood in the middle of the lake, bearing the sword and scabbard in her hands. She was exceedingly beautiful, her hair alive like the sunset. Everything about her seemed to *shine*."

Ninianne, of course; Merlin's unfathomable fairy companion. I had not seen her for almost a decade, but our last encounter on Tintagel's headland lived on in my mind. In one conversation she had told me the truth about Accolon's abandonment and lied through her teeth about Arthur's existence. She vehemently rejected the idea of being Merlin's tool, yet did all his bidding. To know of her was to understand nothing.

"She walked towards me, *atop the water*," Arthur continued. "Like a holy miracle, a myth of old, like . . ."

"Magic," I murmured.

My brother smiled. "I knew you would understand."

Only too well, I thought. I could see it: this endless lake; the billowing mist; Ninianne's slow, captivating movements; the otherworldly glow from her skin.

"When she reached us," Arthur continued, "she handed me the sword and spoke as if we were long acquaintances. I felt we had met somehow, but it cannot be—I would remember such a face. Then she vanished back into the mist. When I asked Merlin, he told me only that she is known as the Lady of the Lake."

Typical of the sorcerer, to withhold for the illusion of mystery, but I would not keep his secrets.

"You have met her, in a way," I said. "Her name is Ninianne. She delivered our mother of you, and helped Merlin carry you off."

It struck Arthur less than I thought it would. "Merlin said she was important to my past and future. Thereafter, he would speak of nothing but the sword."

He lifted the weapon again, turning his wrist; it glowed cold between us, lustrous and deadly. Arthur gazed at the blade as Narcissus beheld his reflection.

"What about the sword?" I asked.

"Its name is Excalibur. Merlin says it is the finest sword in existence, and I am destined to wield it. It cuts through iron as if it were flesh, never loses its edge, and holds untold power. Is it not beautiful?"

There was certainly something about this Excalibur that held Arthur rapt, but the radiating pull I felt came from the jewelled scabbard in his left hand, a siren song I could not ignore. I reached out, wanting badly to touch it again.

Arthur smiled. "Of course, my clever sister. You would succeed where I failed."

He placed the scabbard in my hands. In contrast to the sword's relative simplicity, it dazzled with luxury: thick, pale leather ridged with emeralds and rubies between starbursts of sapphire and diamond. I was ready for it this time, so the cascade of light did not stun, but bathed me in its lucent goodness, sending waves of tranquil power through my body. It was as if I were being remade anew: stronger, confident, vital. Invincible.

"At the lake," he said, "Merlin asked me which of the two I deemed more important. Naturally, I said the sword—it is the symbol of a knight's life, a king's, how we protect what we love and shape the world to our will. Nevertheless, I was wrong. The scabbard is by far the most important of the two, and you knew it at once."

"It's a marvel, singing with life and power. The jewels must be enchanted." I ran my fingertips between the gemstones. "No—the leather. Anyone who wears this would be protected better than any armour."

Arthur beamed with brotherly pride. "Your wisdom is endless. The hide is suffused with old magic, more ancient and complex than even Merlin can explain. He who wears it cannot bleed from wounds, and is healed as he stands. In plain terms, this scabbard is worth ten Excaliburs."

"An object that prevents death itself," I said in wonder. "I can feel it."

"I confess, I do not," Arthur said. "Your learnedness, the astonishing skills you possess, allow you to sense what I cannot. Sometimes

I think that if you could sit down with Merlin and entwine your intelligence with his . . ."

The notion cut a discordant note through the scabbard's joyous symphony. "No," I said. "My mind is for no one's use but yours."

He had suggested it before and my answer had not changed, though for the sake of our bond, I rarely spoke of how I felt about the sorcerer. But what Merlin did for Uther Pendragon led to my father's murder and my mother's violation and entrapment. I would never forgive him, nor spend a moment in his presence that I could avoid.

Arthur gave a bare nod and held his hand out for the scabbard. I prised the precious object away from my body and watched as he slid the sword home.

"According to Merlin," he said, "Excalibur is essential to my strength, my reign. He said I should gird myself with it and be worthy of its great power."

"Yet you have not worn it, nor shown it to the court. Why?"

"I—I don't know."

He glanced down at the fantastical object, his reluctance strangely moving. The grandeur and visibility that came with his status had long been second nature, his command of his kingdom masterful; he understood the responsibilities of power better than most. The sword he currently carried in public was the one he drew from the stone, used to win the battles that secured his crown—hardly inauspicious. What was another impressive talisman to Arthur's godlike reputation?

But he was a man, not a god, and perhaps there, in the space where I knew him deeply, lay the answer.

"Arthur," I said. "You are worthy of this, but it is no sin to take caution. Your reluctance to gird yourself with the sword isn't because you fear it—it's because you want it to *mean* something."

I put my hand on his arm. "Excalibur is *yours*. You can use it however and whenever you wish. The only authority you answer to is God Himself."

The weight on his brow lifted. "My dear sister. Your loyalty, your belief in me, it strengthens my soul, it . . ."

He stopped, looking down at the sheathed sword, then back at me. "Take it," he said.

His steel-grey gaze was so serious it made me step back. "What?"

"Take Excalibur, and more importantly, the scabbard. Conceal it, guard it, keep it safe—with all the wisdom that you have."

My mouth dropped open. "Why?"

"I want you to," he said. "I will not even ask where you keep it. When the time feels right to display Excalibur to the kingdom, I will come for it, and you will know if I am ready because you know me better than anyone."

The idea of having the scabbard in my hands again was thrilling, but the sword was Arthur's legacy, the kingdom's future, and I was one woman, not a vault.

"Truly I am honoured," I said. "But are you sure I should be the one to bear such a responsibility?"

He smiled, both brother and King. "Morgan, there is no one in this world I trust more than you."

It caught me unawares with a bolt of joy, a sentiment that I had often hoped for, but he had never declared with such conviction.

"In fact," my brother continued, "your place should not only be in my heart and high regard—it should be at my right hand. Once all is formalized with King Urien, there will be no need to make excuses for your presence here. Things being well, you must leave the Queen's service and have a place on my official council. What do you say?"

And there it was—a true act of faith, one I deserved, and a pathway to the future I had long envisioned. All I had to do was accept.

Arthur bore up Excalibur, presenting the sword as if on completion of my knighthood. "Please, sister. I cannot do this without you." I bowed my head and offered up my open hands.

*

IT TOOK ME the entire journey back to my rooms with the silkwrapped sword beneath my mantle, and the sight of Yvain's tiny leather slippers by my bed, for reality to pierce my heart. I shut all the doors between me and the outside world, tossed Excalibur and its miraculous scabbard under my mattress, and went to seek my son.

6

I HELD HIM for days—Yvain, my brightest star, the twin beat of my heart—spending every hour by his side, eschewing his routines and my duties, ignoring Camelot in its entirety to absorb every last moment of his presence.

We stayed in my chambers, building towers from his wooden blocks, playing hide-and-seek on the terrace and telling stories until far too late. When his deep-blue eyes began to droop, I would carry his sleepy body to my bed and lie beside him, watching his contented breaths.

Arthur was right, I told myself; Yvain was cheerful, confident and keen for adventure, and between my brother's scrutiny and the spirit of parental competition, his father would certainly treat him well. Later, the Michaelmas negotiations would ensure us a fair and final arrangement.

None of which seemed to matter on the morning of his departure as I faced a gossamer dawn in Camelot's courtyard, my son still half dozing in my arms.

Alys and Tressa stood beside me, castle walls casting shadows across us, as Urien's men waited, draped in the green and gold that had once dominated my world. Yvain's nurses lingered a little way off among Arthur's guards, between dragon and boar.

I shifted Yvain up and was rewarded with a beatific, sleepy smile. "I love you, my precious eyas."

"Mama," he said drowsily, bestowing a butterfly kiss on my lips. "Love you."

I buried my face in his dark-gold curls. Nothing was worth this: no show of trust, no precious sword, no place on a High King's council.

"I can't," I said. "I can't hand him over. Tressa, can you . . . ?"

"Of course, my lady." Tressa swiped tears away and lifted him onto her hip. "Come, my sleepy young knight. Say, 'Farewell, Mama. I'll see you when my quest is done.'"

"Bye, Mama," Yvain said.

"Goodbye, my one love," I said.

As she walked away, a horse whinnied and Yvain awoke, the sight of armoured knights bringing forth his joyous laugh. He reached for his nurses and accepted their praise, leaving as I had hoped, with the sound of his contentment threaded through the air.

*

BETWEEN MY GRIEF and the thick heat, the Queen's solar felt even more oppressive than usual. It was a long, wide chamber, still tapestried despite the temperature, slabs of sun from the large windows bathing the room. Guinevere sat remote in her chair atop the small dais, her attending women gathered at intervals, speaking little and fanning themselves. Alys had been charged to play her lute and sat near the royal skirts, plucking out a languorous tune.

I had taken up a settle in the shadiest corner, my work basket ignored and Lady Clarisse rustling beside me in copper silk. My usual High Table companion, she was the eldest in the Queen's service and arguably the most formidable in position, given she bore Sir Kay and raised Arthur from a newborn babe. She was also my closest confidante outside my own household, and the only one I had told of Yvain's departure that same morning.

"Take courage, my dear," she had said. "You are strong enough to withstand this."

At the time, I couldn't respond, but her words had settled within me as comfort; she had sent her two sons off into battle enough times to understand.

The heat had rendered the ladies similarly listless, with the exception of Lady Isabeau, a bold young woman of vague royal relation, and the only one of us with any spirit left for conversation.

"One of our number has happy news," she declared. "Lady Beatrice and her husband are going to have a child."

The room exhaled a happy gasp, a flurry of congratulations flying towards the blushing Lady Beatrice. My eyes flicked to Guinevere.

"So soon!" she said, an octave too high. "You were only wed at Candlemas."

I watched her form a smile, drawing the grace of a queen about her like miniver. "The High King and I bestow our warmest wishes upon you and your good lord husband."

"Thank you, my lady." Lady Beatrice dipped her head. "Your Highness's blessing is a heavenly gift."

"The child is the gift," Guinevere replied, and the solar fell so silent one could have heard a ghost draw breath.

The Queen held taut her smile, and it surprised me how easily I could still sense the pain behind her poise. A year ago, she would have called for me in private to let me tell her she hadn't done anything wrong, that these things took time and my own healthy son was six years in conceiving. Since then, the whispers had only got louder, but she no longer wanted me there to cast out her shadows.

"How fare you with aversions?" I asked Lady Beatrice, drawing the room's gaze. "I could smell every tiny scent on the air and couldn't bear wine. If you're suffering, Lady Alys has tinctures that will settle you."

Lady Beatrice looked relieved. "Thank you, Lady Morgan. That is very kind."

"Yes, isn't it?" said the Queen. "We are so lucky to have Queen Morgan's vast knowledge to serve us. Not to mention her experience as a mother."

Lady Clarisse cleared her throat. "Speaking of remedies, did you hear of the injury down at the stables? Apparently, a knight slapped his horse on the cheek, and it kicked out at a boy. Ten years old if he's a day."

"Sir Guiomar told me of that," Guinevere commented. "Said he couldn't get sense out of the grooms to have his horse saddled."

"What's the injury?" I asked.

The Queen gave a delicate shrug. "He didn't go into detail. A broken leg, maybe."

"How bad is it? Maybe the Royal Surgeon should—"

"The Royal Surgeon! He has no business attending some stable-boy." She gave me a pointed look. "Nor, Lady Morgan, do you."

To my chagrin, she had read my intentions perfectly. "I just wished to know the seriousness of the damage," I said. "Perhaps I'll ask Sir Guiomar."

Guinevere pursed her rosebud lips. "I must forbid any interference from the Royal Household, and I'm sure the King would agree. The stables will have it in hand. Let's change the subject, shall we?"

Exasperated, I rose and took a turn about the room as Alys began plucking a new song and the women returned to a low hum of conversation.

"Lady Clarisse breaks her fast with the Seneschal daily," I heard Lady Isabeau chirp. "Has he offered any insight into our mysterious champion knight?"

"Time with my elder son is not spent on idle talk," Lady Clarisse said, to looks of mild disbelief; everyone knew Sir Kay's excellent household management relied at least partly on gossip. She conceded a smile. "I *may* have heard that by the time Sir Accolon swore to His Highness's crown, he had won every joust competition for several years. Lords across the Continent were clamouring for his presence at their tournaments."

"Their ladies were clamouring too, I should imagine," said Lady Isabeau. "His fame and prowess aren't news—what of the rest of his secrets?" Her mischievous eyes alighted on me. "Lady Morgan met him a few nights ago. You've seen more of Sir Accolon than the rest of us combined."

Alys's lute quill twanged an errant note.

If only you knew, I thought.

"We were barely introduced," I replied. "If you wish to know things, why not ask him yourself? Sir Accolon is just a man."

"And what a fine figure of one," she mused. "Handsome, well-dressed, noble manners, unassuming charm. Made rich by his own prowess. If I wasn't already married . . ."

"Isabeau!" Guinevere exclaimed. "Camelot is a place of godly virtues. Such talk is not befitting of a wedded woman."

Lady Isabeau grinned. "I do not speak for myself, Your Highness. Lady Joliete is the one with interest in her heart."

Curious heads turned to a pretty, sweet-natured maiden, shrinking behind her loose walnut hair. A recent addition to the Queen's service, Lady Joliete was not yet accustomed to the guile upon which the Royal Court fuelled itself.

"Sir Accolon is very gallant," she quavered. "I met him and he was nothing but courteous and kind. But to speak of tender feelings would be wrong, given he is rumoured betrothed elsewhere."

Betrothed—the word ran down my spine like cracking ice. Alys was diligent enough not to look up.

"He hasn't admitted it," countered Lady Isabeau.

"Gossip serves none of us," Guinevere said. "Sir Accolon is an impressive knight, and the King already admires his skill and potential. If he does well in the tournament, he could be a fine addition to the Royal Court."

I forced my feet to move, away from the meaningless talk. It was odd, hearing Accolon spoken of by others—admired, lauded, desired in a way that I had always considered uniquely my own—but in the midst of my other troubles I had forgotten about his descent upon my life, and was content to keep it thus.

I drifted into a wide window recess at the back of the room, taking in the view of the Queen's complicated hedge maze. Beyond the castle ramparts, my son was already a few miles towards the main road north, and I wondered how far he would be away from me by nightfall.

"What are you looking at?"

Guinevere stepped into the alcove, casting a long slant of shadow. Her sudden proximity was strange, unusual since our breach, but I didn't show my surprise.

"Just the view, Your Highness," I said.

"I suppose having seen it before doesn't mean it loses its interest."

Her tone pricked my curiosity, but I said nothing. Undeterred, she leaned inwards until her shoulder brushed mine, as we had once shared friendlier confidences.

"Do not think," she said in a low voice, "that because you and Sir Guiomar have exchanged a few pleasant words, you are free to converse with him. If you attempt to bewitch him again, you will answer to me."

It made me look at her, but she kept her prim profile facing the window, and I recalled why my tryst with Sir Guiomar had cast us so badly asunder. That Guinevere still considered my private life under her authority was a severed rope that could not be rewoven. She assumed it was her right to rule me as a woman, and I would not be ruled.

"*Bewitching* aside," I said, "if he speaks to me, I cannot ignore him."

"You have a husband, Lady Morgan. Try thinking of him. I hear your son left this morning. Perhaps if you remembered King Urien is the only man God permits you to have, all three of you would be together in Gore."

I swallowed hard. "*Don't*," I said.

She turned, fixing me with her pale gaze. "Still, Yvain returning to his homeland pleases you, I'm sure. It is, after all, so important for a son to learn the ways of his father."

My body lit up with white heat, only the thought of Arthur stopping me from flying at her pretty yellow head. For him had I mastered my fire, and never unleashed it on his beloved wife despite her provocations, nor could Guinevere act upon her dislike in her husband's view. Now, my council seat and future depended on me keeping my temper. I glared at her and she returned it, a futile challenge that neither of us could afford to answer.

"My lady, it's time for the dance lessons."

Guinevere turned to snap at whoever had interrupted us, pausing when she saw it was Lady Clarisse.

"Of course. Gather the ladies," she replied, then regarded me expectantly. "Shall we, Lady Morgan?"

"No indeed," I said. "I'm leaving."

"You certainly are *not*," the Queen snapped. Beyond us, the room held its breath.

"Perhaps, in the circumstances, Your Highness," Lady Clarisse said, "you should let Lady Morgan go."

"She does not control that," came the royal response. "She waits upon my grace."

Lady Clarisse regarded her daughter-in-law with a steady calm. "My dear, there's more to being a gracious queen than giving orders and sitting a throne. King Arthur would wish for greater kindness in our hearts, wouldn't you say?"

Guinevere looked astonished; no doubt she had never been scolded in her life. She grimaced her assent, bound by the unquestionable authority of the woman who had known Arthur longer and better than anyone. I beckoned to Alys, nodded gratefully at Lady Clarisse, and left the solar without another word.

*

"WHAT DID THE Queen say to you?" Alys asked the moment we were within my reception chamber.

"Nothing of consequence." I didn't wish to recount Guinevere's unexpectedly painful goading, so instead I asked, "Did you know about Accolon?"

She raised an eyebrow. "There are rumours, but he hasn't confirmed any betrothal."

I stared at her, aghast. "Not *that*. I meant the possibility he might join the court."

"Oh! It's the first I've heard, but he is garnering considerable favour."

"My God, why should I even have to *care?*" I leaned against the door and put my head in my hands. "What happened to me, Alys? When did I lose sight of it all?"

She regarded me patiently. "Lose sight of what?"

"This—the Royal Court, endless travel and duty—it was never supposed to be our entire life. We wanted to go to my mother's manor, remember? Live there for half the year, to study, heal, work, spend time with my son in peace. Camelot was always part of the plan, but Fair Guard was to be our home."

I went across to Tressa's parchment-covered scribe desk; she was the only one of us who had done any writing in over a year. Beside it, I opened a small trunk and lifted out two manuscripts: the *Ars Physica*, where my love of healing had begun, and another volume bound with blue leather.

"Remember this?" I said. "The manuscript on women's afflictions we began writing in Gore? When did we last look at it?"

An empty lectern stood beside the desk, melancholy in its disuse, and I propped both books upon it. "I didn't burn Urien into submission and flee in great danger so we could sit in the Queen's presence with our minds going fallow. Nor did I drag you and Tressa to Camelot so you could endure the same restrictions as in Castle Chariot."

"Tressa and I would follow you into Hell, but weren't dragged into anything," Alys said firmly. "There are no regrets here."

"*I* should regret it," I said. "Look at how things are. I cannot keep my child with me, or think of love, because I am forever bound to a man I hate. I can't even take a fleeting paramour to bed because the Queen assumes my body is her jurisdiction. There's no time to further our work, nor can I use my skills to help someone if they do not carry the right rank. As if any of that threatens my loyalty to my brother. This is not the freedom we fought for."

"You had to escape Gore. What more could you have done?"

"The question is, what have I *tried* to do since?" I turned from the lectern, resting my fists against the desk. "When we first came here, we talked endlessly about a different kind of life, without protocol. Not only where I can choose my own path, but where you and Tressa can sit beside one another at table, dance with your arms around one another, express love in the myriad careless ways others do. This cannot be what you truly want."

"And what do *you* want, Morgan?" she said. "Only you. Not back then—now. Today."

Her question arrested me, the answer elusive, unformed. My eyes drifted back to the *Ars Physica*, unopened for so long.

To fix all this, I thought. *One broken thing at a time.*

"I want . . ." I said slowly, "to heal the stableboy."

Alys nodded. "Tressa mentioned him earlier. His leg is shattered. They say it's unlikely he'll ever walk again."

"He will if I have anything to do with it," I said.

"You're going to lay hands?" she said in surprise. Aside from Arthur's headaches—a closely guarded secret—I had done little of that kind of healing. Sometimes, the shadows of my old life still loomed large.

"I'll have to. I won't see an innocent boy crippled because some spoiled knight cannot control his temper, or because Guinevere likes to control *me*."

I opened the cover of the *Ars Physica*, turning page after page. I still knew it all by heart, but just to look upon it again brought new pleasure. A loose leaf of parchment caught my eye, an intricate diagram of the human leg in crosshatched ink, one of many sketches I had done under the Prioress's watchful eye in St. Brigid's Abbey.

Four major bones between ankle and hip, the stanchions of all that came above. My hands tingled in anticipation.

I brandished the sketch at Alys. "Will you come? I cannot soothe pain at the same time as mending a fracture, so I need your remedies and keen eye. Though the Queen *has* forbidden it."

She smiled with distinct mischief. "I am with you, always." Then, gently: "What about the rest of it?"

"We're going to heal the boy, Alys," I said. "Damn the rest of it."

7

THE LOWER STABLES were bustling, grooms and stablelads heaving hay, shovelling oats and pulling bucket after bucket of water from the yard's central well. A row of enormous destriers stood in the shade, awaiting the assiduous washing and brushing that horses of sporting prowess required.

"Where's the boy with the broken leg?" Alys asked a passing lad.

He managed a surprised half bow, then called for the boy's father, one of Camelot's senior grooms.

"I didn't expect you, Lady Morgan," he said, ushering us towards a large stone building. "Every leech in the city said they're too busy."

"I will always come—everyone must learn that," I said. "How is your son?"

"Robin's somewhat awake now," he replied. "A barber-surgeon travelling with a group of knights gave him a heavy sleeping draught. I've been watching his breathing all morning."

He guided us into a huge high-timbered barn, hazy light filtering over a long row of stalls occupied by highly bred horses. The entire stable was immaculate, clean-swept and smelling of fresh hay and leather.

"Do you know what was in the draught?" Alys asked.

"No, my lady, nor who ordered it. Some knights complained Robin was crying too much with the pain—they said it was disturbing their competition horses."

She tutted. "How noble."

He pushed a door on our right, which opened into a spacious whitewashed room, cool despite the day's hot air. A truckle bed stood against the far wall, a slight whimper emanating from under the sheets.

"May I look at him?" Alys said.

The groom nodded, then turned to me with wretched eyes. "The barber-surgeon said his leg is in splinters—that it'll fuse twisted if it heals at all. Robin only ever wants to ride and run around with the horses, but they say he might never bear weight again."

"He'll be bounding about in no time now we are here," I said. "I don't make promises I cannot keep. All we need is time alone, and as much quiet as possible."

"Thank you, Lady Morgan," he said. "I'll tell the lads to keep everyone out."

Once he left, I went immediately to the bed. The child wasn't overly small but seemed shrunken by the pain, his pallor greenish-white, red hair darkened with the sweat of drugged sleep.

Alys sat by his side, one hand on his forehead and the other at his wrist. "His essential signs are good, and he's calm."

"Robin," I said, "we're going to help fix your leg. Can you sip some water?"

The boy struggled to wake, so I brushed my thumb across his forehead and chased away the fog in his skull. His eyes flew open, hazel and alert.

"You're Lady Morgan," he said. "I've heard of you."

"All good things, I hope," I replied, because in Camelot such a comment could mean anything. Robin only smiled enigmatically. "How old are you?" I asked.

He thought about it, then declared, "Ten years, nine months and twelve days."

Alys poured a cup of water and brought a vial out of her belt purse. She measured a powder into her hand, eyes flicking to the boy in calculation.

"What's that?" Before we could stop him, Robin wriggled up on his elbows in curiosity, emitting a sharp cry of pain when his leg reminded him it was there.

"All right," Alys soothed as tears poured down his freckled cheeks. "Drink this. It'll help with the pain."

She held the cup and he gulped at it, chest hitching in distress. I considered the misshapen limb beneath the bedsheets, profound damage already radiating forth to my senses. His small body seemed strong but would not be without limits.

I drew up a stool and took his hand. "Robin, you are wise enough to hear the truth. I will fix you, but it won't be easy and there is much left to feel. But if you help me, together we can do it. Yes?"

The boy drew a deep breath, taking hold of his pain, his fear. "Yes, Lady Morgan," he said stoically. "I'm ready."

I folded back the sheets to reveal his leg, which had been splinted on both sides in a rudimentary fashion. The entire limb was mottled with inky-green bruising; his bones hadn't pierced the skin, but several ominous bulges declared this pure luck.

"The horse must have kicked him more than once," Alys murmured. "A curse on whichever petulant knight did this."

I took my falcon-handled knife from my belt and cut through the splint's strappings. Hands on either side of his knee, I closed my eyes and focused, letting my fingertips map his injuries in my mind.

I had healed bones before, though the fractures I had knitted were uncomplicated slivers—the Prioress's arm at St. Brigid's, or my own wrist after Urien had cracked it. The boy's shattered leg was a catastrophe, a broken glass I would have to gather shard by shard and rebuild with utmost delicacy, maintaining both form and strength. It could not be done without complete concentration, or in half measures.

Robin twisted under my searching pressure, his pain so fresh and raw that I felt it like ice water in my veins. Alys stroked his head to settle him, and her hushing whispers were the last thing I heard, vanishing behind the serene roar of my blood turning to light, fanning like tributaries into my waiting fingertips. There, I began.

Splintered bones shivered and rose, fragments shifting at my request. The ghost of Robin's femur remained, and I sought the distinct shapes of absence in layers, some pieces slotting perfectly and others needing more experimentation to fit them into place.

A ripple of sound broke through my concentration. Robin twitched as if disturbed, but I steadied my hands, refocusing my mind to the larger bone fragments I had left until last. One more surge sent bolts of light along the final fissure, bone weaving together like flax on a loom, and I knew it was done.

Another noise clattered into the room, loud and deep, tearing my connection. I pulled away, lungs and muscles pleasantly hollowed by tiredness, as if I had flown far and fast on shimmering wings. Robin's eyes were closed in rest, a dreamlike muttering coming from his lips. Alys sat monitoring the pulse in his neck and gave me a satisfied nod.

A distinct laugh struck the air like an untuned lute.

"What *is* that?" I said. "Keep him soothed."

I hastened into the stable, seeking the disruption. The horses were stirring, heads tossing, ears pricked towards two tall figures striding between the stalls.

"He's surprisingly fresh after the journey," Accolon said. "His legs look good and he's settled. It was worth taking a slower pace."

"You wouldn't be saying that if you'd missed inclusion in the lists," Sir Manassen replied.

"Not true! You know I'd never put competition above the health of any horse."

My heart gave an unwanted jolt at the sound of their particular

Gaulish dialect. Neither of them noticed me, vibrating angrily at the end of their path.

A dapple grey destrier gave an impatient whinny, ears flattened and teeth bared. Accolon paused and regarded it mildly. "Yes, yes, you're very ferocious," he said, producing a piece of carrot seemingly from nowhere. To my chagrin, the animal didn't bite him but calmed at the offering, dropping its huge velvety nose into his palm.

He scratched the horse's forelock and grinned at his cousin. "Today, we rest. Practice drills tomorrow at dawn."

Sir Manassen groaned. "Why so early? I'm not even riding in the joust."

Accolon laughed as they reached the end of the stalls. "You sleep in like the others if you wish. I prefer having the field to myself, in peace and quiet."

"Peace and quiet would be a fine thing indeed," I declared.

They stopped dead, noticing me at last. Accolon glanced immediately away.

"I beg your pardon, my lady?" Sir Manassen said tersely.

I pointed at the way out. "You're not allowed in here. You must leave."

He made to protest, but Accolon spoke first. "We weren't told, Lady Morgan. A mistake, nothing more."

It was courteous enough, but my name again in his mouth struck hard against my nerves. "So I am *visible* to you after all, Sir Accolon?" I retorted.

The Gaul didn't flinch, but Sir Manassen recoiled as if slapped. "My fellow knight was checking his jousting horse. On whose orders is he not permitted?"

I stared at him, this man I didn't know, who didn't know me, and a recollection rose up of our first encounter in the Great Hall—the feeling we were locked in a battle I wasn't aware of.

"*On my orders*," I said, as if he was the greatest dolt I had ever encountered.

His neck reddened. "My lady, I'm not convinced you *can* order us out of here."

Accolon turned to him in horror. "Are you mad? Of course she can. Apologize and let's go."

"Apologize? For what?" Sir Manassen switched back to their native language. "Why does she deserve respect when she offers you none?"

"*Cousin*, you swore you would not do this," Accolon warned. "I told you—I carry this alone. *Apologize*."

I was rooted, fascinated, the healing's tired euphoria held back by a nascent desire for a fight. Sir Manassen's face darkened with brimstone determination.

"Have you forgotten how I found you, *cousin?*" he said in clenched, insistent French. "Half-dead in a tavern, about to throw your spurs down on a game of hazard. *She* did that, *she* put you in that state. You know what she is, and yet—"

"For the love of God, hold your tongue!" Accolon cried.

In all my days I had never heard him shout in such a way, but his intensity dissolved just as quickly. "She speaks our language, you fool," he said wearily. "She can understand every word you say."

Sir Manassen paled, but his hard demeanour did not change. He squinted at me, as if trying to read my linguistic abilities from the bones of my face.

I met his gaze with cold fire. "Please, do go on," I said in their north-of-Paris dialect. "Tell me exactly what I am."

Accolon's shoulders dropped, as if my words in his most intimate tongue—the tricks and quirks that he once taught me—had weighted him somehow, and momentarily I hoped that it had pained him as much to hear as it did for me to speak it.

He turned to his cousin. "Manassen, if you love me like a brother, then you will not say another word." His tired voice contained a distinct, unyielding edge. "*You* want us to join this court; *you* want the opportunities it brings. Do you think this is any way to conduct yourself as a knight of honour?"

A flame of irritation licked up my limbs. "Damn your so-called *honour*," I said. "There's a child in there who has been through a terrifying ordeal after having his leg and dreams destroyed. He and I worked hard to restore them both, and he deserves better."

Accolon paused and for once looked directly at me. "The boy— you healed him?" His sudden interest made me flinch, but I nodded. He smiled and it was gentle, almost involuntary. "I did not know you still—"

A sweet ache drove into my chest, deep and blunt-edged. "There is much you don't know of me," I snapped.

It was enough to turn him cold. Accolon drew his shoulders back, eyes dimming to detachment once more. With a sweep of his arm, he gathered Sir Manassen and they left the stables without another word.

I watched him vanish, golden dust motes settling in the wake of our conflict. So it was true: from The Gaul's own lips, they wanted to join the court. My presence, our dangerous past, had made no dent in his ambitions.

Yet it was not that which caught in my mind, but another phrase, replaying unbidden like an irresistible tune.

I carry this alone, Accolon had said.

And though I pushed the thought aside, the mystery of his words shivered hot across my skin, like moving closer to a wildfire when I should have been running away.

8

THE NEXT MORNING, when dawn had just anointed the horizon, I sprung out of bed and dressed rapidly in an old gown of Tressa's. Hoisting up my mattress, I pulled out Excalibur and drew it from the scabbard before concealing the sword behind a false-backed cupboard in the alcove beside my bed. The scabbard I bundled up in old muslin, savouring its thrill of goodness as I slipped it under my hooded cloak and exited my chambers.

I left the castle by a quiet side gate, hurrying down to a large square that held a gathering of stables, armourers and smiths. Beyond, a twisting series of alleyways eventually led to an unmarked door under a faded sign.

The smell hit me the moment I entered—animals, dung and salt, the unmistakable odour of tanned hides—but the shuttered workroom I stood in was pristine: uncluttered workbenches; neatly hung tools; flagstones still damp from washing. In the glow of the hearth fire, a thin, dark-bearded man sat on a stool, strips of leather in his hand, and staring at me in disdain.

"Who in ten devils are you?" he demanded.

"I have a job for you," I said.

"Don't you know it's a holy day?"

"I can pay." I held out my palm, revealing a chunk of sapphire within a nest of gold chain—a necklace, awarded by Arthur for my last birthday. I was loath to part with it, but there was no other way. "With this, you'll be able to live like a baron for a year, for a task that will cost you only a morning."

The leatherworker rose, eyeing the stone. "What's the job?"

I drew out the scabbard from my cloak and unwrapped it.

"What in God's name?" he whispered.

"I need a counterfeit," I said. "Completely identical. The leather must be exactly the same quality and colour, the jewels positioned with perfect accuracy. You may use the jewels from one to adorn the other, but the original scabbard must remain unharmed. And I need it this morning. A challenge, but I've heard you're the best. What say you?"

He squinted at me, pushing spotless sleeves up wiry forearms. "I'm apt to it."

Turning with surprising grace, he stalked back to his bench and hooked open a pair of shutters, letting down a column of morning sun. He poured a bowl of clean water and scrubbed his hands and nails, then gestured for the scabbard. Its life force tugged at me as I lay it on his palms.

"Come back at third bell," he said.

"I'll wait." I perched upon a wooden storage case, and he shrugged.

For several hours I watched: his search for the perfect white leather; the measuring of Excalibur's scabbard; his flowing hands, removing and reattaching the jewels with the delicacy of a mother tending her newborn child. Finally, he took two strips of blue leather and crisscrossed them around the true scabbard, covering the pinholes where the jewels had been and creating a striking object in its own right, fit for any sword.

Once finished, he brought both scabbards across to me on the muslin. "Here," he said haughtily. "No man within five hundred miles could have managed such a fine job."

I picked up the real scabbard first, confirming it still thrummed with healing, then studied the counterfeit. There was nothing to indicate that it was not the original. Excalibur's death-defying counterpart would be safer than Arthur could have hoped for; no one predisposed to theft would put the true scabbard's value above the jewelled one.

"Perfect," I said. "Take your payment with my gratitude."

The leatherworker snatched up the sapphire, and I took hold of the scabbards, only to be met with a tugging resistance.

"I did consider," he mused, "that with all these other jewels, I could live like a baron for the rest of my years." With his free hand, he drew a slim silver dagger from inside his jerkin and tilted the blade at my throat. "Go quietly now."

A laugh rose up inside me. "You fool," I said. "I don't have time for this."

Flint against steel. Lifting my arm, I struck my fingers against my palm. I hadn't held fire since burning my husband, but the flame roared up instantly, blazing with purpose.

"Christ in Heaven." The leatherworker stumbled backwards, falling onto the stone floor. He pushed the scabbards and the necklace towards me. "Here, take them and go."

"It's too late for that." I stooped over him, holding my crackling hand alongside his cheek. "Leave this place. Forget you saw me, or that you ever set foot in this city. If I hear the slightest hint of this on the wind, I will burn you senseless and throw your body into the sea. Do you understand?"

He nodded, and I extinguished the flame. With a sweep of my cloak, I kicked the sapphire over to him, retrieved the scabbards, and flung open the door.

"Who are you?" he croaked.

I paused to answer, my name poised on my tongue. But I could not risk it, so I pulled my hood up and left without another word.

*

LATER, I WAS pleased to receive an invitation from my brother, requesting that I meet him at dusk in the large ornamental garden outside the Great Hall.

A heavy quiet hung over the castle as I passed through its twilit galleries; there was no banquet that night, in solidarity with the knights sitting vigil in preparation for the tournament. Most were kneeling in St. Stephen's Cathedral or their chamber oratories, some unfolding small travelling altars before retiring early to bed, or partaking of other, private rituals.

I found Arthur on the terrace's balconied edge, overlooking a grove of apple trees. The balmy dusk hung with the scent of sweet cider, paving stones returning the day's heat into the air. My brother acknowledged my arrival with a nod, keeping his gaze on the star-specked horizon.

"I heard you left the Queen's presence rather abruptly yesterday," he said. "Without asking her leave, and missing some duty you were meant to attend."

"Yes," I confessed. "Yvain had just left, and I wasn't at my best. I'm sorry."

He released a brief sigh. "I understand. However, your place in Guinevere's service is what sanctioned your absence from Gore when King Urien formally demanded his Queen's return. Upon her grace do you officially depend."

"Of course," I said reasonably. "Until I sit on your council, that is."

A faint amusement crossed his face. "Maybe so. Nevertheless, the position you hope to hold in the future depends on my ability to justify my decisions. My wife is High Queen, mistress of this house and kingdom, and dearer to my heart than any on this earth. She and her wishes are to be respected at all times. Remember that." He glanced at me, half smiling. "For my sake, at least."

The message was clear: to ensure my seat amongst his councilmen, I must prove myself in more ways than loyalty and intelligence, but his appeal had landed upon my soft sister's heart. I couldn't argue with his show of faith.

"You have my word," I said. "I will change my ways."

Arthur shook his head. "I would not have you change, sister. Your great honesty and dedication to your true self is what bonds us. So long as we have love, trust and regard, we will always be in harmony."

We shared a smile and fell into a companionable silence, watching the swifts wheeling and swooping against the violet-gold twilight.

"Is our secret safe?" he said suddenly.

"Yes," I replied. "And well-hidden, by your command."

It was a relief that I did not have to lie. Excalibur sat snug in the counterfeit scabbard behind my alcove cupboard, itself concealed under a tapestry of Pandora unleashing chaos upon the world. The true scabbard I had taken even more caution with, stitching a hidden panel into my favourite hooded cloak. The thick, dark-blue fabric held the miraculous object snug and undetectable between the shoulder blades, its voluminous hood an extra layer of protection. I could carry it anywhere and no one would suspect a thing.

Arthur exhaled. "I knew I could rely on you, Morgan. After all, who can I trust more than my own blood? Though there are some who would prefer I never trusted at all."

I felt the shift in his thoughts as keenly as if it were pain in his skull.

"Merlin, I suppose," I said. "A man who lives in seclusion and talks mostly to the skies has little use for trust. What can he know of family, love or loyalty?"

"The concerns of the heart are not his strength, it's true. Though Merlin is loyal to me—that I do believe." His fingers twitched atop the balcony, tapping out a fraught, irregular rhythm. "He suggested he attend the tournament, when we last met. I told him not to come."

A bloom of victory flowered in my chest. "He would have only sought to detract from the celebrations. You are to be congratulated for taking such a stance."

Arthur eyed me cautiously, as he always did when I dared criticize his great mentor.

"I'm sure such 'frivolities' hold no interest for Merlin," I added. "Almost two years you did not hear from him, and this is when he times his return? Whatever he wants can wait. It was the right thing to do."

"Perhaps, though he says the situation is urgent." Arthur gazed up, contemplating the sky above Camelot's spires and turrets, now embedded with night. "He says there's trouble brewing among the stars."

Isn't there always? I thought.

"What trouble?"

"He said it will take a long time for him to know what will befall me," he replied. "As his predictions become more serious, the cloudier they seem to be. I am used to it, but the waiting does weigh on me."

"Of course it does, but it oughtn't distract you. Let him seek the answers first." I looked up at the stars that spoke so loudly of Arthur but somehow not the rest of us. "One sorcerer's concept of destiny isn't everything. If you want my view, Fate contains many facets, with possibilities far beyond what Merlin's cloudy prophecies can deduce."

My brother frowned. "Can that be true? It is against what I have been told my entire life."

I took his arm, drawing his eyes down from the unyielding skies. "You are more than the stars, Arthur. Look at everything you've done with your own fortitude. So Merlin rode with you in a few battles, but you were the one who fought and survived, when you were barely of age. You faced rebellion and came out stronger, found your true love and married her despite the doubts of others. You built this castle, this court, and rule this realm according to your own ideals. *Your* vision."

"What about what comes hereafter?"

"Do not think of hereafter," I said. "Think of your successes now. Of your tournament—nine days where so much tangible good will be done for the kingdom. You must move beyond what occupies Merlin and be proud of what you are doing—what we can do—without him."

Arthur's shoulders drew back, his entire figure seeming to expand and glow with the effect of my words. "You're right, Morgan—as ever. How I rule here, what I have built, how I approach my life as a king and man under God—that's what matters."

"It's *all* that matters," I said. "Regardless of what this new tangle of stars claims, you will weather it with the strength that resides within you, as you always have. Nor will you do it alone, for I will be at your side. Whatever comes, we will face it together."

9

I LEFT ARTHUR still contemplating the night sky but standing taller, and walked through Camelot's deserted Great Hall. After a day of industrious work and Sir Kay shouting himself hoarse, the vaulted room was resplendent with ceremonial glory for the tournament's first formal banquet: new dragon banners hanging from rafters and walls with garlands of red and white roses; tables set with gold plate; each name from Kay's strict seating chart inscribed on rectangles of wood.

A pleasant, featherlight peace descended as I wound my way past High Table and its pair of thrones, my own seat nearby. Somehow, despite the grief of the past week, I had begun again, and the rush of hope felt strange, God-given. Nine days, then the future; there was nothing that I could not overcome.

I stepped outside onto the small, pillared courtyard, bright moonlight arching along the tiled path. In the centre, the fountain trickled its delicate song, marble horses obscured by an incongruous shadow. I moved closer and the dark shape refined into a tall, sleek figure perched sideways on the sill, head bent and one hand trailing in the silver-streaked pool.

The half-lit profile I would have known anywhere, the colour of his tunic a deep-blue memory. In my chambers, slipped within the bindings of the *Ars Physica*, was a makeshift kerchief in the exact same shade.

Accolon, my unmet challenge, deep in thought, sitting his own private vigil at the water's edge.

I stilled, but he had already glanced up and seen me, lit boldly by moonlight. He inhaled in surprise, taking me in with an unreadable gaze. I let him do it, watching him watch me, my every sense heightened, poised.

His eyes held mine a heartbeat longer, then, in a graceful arc, he turned his face back down to the water. Whatever it was, this strange communion, it was over.

His dismissal sent a riptide of wrath through my body. For a moment, I had wished only to melt away, leave him to his solitude, but we were far past good will. If Accolon wanted peace, then he should have gone to a church.

I strode directly over to where he sat. "How dare you come here," I said. "How dare you *stay*."

Accolon straightened but did not rise. My height as I stood over him felt lofty, superior.

"My lady," he said uneasily. "I don't wish to argue. Let's stop this."

"I didn't *begin* this."

My tone elicited a hard glare. I sensed argument in the stiff pitch of his neck, but instead, he rose. "To that," he said, "there is no fit reply. I bid you good evening."

He offered me an entirely sardonic bow, then turned on his heel and sauntered away, leaving my body afire with unspent quarrel.

"What's wrong?" I called to his retreating back. "Can't the great Sir Accolon of Gaul form a sentence without his guard-dog cousin here to speak for him?"

He halted as if hearing a sword drawn. "Don't bring Manassen into this," he said over his shoulder. "He seeks only to protect me."

"So he does have a voice!" I exclaimed. "And what could a man like you—so lauded, so charming, *so honourable*—possibly need protecting from?"

Slowly, purposefully, The Gaul turned and walked back until we were two steps apart.

"Is there something," he said quietly, "that you wish to say to me?"

I tilted my chin up, expecting to meet his detached, empty gaze, but for once his eyes were alive, storm-coloured depths stirring with a melancholy anger, and beneath, something wilder, more complicated, that I did not want to decode. To catch him unmasked was a shock, his look of candour an aching note of remembrance, played between two souls. In that sudden, vivid moment, Accolon was not gone, and I knew him still.

It took every tensed sinew of my body not to shy away. *"Leave,"* I said. "Go from here and never come back."

At last, he cut his gaze free, looking beyond me. "Why would I do that?"

"Are you so wilfully ignorant?" I said. "Because *I* am here. This is where I live. You don't belong at Camelot."

"I don't believe that's for you to decide, *my lady*." He kept his tone even, but still he wouldn't look at me, and my blood thrilled a little that I had succeeded in goading him.

"You sound just like your ferocious cousin," I said. "Do not think it's so simple, your grand plan to join the court. One word in my brother's ear about our past, and you'll both be turned out into the road."

"I know enough about the King's ideals. Doing so would destroy your standing alongside mine."

"That's my risk to take. Maybe I am *so galled* with the idea of seeing your face that I would do anything."

Accolon paused—barely, but it was all I needed to see, the thin fissures in his unbreachable guard, lit up and fracturing.

"No," he said. "You wouldn't."

"Are you sure? Enough to stake your good name on it?" I moved forwards, into the orbit of his presence. Up close, I could see the jolt of uneven breaths in his chest, the quick flex of his jaw. "It sounds like you have a good life—fame, riches, your pick of tournaments or command. What's a place in a strict, virtuous court to you?"

"I'm not leaving," he said.

I nodded thoughtfully. "I can ruin you."

Accolon's eyes found mine again, dark and bleak in the cerulean light. He gazed down at me as though he were on a precipice, contemplating what would happen if he let himself fall.

"You won't ruin yourself for me," he said.

"*Try me*," I replied.

For several hammering heartbeats he held my stare, and I felt myself bracing for something I could not name.

I stepped back and cleared my throat. "It doesn't matter anyway. Camelot's court is prestigious and full, with a hundred more suitable candidates waiting to join. You'll compete in the tournament, it will end, and you will leave."

"*Alors*, you have nothing to worry about," Accolon said. "Though the King seems to enjoy my company, and there'll be plenty of other tournaments."

I eyed him, towering over me, his expression unnerved but determined. His demeanour said he would keep turning up, no matter the consequences. He wanted something, I realized; wanted it enough to withstand my threats and the dangers of our past.

And what do you want?

Alys's question echoed back to me, and this time I knew the answer. I wanted to win; to regain everything I had once possessed; to hold power, not just over my future, but anything I chose. First, I wanted to slip myself inside Accolon's arrogance, his weaknesses, and prise him apart until he broke.

"Nevertheless," I said coolly, "the High King takes advice on who would be best to enhance his vision for the realm. You'd have to win the tournament—difficult and unlikely—or receive a convincing endorsement before you're even included in the conversation. Of course, I have Sir Kay's ear and, more importantly, King Arthur's."

Accolon's top lip curled in a half smile. "If I didn't know better, Lady Morgan, I'd say you were trying to wager with me."

"What if I was?" I asked. "Are you tempted?"

"Name your terms, and we will see."

"Very well," I said. "The moment you lose in the joust, you will leave at once, and never come to the Royal Court again. In exchange, I won't sully your name with the High King or anyone else. Presumably, you'll keep your captaincy under Arthur's banner, the spoils he shares out, everything he has awarded you already. That is no mean life."

"Yet it's what I already *have*," Accolon mused. "I wish I could accept your paltry, unfair terms, my lady, truly I do. But I rode a very rough sea to be here."

"Then what will it take?" I asked.

"Nothing too arduous," he said. "If I win the tournament, you will speak to the King and Sir Kay and suggest in *very* positive terms that my cousin and I would be great assets to this court. Make me part of the conversation."

I inclined my head. "And if I win this bet, you swear you will leave, without hesitation or argument?"

"Upon my honour, Lady Morgan. If I lose, you'll never see me again."

He bowed in mock courtesy and extended his hand. I wanted to take it, to dig my nails into his palm, shock his confidence and feel the race of his pulse, but I resisted.

"We are not children, Sir Accolon," I said. "The agreement is made, and let this be an end to it."

"Or the beginning," he said carelessly, but his expression was keen, questioning. Could he trust me, he wondered; did I trust him? Was I more or less likely than him to keep my word? I watched it ignite within him, the spark of competition. He had seen the chessboard laid out between us and chosen, once again, to play.

But for all we had played, he had never once beaten me.

10

THE FIRST DAY of Camelot's Pentecost tournament dawned bright and hot, sun searing in a cloudless azure sky. The Royal Pavilion was large and well-shaded, draped entirely in red and white. Liveried pages stood along the rows of seats, waving great fans of vellum and goose feathers, but it was little help against the dense heat and so much finery.

Proceedings were due to begin at the relentless hour of noon. I left Alys several rows back and took my allotted place at the front of the pavilion, two seats from the Queen's throne. Lady Clarisse smiled as I sat beside her.

"At least we have the view," she said, gesturing to the tilt field. Heat shimmered off the cropped grass and stockade fences, the two-storey spectator stands opposite a blur of faces and colour.

After an endless, perspiring wait, Arthur and Guinevere finally appeared in the arena to rapturous applause. Tall and crowned and dazzling, they walked the tilt field at a regal pace, swathed in ermine and cloth of gold, unaffected by the heat, waving and smiling beatifically at their adoring audience. In the background, Arthur's fabled castle rose up in a gilded blaze, a shining witness to the glory of a boy once foretold as Britain's destiny, now its formidable, unimpeachable High King.

"Well, they've done it," Lady Clarisse said with maternal pride. "The kingdom belongs to them now."

Not a soul could have disputed it. As always in Camelot's great moments, it was impossible not to believe in the alignment of the stars and feel the golden future in the offing.

With a final gracious wave, the King and Queen ascended the steps to the Royal Pavilion. Arthur surveyed his subjects with a deep satisfaction, silenced them with a slight tilt of his chin, and commanded, "Let the tournament begin!"

Another joyous cheer went up as senior squires filed in to ready the field, followed by several heralds, who climbed up onto a silk-draped scaffold to make announcements of welcome.

Lady Clarisse leaned in, her hand fan fluttering a soupy breeze over us. "One hundred and twenty-eight knights in all. Who are you hoping is victorious?"

I hadn't given it a moment's thought. "My nephew Gawain, I suppose. Camelot's main hope of a home victory, now Arthur isn't riding."

"A good choice," Lady Clarisse said. "For a betting woman, however, the winds have shifted. Word has it Sir Accolon of Gaul holds this tournament in the palm of his hand. I lay coin to him days ago."

"I heard he declared himself rusty," I said. "I hope he doesn't lose your bet."

Lady Clarisse chuckled. "So do I, dear. I'll never endure Kay's telling off for betting if I do."

Nevertheless, she was no careless gambler; if Lady Clarisse was right, my own wager may have been hasty. A trickle of perspiration ran between my shoulder blades, so I rose and leaned against the pavilion railing, seeking the non-existent breeze. Across the jousting green, gleaming horses gathered at the stockade gateway, resplendent in multicoloured cloth, knights astride in steel and matching silks.

"For goodness' sake, *someone* has to do it. Sir Accolon is riding first, and he's *your* favourite."

My ears pricked to the strident voice of Lady Isabeau, holding forth within a clutch of the Queen's ladies behind the throne. I slid along the railing, moving closer.

"Maybe so, but . . ." Lady Joliete stood under scrutiny, pretty in white, her dark-brown hair sprigged with daisies. Between her fingers, she held a long yellow kerchief embroidered with gold crosses.

"*All* knights at Camelot must ride with a lady's favour," Lady Isabeau interrupted. "It's the King and Queen's tradition. We have chosen our champions. Would you prefer to disrespect the Crown and doom him to misfortune?"

"No!" Lady Joliete protested. "But if Sir Accolon *is* betrothed, to accept favour from an unmarried woman might cause him discomfort. I cannot do that."

"I can," I cut in.

They swung around in unison, staring at me as if I had been summoned from a cauldron.

"I'm a married woman and a Queen besides," I continued. "If I bestow the favour on behalf of an anonymous well-wisher, there can be no confusion that it's purely a gesture of good fortune. Sir Accolon will have his luck, and tradition will be kept. If that suits Lady Joliete, of course."

The girl nodded enthusiastically as a bell began to clang for the joust pageant. The knights competing that afternoon would ride in to receive their favours, with the first contest immediately afterwards. Lady Isabeau shrugged and flapped the ladies towards their seats.

Lady Joliete handed me the favour. "Thank you, Queen Morgan. To see Sir Accolon ride wearing my token today—even anonymously—will give me great pleasure."

She blushed like a ripening apple. He set her maiden's heart aflutter, that much was clear, and who could blame her? Accolon was easy to adore, when you had not yet learned what he was capable of.

A blare of trumpets sounded, accompanied by an impatient cheer from the crowd.

"Say a prayer for your champion knight," I told her.

At Arthur's nod, the gates opened, and the herald read out the list of names, a complicated order of birth and jousting rank that Sir Kay had been working on for weeks. One by one, the knights rode in, drawing their enormous mounts up to the pavilion's wooden balcony as ladies crowded forwards, dangling sleeves and kerchiefs.

"Sir Accolon of Gaul!" called the herald, to a roar from the crowd.

Accolon emerged, astride a magnificent black warhorse with a white streak in its forelock, wearing a tunic of his eternal Parisian blue over a cowled mail hauberk that glittered like stars. He flowed forth like a river, riding gracefully past the crowd, accepting their cheers of admiration with modest waves and a charming smile.

Turning to the Royal Pavilion, he bowed to the King and Queen and rested a hand on his longsword. It was silver-hilted and exceedingly fine, pommel carved into the shape of a rearing horse.

He had done it: Accolon had become the shining model of a knight, perfect in image and celebrated for his prowess and honour, everything he had wanted to be. Nothing stood in the way of his glory at Camelot but me.

I stood up, but The Gaul had steered his horse away, trotting past the pavilion rail. He had no expectation of a favour, and I had no choice.

"Sir Accolon!" I called, loud enough to turn his head.

His smile stuttered. At my beckon, he glanced at the King, observing us from mere feet away. Eventually, he nudged his mount and drew up beside the pavilion with a heavy sigh. Manners alone had brought him to me.

"Sir Accolon of Gaul," I said formally. "I offer you this favour in honour of your participation today."

He frowned. "*You* wish to offer *me*—?"

"No knight should ride without the bestowal of a lady's luck," I interrupted. "The High King's own tradition. Do you accept?"

He contemplated me sceptically. Then, finding nothing on my impassive face, he muttered, "*Dieu aidez-moi*," and offered up his arm.

I tied the kerchief between elbow and shoulder, polished chill of his mail shirt grazing my fingertips. I pulled hard on the knot and his muscle tensed.

"Sorry, did that hurt?" I said.

He offered me nothing but a glance of stubborn patience. The kerchief's sunny hue looked gaudy against his tasteful shades of ice and evening, and it gave me a devious thrill to see his knightly perfection so marred.

"There," I said, fixing the knot. "May God bless your brave performance today."

He looked down at his arm, then back at me, not quite smiling but loosening, choosing acceptance. "Thank you, my lady, for your gesture of good fortune. Sincerely, I am grateful." It was the least he could do, his tone said, given I had prostrated myself first.

I allowed him to believe it a few moments longer, then smiled like a painted devil. "Sir Accolon, how vainglorious. As if *I* could wish you good fortune. This favour is on behalf of a different lady, who sadly doesn't know better. Still, your *sincere* gratitude has been noted."

He stared at me, thunderstruck, and I offered him my imperious hand. For appearances, he took it.

"Of course, Lady Morgan," he murmured. "I should have known."

He brought me closer with a slight tug, and I leaned into it, savouring the victory of his lips against my knuckles. Up close he smelled clean and vital, like fresh linen and steel. His hair brushed my cheek as I spoke into his ear.

"Try not to break your neck," I said, with sweet insincerity.

His recoil was glorious, his hand torn from mine. Another trumpet blast sounded, calling the first joust competitors to enter and take up their ends. With a last, wild look, Accolon swung his horse away from the pavilion and cantered off towards his squire.

Preferably, a knight's helmet would have been fitted and tied on well in advance, but I had so delayed Accolon's progress that the herald held Arthur's flag above his head, ready to call the first charge. Panicked, he shoved on his helm without tying the laces and grabbed his shield, missing several attempts to fewter his lance against the saddle. I took my seat with an air of satisfaction.

The herald dropped his flag, the crowd roared, and the two knights spurred their horses into a gallop. The opposing knight ran his line with well-practised straightness, whereas Accolon's horse took off on the wrong leg, veering away from the jousting boundary. The crowd gasped, but he leaned in hard, getting his mount back on its charge line just in time.

Nevertheless, his strike missed, skimming across his opponent's shield without a splinter of force. In contrast, the other knight's aim was imperfect but his arm strong, lance plowing hard into the top corner of Accolon's shield.

The Gaul lurched sideways, losing a stirrup and drawing a horrified gasp from the crowd. Limbs flailing, he had no choice but to drop his lance and throw himself onto his horse's neck. Missing the loose stirrup, he slid dramatically in the saddle, his flapping tunic skimming the ground.

The pavilion leapt to its feet, surging forwards. I followed, gripping the front rail. In dozens of tournaments, I had never seen a knight regain his seat in such circumstances on a still galloping horse. Accolon was finished, and I had won.

Suddenly, he lifted his shoulders, risking his little remaining balance to throw himself in the opposite direction and regaining the saddle in one strong, fluid movement. Hooking his feet back into the stirrups, he curved his horse around the jousting boundary and thundered back to his dazed squire, patting his stallion reassuringly on the neck. I collapsed into my seat, exhaling with the crowd, but not joining their applause.

Lady Clarisse tutted. "Our much-admired Gaul looks like he may disappoint, despite all the talk of great prowess."

"Isn't that so often the way with men?" I said, and we laughed.

Accolon opened his visor and surveyed the field, his bottom lip caught between his teeth. Then, with sudden decisiveness, he gestured for a fresh lance and shrugged his shield up. As he did, the yellow favour caught his eye and he raised his eyes to mine. I smiled venomously.

Fall, I cursed him. *Fall and set me free.*

With a look of stormy determination, he slammed his helm shut and set off for the second charge.

Both knights charged a balanced line, but when Accolon raised his lance a sudden calm settled across him, a graceful certainty in the deft tilt of his shoulders. With an artful twitch of aim, he hit his opponent's shield off-centre and thrust up with his own, skidding the other's lance skywards. The clever angle of Accolon's strike drove into the opposing knight's chest, pushing him clean out of the saddle with a great metallic crash.

The spectator stands erupted at the first fall of the day, victory bell clanging. Accolon threw his lance to his squire, removed his helmet and rode past the bellowing crowd in celebration, halting in centre field. As all around me applauded, he looked up at the sky and kissed his hand before laying it over his heart.

I felt a hot pain and realized my nails had dug small red crescents into the flesh of my palm.

"It seems we were ahead of ourselves," Lady Clarisse said above her clapping. "Sir Accolon of Gaul has done this before, and loves every moment of his work."

"Yes," I said faintly, and in one heart's leap I understood. Accolon's first, catastrophic charge I had taken for weakness, a failure of skill, when in reality, his refusal to let it deter him had only shown how great he truly was.

It was not victory or the adoration of the crowd that drove him, but one immutable fact: on the tilt field was where he lived. To defeat him out there would be harder than I thought.

And beneath this truth, another—a dark, singing cry I had tried not to feel; that in the moment, as the storm of our opposing wills raced towards collision, it had been nothing but exhilarating to watch him ride.

II

THE TOURNAMENT'S INAUGURAL banquet went perfectly as planned, including one glorious moment where Arthur called me into a circle with the day's winners and raised a cup to the power of my luck on "Sir Accolon's bold victory." The Gaul was forced to acknowledge my favour, which he did with jaw-clenched graciousness, making it an exceedingly successful day.

Alys, on the other hand, was appalled.

"What in God's blue heavens is going on?" she demanded, when I floated back to my chambers on a wave of my own brilliance. "Tying a favour on Sir Accolon? Conversing at the banquet?"

"It's not how it seems," I said and, with no little pride, explained everything I had done so far, including the wager Accolon and I had made, which occasioned a startling outburst of Welsh exclamations.

"I thought you were going to avoid him?" she said. "Give him the indifference he deserves."

"Trust me, Alys," I replied, with the assurance of a sage. "I know what I'm doing."

*

EARLY THE NEXT morning, before the heat-soaked formality of the tournament day began, I walked through Camelot's rare quiet and headed for the lower stables.

I found Robin in the long row of stalls, holding a feed bucket for an enormous black horse, murmuring compliments into its flicking ebony ear. The streak of white in its forelock confirmed it was Accolon's jousting stallion, shining and contented, seemingly modest about its triumph of the day before. Thankfully, his owner was nowhere to be seen.

"Can't that horse eat from the bucket itself?" I asked with a smile.

"Lady Morgan!" Robin beamed at me, then back at his charge. "This one's special. He won the day at the first tilt—did you see it?"

"I did." I gave the horse's neck a brief rub; he really was a fine, well-mannered beast—it wasn't his fault if his rider was a scoundrel of the highest order. "I'm more interested in how you are, Robin. May I take a look at your leg?"

He nodded and put the bucket down, heading towards his quarters while keeping up a near-constant stream of talk about the previous day's joust. He had been assisting with the horses in the knights' tents away from the stands, but knew every detail regardless.

The quarters he shared with his father were cool and orderly, a new flash of brightness catching my eye above the boy's bed—a long triangular pennant hanging on a nail, white and dotted with yellow suns.

Robin sat on a stool and shook his boot off without a wince. Taking up his leg, I rolled his breeches back and felt the bone all over, seeking anything I had missed, or pressure from normal use. There was nothing, not a whisper of difference between his and a leg that had never been broken.

"You are a marvel," I told him. "So brave when you were in pain, and you've healed good and strong. I couldn't have hoped for better."

He smiled, showing gapped teeth. "Does that mean King Arthur would let me be a squire one day—a knight?"

"I'm sure you can do anything you wish. There's a knight's heart in your chest and no mistake." I pointed at the pennant on the wall. "Speaking of which—what's that? It wasn't here before."

"A knight gave it to me," Robin said proudly. "He said I was brave too. He said he broke his arm at my age and didn't stop crying for a week, so my courage put him to shame." He hopped bootless onto his bed, touching each sun with his forefinger. "It's the Knight of the Sun's flag. One for every year he won the tournament in his hometown."

"And he's here now? Jousting at Camelot?" I had never seen the sigil or heard this dramatic nickname, though many were flying around the tournament stands.

"He's not *here*, m'lady," Robin said patiently, "but it's his *flag*. He gave it to Sir Accolon, who gave it to me. He jousted him once, and never thought he'd beat him, but he did because it was a rainy day. Of all his stories, *that* was my favourite, and—"

I held up a halting hand, head spinning with the torrent of information. "Sir Accolon came to see you? When?"

"The morning after you healed me. He asked how I was, and it made me cry because my leg was still stiff and I thought I wasn't going to be able to ride properly, or be a squire. He sat down and said he was sure I would get better, because he knew you, and—"

"He told you he *knew* me?" I cut in. "Said 'I know Lady Morgan' just like that?"

Robin regarded me as if I were entirely bizarre. "Yes. He said you are the cleverest person he's ever met, and he'd known you for a long time. Why—isn't it true?"

A lie was safer, but I couldn't utter it. "It's true," I said.

"Anyway," Robin continued, "he said never to worry because what you did would work, and he'd found out which knight slapped the horse and broke my leg, and if he faced him in the tournament, he would defeat him in my honour. And he is facing him—tomorrow!" He thrust his arm out, driving forth an imaginary lance, then his face fell. "Though I won't get to see it."

I was glad to grip onto a practical thought. "You will," I assured him. "I'll arrange it that you're at the front of the stands tomorrow."

He lit up like a row of candles. "Really?"

"I wouldn't have you miss it for anything. Besides, how will Sir Accolon ride well without you cheering him on? I've seen how you dote on his horse."

Robin grinned and skipped back out to the stalls, the bounce of his restored leg affording me a swell of satisfaction. He turned and eyed me with a child's precision.

"Will *you* be cheering for Sir Accolon?" he asked.

I smiled at him, and the potential of all I knew now. "We shall see."

*

THE NEXT DAY, the first-round victors rode in to have their favours tied on and I beckoned again to Accolon, waving Lady Joliete's returned yellow kerchief. He approached with distinct reluctance.

I smiled, attempting contrition. "You heard His Highness praise my luck. Dare you refuse the King's will?"

Accolon offered up his arm in silence, but when I leaned over to tie the knot, he turned his face to mine, as if about to share a confidence.

"I thought it wasn't your favour," he said. "Nor your luck."

"It isn't," I replied. "*I* still hope for your crushing defeat."

"Then whose is it?"

I cast my focus back to the knot, and a lock of my hair fell forwards, brushing across his cheek. Accolon didn't flinch and kept looking at me in expectation.

I tucked the offending tress behind my ear. "I'm sworn to secrecy, and abide by my honour," I said. "However, I do have something to show you,"

I pointed across the field, to where a small face with a shock of red-gold curls beamed at us from the lower stand. I gave Robin a subtle wave, which he excitedly reciprocated.

The Gaul's breath caught. He offered Robin an elegant salute, then turned back to me, the flush in his cheeks extremely pleasing.

"I spoke to our mutual friend," I said. "He's very eager to see you ride."

Accolon considered me for a long moment, calculating what I knew, and briefly I wondered if my face, my eyes, were still readable to him.

I pushed the thought away and smirked. "Off you go."

He hesitated, reaching for the gauntlets on the front of his saddle with juddering hands. One slipped away and he caught it, but the sudden movement made his horse leap sideways in alarm, rattling him onto its neck like an ill-stuffed doll. A few shocked gasps came from the pavilion.

My gambit was working better than I had thought possible, but for the small, red-headed face in the spectator stand, eyes wide as the moon, a hope for justice beating in his child's heart. My unsteady adversary gathered his reins to ride away.

"Wait," I said, and he sighed in vexation as I leaned back over the rail.

"Luck is a myth," I told him, "and there's something greater at stake." I nodded at Robin, still smiling, elbows hooked over the stand fence. "If you succeed for anyone, do it for him. *Oui?*"

Accolon looked up at me, a trio of lines forming between his brows, a youthful memory that echoed deep in my core.

"*Oui,*" he said, and his top lip rose, but I turned away before I had to see him smile.

Nevertheless, I saw his joy later as Sir Accolon of Gaul won another day, vanquishing the boy's enemy in two brutal, rib-crushing strikes. Once again, he kissed his hand and covered his heart, then lifted an ecstatic Robin onto the front of his saddle and took him on three victory laps before an adoring crowd.

As he did in his next two jousts, after destroying his opponents in a single, effortless charge, yellow favour whipping in the wake of his speed. Each time, I found myself on my feet with the rest, applauding his artfulness and skill. And much as I tried to conjure outrage, I found I couldn't begrudge him his moments of glory, because out there, in the breathless space between gallop and clash, he was real and true: Accolon as I had first known him, who he had always been.

It came as little surprise, then, when in his next match, he unhorsed Camelot's marshal, Sir Bedivere, in two audacious strikes, without suffering a scratch to his shield, and earned a standing ovation from the High King himself. More inevitable still that as we stood in the evening to raise our goblets to the day's most impressive victors, Arthur declared Sir Accolon of Gaul his Guest of Honour, awarded him a fine chamber in the castle proper, and invited him to stay with the Royal Court for the rest of the summer.

12

MAYBE I SHOULD have felt I had lost. Indeed, Alys called Accolon's elevation "a disaster"—especially when Tressa informed us that his new castle chamber was only two corridors and one small stairway from ours—but all else was going too well for me to dwell on it.

Arthur was happy; he had told me so that afternoon as we walked the rows of hooded birds at the falconry competition we were judging. During the banquet, after the formalities, my brother called me to his side and we spoke at length of his satisfaction with the tournament and our hopes for the future, and I felt his contentment as my own.

"There is also good news from Gore," he said. "Yvain reached Castle Chariot safe and well a few days ago, and by all accounts is thriving."

To hear much-awaited news of my son so casually threw me for a moment. "When was this?" I asked. "Was it from Urien, or the nurses? Did it come by letter or messenger?"

"A messenger came with letters as the bell rang to dine. He brought a missive from King Urien to myself saying all is well, and two for you from the nurses, I assume containing a full report. We must meet and view them together."

"Tomorrow?"

"As soon as I can." He put a hand on my shoulder, his grey gaze reassuring. "I promise you, all could not be better. I know to tell you like this is not ideal, but I assumed you'd want to know the essential points with haste."

"I appreciate it, brother," I said. "Was anything else said? Has Yvain—?"

Arthur glanced up, cutting me off as the Queen glided into our vicinity. She lay a proprietary hand on his arm, and he beheld her in adoration.

"My lord, the first dance is due to begin," she said. "The musicians wait upon our presence, and I await my husband's embrace."

"And I yours, my beautiful wife." Dropping his hand from my shoulder, Arthur put an arm around Guinevere's waist and cast his happy light back on me. "You know what I know, Morgan, and I'm sure everything else will be in the letters. But for now, this night is so glorious, I wish all of those closest to me to enjoy it. Sister, we must have you dance!"

Such was his aura of joy, even Guinevere offered me an encouraging smile. She didn't realize I had avoided the tournament's fashionable formal dances because after storming out of her solar, I still hadn't learned them.

"Alas, brother," I said. "I have no partner."

"That's easily solved."

"*Suitable* partner, for such a ceremonious occasion," I added. "As a married woman and Queen."

I felt a mild shame at my invoking Urien as an excuse, though I supposed he might as well be useful for something.

"It's a consideration," Arthur mused. "Darling, whom do we have befitting my dear sister's grace and status?"

"Oh, I'm sure no one would be good enough for Lady Morgan," Guinevere said.

Arthur failed to catch the tartness in her voice. "You are generous as ever, my love, but I'm not yet defeated." He stepped away, casting his eyes over the room.

"What a shame," Guinevere said. "It seems you will not be joining us after all."

"It's kind of you to spare me," I replied. "Given I didn't waste time on Your Highness's dance lessons."

Her eyes flashed, but before I could enjoy her affront, she went directly to Arthur's side and murmured in his ear.

"How perfect!" he exclaimed. "Why didn't I think of it myself?"

The Queen spoke to a page, and within moments a tall, familiar figure strode up and bowed to the King and Queen. He wore a blue silk tunic crisscrossed with silver thread—his favoured shades and a reminder of his sporting success.

"Sir Accolon," Arthur said. "I have a request to make."

No no no. I looked frantically around the room for escape, but my brother's gaze held us trapped. Guinevere smiled like a cat in a milking parlour, though she had little concept of how thoroughly she had bested me.

Accolon bowed. "Of course, my lord King. What do you wish of me?"

"My noble sister seeks a suitable dance partner, and you are a man who dances as well as he rides," Arthur said. "My esteemed Guest of Honour and his Lady of Luck—what could be a worthier pairing?"

"My lord, I'm not sure—" I began.

"I'll hear no refusal!" Arthur's tone was both genial and defied argument. "Come, it will please me greatly."

Offering Guinevere his arm, they walked regally down the dais's central steps and to the rose-garlanded dancing area, Accolon and I following in unwitting obedience. Other pairs crowded the floor, eager to dance the same round as the royal couple.

My brother pointed us to a place near the musicians' stage. "There, now we may begin. I commend you both to God."

Arthur and Guinevere glided off to the centre spot, minstrels awaiting his command, as the participants shifted into dancing hold, entwining fingers and moving close. I looked up at Accolon's grim face. This would never work; aside from anything else, he wouldn't be willing to take me into his arms for all the sunken treasure in God's blue oceans.

He sighed. "Know that I would not have chosen this."

"As if the thought ever crossed my mind," I said. "What should we do?"

"I don't think either one of us wishes to disappoint our King."

"Not *that*," I hissed. "I never learned this dance and don't know the steps."

"I do," he replied.

I rolled my eyes. "Of course. It's all very well, *you* knowing."

"*Sang de Dieu.*" He exhaled in impatience, then looked at me. His eyes were so dark within our shared shadows that I caught my insolent, upturned face in their reflection. "What I meant, *my lady*, is if you hold on to me and allow me to take you . . ."

"I hardly think so—" I began.

". . . then not only will the King be pleased, but no one will wonder why we are disobeying a royal request. We are already delaying the entire dance."

He wasn't wrong; the music waited on Arthur's command, and my brother was awaiting our readiness with a look of confusion. We were the last couple not in hold. If we walked away now, there would be no stopping the whispers, and I was so close: to being rid of The Gaul's distracting presence, to Arthur's council table and my entire future. Still, to touch him felt like a bridge I did not know how to cross.

"Do not misunderstand," Accolon said softly. "I will weather it—we both will—if the answer is no. I do this only with your full consent."

I looked back at him and within his honesty, his mirrored doubt, I found my path.

"You have it," I said.

Swiftly, he took hold of me, his warm nearness a surprise as he threaded his fingers through mine and raised our arms into the first dance position. Arthur observed with a satisfied nod, lifting a hand to the stage, and all at once the music was upon us, swooping, rhythmic, irresistible, and it was far too late to do anything but dance.

Led by Arthur and Guinevere, dancing pairs fanned outwards to stand side by side, splayed towards the centre of the room. Starting with the Queen, each lady was drawn towards her partner in an elegant crescent, following an order I could not discern. I had never felt the lack of a dance lesson more.

"*Alors*," Accolon said. "Follow me and watch your feet."

"Yes, thank you," I said sarcastically. "I am perfectly capable of—"

His firm tug on my arm caught me unawares, and I spun too fast, feet tangling with the hem of my gown. I careered inwards in a half fall and collided with Accolon's hard torso.

An involuntary gasp escaped my lungs. We stared at one another, stunned at the impact, the sudden heat of our bodies touching from collarbone to thigh. Our eyes held the same stricken thought: that the last time we were this close was nine years in the past and we were—well, it did not bear thinking about.

"*Pardon*, my lady," he said, quickly stepping back. He put his hands to my waist and held me at bay, picking up the music with a deft corrective step. "Place your palms against my chest and follow me—south to north, west to east. It stays this way for a while."

Cheeks burning, I did as instructed, resting my hands on his silken chest and following his feet. This phase of the dance was slow and intricate, but we found our rhythm with astonishing quickness, our movements instinctive, natural, even enjoyable. Like celestial bodies we wove in and out, and for that long, flowing moment, he and I were luminous, all we needed to be.

"There, it's not so difficult," Accolon murmured. "Even for us."

The notion ached unexpectedly in my chest. *After all these years,* I thought, *we are finally dancing together for the first time, and it is under these circumstances, when we can hardly bear it.*

Accolon glanced down with a slight frown, as if feeling my mood shift.

"What's wrong?" he asked, and I found myself wanting to tell him the truth, to acknowledge the strangeness of this current moment and the star-crossed events of our past. I reached inside, seeking the words, but they were too far away, caught beneath the impossible pain in my sternum.

"Nothing," I said. "I was only thinking that you do know this dance as if you were born to it."

It was the best I could offer, inconsequential small talk that said nothing, meant nothing. Accolon studied my face a moment longer, then offered a smile of concession that fluttered within my gut more than it ought.

"Tomorrow we conclude, Lady Morgan," he said. "I assume your favour resides with my opponent in the final joust?"

It was a relief to return to my idle scorn. "I have a bet to win, and Sir Gawain is my nephew. I hope he grinds you into the dust."

The smile widened to a grin. "Then I'm afraid I may have to disappoint."

"I am well accustomed to that," I said archly. "You are a man of many mistakes."

"Indeed?" he exclaimed. "How so?"

"Your beard," I said. "It does not become you."

He laughed aloud, and it rang through me, bright and liberating like a bird's wing catching the air. "My lady, you wound me! With a sin so grave, how will I ever atone?"

"Well, when I win our bet and you leave, I'll never have to see your inadvisably barbered face again. The thought of you atoning elsewhere will be enough." How was it we were speaking without venom, our former sharpness translating into an exchange of jest?

"*Bien sûr*, Lady Morgan," Accolon replied. "But can I ever truly lose if you admit you will still be thinking of me?"

My breath caught, and before I could retort, the music changed, holding us suspended for a long moment, and I was once again thrown away from his warm hold. This time, I anticipated the swinging movement, returning to him with smooth ease.

Accolon smiled at our perfect rhythm, softly, privately, as if nothing outside this serene moment existed but his assured touch at my waist, and his heartbeat, fast and strong under my hands. Again, it occurred to me that perhaps there was another way, a new world of cordiality where our fraught and desperate deal ceased to matter, and no one was the victor, or had to live in defeat.

I could do it—we could—if he managed to find the words I needed to hear. A simple, honest apology, spoken aloud, to release me from my fury and heartache. Maybe then I could begin to forgive.

I spoke before I could change my mind. "Have you ever thought that neither of us needs to lose? That perhaps it . . . wouldn't be fair?"

Accolon's step took a slight hitch, but he quickly recovered. "You mean a sort of truce?"

Apologize to me now and we can move beyond this was what I wanted to say, but I was not as bold with him as I once was. "If the conditions were favourable, possibly," I said. "The right words, spoken in the right way, and I think it could settle things. Don't you?"

He gave me a long, discerning look. "'The right words' meaning?"

"An apology," I said.

"Prepare yourself," he said, to my confusion. Abruptly, he stopped and slid his hands up my back, tilting me backwards in what I realized was the dance's closing flourish. His body arched over mine, our faces so close I could almost see the thoughts whirring behind his eyes.

"Of course I agree," he said. "If it's truly what you wish."

The motion and his reply made me feel as though I had been plunged underwater. He eased me back up and I nodded, a door swinging open to our new path. "It is."

Accolon drew a deep breath. "I appreciate the gesture, Lady Morgan, but in truth, it wouldn't be knightly of me to belabour this concession. You needn't speak it aloud—I accept your apology."

"You . . . *what?*"

The music trounced its final note to immediate applause, drowning out my exclamation. Accolon took my questioning expression to mean I hadn't heard him.

"I accept your apology, my lady," he repeated. "You're right—honest words are fairer. Manassen said engaging with you would be a waste of time, but I knew if I was patient and allowed us to converse enough, we could end this. Now you are unburdened, and I am free to join the court. This truce can signal our conclusion, once and for all."

"Once and for all?" I echoed, wondering if I had misheard him amidst the applause still ringing out for the musicians.

"Of course," he went on, "whatever happens tomorrow, you're no longer under any obligation to speak to the King on my behalf. My dancing with you should shore up his approval. But in truth, I'm impressed. I never dreamed you would apologize. I didn't think you believed it owed to me."

This I heard clearly enough. "Are you mad?" I exclaimed. "I owe you *nothing!*"

I pushed his hands from my waist, breaking away from his confident hold. "Is that what this was—accepting the joust token, offering greater civility, this dance—it was all a ruse to curry favour with my brother then never *speak* to me again?"

His brow clouded in apparent confusion. "It seemed the only way," he said. "I thought this was what you—"

"My God," I cut in. "To think I was almost persuaded you might have changed. Apologize, to *you?*"

"I don't understand," he began, but I'd had enough and made to storm off.

Accolon caught hold of my sleeve. "Morgan, wait," he said.

Standing as we were in the middle of Camelot's Great Hall, I could not slap his hand off me, but turned on him fiercely. At the sight of the cold fury in my eyes, his faint grip fell away and he recoiled, stiffening like I held Medusa in my stare.

"Don't you *dare* speak my name," I said, and stalked away, wishing I too could turn into stone.

13

THE ROYAL PAVILION was packed with bodies, including the joust-vanquished knights from the Royal Court and several new faces invited by Arthur. On my way to my seat, I encountered a grinning, long-defeated Sir Guiomar—who kissed my hand solicitously as I passed—and caught the cold, lean stare of Sir Manassen.

His shameless cousin had already disturbed my night's sleep, my mind replaying every moment of our catastrophic dance. Accolon had once again made a fool of me, but the tournament wasn't over yet, and he was still bound by the terms of our deal.

The seating arrangements had changed—Lady Clarisse was at Arthur's side next to Sir Kay, and my dubious privilege was to sit beside the Queen's throne, so we could bestow our favours on the finalists in ceremonial conjunction. I took my seat, missing the breeze from Lady Clarisse's dove-feather fan. The air between the draped silks was more oppressive than ever, weeks of heat baked into the parched soil and rising up to meet the relentless sun. My tightly pinned hair ached atop my head like a coil of pythons. Today, at least, it would all be over.

Amidst the usual blast of trumpets, we were called to our feet as Arthur and Guinevere arrived, still golden and unwearied, gliding along the tilt field before the applauding crowd. The couple ascended to their waiting thrones for the final time before another blare of pompous notes announced the arrival of the tournament's two finest combatants.

Sir Gawain—my sister Morgause's eldest son, and mine and Arthur's nephew—was called in first, his alabaster destrier reflecting the plain white silks he wore as Queen's Knight. Young, bold and strong, he looked like his father but carried my sister's tenacity, riding twice around the arena to the sound of roaring popularity, and pulling up at the pavilion with the brisk confidence of a born prince.

He dismounted and waited at the bottom of the steps as the herald announced, "Sir Accolon of Gaul!"

The crowd cheered even louder, and Accolon rode in, sitting relaxed atop his prancing black horse, silver-blue armour incandescent in the high sunlight. He took his lap slower so the audience could admire him, arm lifted in a gracious wave. Even the way he approached the Royal Pavilion was presumptuous, swinging down from his mount and shaking Sir Gawain's hand in a careless, masculine fashion, laughing heartily at some shared amusement as they climbed the steps.

King and Queen greeted the finalists, Arthur thanking the former competitors, the crowd, and the "two valiant men who deserve so much praise." Guinevere stepped forwards, tying her pristine white favour around Sir Gawain's arm and accepting his kiss of homage upon her regal hand.

Accolon looked at me expectantly, and the memory of the dance, his audacity, spiked along my spine. In the purse at my belt, the yellow favour sat waiting, but I made no move to reach for it, returning his gaze of entitlement with a stare like knives. He would learn the hard way that I owed him nothing but vengeance.

"Queen Morgan," Guinevere said. "Please, do your duty by this worthy knight."

"I cannot," I told her. "I don't have the favour."

"Don't be silly," she said. "This is no time for jest."

"Then it's just as well I am sincere. Unfortunately, the favour caught on a candle and burned to ashes."

The Queen's delicate nostrils flared. Beside her, Arthur bestowed his blessing upon Gawain and turned enquiringly to our procrastination.

"Lady Morgan," Guinevere warned. "Traditions must be kept."

With a subtle exasperation only I saw, Accolon propped his wrist on his sword pommel and sighed skywards. His impatience struck me like lightning.

"*I don't have it*," I snapped, and sat down.

The full force of realization arrived, painting both Guinevere and Accolon's cheeks an indignant red. The final trumpet blast warned the jousters to take their places, and Arthur half raised his hand to signal a delay, but The Gaul shook his head.

"It's all right, Your Highness," he said tersely. "I will not hinder proceedings. I commend my lord King and lady Queen to God."

Arthur gave a stunned nod, and Accolon swept away to mount his horse, while I tasted the bittersweet darkness of satisfaction.

Guinevere glared down at me. "This is unacceptable. Give him something else." She turned to the King. "Call Sir Accolon back for a favour—it's tradition."

"I'm sure it's an honest mistake." Arthur shifted his gaze to me, and I had to rise. "Have you an alternative, sister?"

"No, my lord," I said.

"Honest mistake!" Guinevere said. "She must have *something*, but wishes to make me look a fool, on this, of all days. I will not have it."

She snatched at the purse at my belt; I had no choice but to grab her wrist.

"Don't *touch* me," I snarled. "High Queen or not, my body and mind are *no one's* to control."

"Morgan, good God!" Arthur stepped between us, his expression horrified.

"You see how she is," Guinevere hissed. "How many times must I say it?"

Arthur put a reassuring hand on her elbow. "Take your seat, darling. Morgan, come with me."

Grim-faced, he pointed to the other side of his throne, waving Kay to stand up and ushering me into the seat beside Lady Clarisse. He signalled for the heralds to start reading the joust rules, and sat down with an air of hard-won composure.

"What in all Heaven was that?" he muttered.

"Don't ask me," I said. "I had nothing to give, and the Queen wouldn't listen."

"She is *upset*, Morgan. By your behaviour, and for failing to keep Camelot's tournament tradition. These things are important."

I suppressed an eye roll, but my brother noted it.

"I am well used to your stubbornness," he said, "and often weather it because of my high regard, but it has no place here. There's an order to things, and duties we promised to perform. What is the *matter* with you?"

I was about to argue I had never promised to be the midwife of The Gaul's luck, when I sensed a whisper of observation across my skin. Glancing up, I spotted Accolon walking his horse in an anticipatory circle, his eyes fixed on my conversation with Arthur. The look of suppressed panic on his face said everything; he believed I was telling the King exactly what I thought of his Guest of Honour.

I put my hand on my brother's arm. "I didn't mean to react that way," I said. "You never called me to receive the letters from Yvain's nurses, which has been a source of agitation today."

Arthur sighed, drawing down a veil of brotherly sympathy. "I see. But I cannot excuse such scene-making, much less on the tournament's most important day. For now, there are other things at hand."

He sat back in his throne, and I retreated with the same dignity. Across the arena, Accolon tore his eyes away, pushing on his helm and accepting the first lance.

"No favour for Lady Joliete's beau today?" Lady Clarisse asked.

"No," I said airily. "Though I wouldn't worry for your bet. He has confidence enough."

She chuckled. "Let's hope your luck isn't as potent as they claim."

The thought relaxed me somewhat. Gawain's tournament record was almost as impressive as Accolon's, and his anxious spying proved I had crept under his skin. Victory might yet be mine.

At the hush of the crowd, the herald's flag came down. The first charge was typical of Accolon—explosive, intense, daunting to most competitors—but Gawain met him at pace. Accolon's strike connected first, but the speed from both sides was too great, and it merely skidded across his opponent's shield. In turn, Gawain held firm, his lance shattering against Accolon's shoulder and rocking him backwards.

The crowd gasped, but The Gaul pulled his balance back to centre saddle at once, cantering back to his squire. He tossed down the lance and pushed his visor up, grimacing at his stricken shoulder. The left pauldron was badly dented, so he tore it free, shrugging his shield higher.

Both knights rode more steadily into the next charge, the second clash clean but tremendous. In the same heartbeat, their lances hit the centre of the other's shield, coloured splinters raining onto the grass. The crowd cheered at the ear-splitting crash, then groaned as both riders easily stayed ahorse.

"They're sitting well," Lady Clarisse remarked to Sir Kay behind us. "It seems your father may get his wish to adjudicate a draw."

"Not as it stands," Kay replied. "Gawain took a pauldron. So far, the contest is in his favour. Sir Accolon has no choice but to unhorse."

"Or land a strike far worse," I put in. "The helm."

"If he missed, he'd be unseated for certain," Lady Clarisse said. "Surely he won't risk it?"

Sir Kay shrugged. "Gawain will likely not fall for any lesser strike."

The final charge bell rang and the Royal Pavilion stood in unison, even Lady Clarisse. Accolon swapped lances and snapped down his visor, and as he gathered the reins I had the sudden, overwhelming conviction that whichever of us proved the victor here, something definitive would also be lost.

The flag dropped; Accolon straightened his horse, gave a twitch of his golden spurs, and charged. Lifting the lance, he tilted it slightly upwards, seeking the helm.

I knew it, I thought, heart leaping at my innate knowledge of him.

Such a move was fearless and foolish—too much height and the opponent's shield would parry it easily; too low and it would miss the small target and leave him open to an easy counterstrike. My hands gripped the railing, knuckles white.

Gawain noticed the move just in time, pushing his body up in the saddle and taking the hit squarely on his shoulder. The evasion sent him sideways, but his Orkney determination held true, lance grazing the surface of Accolon's shield enough to count.

The crowd held its collective breath, hoping for something decisive, but Gawain stayed ahorse. At the end of the barrier, both knights wheeled around to the judges' pavilion, where five fair-minded adjudicators were already huddled in discussion.

Eventually, Sir Ector stood, thumbs hooked in his gold belt.

"Worthy knights!" he shouted. "You have competed valiantly and are equally matched! Therefore, the victor will be decided by sword combat, until one of you yields."

A deafening roar took up in the stands. To finish a drawn joust on a sword fight was an old custom from harsher days, where death often chose the winner. At Camelot, they would fight with blunted blades, but it was still a rare spectacle.

Arthur leaned across. "This will be interesting, though Sir Accolon doesn't look pleased. Perhaps you could bestow a favour upon him now, sister."

"Sir Gawain is your nephew," I replied. "How will he feel if he sees you showing favour to his opponent?"

"It would not be my gesture," he pointed out. "Now is the opportunity to right a wrong."

The word *wrong* prickled hot up my neck. "No, brother. It would not be right. If you wish to call your well-known fairness into question, then I suggest you tie the favour yourself."

He recoiled and I regretted it, but I was deep in the tangle of thorns I had planted now; the only way out was through.

On the field, the knights had dismounted to prepare. Accolon chose to fight without his helm, mail hood gathered into a cowl around his neck. He tested the round-pointed sword's weight as the audience bayed in excitement, stamping their feet to the royal drums in an irresistible, blood-pounding rhythm.

A deep horn sounded; Accolon pushed his hair off his brow, spun the blade in his hand and strode forth.

The first blow came from Gawain, a hurled, overeager attempt that The Gaul comfortably blocked, throwing it sideways with casual force. My nephew threw another, and another, pushing forwards in furious purpose while Accolon parried with little effort, as if he could duel this way for a week and not tire. Someone in the crowd hooted, and he smiled.

At length, they fenced their way past the King and Queen until they were below my seat, Accolon idly blocking a slash towards his bare head. I leaned over the railing and my movement made him glance up, our gaze locking like a turned key.

The ease in his eyes drained, joylight of duelling dissolving into blue-black hardness. I glared down at him in challenge as Gawain swung his sword once more, laying a two-handed blow against Accolon's hip. Shocked, he crumpled, and my gut lurched, but instead of letting himself fold, The Gaul came violently to life. Eyes still on mine, he tossed aside Gawain's next shoulder strike and returned the blow, smashing my nephew on the arm and causing him to drop his shield.

Accolon threw down his own shield, raining blows across Gawain's body and avoiding a ferocious counterstrike with a graceful sidestep. He looked up at me again, breathing hard, no longer angry but sad, tired, wanting only to be done, and for a strange, quick moment I felt I had got everything terribly wrong. Our gaze held for a heartbeat, then Accolon cut his eyes away, and with savage proficiency brought the blunted blade in an elegant arc, dealing his opponent a stunning blow to the side of the head.

Gawain fell like a rock, sprawling on his back, to the collective gasp of the crowd. The side of his helm was dented, tournament sword flown feet away. He stirred, pushing his visor up and gasping for air. Accolon levelled his swordpoint at Gawain's chest.

"Yield," he said quietly.

Gawain nodded and croaked, "I yield."

Swiftly, Accolon reached down, unlacing the leather ties under my nephew's helm and pulling it free. He slung his shoulder beneath Gawain and heaved him upright, turning them both to the largest spectator stand, noise growing even louder at the display of knightly honour. The former opponents embraced in a musical clash of mail, then Gawain—smiling, dazed, his nose beginning to bleed—ushered his vanquisher up the pavilion steps.

Finally, definitively, I had lost.

All at once I knew why. My lethal mistake wasn't within our game, but entering into battle with Accolon at all. I had assumed we were playing anew, when in reality, we were halfway through a conflict I could never win.

After a rousing speech in celebration of a brilliant, hard-fought contest, my brother turned to his winner in private. "Such an impressive performance, Sir Accolon," I heard Arthur say. "Though I must apologize on behalf of my sister's forgetfulness. Such a lapse should not have happened at my tournament."

"Think nothing of it, my lord." Accolon cut his eyes to me and then away. "Luck is an unreliable mistress. Better to depend upon my skill than her inconstant heart."

Arthur smiled and put a hand on his victor's shoulder. "A gracious knight, as ever. Nevertheless, we will find a way to make this up to you. Bring your best bow and spear on the hunting trip—we have much to discuss about your future."

Ever obliging to his King, The Gaul knelt with a swift, familiar grace that sent a shiver across the back of my shoulders. In turn, Arthur raised his tournament champion up and embraced him like a brother, and though I stared endlessly at the side of his head, seeking a look of triumph, pride, fury, anything, Accolon did not look at me again.

14

I WOULD NOT for anything be compelled to go to the final banquet, nor did anyone summon me in my absence. The following day, a page brought the letters from Yvain's nurses to my chambers—detailed, blandly informative missives, positive enough. My son was happy and healthy, his father attentive, good-tempered and generous, which I found both infuriating and reassuring. Arthur had obviously deemed there was nothing further to discuss.

After a while pacing wrathfully around my thoughts, I had decided: I was in no mood for revels, and if the hunting trip was to be spent fawning over Accolon of Gaul, then I would not go. Time alone was what I craved. Fortuitously, Alys's study-sister at St. Brigid's before me was now prioress of a nunnery near the Kingswood, with an infirmary, good teaching and several female scribes, so I instructed her to accept the long-standing invitation to visit with Tressa, saying I had promised to take up the task of organizing Arthur's library.

Camelot reverted to a less frenetic hum of activity, tournament guests streaming out of the city under the still-blazing sun. Those left became absorbed by their arrangements for the Royal Summer Hunt, or returning to their own, quieter homes. Within days, aside from a scattering of servants, stablehands and a few guards on the outer walls, Arthur's great golden fortress would be deserted. The only obstacle was, I hadn't informed my brother I intended to remain.

My innate stubbornness held firm until the evening before the hunting party was due to leave. I sought Arthur in the hour before Evensong and guessed he would be in his Great Chamber, it being the time and place we had always spent our daily meetings. The Council Room door stood ajar, so I entered that way. An enormous rectangular table stretched the length of the room, a map of Britain painted upon its surface in green and blue—no longer the entire scope of Arthur's domain, but his kingdom's beating heart.

Walking along the coast, I passed the Crown's major palaces and strongholds, seas mauve in the rose-gold sunlight. Another gilded chair defined the head of the table by its proximity to Cornwall, mine and my brother's shared birthplace. I placed my hand over Tintagel Castle and felt my home like a storm in my chest.

"Morgan. I didn't call for you."

I looked up to see Arthur standing at the interior door. He glanced at my hand on the council table.

"I know," I replied. "But I thought I should come. Can we speak?"

"Briefly, yes. In here."

He led us into the Great Chamber, towards a table in a deep window embrasure, where a gold wine tray sat beside piles of parchment covered in the Seneschal's precise hand.

"Thank you for sending the letters from Yvain's nurses," I said. "They allayed my worries, just as you said."

"Good." He picked up the gold jug and hooked forth two goblets. "To what do I owe your unexpected company?"

My throat felt dry; preferably, the wine would have come first. "I've decided not to go on the Royal Summer Hunt."

He stopped pouring. "Is that so?"

"With your leave," I said automatically. "I have much to do here. The library, for one—you gave me the honour of ordering it months ago, and I haven't had time."

There was a leaden pause. "The Summer Hunt is a bright spot in my calendar, and I wish to share it with all of those whose company I enjoy. The library can wait."

"It's not just that," I said. "After reading the letters from Gore, I wish for some time alone to think about Yvain, the negotiations. Urien is a game player—not a very good one, but he will seek to prevaricate. If I'm prepared with my requirements, it will save time and trouble at Michaelmas. I'm sure you will not miss my presence in the Kingswood."

"That's not true," he replied. "I always wish for you to be near me, in case I am in need of your wisdom and skills."

His casual honesty unseated my convictions. What man, what king, had ever condescended to admit he needed my skills? Was I truly going to throw over my brother's plea just to shelve manuscripts, or because Accolon of Gaul won a specious bet?

"Perhaps you're right," I relented.

Arthur smiled and took a swig from his goblet. "Of course I am. Negotiations are a six-month away—there's plenty of time."

"Six months?" I made a quick calculation. "Michaelmas is in twelve weeks."

His eyes flashed then flickered away, roving the table, the sky outside, looking anywhere but my face.

"Arthur?" I said, and it hit me like a stark wind: that my brother was profoundly unskilled at subterfuge and I had never known it, because before now he had only ever given me the truth.

He let out a guilty breath. "King Urien's letter stated that he cannot come to court at Michaelmas. The meeting has been pushed to Christmastide, and Yvain will stay with him."

Gooseflesh crept over my skin, despite the room's oppressive heat. "But that was days ago. You told me everything was well."

"It is," he said. "You've seen the nurses' reports. There was no gain in telling you the details before the final joust. My focus, everyone's focus, needed to be on the tournament."

"So you *lied* to me?"

Arthur stiffened. "I did not lie, sister. I merely decided not to share the contents of a private message with you. As is my right."

"Oh, don't try that twisting kingly talk with me." I walked in a tight circle, trying to think beyond the building roar inside my head. "Urien suggested September. He *agreed* that it was time to resolve things. He cannot just change his mind. If you say he must come to court, he has to attend. Why can't we—why can't *you*—deny him this?"

Arthur shook his head. "I can certainly order him to court, and hold him in my service for forty days. But I cannot demand he bring Yvain, or force him to negotiate terms for your son unless he is willing. We've discussed this, Morgan. The rights of the father are—"

"God-given and absolute," I snapped. "I know. I've heard it a thousand times."

He sighed and gestured to a chair. "Let's sit down."

"Why? So you can persuade me that everything is fine, and legal, and I should go along? It's not good enough, Arthur. All this power and influence, yet we must let Urien take Yvain the moment he is old enough to interest him? You don't know my husband as I do—too much rein makes him bolder. He fears your authority, and if you refuse to wield it—"

My brother held up a silencing hand. "There are a hundred ways to solve this without force or causing offence. It doesn't always have to be about wielding power."

Easy to say, I thought, *when you already have it.*

"Then what do you suggest?" I asked.

"For one, you could go to Gore when we travel north," he replied. "King Urien has offered many times, despite the . . . difficulties between you. There would be no expectations of marital accord, of course, and the guard I sent would be there for your use. If more time with Yvain is what you wish, it is worth considering."

I stared at him, aghast. "That is *not* the answer."

"Another solution that you refuse!" he said. "In that case, you may have to get used to being apart from your son sometimes, as with many women of your class. I've tried to help you, sister, but perhaps it is less the choices than your uncompromising mind. Lately, there are many things you are simply unwilling to do."

"Such as?"

He raised a hand, counting off my sins. "Your presence at my wife's side has been much diminished, not to mention the lack of regard she says you show her. During the tournament you arrived late and left early, delayed events and refused to participate in some traditions. You missed the final banquet altogether. And what you did to Sir Accolon . . ."

"Sir Accolon!" I exclaimed. "What has he to do with any of this?"

"You know what I speak of. Your forgetfulness, or refusal, or damned wilfulness—whatever it was—with the favour. How do you think it looked?"

"I don't see how that matters," I shot back, "given he won anyway."

Arthur shook his head in exasperation. "Precisely my point. You hold a complete disregard for anything that does not immediately matter to you. How do you think my wife felt, bearing the brunt of your public disrespect? How I felt, having to prevent your unrest? How do you think Sir Accolon felt, ignored and having to ride off without Camelot's good wishes? It shamed us all."

"How *he* felt? Are you telling me that Sir Accolon winning the tournament with a piece of cloth around his arm is more important than your own sister? You lied to me about my son, and for what—so you could enjoy *yet another* banquet in your glorious honour?"

"Do not say that, Morgan," Arthur warned. "Don't accuse me of harms I did not cause. This tournament meant a great deal to me— the commemoration of my marriage, the benefit to the realm. All I wanted was for it to go forth as I long planned."

"Oh, a plague on your precious tournament!" I cried. "I am sick to the back teeth of hearing about it!"

We stared at one another, stunned. I had never before raised my voice to him and could not have imagined doing so in a hundred years. My limbs began to shiver and I shut my eyes, willing our disharmony away.

"There is no gain in this," Arthur said. "I think you should leave."

When I looked again he had changed, animation replaced with an eerie stillness. "Brother, I didn't mean—" I began.

"In fact," he interrupted, "perhaps it's best that you do not come on the hunting trip. It seems some time to consider your actions, and your future, is exactly what you need."

I shook my head. "No, Arthur—we are better than this. We share one vision, one mind. We transcend these things because we share blood."

"*Half* our blood," he said.

The cold cruelty of it struck my chest like a dagger, but his forbidding, steel-eyed posture didn't waver. With a hurt, furious glare, I turned on my heel and fled.

15

I DIDN'T KNOW where I was going, only that I was running, up
staircases, through passageways and past my own chambers, burning
on the fuel of my rage, until I found myself pounding on an unfa-
miliar door.

There was no answer at first, but I kept battering until I heard an
impatient call from within. At length, the door swung lazily open.

"You," I said accusingly.

Accolon stiffened as if shot with an arrow.

"It wasn't enough to win, was it?" I said. "You had to make me
look a fool."

With a wordless scoff, he made to shut the door. I slammed my
hand against it.

"I am a lady of King Arthur's house—you are bound by your
knightly code to show me courtesy. Unless you wish me to shout my
grievances through a closed door?"

"Grievances?" he exclaimed. "What in all Hell—?"

A white flash caught in the tail of my eye: a liveried page emerging
at the end of the hallway, seeking the noise. I grabbed Accolon's
elbow and bundled him inside.

It was a generous chamber, low-beamed but well-furnished, with
a separate dressing room. The jewelled victory chalice he had won in
the tournament stood on a nearby wine table.

Accolon stalked a wide arc of the room, coming to rest beside a large bed draped in blue hangings. He wore breeches and a loose linen shirt, and the coverlet behind him was rumpled, as if he had been lying down.

"Well?" he said, leaning against the bedpost. "What do you want?"

"You know what I want," I replied.

"Believe me when I say I do not."

"I want you to *go*," I said. "Give up your plans to join the court and disappear from my sight once and for all."

Accolon stared at me in astonishment. "I don't understand you. I tried to keep my distance, and that didn't work. We made a bet, which I won fairly despite your efforts at sabotage, and *still* you come for me. What is this truly about?" He threw up his hands in surrender. "Never mind. *C'est foutu.*"

With decisive grace, he strode towards the door, reaching past my shoulder for the handle.

"Go then," I said acidly. "After all, leaving me is what you're good at."

The door thudded shut. "I . . . *What?*"

"You heard me," I snapped. "You said you loved me, came to my bed and swore your heart was mine; then when you had enough you ran, abandoning me at Tintagel without a word."

He recoiled as if I had struck him. "I *abandoned* you? Morgan, you married a King! *You* left *me!*"

The sheer wrongness of his declaration knocked the power of speech from me. Accolon swung away, pacing back and forth like a wolf at a cave mouth.

"God knows I didn't want to believe it," he said. "Even after the betrothal announcement, I thought no, not after all we've done. Morgan *loves me*—there will be an explanation."

He stopped and looked up, the lines of his face drawn grim, as if he had aged ten years since I first chased him into the room.

"And then," he said, "I saw you with him. Standing with your King, smiling, laughing, holding his arm. Looking like a pair already wed."

The colours we wore, I thought. *Urien's cursed green and gold.*

Accolon shrugged into my silence. "I knew at once you were gone."

So it was true—he had seen my meeting with Urien and simply fled. Ninianne's assumption on the headland was correct: his betrayal was nothing but a failure of love.

It should have been a triumph, to hold the truth, the power to destroy his righteousness, but I only felt raw, scorched anew. I turned away from his conviction, walking a slanting path of sunset to the high-silled window. Two panes sat open against the day's heat, but in the sky the light had turned, igniting the clouds and casting the castle walls in a strange, sulphuric yellow. An errant breeze gusted across me.

"You're wrong," I said. "Back then, as you are now."

"No," he replied. "I'm not. He was the life you wanted, the one who could provide you with everything you deserved. I was a mistake, a complication you didn't want. So I did the honourable thing and left, for your own good."

The destructive weight of the word snapped any patience I had mustered. I spun around, blazing. "The *honourable* thing?" I cried. "Is that what you've spent the last nine years telling yourself? All this time you've been living without an ounce of guilt, glorying in your suffering like some lance-carrying *saint?*"

His eyes hardened with offence. "How am I wrong? You married him, did you not?"

He fixed me with his dark, flat gaze, mouth pursed, awaiting my defeat, the justification for everything he had done. His insolent, sanctimonious expression sent a tidal wave of fury through my body that drowned every shred of my sadness.

I raised a shaky finger. "Listen to me, *honourable* Sir Accolon— you don't know a damned thing. I never wanted to marry King Urien of Gore. Not the day you saw us together, the day I spoke my marriage vows or any day since. *I did it to save you.*"

He didn't flinch, but I watched his face change, eyes flashing with a sudden, febrile doubt.

"Uther Pendragon was going to hunt you down and *murder* you," I continued. "He gave me a choice—marry King Urien or find your burned and quartered body hanging from his gallows one day. So I chose you—over myself, or any life worth living. All so *you* could be safe, and free."

Accolon had paled in the time it took me to upend his worldview. "No," he said hoarsely. "Why would you say this?"

"Because it's the truth."

There was a long, aching silence. Then, inevitably, "But how did he know?"

I sighed in concession. "I told him. Commend yourself to God for my error. But you weren't there—you don't know. I said I couldn't marry because I'd given myself to another, then recanted everything when he tried to force your name from me. There was time to find our way—right up until you took your horse and arms and godforsaken pride and rode out of Tintagel, putting your name in Uther Pendragon's mouth."

Warm tears pricked the corners of my eyes, but I refused to let him see me cry. "I was trying to save us. Back then I would have done *anything* to keep you from harm. I loved you more than my own life."

A sharp, humourless laugh escaped me. "Sweet Jesus, how wrong I was! I misjudged everything—my own cleverness, that monster Pendragon, and most of all I misjudged *you*, didn't I? All of our talk, the intimacy, the love we gave so fiercely, and in one jealous glance you believed I had thrown you over for some popinjay with a crown."

Accolon's long body swayed, breaths drawn hard, the truth like a poison seeping through his veins. "I can't—I don't . . ."

He stumbled to the bed, dropping heavily onto the mattress, head in his hands. I retreated to the window, steadying myself against the cool stone sill.

"So now you know," I said. "I saved your life and lived with the consequences, while you jousted and revelled your way across the Continent with your honour shining, fuelled by your hatred of me."

"No," came a firm, muffled voice.

It turned me back. "No *what?*"

Accolon raised his head, eyes holding the same startling look as in the fountain courtyard, stormy and honest. "I never hated you, Morgan. I've felt many things when I think of you, but not hatred. It—it's not in me."

His sudden candour played a melody across my nerves that I wished I didn't feel.

"Have you . . . hated me?" he asked.

I wanted to snap "Yes," crack a whip across his feelings and regain control. Yet to look at him then was to remember us at Tintagel, a time and place long gone, but still home in my very depths; the memory of a love wild and real, and a pain that could not have cut so deep if there wasn't something extraordinary to grieve.

"No," I said, and it came as a sigh. "I tried very hard—Lord knows it would have been easier—but I couldn't hate you."

"I'm glad." His brow cleared, as if it was all he needed to feel better, when I still felt like a glass vessel thrown against a wall.

"Do not mistake me, Accolon of Gaul," I said forcefully. "I hated what you did, and what happened to my life in your wake. Whatever my heart wanted to feel, I did my best to silence it. And if you had any decency, you would leave me in peace. Go back to your fame, your knightly glory and your betrothed."

He frowned. "My . . . who?"

"Don't waste your breath on denial. Just go from here, dedicate your victories to your beloved somewhere else, and I hope to God you are better to her than you were to me."

"For the love of Christ, Morgan, I'm not betrothed!"

He was up and across the room in three strides. "The truth is," he said, then halted with a sudden look of self-doubt. I regarded him, unyielding, and he drew a deep breath. "The absolute truth is . . . that my every victory is dedicated to you."

My heart leapt, bruising itself against my sternum. "Don't be *ridiculous*," I said.

Accolon raised a slight, forlorn smile, the first flutter of amusement we had shared since our disastrous dance. "*Incroyable, non?* But it's true."

"No. All these years you thought I left you for another man. Why would you?"

"For a long time you were all I could think about," he confessed. "My first joust victory was scrappy, an ignoble challenge at a forest bridge, but in the relief of success I put my hand on my heart and your name flew out. In defiance, maybe. To prove that I was worth something."

He winced, but his eyes didn't waver from mine. "From then on, I jousted, I won, I sent it up to the heavens in your name. For better or worse, you have been with me these long years. Only you."

A hard lump had formed in my throat. "The Devil take me," I muttered, swiping shameful tears away. They kept pouring anyway, a hot torrent I couldn't control.

"Morgan . . ." Accolon moved towards me, but I held up a warding hand. "What can I do?" he said hopelessly.

"Go back to Gaul," I said. "For both of our sakes. Keep believing in all my wrongs. Tell yourself that I am a liar, an ambitious seductress who ruined your life, and forget about me. And I will forget about you."

A wave of pain crossed his face. "Is that what you want?" Accolon said. "To forget about me?"

I found myself raising my hand, wanting to smooth the suffering from his brow, realign the mask that had protected us both. Or maybe I just wanted to touch him, to feel his bones, his skin, his heat, under my fingertips and remember how things had once been.

It was too much, and not enough. Instead, I dropped my fingers to my neck and let them fuss with the fine gold chain.

"Yes," I said, and knew it was a lie before it left my lips.

His eyes flicked to the fretting at my collarbone. Gently, he lifted his hand and slipped one finger under the tiny glittering links. I fell still, allowing him.

In slow loops, he wrapped the chain around his fingertip, watching my face all the while. The pulse in my neck throbbed so hard I wondered if he could feel it vibrating against his knuckle.

The Gaulish coin shifted, resisting briefly against my skin before yielding to him. Like a tiny sun, it rose from my gown, sliding across Accolon's open palm. He studied one side and the other, then closed his hand around its warmth. When he looked up, his eyes were like the surface of a lake.

"You kept this?" he said.

"Yes," I said.

"Why?"

"I couldn't bear to take it off."

I watched my words dawn on his face, everything it meant. He reared back, hand dragging through his hair. The coin plummeted, sounding a faint chime against my bodice.

"I am a knave, a reckless fool," he said. "All these years, I have carried you with me, and you have carried me. Our lives spent apart, wasted, because I— *What have I done?*"

In a swift reversal he was back with me, arms outstretched, a hopeless sinner awaiting absolution. In slow motion, I laid my palms upon his and let his hands close around mine.

"I'm sorry, Morgan," he said, and a single tear ran down his cheek like a diamond.

I followed its descent along the face I had once studied, and kissed, and loved so much, but in its wake came cold futility, clattering hard against my body.

"Don't say that—what good does it do!" I pushed his hands to his chest. "Say that I never meant anything to you but a moment's pleasure, that we would have tired of one another and you wouldn't change a moment of your life. But for the love of God, do not say you are *sorry*."

I felt him slump against my resistance. "Take it back, *now*," I urged.

He shook his head. "No."

Another tear fell, cutting a silvery track over his cheekbone. I reached up and brushed it away. "Do not be good to me, Accolon. Call me a liar and a vixen and a witch, but do not say you wish you'd trusted me and regret these last nine years, because I don't think I can stand it."

He leaned into my touch, soft and stubborn. "I can't do that, Morgan. You were right and I was wrong, and I will be sorry for the rest of my life."

All I could do was let him go. I turned back to the window; night had descended quickly, thick tendrils of cloud blocking out the summer stars. The wind blew definitively now, sparring with the torches on the castle walls, flags twisting and snapping. The air felt fit to burst, a vital, metallic scent cutting through the stagnancy of heat.

At length, Accolon appeared beside me, resting his hands on the windowsill. "Please, say something."

"What's left to say?" I asked. "It was all so long ago—we're not the same people as we were then. Can either of us remember how it truly was?"

There was a long, fathomless silence, so pervasive that I wondered if he had ignored me, before I heard his breath let out.

"I do," he said. "Every word, every smile, every breath we took—all of it. As if it were a moment ago."

I kept my eyes on the glass, on the iron blue clouds beyond, whipping breeze mirroring my heart's quickening beat. My hand strayed across the sill, weaving one finger between his, then another.

"Tell me," I said.

His voice was a low, beautiful music. "That first night. I have it so clearly. Your face, when you saw it was me. The wine we poured and forgot to drink. Your hair as I held you, like a waterfall over my body."

Hands entwined, I let him turn me towards him, his clear, dark gaze as intense and unguarded as it had been on those precious few nights, solely for me. In his remembrance I found my own: conjuring touch and whispers and skin under candlelight; pale mornings and long nights where our blood was only fire; moments that were endless, until they were not. It felt like hours since I had last drawn breath.

"You smelled of lavender," he said. "Like the fields around Rouen in the sun. But you tasted of the sea."

Our inevitability crashed through me like high tide; I put my hands to his face and pulled him down into a kiss.

We were everything, all at once: tender and furious; the shock of the new colliding with a rush of deep knowledge and desire long held; of intimacy scored into our bones, as if we had been lovers all this time but our touch had never lost its thrill.

Our embrace took on a rapid, desperate intensity; my arms went around his neck, fingers twisting in his hair, cleaving him to me so tightly a feather couldn't have slipped between. In one swift jolt, Accolon lifted me onto the windowsill without letting our mouths break contact, hands fast to my back, no proximity close enough to sate us.

White light filled the window embrasure with a loud, cracking flash. We stopped, breathless; my eyes slid to the bed, steps away, and his followed. It would be so easy to take us there, to exorcise the ghost of our loss by returning us to ourselves in the way we had long craved. We looked back at one another, hungry, unsure, and the thunder caught up with the lightning in a rumbling crash.

It was not so simple. Much as my body sang out for him, my passion felt heedless, uncontrollable. I had lost too much, too often, to withstand its failures again.

I withdrew my arms from his neck and held him at bay. "We have to stop."

"Why?" Accolon said, and his willingness surprised me, bringing another surge of desire that was difficult to resist. I studied him at arm's length—older, broader, made hard and strong from battle and sport—and for a moment I wondered how he looked now, how he felt beneath his experience and the confidence he had found in his calling. Was he different, changed as a lover as he had as a man? Would he be mine, still?

It didn't matter, anyway; if we were unsuited, or as good as ever, we were doomed regardless.

"You know why," I said. "This is untenable, in all ways."

"Morgan, no," he protested. "I've heard those words—I've *said* those words. They began what tore us apart."

"Yet they are true," I said. "We cannot go back in time."

Another sheet of lightning illuminated us, thunder crashing like a portent. Accolon nodded reluctantly, easing me off the sill. I leaned my head on his chest.

"I would have gone anywhere with you," I said against his heart. "We were supposed to be together."

He said nothing, his breaths deep and heavy under my weight. I lifted my head and saw the strain of our shared grief between his brows, the three lines that had always been there cut deep with sorrow and longing.

"*Mon coeur*," was all he said, and I was weak for him, letting him kiss me with a slow, unfaltering tenderness that I felt deep in my veins.

When we finally parted, he rested his forehead against mine, and we stood that way for a long time, knowing this moment, too, would soon be over.

"How could you?" I whispered.

"I don't know," he said.

Our time was at an end, and we both knew it. But as I tore myself away and slipped through the door, Accolon's fingers caught mine, his touch crackling across my skin as new lightning lit the window. He held on for the length of another thunder crash, then with a last unreadable look, he let me go, as outside the first drops of storm rain began to fall.

*

NEVERTHELESS, I COULD not sleep, watching the windows ablaze amidst deep roars of thunder, the clatter of rain against glass, telling myself the weather's exhilarating turn meant nothing; that my sharp, bright nerves were only answering the natural uproar, and the reckless gallop of my heart would calm.

I turned over, away from the skies, and a tug of resistance caught at my neck: the gold chain tangled in my hair. I drew it free, and a streak of lightning lit the room, Gaulish coin incandescent in my hand. I snatched up my robe and ran into the night.

His door yielded without resistance. Accolon stood in the middle of the room, mid-pace, bare-chested, hand at his jaw in deep thought. At my entrance, his head flew up and lightning filled the window behind him, illuminating the chamber, the bed, sheets twisted and thrown back where he too had sought rest and failed.

I paused, suddenly stilled. Thunder drowned out the possibility of words, but his eyes on mine were enough—alive, desirous, deep as midnight, so full of want I felt I might turn into vapour if he did not move soon.

But he did. In one long stride he came, pulling me to his chest as I reached for him, hands seeking his shoulders, his neck, his face, no time to draw breath before my lips found his and I was kissing him, and he was kissing me, and it was far from enough.

Keeping my mouth on his, I put his hands to my waist and urged him to guide us, like the dance but better, surer, until the bed pressed against my back, and I pulled him down, arching over me. My legs entwined with his, our hands impatient, rapidly baring skin, mouths hungry and hot, bodies colliding with nine years' unspent desire under another furious storm.

The windowpane slammed open, rattling like bones as the tempest rushed in. Cool air surged across us, water hitting the sill in slick, relentless rhythm, making us inevitable.

We never could resist the sound of rain.

16

I WAS STILL in his arms when I awoke, roused by a breeze like feathers across my bare back. Sometime during the night, the raging storm had blown itself out, taking the oppressive heat with it, leaving cool, sweet air through the open window and benign sunlight dawning in a fresh blue sky.

Accolon lay fast asleep, handsome face tilted into the pillow, chest rising and falling with the depth of his breaths, one arm slung across my waist in casual possession. Mine again—or so it had felt hours earlier, when we collided like dark and light. Our reconciliation was not destined to be brief and we had savoured it, moment by moment, every kiss, every hungry touch and snatched breath an act of contrition against lost time.

The memory trembled through me, and he stirred, limbs loosening into a stretch. His eyes opened, blinking against the light, considering my presence through sleepy lids. Then, like a fleet breeze, he smiled, wide and genuine, so unexpectedly beautiful I felt it as an exquisite pain.

"Good morning," he murmured. "What better sight could one awake to?"

"That depends on whose sight," I said archly. "I still don't like your beard."

He laughed, sweeping me to his chest and kissing me with languorous grace. The scent of sleep and heat lingered on his skin, heady in my senses.

"For you, I'll shave it off," he said when we parted.

Unease drifted through me, soft and chill like first snowfall. "Don't make rash promises on my account," I said.

Extracting myself from his arms, I swung my legs out of bed and cast about the floor for my robe. My fingers found the crumpled silk and I pulled it on.

"Wait, wait, wait." Accolon caught hold of its edge. "The sun isn't at the window yet. There's no need to rush."

I said nothing, tying the belt in a knot. A shadow of realization crossed his face. "You are in a hurry to be gone."

He let the robe slip from his fingers and sat up, leaning bare-chested against the headboard, sheet taut across his waist. In the blurring ochre light of the night before I had not seen him so clearly, and the sight of his body in repose fluttered hot in my abdomen.

I knelt back on the bed and sought his hands with mine. "I'm just . . . not where I should be."

He smiled. "And if Lady Alys finds out, she will have me conveyed to the dungeon and order them to cut off my . . . head."

"If you're lucky," I jested, though the thought of Alys finding out settled ominously on my shoulders. "Besides, you are leaving for the King's hunting trip."

"So are you," he replied, and I shook my head. "You're not coming? Why?"

His disappointment thrilled up my spine, but I could not let myself feel it.

"Many reasons," I replied. "I have work to do in the library, and some peace is long overdue. I've even sent Alys to visit an old friend."

"Six weeks without seeing you. What will I do?"

He rubbed a thoughtful hand across his abdomen, over a long, silvery scar that ran between the ridges of his stomach muscles, its origin unknown to me. So much of our lives, our older selves, were a mystery now, our connection tied mainly to memories a decade old or more—though it hadn't felt that way back in the stormy depths of the night.

"You'll survive, I'm sure," I said. "Things will feel different the moment you ride out of Camelot's gates."

Accolon considered me with frank intensity. "I cannot imagine things feeling different to how they did last night. After this . . . how it was . . ."

The thought hovered in the air, enough to undo us both. Slowly, he lifted my hand and kissed the centre of my palm, then lower, where the lines of Life and Fate cross. His touch rang through me like a nightingale's cry.

It took all of my strength to pull away. "I have to go."

"Morgan," he called as I reached the door. He sat forwards, hair dishevelled, arms still outstretched in the motion of letting me go. "Do you regret this?"

"No," I replied, so quickly it must have been true. "Never regret, not with you."

I opened the door and slipped out, before he was fool enough to say the same.

*

LATER, I KISSED Alys and Tressa farewell in Camelot's Entrance Hall and sent them off with a stab of guilty relief that neither one had noted my distraction, or sensed the remnants of Accolon's touch, which I still felt like fever on my skin.

The hunting party would pass the priory and leave Alys and Tressa there, returning for them on the way back. I watched from a high window as they rode out of Camelot's courtyard amidst a long line of guards, knights, ladies, heralds and servants, passing under the portcullises of the towering gatehouse.

In the centre of the procession, Arthur rode proud on his pure-white courser, gold-clad and surrounded by red dragons—on his guards, draped across his horse, carried aloft by standard-bearers enclosing the royal party. Guinevere rode beside him on a highly bred palfrey, her snowy mount and gold mantle matching her husband's.

Regret plucked at my heart at my brother's distance, our irresolution. It had never been this way between him and me, nor did I know how to fix us.

On Arthur's other side, clad in his cool, vibrant blue, was Accolon, talking amiably with his King, charming smile high on his face, riding away from Camelot, and from me. I watched until they vanished, then turned from the empty glass.

*

CAMELOT'S SPRAWLING LIBRARY was in disarray—half-empty bookcases, tables piled with disordered, unbound pages, unopened storage trunks still full of the valuable manuscripts given to the King and Queen as gifts.

It was partly my fault; I hadn't had time to go there in the year since Arthur entrusted its organization into my care. Gathering up a pile of pages, I settled at a table near the front of the room under a large window and the advancing afternoon light. What my brother wanted was a fine Royal Library; what I had was chaos. However, there were worse ways to spend a six-week than in the company of books.

I took up the unfiled pages and read awhile as the sky outside softened, sun tilting towards a golden evening. Camelot's riding party would have reached Arthur's Kingswood by now, arriving to red and white pavilions amongst the trees, lanterns strung above banqueting tables strewn with meadowsweet and dog violets. Goblets of pear wine would greet them from barrels cooled in a nearby stream, the smell of the huntsman's venison already mouth-watering. Later, bards would spin tales of fairies and woodland trysts, followed by music and dancing late into the night, under leafy branches and starlight.

I thought of Accolon, full of wine and good humour, and missed him so completely that it hit like a hawk strike. His life was out there in Arthur's wood, amidst sporting talk, flower-crowned ladies and air enchanted with possibility. Soon, he would realize that the lure of past fruit could never taste as sweet as the orchards before him now, no matter how intoxicating, how transcendent, one night could feel.

Biting my lip, I forced my eyes back to the pages, but the words ceased to flow, the tale dull and inevitable; the same heroic story that always ended with the world returned to a pre-ordained ideal, no matter how much those within fought or wished otherwise.

I leaned on the table, drawing a tired hand over my face. Beyond my fingers, a blur of shadow disrupted the stillness, falling across the lavender evening light.

I glanced up, breath catching in my throat.

Accolon stood in the open doorway, one shoulder leaning against the frame. A slow smile rose on his face.

"I could watch you read all day," he said, and I ran to him.

17

"HOW ARE YOU here?" I asked him, as we sat breathless amongst the empty bookshelves, dust settling after our hurried reconciliation. "Arthur couldn't have let you go."

I assumed some sort of secret flit, where he cut loose from the hunting party without word, his only thought being back in my arms.

"Actually, he did," Accolon said, toying with a lock of my hair. "After the tournament, the King offered me and my cousin a quest. I was undecided, but before we reached the forest, I said I'd accept if he gave me leave to attend some business around Camelot. I told Manassen the King had sent me on a personal errand. *Me voici.*"

His clever planning left me impressed. "What sort of quest?"

"Tying up the ends of the wars in Benoic and Gaul, overseeing treaties, rebuilding—good work, safe and easy. It will guarantee a place in the court, maybe even in King Arthur's new order of knights."

"How long will it take?"

"A year," he said quietly. It was then, upon learning that his presence came with a cost and an ending built in, that our passion became a predicament.

What it meant I could not define, but his eyes were tempests, without regret.

"That's how badly I wanted to come back here," he said.

*

WE WERE CAUTIOUS, as much as we could be. Nor could he and I keep apart. The next morning, after unmaking the bed in his chamber and checking on his horse, Accolon wandered through the library shelves to where I stood collating a collection of Welsh poetry.

"I'd rather be here," he said. "If you are content to have me."

"Only if you don't hinder my work," I replied.

Thereafter, he stayed, and I was content, alarmingly so.

We took up residence at a different table at the back of the library, fortressed by shelves and dusty peace. I sat with a pile of pages and he reclined in the long, low window, legs stretched along the sill. It was impossible to not think of the sacristy in Tintagel's chapel, where Accolon had first observed my insistent reading, and I had battled with the call of desire. We could not go back, yet in many ways we already had.

One day, I glanced up into our companionable silence and watched him tracking the flight of a wild kestrel. He met my observation, and his idle smile fluttered within me like a weakness.

"Listen to this," I said. *"Of all parts that make the body in the Lord's own image, there is none more noble or important than the heart. For etched here is the record of existence from birth to holy judgment, bearing all good deeds and bad, to be displayed and relived at Heaven's gate."*

He nodded thoughtfully. "When knights die in faraway lands, it's the heart they ask to be sent home. They say the soul is contained within."

I picked up my quill and made a note on the parchment I kept for interesting ideas. *"Every life, in its entirety, can be found written upon the heart. So it can be read there in death, and lived again.* I wonder if there's any literal truth to it."

"Ever the physician," Accolon said, with such proud affection I felt myself blush. He put a hand to his chest. "Perhaps that's why the purest joy or pain is felt here."

I put the page down and moved to sit beside him on the window-sill. "Tell me, Sir Accolon, what is written upon your noble heart?"

He gave a gentle shrug and smiled handsomely.

"Your name," he said.

So quickly had he fallen back into the idea of us.

*

"WHAT DID YOU do?" I asked him, some time later. "After Tintagel. After me."

"Mainly, I suffered," he said.

I cuffed him on the chest and he laughed. We sat curved together under the trailing vines of Alys's cushioned arbour, gazing out onto a tranquil morning. Accolon had discovered he could reach my chambers by climbing the steep bank and vaulting over the terrace balustrade, negating the need to sneak in and out at dusk and dawn. It meant we were even less apart, sharing our meals and sitting on my terrace late into the night, drinking wine and talking, surrounded by solitude and stars. Only ten days had passed, but our new harmony felt lifelong.

Serious again, he looked down at me, threading his fingers through mine. "Anything you wish, I will tell you. But my mistakes, things I did—are you sure you want to hear?"

I considered him, trying to withstand the intimacy in his eyes, his beautiful face, all I knew I could feel if I allowed it.

"Yes," I said. "There must only be truth between us."

He began with what I knew: how he left with little—his arms, his hunting hound, the few things he possessed. His father had kept his promise and sent him two horses upon achieving knighthood, so he chose one and sold the other for too little coin.

"I rode south along the coast, reached a fishing town and bought passage across the Channel, then started towards Paris. My progress was slow, torturous. I was hollow, flayed with grief, and couldn't rest for wondering if I had made the greatest mistake of my life. I almost turned back hundreds of times."

I leaned my head against his shoulder. "I wish you had."

"So do I," he replied, and we were silent for a long, sad moment.

"Keep going," I said.

"I barely ate, couldn't sleep, so I rode instead," he continued. "Trying to outrun thoughts of you—my guilt, my doubt. Until one night, I stopped in a tavern and discovered that even the most potent despair cannot withstand the right amount of clouded ale. So that's what I did, for a while—I hired out my sword for petty tasks, took on forest jousts to win horses and armour to sell, gambled with varying success. I drank until my coin ran out, before doing it all over again. Choosing oblivion, like the coward I was."

A memory of my earliest days in Gore floated up, my craving for Urien's body against mine in the darkness to combat the loss of Accolon. "And you were alone?" I asked.

"Before Manassen came." He shook his head ruefully. "My God, if he only knew where I was now, and with whom."

"It at least makes sense now why he hates me," I said.

"He doesn't *hate* you. He just . . . was there, afterwards. He thinks you're trouble for me." Accolon smiled with his usual handsome charm. "I can't imagine why."

He had concluded, but I knew there was more, missing pieces not so easily given.

"That day in the stables," I pressed. "Sir Manassen said—"

"That I was half-dead, about to throw my spurs down on a game of hazard?" He grimaced. "I could have thrashed him for saying that in front of you."

"Then it's true?"

Accolon tilted back and studied me, lip caught between his teeth. "*L'enfer*. Yes, though I'm not proud of it. One night, a game of dice turned violent when I didn't have the coin to pay my debts. The man I owed got angry, I was too drunk to best him in a fight, and he took a knife to my gut."

He traced a thumb across his abdomen. "Hence my scar. The tavern keeper stepped in, patched up my wound and made me swear upon my knightly honour that I would repay the debt. I swore to it, only to find myself at a different gambling table a few nights later, losing again."

His fingers trailed restlessly through my loose hair. I put a comforting hand on his thigh, but he didn't seem to feel it.

"By then I was exhausted, lost, so far from the knight I had wanted to be, undeserving of the spurs that Sir Bretel had fixed to my heels. But the spurs were enough gold to cover my losing game and one more roll. I was rattling the dice in my hand when . . ."

His voice cracked, as if the memory had swallowed his breath.

"Sir Manassen found you," I said.

Accolon nodded. "Came in like an avenging angel. He dragged me away by the scruff and commanded me to stick my head in a bucket of icy water until I was sober. While I did, he settled my debts, picked up my spurs and took us to a quiet inn, where I slept for a week. Apparently, he heard I'd left Britain in a hurry and came to find me. Two years he searched and never gave up."

"Then you became who you are now."

"Because of him. It was a hard road, but my cousin made me face my despair, my failures. He showed me I could become the knight I wished to be, asking nothing in return. His belief, his loyalty . . . it humbles me still." He sat straighter, eyes bright with emotion. "Manassen saved me that day. I owe him my life."

I gazed at him, moved, unsettled by his gravity. "What will you tell him?" I asked. "About this."

He met my eyes with interest. "What would you say there is to tell?"

Still I couldn't answer.

*

AFTER THAT, ABANDON. Time stretched itself around Accolon and me, bending days into nights and back again, driven by my eternal impulse for him.

"Do you ever think about the future?" he asked, late one sun-drenched afternoon, as we lay in the aftermath of love.

"Doesn't everyone?" I said.

I felt him shrug under my cheek. "I didn't for a long time. Now I do."

"Then I was right."

He gave a soft laugh. "Very well, my lady of logic. How do you envision yours?"

The answer was easy. "I want to sit on Arthur's council, officially help run the realm. See my son flourish and become a knight of Camelot under his uncle's wing. I'd like to finish my manuscript and start another. To take the manor my mother gave me and make it a home with Alys and Tressa, where we can be safe and free."

My skin prickled with an excitement I rarely felt, the power of my life's plan spoken aloud. Accolon took a deep breath and held on to it so long I was compelled to look up at him.

"And when you imagine that future now," he said, "am I ever there?"

"Sometimes, yes," I said slowly. "You are there, and happy."

"And other times?"

"I have done what is best for you, and let you go."

*

"MORGAN?" HE SAID, in bed late one night.

"Mmmm?" I replied, eyes half-mast. Soft candlelight still lit us, his fingertips drifting up and down my arm like the slow strumming of a lute.

"I know what's best for me."

In my state of relaxation, I didn't catch the significance. I let my hand stray over the raised white slash across his stomach. "This impressive scar from a gambling den stabbing suggests otherwise."

"No," he said patiently, "I know what's best for my life *now*. And that is you."

I jolted up, suddenly awake. "You don't know enough to say that."

"What more do I need? I know you are married, a mother, with an important place by King Arthur's side. That your skills and quest for knowledge never stop calling to you, and you want to live life in your own way."

"That's not all there is," I said, "but I—I cannot find the words."

He put his hand over mine and brought it to his chest, his heartbeat steady and vital beneath my palm. "I know your scars are deep within and difficult to speak of. Perhaps you and I don't need words."

A ribbon of epiphany shivered along my spine. For better or worse, I knew what he must see.

I lifted my hand, fingers curled, and he frowned. "Morgan, what . . . ?" he began, but I shook my head. With a silent flick, I struck my palm and lit the flame.

Accolon bolted upright, fists against the mattress. He stared at the small red-gold blaze, then up at me.

"Now you know," I said tremulously, awaiting his repulsion.

Instead, he leaned forwards, dark eyes reflecting fire, lip curling into a smile. "That you are extraordinary? This I have always known. Can I . . . touch it?"

He raised a fine, unmarked hand. The flame surged with my burst of panic.

"Only if you want to get burned," I said, and snatched the fire out, leaving our shadows blurring together on the bed.

He caught my wrist, gentle, unflinching. "Don't shy away. You showed me for a reason. Why?"

I dropped my gaze, unable to withstand his calm acceptance. "Because you should understand what I've become. To you, my hands heal, they restore, but you don't know what life has made of me . . . what I've done. I've been frightened, and despairing, and violent. Fury has always been in my blood, but this fire—it's the opposite of healing. It is rage and vengeance and destruction, and sometimes I fear what it could do."

"Morgan," Accolon said, and I made myself look at him. He regarded me with a serene certainty. "I am not afraid."

"Perhaps you should be."

"No," he said. "I love you. Every part of your being."

Nine years since he last said he loved me, and so much gone between, yet I was as hungry for the taste of it as I had been the very first time.

His thumb slipped under my curled fingers, opening my hand like a new leaf.

"Show me," he said.

It should not have been possible with the cloudburst of pleasure in my heart, but I reached inside for other fuels, the joy and belief that burned like beacons.

"I love you," I said, and struck up the fire in my hand.

Accolon smiled, lit gloriously by my flame, light pulsing between us in a new shared rhythm. *This is enough*, it seemed to say, with the rise and fall of our breaths; *we are enough*.

18

A MONTH TO the day that Accolon had appeared at the library door, I was up and enjoying the honeysuckle breeze through my bedchamber window as he sat dressing on the edge of our bed. He leaned down, retrieving his linen shirt from the floor with one elegant hand; with the other, he caught hold of my fingers, glancing up and smiling as if it were the first time seeing me that day. It was then I knew.

"This cannot end," I said.

He regarded me in curiosity. "What do you mean?"

"We should be together. Somehow. Always. If it's what you want."

Tossing his shirt on the bed, Accolon leapt up and took me into his arms. "Come away with me," he said. "To Gaul, to my manor there. It's beautiful, fully moated—like our own island. Anything you wish for, I can now provide. We can make a home, live the life we were meant to have."

The thought was sweet, dreamlike, futile.

"We can't," I replied. "My son is here. I cannot be a sea away. But there's a path for us, a place. Fair Guard, my mother's manor that I told you of—we can live freely there."

He brightened. "Then that's where we will go."

"This won't be easy, Accolon," I warned. "My life is complicated. I am still married by law, and I have a place by my brother's side. Then there's your quest, the year you've promised to Arthur. None of this is straightforward. It'll be dangerous, and difficult, and imperfect."

Accolon leaned his forehead against mine. "It'll be worth it," he said. "Because it is you."

From his silver tongue, it all sounded so simple. His arms tightened around me and I kissed him, his surety making me want to enfold him back into our bed, our love, and prevent him from leaving even for a short while.

"I should go," he said. "Before anyone finds my bed unslept in."

"Or stay," I suggested. "And the Devil take it all."

He kissed me again, bestowing his smile on my lips. Somewhere beyond, brisk footsteps and the distant cry of hinges declared Camelot somewhat alive.

"The sooner I go, the sooner I come back," Accolon said. "Then we will drink wine, sit beneath the sun and make plans for our future."

Still I held him. "I love you."

"And I love you, *mon coeur*. But if I don't go now, I never will."

He slipped free, retrieving his shirt and pulling it over his head. Playfully, I caught its edges, tickling my fingers across the taut skin of his abdomen and making him laugh. More footsteps sounded nearby, closer than they should have been.

We barely had time to glance at one another in confusion before the interior door flew open, admitting a sudden draft and a tall, longskirted figure.

"Morgan? We're b— By Almighty *God!*"

Alys froze, eyes wide as an arrow-shot deer. Accolon and I leapt apart, him rapidly tucking his shirt into his unbelted breeches, as if doing so would look any less damning.

"Alys, I can explain," I began.

"Why is *he* here?" she said. "Tell me this is not what I think I'm seeing."

"Dear heart, I cannot lie to you," I said as calmly as I could. "This is exactly how it appears."

She stared at Accolon, still half-dressed across our rumpled bed. "For how long?"

"Since the hunting trip left. We—it happened just before."

"That's over a *month!*" She pointed a shaky finger at Accolon. "*You* were in the hunting party—I saw you ride out."

He offered the faintest of shrugs. "I came back for her."

If there had been a blade to hand, I might have feared for him then, such was Alys's look of wrath. I went towards her, but she swerved out of my reach.

"How can you say you wouldn't lie to me?" she said. "You insisted you were staying to rearrange the library."

"I *did!*" I replied. "This wasn't planned."

She huffed in disbelief, and I ducked my head, which made it look like a lie. Maybe it was; when I watched Accolon ride away after our night together, perhaps part of me *had* known he would come back, that he would choose me over everything.

"Lady Alys, I beg your pardon," Accolon put in. "But this is not Morgan's doing. She never knew I would ride back."

"Do *not* speak to me," she snapped. "I cannot bear to hear your lying voice."

"Alys," I said in a cautionary tone.

"No, Morgan. Of all the people—after what he did to you." She thrust her hand out in disgust. "*Him?*"

A prickle of defensiveness ran across my skin, mixed with the overwhelming urge to throw my arms around Alys and explain until she understood.

I turned to Accolon. "Go. I will find you later."

He gave me a long look, projecting love where he could not say it, then picked up his boots and left. Alys jumped when he passed outside my bedchamber window, heading for his secret escape route.

"My God," she exclaimed in renewed outrage. "He hasn't been coming and going by *climbing the terrace?* You are fully grown people with real lives and responsibilities, not a pair of lovelorn youths in a troubadour's ballad. What possessed you?"

The scorn in her voice pierced me. "Do you truly want an explanation, Alys? Or do you just want to hold forth on how dreadful you think I am?"

"Not dreadful—foolish," she replied. "Do you even know why we're back? The hunting party is returning today, on King Arthur's orders. Tressa and I arrived faster, but imagine your brother's reaction if he discovered his married sister's moral lapse with his tournament champion. Mother of God, the risks you have taken, and to be with *him!*"

I stiffened; she had never once commented on my supposed morals before. Since the day we first met at the nunnery, Alys had only ever judged by what she felt was good and true in her heart.

"*That's* what it's about, isn't it?" I said. "Not the risks, not the morality of it all. You never cared about my going to bed with Sir Guiomar. You're angry because it's *Accolon* I've been with."

"What of it? I have spent the last nine years hating that feckless Gaul for what he did to you, what you endured in his wake." Her eyes met mine, wide and glassy. "He left you, Morgan. You trusted in his love, his word, and he left you a chess set, his petulance, and broke your heart. I can never forgive him for that."

"Alys," I said with a sigh, but there were no words I could offer, no justification, because everything she said was true. Her amber eyes pleaded with me to agree, to concede, so she could move on to forgiveness. How much easier it would be if I could give her what she wished for, but for him; but for the truth.

"I would never ask you to forgive him," I said. "What you feel is inarguable and there is nothing I can do to change it. But in turn, you must accept that my feelings also cannot be changed."

"No," she said. "I won't hear it, and you shouldn't say it."

"I love him, Alys. We love one another. The moment I laid eyes on him I knew that he still lived within me, even when we were at odds. This is not weakness, or a madness, or a return to youthful infatuation. When I look at Accolon, I see love—he *is* love. I forgave him. I *chose* him. He is part of the future I want."

I gathered her hands in mine; they were cold, and I held them to my chest.

"Dear heart, you know love—you have love. We can no more change how we feel than we can extinguish the stars in the sky."

"Then why can I not imagine ever doing to Tressa what Accolon did to you?" Alys shook her head, pulling her hands away. "When life became challenging, that knave cared only about himself, and it's more than your heart at stake this time. Can you really trust him to bear the weight of your reputation, your complications, our entire lives?"

I stared at her, my insides chilled. Earlier with Accolon, wrapped in the warmth of our love and intimacy, I had believed in everything, down to his quick assurances that our difficulties were of no consequence. Yet we had been here before: the paradise of an empty castle; our youthful, passionate haze; the important questions we had failed to discuss. He was due on a year's quest at any moment, and we had barely given it a thought.

"I know my own mind, Alys," I said. "I know who Accolon is."

"I sincerely hope you do, Morgan. For your own sake."

I caught the flicker of feeling in her voice before she left me standing alone in the room, with nothing but the ghost of Accolon's presence imprinted upon the empty bed.

*

THE ROYAL HOUSEHOLD arrived as Alys said they would, late that same afternoon. I managed to catch Accolon long enough to confirm that the King expected him to leave for his quest the next day, and agree that for safety's sake we should keep apart.

But that night, as I tried to lie still, I felt the hum of my blood, singing through my greedy heart and filling my body with restlessness. There was only one way for my soul to be soothed.

"*Sacredieu*, what are you doing here?" Accolon exclaimed as I slipped through his chamber door. He was still awake, polishing his sword by the window under the light of candles and a high yellow moon.

"Come back for me," I said. "Swear that you will."

He regarded me as if he had considered nothing else. "I will, *mon coeur*. Even if I have to walk the roads barefoot and swim the violent seas. One year and I'll be back, then I'll never leave you again. Trust in that."

"I trust you." I exhaled, pausing. "Shall I go?"

Slowly he stood, taking in my impetuous, contradictory presence, my fingers still gripping the door handle. His elegant hands slid his sword into its scabbard and leaned it carefully against the wall.

Then, as so often it did, his recklessness rushed forth to match my own, and he was across the room, pressing me hungrily against the door, his arms, his mouth, his body all around me, as if we were long overdue.

"Stay," he said, and inside I felt myself give; even as I said "I can't" and he said "I know"; even as I kissed him and we gave ourselves over anyway.

By the time I awoke in my own bed late the next morning, with my skin still sparking from his last caress, Accolon had cleared Camelot of all traces of his presence and was gone.

19

BEFORE I EVEN had the chance to fathom Accolon's absence or the year ahead, Camelot's official bells started ringing like a May Day Mass, calling the household insistently to the Throne Room.

Alys wasn't speaking to me, so I went alone, arriving among the bustling court with the deep bell strikes clanging dents into my nerves. At the final echoing stroke, Arthur strode in through a door behind the thrones. He was sharply crowned and dazzling in red and white, a gold ermine mantle trailing from his shoulders, Guinevere on his arm in matching colours. He handed her into her royal seat, kissed her fingers, then turned to the front of the dais and took a long look at the room.

"Since so many of you have seen fit to arrive at a leisurely pace, perhaps I should be brief." His voice rang out, cold as a winterburn. "I, Arthur, High King of All Britain, call this court in the royal city of Camelot *to order.*"

The last murmurs and shuffling feet fell to immediate silence. Arthur gave a terse, regal nod.

"Then we may begin. Change is coming—to Camelot, to this court and this entire kingdom. Our nation has advanced in its glorious purpose, but the work is far from done. Now is the time to build this noble and ancient realm into everything it can be—a sacred bastion of honour, prosperity and peace."

He held the court rapt now, not a breath or movement under the Throne Room's golden arches.

"There will be oaths to take, quests to answer, ideals to be sworn to and upheld. You will come when I ask it of you. Tell your liegemen to expect to be called. What we do hereafter will shape the country for centuries to come and advance the greater good in the name of God and the Crown of All Britain."

With a sweep of his trailing gold mantle, he turned away, dismissing the room's undivided attention.

It took several heartbeats for the congregation to recover, mood dissolving into a muted excitement. Above them, Arthur roved before the throne, speaking confidentially to the Queen, Sir Kay, a few others in his closest council. I hovered at the edge of the dais, trying to judge my brother's true mood, but I could never read him fully from a distance. To know where I stood, I had to look into his eyes.

Arthur took me in as I ascended the steps, Guinevere viewing me from just beyond.

"My lord," I said cautiously. "It's good to see you back in Camelot."

He accepted my bow with a brisk nod. "I'm happy to have returned. I hope your time here in my absence has been restorative."

"It has, my lord, and productive as I'd hoped. The library is much improved."

"Good," he said. "I must make time to see what you've done."

"I'd like that." I paused, drawing a breath of courage. "Arthur, I—"

"Queen Morgan, how pleasant it is to see you," Guinevere said, her smile devoid of all pleasure. She turned to Arthur. "Not to interrupt, but my father awaits your attention."

My brother glanced at me, the words of my appeal still hanging unsaid. "Will you leave us?" he said to his wife.

The Queen bridled, her recovery immediate. "Of course, my lord. Though please, do not keep us waiting."

I watched her sweep away. When I looked back at Arthur, his focus was on me, and I felt a strange, unfurling relief.

"How have you been, sister?" he said. "When we last saw one another you did not seem contented."

"I know," I said. "I hadn't been thinking clearly, but for my troubles to come between us was the last thing I wanted. If I've disappointed you, then I deeply regret it."

Arthur sighed. "I never wish for us to disappoint one another, Morgan, though it's inevitable that we sometimes will. What matters is that our bond is restored in good faith."

"That's all I want, brother."

We shared a tentative smile, and I saw a flicker behind his reservation: relief, perhaps, or something greater—the light of returning trust. "Then we must talk, soon and at length. Like we always did."

"Any time you wish, I am here," I said. "How was the hunting trip?"

"It went well," he replied. "Time away from Camelot has been enlightening, clarifying. As soon as I was outside these walls, I saw the great amount of work that needs to be done. I must begin at once."

"Is that why you returned early?"

His eyes drifted, clouding slightly, and I felt his answer in the instant before he opened his mouth.

"Merlin came," he said under his breath. "Appeared to me in the Kingswood one night. He told me to return to Camelot in all haste."

It was always *in all haste* with the sorcerer, a test to see how quickly Arthur came to heel. I bit back on my natural dissent. "It sounds important. What was the purpose?"

Arthur's expression relaxed, hand reaching up to rest on my shoulder. "Can we speak now, in private?"

My heart leapt with hope. "Of course."

With a ghost of a nod, he hurried us out of the Throne Room by a rear door, unheeding of Guinevere's stare of pique as we passed.

To my great surprise, we went to his Council Room. The large chamber was dustless but gloomy, clouded skies letting in a grey-white light. A thick scent of cold lingered in the air, incongruous given the day's humidity.

Arthur put a hand on the back of his gilded council chair, casting a crowned shadow across the map of Britain, then turned away, indicating two armchairs before the hearth. I sat down opposite him, glancing at the council seats; it would not be long before I was at the table proper.

I looked back at my brother. "What did Merlin tell you?"

"Much the same as before," he said. "There continues to be unrest among my stars and I must prepare to face what comes. He told me to return here and await him."

"Merlin's coming to Camelot?"

Arthur nodded. It was unusual for the sorcerer to come to court. To my knowledge he had not done so since King Lot's funeral and the reveal of his life candles two years ago. That day, he had also taught me how to hold fire and I had spurned his offer to further teach me his ways.

"He's not usually so reliable," I said.

My brother shot me a disapproving look. "I know you don't agree with Merlin's methods, but you must concede he is wise, and learned, and has given many years of service to Kings. Myself and my father, Uther Pendragon, before me."

The name of his warmongering, brutal sire, so rarely invoked, hung between us like a demon's curse. Arthur looked away; without Uther's monstrous appetites and Merlin's machinations he would not exist, yet recalling it conjured the fate of his mother. *Our* mother.

"What I don't agree with is his *influence*," I said. "Merlin beckons and you run to him. He tells you to cut short the hunting trip and you drive the entire court back to Camelot on Boreas's coattails. His hold over the Crown has been too great. I fear his wants will counteract your own plans."

Arthur regarded me in imperious fashion, a look that silenced the boldest lords. "The plans I have are *because* of Merlin. This country wouldn't be half of what I have made it without his wisdom and foresight."

Annoyance uncurled within me like a dragon's tail. "It isn't true, Arthur. I'll say it as many times as is necessary. This is *your* kingdom, and you know well enough how to run it. Merlin's prophecies, his rules and demands, only interfere with your vision. You and I, alone in this council room together, could rule the realm with clearer purpose than waiting on the stars. Don't you see? You don't *need* Merlin."

The moment I stopped speaking, silence fell between us like a stone. Suddenly, Arthur rose, hooking his hands behind his back and taking long, concentrated strides alongside the council table, and for the first time, I had no concept of whether he was in agreement, furiously opposed, or something completely other.

"I don't think you understand, Morgan," he said eventually. "So let me explain in no uncertain terms. Merlin has been with me for most of my life. In my childhood he taught me, watched over my progress and ensured I was cared for by a loving family. It was he who made the sword in the stone appear, knowing only I could pull it free. When I rode off, crowned but still a boy, it was Merlin who stayed beside me, who oversaw every battle, every peace treaty, every victory I secured on my way to becoming a man and a true King."

His voice betrayed no emotion, severe crown glinting as he paced. "What reason do I have not to go where he leads me? In many ways, I am his creation. Without Merlin, I would have nothing—I would *be* nothing."

I stood, swallowing the rising mutiny in my throat. "You owe a debt of gratitude to Merlin, I'll not deny, but the man you strive to become, the King people follow, love and respect, is *your* creation. Your courage and honour come from within. No one gets to claim they made—or could unmake—you."

"I appreciate your faith, sister," Arthur said, "but we did not know each other in my earliest years. As the realm grows and my life becomes more complicated, I need you to understand me in full."

"I want to," I said. "I'd do anything to help you and the realm, you know that."

He nodded with serious purpose. "Then you and Merlin must finally meet."

To my shame, I had not seen it coming. "No, brother. I've said it before. He and I operate in different spheres. Our interests do not align."

"Not true," Arthur insisted. "Your interest in my future is shared, not disparate. My God, think of the potential if you gained Merlin's knowledge and applied it to your everyday wisdom. My sister as my closest court adviser—what a wonder it could be."

It was an image I had long imagined, Arthur and I side by side, overseeing the kingdom: my brother happy and fully in command of himself and his realm; I using my skills and intelligence to help him, with the power to carve out my own existence. But in my dream, the sorcerer was excised from Arthur's life, not embedded in my own.

Arthur strode around the table and pointed at the north coast of Cornwall. "I want you to sit *here*, Morgan, close at hand, and feel deeply what I feel. Do you want to sit on my council and be indispensable to my Crown?"

"You know I do, but—"

"Then you must accept the one true way to gain full understanding of who I am."

He moved to the Great Chamber door and pushed it open, bringing forth another stream of claggy chill.

"Is Merlin *here?*" I exclaimed.

"You said you would do anything to help me, sister," Arthur said.
"One conversation is all I ask."

In fairness, he didn't know why I hated the sorcerer; we had never
discussed what I experienced as a child, and Arthur had little awareness of what Uther Pendragon had visited upon my mother. I had
allowed my resistance to the sorcerer to remain abstract to protect
my brother from horror, and would keep doing so. I closed my eyes
against the inevitable.

"All right," I heard myself say.

Even in darkness, I felt him the moment he entered the room.
When I raised my lids again, Merlin stood before me, twisted staff
in hand, his mist clinging to the hems of a voluminous black robe.
Two years had done little to his pointed, ageless face, his hair and
beard still wild and lead grey. Liquid black eyes took me in with
smooth efficiency.

"Lady Morgan, Queen of Gore," he said in his waspish drone.
"How pleasant it is to see you again."

His mouth stretched into a self-satisfied smile, but for the first
time, no cold wave of fright assaulted my senses. Somewhere along
the tumultuous path of my life, I had been freed from fearing him.

"You've met?" Arthur said.

"Why yes, Your Highness," Merlin drawled. "Lady Morgan and
I go back far indeed. Farther than you, almost. I have long been
impressed by her remarkable mind. To teach her is one of my greatest wishes."

My brother regarded me with a youthful amusement. "What an
intriguing idea! It suggests great potential for the realm. Did you not
consider it, sister?"

"I was heavy with Yvain," I said. "Not convenient, and my husband would never have permitted it. Now I couldn't possibly imagine having the time."

"I wonder what you would learn," Arthur mused. "I'm sure if it interested you, an arrangement could be made."

I was about to protest when the sorcerer cut in with surprising quickness.

"Minutiae, my lord," he said dismissively. "Not a High King's concern. Your Highness should leave Lady Morgan and me to discuss our similarities and differences, without boring the royal mind."

"I don't mind staying," Arthur said. "It's perfectly—"

"It is *beneath* you, King Arthur," Merlin cut in. "You were like this as a boy—questioning too much and distracting from greater things. I insist my lord take himself elsewhere."

I expected my brother to reprimand the sorcerer for his presumptuous tone, or certainly refuse to leave, but to my chagrin, he only nodded with a conciliatory smile.

"Of course. I have much to attend to. I will leave the two of you to your renewed acquaintance."

Like a wine page who has filled every cup, Arthur left without pause, closing the Great Chamber door behind him.

The sorcerer turned to me with a vulpine smile. "Lady Morgan, alone at last. You look exceedingly lovely, if I may say so."

It was as if he sensed my lack of fear; he had never once commented on my appearance, and I felt exposed, as if to a sudden cold.

"You may *not*," I snapped. "I'm not about to share pleasantries with you, Merlin, now or ever. Nor did I consent to this meeting."

"You must have, my lady." Merlin inclined his head towards the door. "Unless you wish to tell the High King you have changed your mind. Though I doubt it will please him—he considered my idea to meet such a good one."

"*You* asked for this?"

"I have posited it on occasion," the sorcerer said. "You have avoided me so assiduously throughout your life, never even enquiring what work I am doing."

"That's because I don't *care*," I retorted. "Stars and prophesying and fogging up my brother's mind—if I could put an end to your so-called work I would."

The sorcerer cocked his head, considering me like I was a delicacy he had not yet tasted. "And how has your time in Camelot been, my lady? All those hours sitting at our lady Queen's knee, listening to gossip and stitching bed robes for lonely nights. Have you felt the sting of your wasted time?"

I glared at him; he knew how to prick at my weaknesses, that much was true.

He smiled with a demureness that made my skin crawl. "If you had consented to let me begin teaching you two years ago, imagine the skills you would have honed by now, the powers you would have unleashed."

"Is that what this meeting is about?" I said. "Your vain desire to teach me? I want nothing you have to give. Anything I wish to learn I can seek out for myself."

He laughed, a harsh, rasping sound. "Forgive me, my lady. No one admires your intelligence more than I, but you wouldn't know how to *begin* seeking the knowledge I have."

"I'm sure I'll endure it," I said.

"That's a shame. Particularly when King Arthur himself is so keen on the idea. Think how much more he would trust and appreciate you if you were as learned as I am."

"My brother trusts me in ways you cannot comprehend," I said petulantly. "In fact, you don't *want* me in your vicinity, Merlin. I will never cease trying to make Arthur see you for the scourge you are. I would want to keep me *as far away as possible*."

My tirade was just beginning when a sudden, nauseating ache took hold of my body, dust motes blazing like stars in my vision. I leaned against the council table, drawing deep breaths.

"Is something wrong?" Merlin said.

I glared at him in accusation, but he stood impassive, feet away, black eyes mildly curious. Another wave of unpleasantness washed through me. With great effort, I pushed myself upright and stalked to the door.

"Stay out of my way, Merlin," I managed. "Never mention us in the same breath, or speak of teaching me, to Arthur again."

The sorcerer rested his hand on the back of the throne and smiled. "Farewell, Lady Morgan. I will tell His Highness you are thinking about it."

20

I DON'T KNOW when I began to suspect: the first goblet of red wine that I assumed had gone bad; how many mornings I slept late instead of rising with the lark; the high scent of the honeysuckle clambering over my terrace that I noted, not realizing I could smell the sun-warmed stone distinctly as well.

The Queen's solar became more stifling than usual, myriad perfumes mingling with too much breath, starched linen and the scent of decaying flowers. By the time a second month arrived without my courses, undiluted wine was unpalatable and I was napping through any spare moments of the day. Still the thought was too great to let it take hold.

Nor could I discuss my suspicions with Alys; she and I were on speaking terms but barely, and only where her duties were concerned, my great Gaulish transgression between us like a wall of glass. Tressa treated us with her usual wise equanimity, but I would not burden her with keeping secrets from her beloved.

Then, one muggy morning, I awoke with my queasy stomach hitching beyond my control. I had just enough time to fly out of bed before expelling the meagre contents of my stomach into a wash-bowl, and I couldn't deny it any longer.

I was with child, trapped in Camelot, and completely alone.

*

"YOU HAVE A lover."

The words were low and unclear, and came from beside me at High Table. With Lady Clarisse returned to her quiet forest castle, my seat was now next to the Queen's, but she so rarely glanced in my direction it was a surprise to look up and meet her greenish scrutiny. I was sure I'd misheard her.

"I beg your pardon?" I said.

"You are an *adulteress*," Guinevere murmured. "There's a bed you frequent that is not your own. Broken marriage vows. Some careless man caught in your web of immorality."

Her words coincided with a queasy swoop in my gut. Controlling the sickness had become increasingly difficult, and to sit in the Great Hall amidst smells of roasted capon, spiced fruits and dripping candlewax was almost more than my senses could bear.

"I don't know what you mean," I said uneasily.

She leaned in, and her sweet, expensive perfume caught in my nostrils, violet oil and ambergris. "Oh you do, Lady Morgan. Once again your bodily sins threaten this court's good name."

I turned away, inhaling from the packet of dried herbs concealed within my sleeve. Somewhat restored, I levelled my gaze at her.

"Where did you hear such a fabric of lies?"

Guinevere fell silent as a wine page appeared, filling both of our cups and affording me time to think. Accolon had been gone for a month—in the unlikely event we had been discovered, why the delay? Since his departure, I had sought no particular contact with men, other than the occasional dance with Sir Guiomar to vex the Queen. That I was being accused of this now, and so vaguely, made little sense.

The fresh wine aroma made my stomach churn, and I put a hand over my goblet. "Who is it, then?" I demanded. "Name my supposed lover."

She paused, eyes flickering away just barely, but it was enough.

"You cannot, can you?" I said.

"That doesn't mean it's untrue," she replied. "There's been something amiss with you for weeks—not unlike when you did this before. And when Arthur hears how you have betrayed his trust and disgraced his Crown, he will never forgive you."

"This is absurd," I snapped, though how she had sought a transgression of mine and hit on the truth was a dreadful sort of wonder. "You have no proof."

"Proof can always be found," Guinevere said.

Another lurch assaulted my gut. "Arthur is my brother, and we share a deep bond. It would take more than some ridiculous claim to damage his regard."

"Do not be so certain," she said. "Your disagreement over the Royal Summer Hunt was an awakening for him. My husband is inching ever closer to seeing you for what you really are."

Her suspicious gaze slid to my hand, still covering my goblet, so I gripped the stem and lifted it to my lips. The wine's bloody, ironish scent hitched in my gullet, but I took a defiant sip.

"Tell him what you wish, my lady," I said. "I have nothing to hide."

She held my eyes for a long, sickly moment as the wine hit my gut, then pursed her lips and turned away. I tried to take hold of the nausea, pulling deep breaths against the herb packet, but the aversion was too strong, along with the room's warm air and the Queen's rich perfume. With as little ceremony as possible, I hurried from my seat and out to the Great Hall's terraced garden.

I ran as far from the door as I could and purged into a small shrubbery. When it was over, I slumped onto a bench between two twisted hedges, sweating and trembling. It had not been this violent with Yvain, and I was not used to lacking control. I needed to tell Alys and soon; the thought of her perfectly blended tinctures far outstripped my worries over her reaction.

"Now I see what ails you."

A tall shadow cut across my shuddering body like a knife. In the angular torchlight, Guinevere looked older, her rosy beauty uneven, yellow hair made gaudy in the unflattering glow. "By God, you are with child."

It took all of my strength to stand up. "I am unwell, nothing more. Excuse me."

I made to step around her, but she grabbed my elbow. "Admit it," she said.

She had hardly condescended to touch me since we ceased to be friends, and her authority brought a flare of indignance.

"Do not presume to know my life," I said, pulling out of her grip. "You are severely mistaken."

"Mistaken?" she said. "You think I cannot recognize what's in front of my eyes? Why—because I'm not as clever as you? Or is it because I have not yet given my husband a child? Do you think I haven't learned *every possible sign?"*

There was a sudden wildness to her I had not seen before, a white-eyed, bared-teeth quality that spoke of strain far beyond what I knew lay beneath Guinevere's surface. For the first time, I saw the depth of the fractures in her, the guilt inherent in both her joy and pain, the confusion of what she was allowed to feel. She was so young, so scrutinized, elusive in her complexities, yet still firm in her belief in a queen's perfection, a woman's. It was too late for me to tell her that such a state didn't exist.

"I didn't say that," I replied. "I would *never* say that."

"You claim you would never do a lot of things." She straightened, drawing queenly composure about her as she always did. "You lied to my face about having a lover, and you're still lying now. But I *know* you—I've watched and listened. You told the entire solar that pregnancy made you averse to wine. This makes your adultery indisputable."

"To what end?" I said. "My private life is none of anyone's business."

"Your behaviour *is* the realm's business," she replied. "I didn't make the rules, the laws, nor did I break them. Last time, you were spared redress, and you have exploited my leniency. You are reaping what you began sowing a year ago."

"So that's what you wish for—my punishment, my ruin? You believe it's fair to put me on trial for adultery, despite the good I've brought to Arthur and the kingdom?"

"Lord in Heaven, your arrogance never ceases to astonish me," she exclaimed. "The constant certainty that everything you do, every rule you choose to disdain, is justified by the absolute rightness of your every thought. *I'm* not permitted to sit on Arthur's council, yet *you* believe you have a place?"

A resurgent twist of nausea gripped my stomach, and I put my hand to it. Guinevere shot me a look of blazing significance.

"You do not *deserve* Camelot," she said. "You haven't truly earned Arthur's regard. Every time he finds clarity and begins to see the truth, there you are in his ear again. And he listens, and forgives, because he is good and you are his *sister*. You have a *bond*. When he doesn't know the half of who you are, or what you've done."

Head spinning, I sank back onto the stone bench. I was trapped, that much I knew, but had never known how to walk away from a fight.

"Then it's decided?" I said. "Whatever I say, you'll tell Arthur and let Fate do as it will?"

The Queen clasped her hands together, emerald rings winking at me like cat eyes. "I do not have a choice, Lady Morgan. You may be willing to lie endlessly, but I cannot live in dishonesty with my husband."

I considered her words. The adultery stake was not certain but likely. Urien would be told and inevitably make the complaint, and after the child was born, there was no law that Arthur could use to circumvent a trial. Accolon would return and insist on being my champion, damning us both. There had to be another way.

I continued to rub my roiling belly in soft, pensive circles. Glancing up, I caught Guinevere watching the motion, and her hard expression wavered, as if she was contemplating sitting beside me. With equal suddenness, I wished that she would, a faint sense that if she gave in, then so could I.

The chance hovered in the air, then she cut her eyes away, leaving us adrift in the harsh torchlight. I had never played a game of chess to stalemate, until her.

"Is this truly what you want, Guinevere?" I asked. "To destroy me and damn the consequences? We were friends once—you said you loved me as a sister."

She sighed impatiently. "I cannot remember when I last had any regard for you."

"Yet you did. What you toy with now is my life, my future. There's no coming back from a betrayal like this."

The doubt in her eyes turned to stone. "The betrayal is *yours*, Morgan. What I'm doing is for Arthur, the Crown and the greater good."

"Very well, Your Highness." I stood up, facing her as if answering a challenge of honour. "I admit I have a lover and am carrying his child—there you have won and I cannot escape it. But are you sure you're ready to hear my full confession?"

A slight confusion winnowed across her brow.

"After all, it takes a pair of lovers to form a tryst," I continued. "Two people to make a child. It's clear in your righteous quest to capture me, you have not considered there is another side that you might not want brought into the light. What if my partner in sin is someone *you* love and wish to keep safe? What if I told you my lover is Sir Guiomar?"

Guinevere's face drained to ashen. "N-no," she said. "I put an end to that. You may not know how to obey, but he does. He would never enter into anything so sordid."

"Yet he did, before," I replied. "I will not claim it's any great love affair, but I'm sure my lady has seen us dancing together, and lust is a powerful temptation. Old connections do not die just because you force them apart."

"I won't believe a word of this. What proof do you have?"

"Proof can always be found," I said pointedly. "Of course, if you must tell Arthur of me, then I in turn must name Sir Guiomar. The whole truth. Perhaps he'll be pleased to hear he will become a father."

The Queen glared at me, bottom lip protruded, like a child contemplating a tantrum. "You would still be destroyed in Arthur's eyes. You would still go to the adultery stake. Why curse a good man's reputation when you should be begging God for forgiveness?"

"What choice do I have?" I said. "As you intend, I will face the severest consequences, but what of your dear cousin? Who knows Arthur's ideals better than you? Maybe, after a decade or so in a dusty, far-flung fortress, Sir Guiomar will find a way back into the King's righteous heart. I'm sure he will not blame you, nor will your family question why you couldn't prevent the collapse of his fortunes."

"You—how can you . . . I am the *High Queen*."

"Indeed you are, my lady," I replied. "With all the scrutiny that comes with such a crown. Do you think Arthur will thank you for exposing my scandal in such a public way? It could set the realm back years. How will he bring forth his vision for the kingdom if my sins are all anyone can talk about?"

Guinevere looked down, smoothing her damasked skirts, her face half turned from the light. "What do you *want*, Lady Morgan?"

Again, I wasn't sure of the answer, my mind tired out by sickness, fatigue and the race to outwit the Queen's unexpected manoeuvres. Still, I had come this far, and I had her in check.

"If you wish to protect Arthur and your family's reputation," I said, "you will forget you ever knew this, and understand that my private life has never been any of your business. That I am no more yours to control than I am anyone's."

I crossed my arms and awaited her concession. She met my gaze and held it, pale eyes strangely calm.

"No," she said. "I cannot do that."

Her refusal was an arrow in the dark, striking without warning. "W-what?" I said.

Guinevere straightened to her full height, resplendent and righteous as an archangel. "I am a good and generous Queen, Lady Morgan, but I am not as meek as you have assumed. For Arthur's sake—for the realm—I must do what's right. Understand that it's not for *you* to give me a choice, but I am offering you one."

Once again, inexplicably, the air hung with her advantage. "What *choice?*"

"Either you persist in exposing your own scandal and go to the adultery stake," she said, "or you can save yourself. Relinquish your place in the court and raise your child in peace elsewhere. Leave Camelot well enough alone, and keep your distance from Arthur. I will not tell my husband of your sins, and you won't risk death for your transgressions. Accept my mercy, and be thankful."

I hadn't yet decided how I wanted things to be, but this wasn't close to it.

"Be sure of what you are doing, Guinevere," I warned. "I am not an enemy you want to make."

"Perhaps it's time to learn, *dear sister*, that you do not hold anywhere near as much power as you imagine." She leaned close, her dense perfume raising my gorge. "You choose, Morgan. Leave this court, or burn."

21

LATER, DEEP INTO the witching hour, I was hunched over a bowl in my bedchamber when Alys came in through the interior door. She was in her bed robe, hair braided into a pair of night-time plaits.

"I heard you get up," she said. "I see now why you've been pale and overtired."

"I didn't mean to disturb you." Nausea abating, I staggered to the bed and sat. Alys took a tentative step closer.

"Morgan," she said, "are you—?"

"Pregnant," I confessed, at long last. "Yes."

"Oh," was all she said, and it occurred that she must have guessed weeks ago. No argument or distance could change how attuned she and I had always been.

"It's Accolon's, of course," I added.

"Is that why he left?"

"Alys!" I exclaimed.

"You cannot say I am unfair to ask!" She gave a rueful sigh and sat beside me. "I'm just making sure you're all right. I haven't been in the most generous of moods, and if he . . . you may not have felt you could tell me."

I gave her a stern look but couldn't make it last. "I didn't even suspect my condition when he left. Which is just as well, because he owed Arthur his quest duty, and if he'd known he never would have gone."

"I told her that, but she wouldn't listen," said a sleepy voice. A robed Tressa came into the room, rubbing away a yawn. "How are you feeling, my lady? I can brew you some peppermint tea."

I shook my head and smiled. "Clearly, Tressa knows all."

"Doesn't she always? She was the one who first spotted the signs." Alys fixed me with a searching look. "Morgan, I have to ask. Is this . . . what you want?"

"Yes," I said without pause. "It's Accolon's child, and I love him. We've chosen to finally be together and live the life we should have had. This predicament makes things more difficult, more urgent, but at least he's safe from trouble."

"What trouble?" Tressa asked.

My stomach hollowed again, nausea mixing with dread. "The Queen knows. She caught me being sick and guessed, after accusing me of having an unknown lover. She said she had no choice but to tell Arthur, and I'd go on trial for adultery."

Alys's eyes widened. "Can she do that?"

"Urien would be told, and ensure it," I said grimly. "Not much wanting to burn at the stake, I confessed to having a lover, and suggested the father of my child of scandal was Sir Guiomar. Preserving her cousin's reputation scared her off my death sentence, but she told me to leave the court."

"For good?" said Tressa.

I nodded. "And to keep away from Arthur. The worst part is, she's right—I can't stay in Camelot and bear a child. If I did, an adultery trial would be unavoidable, and I won't force my brother to suffer for my choices."

"I see," Alys said. "So what shall we do?"

Her decisive, natural use of the word *we*—the assurance I was no longer alone—spun through my body in a whirlwind of relief.

"Alys, does this mean . . . I thought you were angry with me."

"I was," she said. "I thought you were reckless, and I was worried—about you, myself, what it meant for our lives. When you implied I didn't care, it hurt me, because it's the opposite. I care about you and your happiness very deeply."

She extended her hand to Tressa, who came and took it. "Of course, Tressa pointed out that the reverse was true. You've always cared fiercely about me, and Tressa, and our happiness. You've done so much to keep us safe and comfortable, and only ever wanted the best for us. Who can I trust more than you?"

My throat was thick with tears. "I don't know what to say."

"There's nothing to say, my lady," Tressa said. "It's the truth."

Alys nodded. "Your future is always our future."

A wave of gratitude crashed over me, followed by a backwash of fatigue. "I wish I could say I knew where to begin. This child wasn't part of the plan, and the complications are so great, I . . ."

I hung my head, but they each took up one of my hands, joining us in an eternal circle.

"We'll go forth in this together, *cariad*, like we always have," Alys said. "For you, I'll even withstand dealing with the faithless knave I spent years wishing vengeance upon."

It made me laugh, at least. "You may have to stop calling him that now."

"Only when he proves worthy," Alys replied. "Sir Accolon aside, I will be overjoyed to have a new child to dote on."

"The child is the easy part," Tressa said. "I've spent enough time in servants' halls to know there are a hundred ways to conceal this, and it is often done."

I didn't doubt her; she was ever knowledgeable on the practicalities used to address human frailties, though Alys balked at her next suggestion that she wear heavier layers and pretend the child was hers.

"One dubious association with Sir Accolon is quite enough," she sniffed.

"My sister's, then," Tressa forged on. "Born out of wedlock and taken in as your ward."

There was much more talking to do, but my mind was sparking. Now that I had Alys back and Tressa's unruffled strategic mind, I could face it all, fix anything. I could see the future again, a slim bright dawn broaching the horizon.

"Fair Guard," I said. "It's what we've spoken of all along. We should go there."

"How?" Tressa said. "We'll need to be granted leave."

"And if you reveal possession of the manor, it'll be considered marital property," Alys pointed out. "Your husband will snatch it away."

Of course he would, or I'd already be free and living there part of the time. More and more, leaving Urien alive had felt like a mistake, but wishing for my husband's serendipitous death was not the only move I had.

"I'll go to Arthur," I said. "It won't be easy, and I must take care what I reveal, but if the love we have holds true, this begins and ends with my brother."

*

ENSCONCED AS HE was with Merlin, it took Arthur several days to accede to my request for a private audience. I kept to my chambers under the auspices of sickness, Alys, Tressa and I deep in discussion on possible plans; another escape from another place.

The Queen let me be, presumably due to the misbelief that I was preparing my permanent exit from Camelot, when the truth was the opposite. I had earned my place at Arthur's side and he needed me; I would not let Guinevere best me so easily.

My brother and I finally met on an afternoon surprisingly hot, summer resurging in defiance of its dying moments. Arthur gestured for me to sit in the window seat overlooking the courtyard, and I was reminded of the febrile, blazing day when he told me that Yvain had to leave.

We sat facing one another, like reflections in a mirror: posture upright, hands flat atop our laps, our tiredness dark-eyed and bone-deep, shared but entirely different. Neither of us wanted to be there, but for me, time had become essential; the child would be born in spring, its father due back the week before Lammastide.

"You asked to see me?" Arthur's tone was polite but strained, as if he would rather recline on a bed of spikes than speak a single excess word. Whatever Merlin had wrought on him had taken a toll like nothing I had seen before.

"Yes, I . . ." My words vanished, as if I hadn't rehearsed them at all. "A-after Carduel, I would like to take some time away from the court."

Arthur's drifting gaze snapped back. "Why?"

"It is usual," I managed. "The rest of the court retires at intervals."

"But you are far from usual," he said. "There is nowhere for you to go."

With the speed of a falcon's stoop, he had made me feel special then snatched it away. The explanation of Fair Guard sprung to my lips, but an odd belligerence in his demeanour made me hesitate.

"What matters is I have the choice, wouldn't you agree?" I replied. "My ambitions for the future—to sit upon your council, to study and gain knowledge in service of your Crown, to bring forth your vision for the realm—all of that depends upon my having the freedom to think, time to step away and work in peace, then return to Camelot with a rested mind."

"How nice it sounds!" Arthur threw up his hands, laughing completely without humour. "How pleasant to be able to think of *time* and *rest* and *quiet*. To not look over one's shoulder every moment of the day, awaiting the next meeting, or hear the very stars in the sky have decided your fate. *I wonder what that is like!*"

He reared up, stalking away with his hand to his forehead. I knew what this was—not from my own experience, but Sir Kay sometimes spoke of their early battlefield days, when to enter a room with Arthur after Merlin had left was to walk into the lair of a snake-bitten lion.

"Brother," I said calmly. "What's happened since we last spoke? What did Merlin tell you?"

"Nothing," he growled. "That is none of your—none of *anyone's* concern. I am alone in this. I always have been, I . . . *Sweet Christ!*"

He fell to the floor with a thud, cradling his head and groaning in agony. I flew across to him and fell to my knees, taking him in my arms.

"Hush," I said. "Let me see, let me feel."

Drawing hard breaths, Arthur dropped his hands and let me put my fingers to his temples. I expected to feel the usual stone wall of tension, but this was different, an intangible haze, opaque, shifting, twitching at his brain until it quivered with exhaustion. Every time I reached for it, the fog bent away as if blown, clustering elsewhere.

I focused harder, gathering the healing force in my fingertips until it was a golden gale, then sent it forth, banishing the darkness and illuminating his mind. Arthur's head sagged onto my shoulder, seemingly in relief, but I turned his face sideways to ensure he was conscious. His eyes were clear and he no longer appeared in pain, but he looked up at me with abject exhaustion, his face younger and more anxious than I had ever seen him.

"You can't go, Morgan," he said. "Can't you see that? I need you here."

"Arthur, I . . ." There was no way to explain that I didn't want to leave him, or ever be out of his reach, but his world, his laws, his wife, had made it impossible. "I can help you avoid the headaches, but you'll have to trust that I'm—"

"No," he said, hoisting himself into a sitting position. "It's not the headaches. The time ahead is precarious for me, and my reign. I know you do not hold much faith in prophecy, but Merlin has never steered me wrong. I must find ways to strengthen my weaknesses, be prepared for any kind of threat to the realm's stability. How will it look if my supposedly loyal sister runs off for half a year? Now more than ever, it is crucial we remain united. My future, the kingdom's future, depends on it."

I was stumbling, but there was nowhere left to fall, caught between two immovable rocks: my brother's insistence I not go, and the absolute necessity that I leave. The last thing either of us wanted was for Arthur to be forced to face my complications, and unless I kept this from him, he would resent me forever for tearing everything down.

There was only one avenue left to me. I closed my eyes and sent a silent prayer up to Saint Jude.

"There is another way," I said. "It requires me leaving for a year, but will not suggest trouble at court. Quite the opposite, in fact. It will make Camelot yet more formidable, and your legacy even stronger."

"What is it?"

As I told him, I watched him grow in strength and vigour, and in a strange way it pleased me, though the words caught like burrs in my throat.

"Granted," he said immediately, as I knew he would. "This is a great thing—for you, for the realm, for us both."

I nodded with reluctance. "If I do this for you, there is one thing I need assured."

"Name it," my brother said.

"When I return, Yvain must be in Camelot waiting for me, along with Urien. No delays, no excuses. The moment I am back, we will sit down in negotiations and secure mine and my son's future for good. Promise me, Arthur."

My brother placed his hand on my shoulder and looked at me, his eyes dark steel within our ring of shadow. "I promise, sister. By the honour in my heart, it will be done."

22

I KNEW WELL enough where to find him.

Merlin was prowling the Council Room and greeted my entrance with a knowing smile. I watched him stalk the length of the map table, thin hand moving from one chair back to another, tracking down the country towards the throne. The chill of his mist settled uneasily on my skin.

One route to solve everything, I told myself: my brother's suffering and exhaustion; the pouring hourglass of my condition; Guinevere's threats and Urien's control; the future I wished to build with those I loved. Better still, if I was artful enough, I could wrench the sorcerer's grip off the Crown of All Britain forever. One sacrifice to gain the freedom I wanted, and secure my place at Arthur's right hand.

"Quite a feat, to hold these lands, all of this loyalty, within the golden circle of one crown," Merlin said lazily. "King Arthur carries the world with such grace, such ease. All because of the effort taken in keeping him safe and making him into the ruler he is today. All because of me."

The notion was repulsive to me and he knew it. "So you like to think," I replied. "Some of us feel that the more Arthur learns to be his own man—his own king—beyond the inconstant stars, the better he is for this realm."

"Yet you are not here to discuss the philosophies of rule," Merlin said. "Or to compete with me for King Arthur's true heart."

He came to rest beside Cornwall, face still carrying its infuriating smirk. He put a hand to the painted surface, trailing long fingers across Tintagel Castle.

I was losing before I began; I marched forwards and slammed both palms on the council table.

"If I consent to let you teach me," I said, "what is it worth?"

The smirk stretched into a mocking smile. "It's worth a great deal, Lady Morgan—to you."

"Very well, then there is nothing more to say," I replied, and walked away.

I had the chamber door two inches ajar before the call came like a wasp sting. *"Wait."*

My every instinct still strained to escape—from this room, the sorcerer, my intentions—as fast as I could. Yet what was the alternative if I did?

"Forgive me, Lady Morgan, for jesting." Merlin was at the head of the table now, beside Arthur's chair, his face neutral, conciliatory. "If you are genuinely considering letting me teach you, then it means a great deal. It would be of huge benefit to you, of course, but the chance to explore the reaches of your mind means far more to me. Most importantly, it would mean a great deal to your brother."

I swallowed hard, wishing it wasn't true.

"The High King has long expressed the desire that his two closest advisers should pool their skills, become stronger. I cannot be what you are to him, but you can learn to be what he needs when I am not here."

He pulled a chair out from the table, inviting me to sit.

"I'll keep to my feet," I said. "I may yet wish to leave."

He conceded with a tilt of his head. "Go ahead, my lady, give me your terms. I'm sure you have them."

I shut the door, moving back into the belly of the room. "I can offer you no longer than a year," I declared.

He shook his head. "That's not enough time."

"You must take it or leave it. I'm a fast learner, and if you cannot teach to keep up with me, become quicker. A year to the day that I arrive, I will leave."

"I see. Why?"

The question arrested me—I did not expect his curiosity, and it occurred to me that I would soon have to tell him the secret of my unborn child. Once again I felt like running for the door.

"I cannot be gone from the court longer than that. I have a son, responsibilities to the realm. Arthur will miss my presence. A year is all I am willing to give. There is no negotiation to be had, so do not try."

Merlin nodded thoughtfully. "Very well, Lady Morgan. I will accept your year, and you will have to prove yourself as quick as you claim. In turn, I have some terms of my own. You will come alone."

The thought of being without Alys, of delivering a child without her comfort and knowledge, left me cold to the bone. "Impossible," I said. "I need my closest woman. I cannot be expected to—"

"I'm sure a lady of your vast gifts is capable of brushing her own hair," Merlin interrupted.

"How dare you suggest my concerns are shallow," I spat. "When the reason is that I won't consent to being alone with you."

My insult blew through him. "You won't be alone. Ninianne will be there. You've already met, and she will answer all your *female* needs."

"She's not all that I require," I protested.

"With only a year to learn, there will be no time to keep company with another." Merlin's gaze took on a reddish, inquisitive gleam. "No, there is something pressing. Why all these demands, my lady? What do you hide?"

My entire body felt like it was rejecting my plan, straining to recant, but instead, I levelled my gaze at the sorcerer. "You *want* to teach me, Merlin. I will listen, and learn, and hang rapt on every word you say, but first I need a vow that what I tell you goes no further than us. A guarantee of yours that I can trust."

"There are ways to prove my secrecy," he said. "The most *trustworthy* is a pact of magic that will bind us. This cannot be done in half measures. If you wish to make a deal, we must agree terms and set the bond. I cannot merely promise to keep your secrets—a pact requires an exchange."

He extended his darkly robed arm, fingers splayed. I didn't move.

"Come," he said. "If we are to trust one another, this is the only way."

I took two halting steps. "What must I do?"

"You will put your hand around my forearm, and I yours, then we will both agree our terms and I will fix us with a binding spell. Thereafter, you will tell me your secret, and I will have to keep it. Whatever you say will remain unspoken for all time."

"How do I know you're telling the truth?"

Merlin smiled like I was a newborn lamb. "To be bound by magic is no small thing. You will feel it." He gestured impatiently with his outstretched hand. "Well?"

His urgency did not convince me, but I knew in my bones that now was the moment. I reached out and wrapped my fingers around the sorcerer's wiry forearm. The pile of his robe was rich and soft, and I felt momentarily grateful that we would not be required to touch skin.

When Merlin gripped on, our arms went rigid, hands fusing tight. A strange sensation slithered around my wrist, a slim invisible rope slipping coil after coil around my arm, tightening as it went. The phantom cord pulled taut, and the sorcerer drew a deep breath.

"Look at me," he said, and I obeyed, pulled irrevocably into his tar-pit eyes. "The terms are this: you will come to my residence and be taught by me for no less than one year. I will guarantee Ninianne will be there for this time, and provide whatever care you require."

"If you swear she will not spy on me, or repeat my words, nor serve your interests in any matter where I am concerned."

"That I can swear to," Merlin said. "She would never do so."

"Then I agree."

"So it will be. Now, some terms regarding what you will learn from me—"

"No more," I cut in. "Until you have assured the safekeeping of my secret. Proceed on that basis, or I will not continue."

After a brief, searching look, his fingers tightened around my arm and he muttered some words in a rapid Latin that were not unlike the oaths knights take to their lord. The invisible rope hardened and shifted, shaping into hot metal links, like a chain recently forged. Deep in my body, I felt the *thunk* of a lock pushed home and knew, with unexplainable certainty, that I could not go back on my promise if I tried. Merlin and I were bound.

"The magic has fettered us," he said. "Give me your secret."

The force of the binding meant I could give no pause. "I am with child," I said. "To a man I will not name. During the year you will teach me, I will carry this baby and give birth, and when it is done, Arthur cannot know. Anyone I choose not to tell must not know, nor can anyone with prior knowledge expose me. I cannot be punished, nor lose my place in the court because of it. Arthur's reign or reputation cannot be affected. Swear that you will ensure all this."

"It will be done," Merlin said. "In exchange for teaching you, your child will be the best-guarded secret in the realm. King Arthur's glory, and that of his Crown, will be preserved. Your return to Camelot, on these terms, will be unimpeded by this secret. Make this pact now, and I will ensure every word."

"I need more," I said. "Swear no harm will come to me or the child."

"I swear it," the sorcerer said. "You will deliver safely in the sanctuary I have promised, and Ninianne will become all that you need."

The words caught on my consciousness, echoing back from two decades ago—of myself as a child, overhearing Merlin telling a girl-like Ninianne to become all my mother needed to deliver Arthur. My mother, too, had agreed out of necessity, but I had learned from her; my sacrifice would be rewarded with liberation.

"Do you agree?" urged the sorcerer. "Quickly, or the bond will not hold."

"I agree," I said.

The invisible chains seared, melting into my skin with a sizzling hiss as the binding took hold. Just before the burning turned into pain, it ceased and dissolved.

"Thus our pact is formed," Merlin said. "Immutable and eternal. I will keep my side of the bargain, and you will keep yours."

I pulled away from his hands, feeling a tugged thread of connection as we parted. "Of course," I replied.

And much more than that, I did not say. *For I will save Arthur and me both.*

23

TO ACCOLON, I left a letter, somewhat explaining my absence, and the date of my return a few weeks after his. It instructed him to secure rooms in an inn of Alys's choosing, and escort her and Tressa there on the day of my departure from the sorcerer's clutches. It held no mention of the child, and they were not to tell him, partly for safety, and partly because I wished to see my revelation dawn on his face.

To Alys, I entrusted several things: firstly, Excalibur's hiding place and the mantle containing the scabbard, along with its death-defying secret. If Arthur came looking, she was to give him everything, but strictly tell no one else. Secondly, so she could guide Accolon to the best inn, I gave her a rough description of where Merlin's was, though only the sorcerer and Ninianne knew its exact location. Last of all, I gave her my father's ring with its trio of sapphires, and copied down my mother's directions to Fair Guard, just in case.

"If anything happens to me, take Tressa and go there," I said, slipping the gold band onto her thumb. "The ring and my name are the key."

Upon her and Tressa, I bestowed final farewells, and enveloped them in embraces I found hard to let go, assuring them I would survive this, as I had survived everything else.

To my brother, I left my sisterly love and faith, my solemn word that we would reunite in greater strength, and an unspoken promise that soon we would both be set free.

"Look for me in a year," I told him, and so I departed.

*

NINIANNE MET ME in Camelot's main courtyard, mounted and swathed in a hooded cloak of deep violet that concealed her irresistible gleam. The guards and courtiers that milled around seemed not to notice her at all—some fairy trick, I assumed.

It had been almost a decade, but she looked no different from when I had last seen her on Tintagel's headland, explaining that Accolon had abandoned me, and the best thing for my life would be to renounce love altogether. I wondered, as I mounted my palfrey under her unreadable emerald gaze, how much she sensed of my circumstances now.

I looked up past the huge steel dragon to the Great Chamber window where Arthur stood watching my departure, his expression half urging and half bereft, as if both wanting and not wanting me to go. I waved in farewell, he returned the gesture, and we shared a warm, strength-giving smile before his face fell to sudden seriousness. A presence rose up beside him like a shaft of shadow: Merlin, still in Camelot. He flicked his shining black gaze over me and Ninianne, then reached for my brother's elbow and turned him away from the glass.

"Let's go," Ninianne said and nudged her horse forth, giving no indication whether she had seen the sorcerer or not.

*

IT WAS ALL she said for many hours. After some time on the road, we cut into a dense old forest and followed a trackless route, passing not another soul on the way.

"Where are we going?" I asked as soon as we left. No answer.

"When will we get there?" I tried again, much later, and silence.

Very well, so she had nothing to say to me, but I had a decade's worth of thoughts to share with her.

"You lied to me," I said. "The last time we met, you told me you weren't Merlin's servant, yet here you are again."

It drew a sharp sideways glance, but she didn't condescend to a response.

"You told me outright that Arthur had died as a baby," I continued. "What was that, if not doing Merlin's bidding?"

Still she could not be persuaded from her self-contained silence. I had almost given up on the belief I could goad her when her voice came, sweet and sonorous on the woodland breeze.

"It wasn't for him that I did it," she said. "It was for the kingdom."

"Merlin believes he runs this kingdom," I retorted. "What you did was by his design."

"I've told you before, I do not belong to him." She turned her full green gaze on me at last. "I have for many years followed his ways because of King Arthur. From the moment I delivered him, I believed in the child, and the man he has become—that everything the stars claimed could be proven true."

"The stars are not immutable," I said. "They cannot be, or Merlin's prophecies would not be so vague."

"That is one way of looking at it," she replied. "Or perhaps prophecy is a more complex art. I believe the stars show us the potential in a person to intersect with certain events and touch greatness, but being a mortal man is filled with obstacles—disruption, distraction, emotion—human weaknesses. That is why potential needs guidance. Intervention."

"So that's your excuse for snatching Arthur away from my mother."

"*And* his father," Ninianne said pointedly.

I fell silent; I couldn't dispute that Arthur had been better off with Sir Ector and Lady Clarisse than being devoured whole by Uther Pendragon.

"Arthur was needed to save Britain," she went on. "Which he did. He has unified the realm and works tirelessly for the greater good. The son of a selfish, brutal father became a force for fairness and peace because he was kept secret and protected from influence."

"Not from all influence," I replied. "There is your sorcerer, by his side since boyhood."

Ninianne looked away, whether in disdain, agreement or because she was bored of looking at me, I could not discern. She pushed her hood down, her hair a sudden fiery crown in the softening light.

"The sun is falling," she said. "We will not be long."

True enough, we soon reached a deep cleft of stream, roaring in a frothing, rocky moat around a large grey house. The building was a confusion of heights and features, gabled and several floors high at one end, the other half long and low, culminating in a tall, square tower, top open to the sky like a castle barbican. Two enormous, ancient trees, an elder and an oak, stood sentry at each end of the island.

My horse tossed its head, refusing to move within six feet of the craggy, torrential moat. Ninianne alighted from her saddle.

"We dismount here. Horses will not cross."

"Cross what?" I asked, but she was already at the water's edge, moving her lips in soundless command. To my astonishment, a white marble bridge rose slowly out of the foam, streaming water. Ninianne offered no explanation but beckoned, so I left my palfrey and followed her across. As we landed footfall on the island, the bridge glided back beneath the moat, sealing us within.

"That waterway cannot be natural," I said above the pounding rapids.

"It is and it isn't," she replied with infuriating vagueness.

She led me into a dim entrance hall crowded with passageways and closed doors, then up a narrow staircase and into a large, better-lit chamber containing a well-quilted bed and a jumble of various furniture. A small anteroom stood off to the side with a washbowl on a stand, and the trunk sent ahead containing my clothing.

I paused in front of the windows, edged with ivy and the fat-lobed fruit of a hops vine. Below, a kitchen garden had been dug, staked and planted to the edge of the churning moat, the forest thick and protective on the other bank.

"It's better than I expected," I said. "You and Merlin live here alone?"

"Yes, and in safety," Ninianne replied. "No one can cross the stream without one of us to raise the bridge, lest they get swept away and dashed onto the rocks. And Merlin has guarded the forest, to stop anyone getting too close."

"Guarded it how?"

"That need not concern you, unless you intend on attempting to travel without one of us, which I wouldn't advise." She unfastened her cloak, warm light filling her side of the room like a corona of sun. "In fact, I wouldn't have advised you to come on this journey at all, Lady Morgan, but you are here now. Rest tonight, then I will show you the house in the morning."

"I'm not tired—" I began.

But she had already left, taking her light, the thud of the door juddering a quake across my nerves. I walked around the room to try to settle my mind, but doing so only increased my restlessness.

Throwing off my travelling cloak, I pulled the door open and marched down the staircase. A soft shaft of evening emanated from a door now ajar, and I went to it.

Ninianne stood in the centre of the room, gazing at the space above the fireplace, painted dark blue and marked out with the stars. Behind her, a large half-circle window took up most of the wall above a long marble worktable. The rest of the chamber was lined with pale, neat shelves, stacked with manuscripts, ink bottles and vases of swan quills. There was only one chair, pure white and remarkably carved into the shape of flowing water.

"Lady Morgan, you startled me," she said, though her demeanour was completely without surprise. "Come in, since you're here."

I stepped inside, agitation relenting within the scope of her light. "You said you would not have advised me to come on this journey. Why?"

She sighed. "It was not my place to say that. Merlin told me I must convey you here and remain for a year. More than anything, I wondered why I was involved."

"Merlin forbade me to bring my women, and I said I wouldn't consent to being alone with him."

"You had that concern," she said, "yet you wonder why I would have advised you not to come."

"Merlin has repulsed me since I was a child, for good reason," I said. "I asked why *you* think such a thing. You and I are to live together in this house for a year, and you will deliver my child. I'd like there to be at least some honesty between us."

Amusement whispered across Ninianne's beautiful face. She said nothing, instead unhooking a chain on the wall and lowering an unlit silver chandelier.

"The child's father is the man I loved before," I offered. "From Tintagel. Our weakness of the heart, as you call it, returned and remade."

"I know," she replied. "His presence, the love that you wore about you when we last met—it hasn't changed. I would guess you never stopped carrying it."

The thought of Accolon made me smile. "I suppose you'll call me foolish now."

"It is not for me to judge either way," Ninianne said. "My part is to fulfil the duties agreed."

"Very well," I said. "When is Merlin coming? I assumed he would travel with us."

"He says he must remain at Camelot for now. He has much to tell the King, and it's unclear how His Highness will react. The delay could be days, possibly weeks."

With a deft flick, she lit a flame on her thumb and proceeded to light the chandelier candles, then glanced up for my reaction.

"*That* I can already do," I said. "Merlin taught me to hold fire once, though it required making myself miserable. Quite the opposite of my other skills."

"Ah, yes," she said. "I can feel you have something—an affinity naturally held, but honed by learning."

"Yes, it's—" I began to explain my healing, but she snapped out her flame and grabbed my hand. It was the first time she had ever touched me, and it drew my entire being to her like a flower towards the sun.

"Don't speak of it," she said. "Your skills, your power. Learn what you can from Merlin and see out your year, but do not reveal your inner self. That is the only advice I can give."

Her touch made it impossible to disagree. "I won't. But why can't I tell you?"

"Because you should not rely upon trusting me." She released my hand with a sigh, and I felt her absence as a small chill of grief. "You should go, Morgan. I will show you the house and fulfil my duties, but outside of that, perhaps it's better if we keep apart."

She hoisted the chandelier up and hooked the chain to the wall, then went to the marble table as if I had ceased to be in the room. I made to leave, but as I reached the doorway, something pulled at me, a possibility I wasn't ready to abandon.

"Ninianne," I said. "I don't trust you, and I never have. If I agree to remain suspicious of you, is that enough to earn *some* company?"

She turned, a vision in violet and copper, silhouetted against the dying remnants of the day. I didn't expect to see her smile, rare as it was, but she laughed too, and it sounded like the surface breaking on a lake.

24

THE TOUR OF the house was brief, culminating in the long, low-beamed classroom where Merlin would teach me. The room contained a dark refectory table, a wall of shelved manuscripts, and the locked door to the sorcerer's tower, which was strictly out of bounds. After that, we returned to Ninianne's light and airy study; she had brought in a second chair and invited me to sit down.

"What now?" I said. "Shouldn't I begin learning something?"

Ninianne offered a shimmering shrug. "I can give you books to pass the time."

She drew out a large, white-leatherbound manuscript and placed it in front of me—a detailed guide of ancient elemental deities and their affinities with the land. It wasn't the answer I wanted, but the act of reading drew me naturally towards contentment, until a sudden wave of nausea clutched at my stomach. I sat back and gave a slight groan.

Ninianne looked up from her book of maps. "The child—does it bother you?"

"Just a little unease," I said, though in truth I had been up since before dawn duelling the same sickly waves. "My sworn woman sent some herbal tinctures with me, but they're diminishing in effect."

Her eyes swept across my body. "The child is growing, becoming stronger. This part will soon be over, but until then he or she must draw on your life force."

I gave a wan smile. "The pleasure of having children."

"I wouldn't know," she replied. "Nor will I in this lifetime."

It was a more personal comment than I was used to. Gracefully, she rose and took a glazed stoneware cup from a shelf, filling it with water from a silver jug.

She flourished her fingers over the rim. "Drink this. Perhaps it will help."

The water had poured cold, but to my astonishment, the cup was steaming hot. "What is it?"

"A tea of sorts," Ninianne said. "The water is full of untapped goodness. I can ask it to . . . do more."

"Because you are a water fairy," I said.

"If you like, yes."

I raised the cup to my lips and sipped. It tasted like peppermint tea, but brighter, clearer. It ran into my stomach with crystal surety, the nausea and strain from my sleepless morning dissipating at once.

"Good?" Ninianne asked.

"Good," I agreed. "How did you make it hot?"

"Fire and air are elements too. They can all be conversed with to various effect."

"And with such ease, for you," I said enviously.

She regarded me with her usual enigmatic gaze. "It needn't have that draining effect, you know—when you held fire. It's Merlin's method because he struggles with the elements. His efforts require harsher spells, greater cost."

"Are you saying the great and powerful sorcerer has *weaknesses?*" I jested.

Again her shoulders rose and fell, noncommittal. "Merlin's strengths lie with his interests—in foresight, concealment and alteration. Perception and prophecy. But for you, with the sea in your blood, your natural connection with water, there are better ways to the elements. Joyous ways."

I thought of conjuring fire for Accolon as the exhilaration of love sang in my blood; it had not been what the sorcerer taught me. "Could I learn it? Would you—?"

"I am no teacher," she cut in. "What's more, Merlin would never permit the time."

"He's not here now," I pointed out.

Ninianne made no reply, instead leaning across to the silver tray and retrieving two goblets. She waved a swift hand over the jug and poured. The liquid emerged cloudy and golden, scented with high summer.

"Now that you feel better, try this. It's a favourite of mine."

We touched goblets and she watched me sip with a calm interest, as if she had never shared a drink in company before. The sweet liquid ran warm down my throat, singing of wildflowers.

"My goodness, that's delicious." I drained my cup and smiled wryly at her. "My old nurse used to say that one should not partake of a fairy drink, lest one be stuck in this realm forever."

"This is not my realm," she said, with a flicker of melancholy, then sipped thoughtfully at her goblet. Everything she did seemed to invite and discourage candour at the same time.

"How came you to be here with Merlin?" I asked.

"I've told you. I wanted to learn from him, gain all the knowledge he has."

"You've been with him a very long time."

"Learning has no limits," she said. "Now there is King Arthur to consider. If I wish to help guide the High King through his destiny, who better to stand beside than Merlin?" Her glow darkened a shade. "Are you suggesting, again, that there is more to my place here?"

"I'm just . . . trying to understand."

Ninianne regarded me curiously, her light building again until it shone like a polished golden shield. "Yes, that *is* your wish, isn't it? To know everything, to understand."

Before I could respond, she reached across the table and plucked a tall foxglove stalk from a vase. "To comprehend how the elemental forces work is to hear a flower speak. This foxglove has been influenced by them all. It grows in the earth, under the fire of the sun, and draws from water and air to live. But there will always be a dominant force."

She laid her fingertips across several petals and gestured that I should do the same. I obeyed without words, in case speaking broke her sudden willingness.

"To find this primary force, you must concentrate and seek to connect with its essence. Ask the elements to show themselves and listen intently to what they say. Therein will lie your understanding."

"How will I—?" I began, but she shook her head.

"You'll know when you find it."

I traced my fingers along the foxglove's speckled bells. Inexplicable but distinct, water came to me first, then hints of air in the green, downy stem, a tiny hum of sun. Loudest of all, however, was a dark, rich presence, redolent with life and a warm, mossy scent.

"Earth," I said. "The most important."

Ninianne smiled in genuine pleasure. "Your elemental connection is stronger than I thought. Now you can have a little fun with form. Ask it to shift and change, like so."

She held the foxglove aloft and the tubed petals stiffened, purple fading to grey and hardening before my eyes. Ninianne dropped it on the table, where it clattered like a bag of marbles.

I picked up the stem, flowers clicking together pleasingly. "Mother of God. It's stone from the inside out."

"Not perfect, given it was quick," Ninianne said. "But yes. I asked the earth within to shift to another of its states, and it yielded to me with utmost courtesy." She hooked a fresh foxglove from the vase. "Now you."

I stared at her. "I couldn't."

"*Try*. Ask the element to grant your request. What have you to lose?"

I put my fingers against the soft, unresisting petals and felt the same swirl of elements sing out at different pitches. In my mind, I asked the earth if it would kindly turn to stone, which felt ridiculous. Beneath my hand, nothing happened.

Burning with failure, I tried again, demanding this time. Again, the foxglove remained a foxglove.

I huffed and crossed my arms. "This is pointless. It doesn't work."

"Patience, Lady Morgan," Ninianne said. "Composure is essential in elemental magic. Not in denial of one's nature, but as master of what fuels you. Be truthful and use your own voice. There you will find your power."

I had little idea of what she meant but placed my hand back on the foxglove. A simple, genuine request, I told myself; no different from asking Alys to pass me a quill. Gradually, the foxglove grew cooler, pebble-like. Then, before I could push further, the connection broke free, leaving me bolstered, invigorated.

Ninianne picked up the stem; it was still purple and green, but when she dropped it on the table, it made the same satisfying clatter as hers.

"An excellent start," she said, beaming from every pore. "Far better than idle talk, wouldn't you say?"

I let myself bask in her praise, though I couldn't help wondering if her sudden forthcomingness had all been to distract from questions of Merlin.

So what if it did? Ninianne's serene smile seemed to say, and I found I didn't care.

*

STILL THE SORCERER did not return, but I had ceased to think about him, so enraptured was I by Ninianne's teaching, her deep wisdom, the enthralling way she demonstrated and explained; her glowing satisfaction as my skills rose to meet her elemental challenges.

She taught me to produce fire in my palm without needing to mine my darkest thoughts, showed me how to capture the air and channel it into a gust, and persisted with my lesser abilities with earth and stone.

"It'll come," she told me, a month into my stay, as I coaxed lily of the valley into hard white bells but failed to turn them grey. "One day you will reach for it, and it will simply be there."

I abandoned the lily sprig with a sigh. We were in the long, narrow classroom, where we had come so she could select new reading for my evening.

"What about water?" I said. Strangely, we had yet to do anything with her dominant element. "When we spoke on the headland, you said I share your affinity."

"I remember," Ninianne replied. "Though we do not share the connection as much as we both possess it, in degrees, from different sources. I am of the lake . . ."

"And I of the sea."

"Yes." She leaned forwards with an air of confidentiality. "Do you miss it, Morgan? Living within the waves, the tides?"

"Every day," I replied. "Though I can still . . . conjure it. Being in Tintagel, with the sea all around me, salt spray in the wind, the constant crash of the waves on the cliffs."

Ninianne's face had taken on a dreamy look. "The bond is strong. Maybe it's time."

Swiftly, she rose and fetched a wide, shallow bowl, placing it between us and filling it to the brim with water.

"Water is elusive, mercurial, often disobedient. Communication is less a polite conversation than it is a dance." She extended her hand above the bowl. "At all times one must feel its fluidity, its wildness, as if your entire self has rained down with it."

She began moving her fingers through the air in a slow stroking motion. The water in the bowl shivered then curved upwards, like the arching spine of a cat. "Once you are in harmony with the water, you can feel its essence and ask it to converse. It won't yield to control, but it will answer to respect."

With a flick of her wrist, Ninianne sent a stream up in a glittering leap, splashing it back down with a musical trill.

I laughed in surprise. She offered me a rare, broad smile and slid the bowl across. "You try. Let your mind be taken into the water, sense its form, and follow wherever it wishes to go."

I held my hand a few inches above the bowl and looked at the water, conjuring thoughts of rain, of rivers and lakes, of the crystal pool I had once found in an enchanted glen and the cascade that fell into it, churning and alive. Last of all, I envisioned the sea embracing Tintagel, swirling eternal in my veins.

The water beneath my hand grew calm and glassy, a mirror containing my image. With a slight twitch of my mind, I shuddered the surface, until the water rose in tiny clear peaks.

"Good. Try more, go farther." Ninianne placed her hand over mine and guided my fingers into making the same cat-stroking motion she had. The water shifted sideways, rising up one side of the bowl, but struggled and soon collapsed. I released a hiss of frustration.

"Again," she said. "Offer more of yourself. Do not hold on—let go."

This time, I let myself breathe, in and out, my eyes fast on the water, our hands drawing it up and back. By degrees, Ninianne eased her touch away, until the water answered to my effort alone. I kept moving, raising it into the air in a high, rippling stream, and all at once I knew I was not holding it in place—it was as much a part of me as my own arm.

"How do you feel?" she asked.

"Incredible," I replied. This was a euphoria comparable to heal-ing, but utterly different: silver where healing was gold; cool, assured and eternal instead of a warm, youthful thrill; and powerful, as though I had not so much achieved something, but *become*. "It feels as if I should have known this, been this, all along."

"That is because you have," Ninianne said. "Elemental work is where your strength lies, alongside your other talents, two powers intertwined. What you might do with such a force . . ." She swept her hands in an elegant arc. "It is limitless."

I looked back at the water, smile rising on my face. Healing and the elements combined, coursing within me. *Limitless*.

A loud bang cut into our peace, water leaping between us and splashing over the table. At the opposite end of the room, the tower door flew open. A slim, sharp figure stood in the archway like a slice of night.

"Ninianne. Lady Morgan." His voice was a knife on a whetstone. "How wonderful it is to finally see you both."

25

"MERLIN," NINIANNE SAID, "when did you return?"

Her voice gave nothing away, but I sensed her shock like heat. The sorcerer advanced into the room, taking us in with his usual wolfish amusement.

"Oh, very late," he replied. "Almost dawn, I believe, so I retired directly."

At first glance, I hadn't recognized him. This was a Merlin I had never seen: neater, serious, honed, his robe cut stiff and narrow from dark-green silk—none of his typical billowing sleeves or dragging hems. His lead-coloured beard was clipped into a neat point, usually wild hair braided into a grey, rope-like plait, like a Norseman of centuries past. He strode through the classroom with a sense of purpose that suggested no nonsense or theatrics and cast curious eyes over the water bowl.

"Interesting," he said tonelessly. "My dear, I did not think you liked to teach."

"I wasn't." Ninianne turned to him, her demeanour imperious. She felt tricked, disrupted—I could feel it as surely as I had intuited the shape of the water. "We were passing the time. Lady Morgan didn't expect to wait so long for you."

"My business in Camelot did not conclude as quickly as intended. The High King was in greater need of me."

The mention of Arthur seemed to soften her. "How is he, in the wake of . . ."

"Becalmed, for now. But there is much work for me to do." Merlin's black eyes flicked to my face. "Still, my purpose is here. Lady Morgan and I only have a year."

"Eleven months," I pointed out. "Since you squandered the rest."

The sorcerer chuckled. "Then wait no longer, Lady Morgan. Ninianne will leave, and your education can begin right away."

"Can't she stay?" I asked.

"No," Ninianne replied without looking at me. "I have my own work to do." She tilted conspiratorially towards Merlin. "I have assessed her abilities. She knows nothing of magic aside from the fire sphere you taught her previously. The rest—the Seven Arts, languages, basic physic—is nothing but the usual nunnery fare."

Despite her concealment of our learning, which I supposed protected us both, her dismissive tone rankled, so suddenly had she turned from confidante to disapproving classroom mistress. I opened my mouth to protest, but her eyes flashed wide—a warning not to reveal myself.

Merlin noted my indignance. "Do you disagree with Ninianne's view, Lady Morgan?"

To deny my skills stung, anathema to my pride. I looked again at Ninianne by his side, her matchless face open and bright moments ago, now muted and impenetrable. In that moment, I knew less than I ever had before.

"I object to being summed up in so few words," I said coolly, "but I cannot disagree."

He glanced between us with faint suspicion, then sent Ninianne away with a flick of his hand, leaving me alone in the sorcerer's domain.

*

MERLIN INTERROGATED ME anyway, asking endless questions about my time in St. Brigid's and in Gore, enquiring of my childhood education and the subjects, theories and manuscripts I was familiar with, while mocking the quality of teaching I had received. I told the truth about some of it, lied about the rest and, in turn, slyly uncovered a few truths of my own. It seemed he did not know of Arthur's headaches and my healing of them, or of my safekeeping of Excalibur, which meant, at the very least, that my brother did not tell him everything.

"Glamour in all its forms," he declared the following morning. "A broad and complicated art, a speciality of mine, and a subject of which you already have experience. We begin with the concealing mist, which you can so cleverly see through. It's only apt you should learn to conjure it first."

There was no more boring a prospect, no skill I wished to learn less, which became increasingly frustrating when I discovered I was bad at creating the damnable mist. The incantation was easy enough, but its key was based on the desire to conceal oneself, a dishonesty of intention that I could not seem to invoke. Day after day I sat there, gathering the cold, damp fog at my heels, only for it to sink back into itself and disappear.

"I'm surprised," Merlin said after another week of filmy, shredded wisps. "I expected wondrous clouds from you."

"Teach me something else," I demanded.

"We cannot move on to greater things until you learn this. Remember, the key to any glamour skill is belief. *Believe* you want to disappear. *Intend* to exist outside of mortal sight."

In the end, through the sheer force of wanting to disappear from the sorcerer's tiresome presence, I conjured a large enough column of mist to step into and demonstrate I could carry myself hidden for a fair distance.

"You will never fill a ravine, Lady Morgan," Merlin sniffed. "Perhaps I must learn to accept your limitations. That is, unless you have some particular affinity you would prefer to explore?"

The thought of healing made my hands prickle. "No," I said. "What's next?"

Pure glamour it was to be: controlling not, as I thought, the true appearance of things, but rather what others saw. It was once again based on belief, but exploiting the expectations of others to create a false image.

"It's not easy to learn," Merlin said. "But you will soon see that few forms of magic have as much value as this one."

Sweeping a thin hand over his face, he overlaid his own visage with that of his younger self, then changed into a man I had never seen, a pretty young woman and, last of all, alarmingly, Arthur's smiling, brotherly face.

Despite my disgust, whatever liar's talents resided within me were well suited to pulling across the veil of glamour. Not with enough finesse for Merlin's applause, but well done enough that he felt satisfied in his own teaching and we could faster move beyond a subject that didn't impress me and I never envisioned needing.

It was a haste I would soon come to regret, because one grey, gusting morning, two months after we had begun our dubious journey into magical lies, Merlin decided to test my resolve.

"Transformation," he announced. "The most difficult and involved of our arts. Not concealment, not glamour, but how to make one man's face and body look and feel entirely like another's. You know how impressive this can be."

A cold rush of memory assaulted me: a Tintagel Castle corridor in the dead of night; the absence of the sea's comforting roar; a hulking figure in ill-fitting skin, trailing mist; the face of the father I loved dearly worn by the man I would hate the most. Uther Pendragon, on his way to my mother's violation and the destruction of our entire lives, enabled by Merlin's corrupted skill.

Gall rose in my throat. "I will not learn that. Such devilry belongs in Hell, with Uther Pendragon's rotting corpse."

"My work at Tintagel was the most complete and wondrous transformation I have created—perhaps my greatest magical achievement so far." Merlin's voice was a drone, the sullen light making spikes of his advancing shadow. "What a way to describe the glorious feat of magic that brought forth King Arthur, whom you profess to love and consider a saviour of this world."

"It's not Arthur's fault, your meddling in his birth and entire life," I said. "He is a better man than the horrors you used to bring him forth. And I am a better woman. I won't participate in this abomination—the knowledge can die with you."

My vehemence didn't move him. "You surprise me, my lady. I thought you were more ambitious than that. Not that you could learn anywhere close to that level of magic. The feat I performed for King Uther is a far more complex process than can be taught in a year. If you could master it at all."

"Do not *taunt* me," I warned. "I could master your demon magic and many other things if you were a decent teacher, but instead you only wish to goad me for your own amusement."

Merlin put a hand to his chest in affected shock. "My desire to teach you is long-held and genuine—you know that. It's *you* who cannot offer your intelligence in return."

"There are a thousand subjects where I would excel," I said. "Yet you have not sought to find them. You haven't mentioned a word of the work you're doing for Arthur, and it's why he wanted me to come here."

"Oh Lady Morgan, I *wish* I could enlighten you on the crucial work I am doing for the King, but I cannot help it if your abilities have been a disappointment."

His mocking sympathy lit me up like a bonfire. Before I knew what I was doing, I reared out of my seat and charged towards him.

"My abilities are greater than you can imagine," I snarled. "It's *you*, Merlin. You're holding back."

He stepped closer, his narrow figure seeming to grow unnaturally, looming over me. "If I am so wrong, my lady," he said, "then tell me what you have that is so valuable to my work. Show me why I sensed such potential in you."

I glared at him, resentful of his insults, hindered by my limitations, furious that I was forced to come to this place at all.

Don't, Ninianne's voice intoned in my head, pausing me just enough.

Merlin sighed impatiently. "Clearly, my lady, you have nothing to say." He turned away, heading for the tower.

"Where are you going?" I said. "This is the third time you've abandoned our lessons this week."

"Go and play your games with Ninianne," came the careless reply. "I have important work to do."

He opened the door and departed without looking back, leaving me in my outrage and frustration, and smarting with the edge of my ambition.

26

MERLIN STAYED AWAY from the classroom for several days, stoking my silent seething and putting me under Ninianne's quiet supervision once again. With her, I could bend water, air, fire and earth to my growing will, a process for which I did not have to sacrifice parts of myself or relive my worst memories; a power that gave, not cost, and cleaved to my spirit like the finest suit of armour.

Yet somehow it was not enough. Merlin's dismissal, the knowledge that he purposefully kept the keys to Arthur on an impossible shelf, continued to seep through me like venom.

"Morgan?"

Ninianne's hand warmed my forearm, drawing me back into the room. She rarely touched me, due to her natural lack of intimacy and an awareness of the effect her fairy presence had on us faint-hearted mortals. I could understand why: in times of frustration, despair or longing for those left behind, the idea of resting bare fingers against her glowing skin was almost irresistible.

"You should master this today, but for your distraction," she said.

A heart-shaped cabbage sat on her marble table, a tight teardrop of layered, shirred leaves. I had been trying to turn it to stone for an hour, but aside from a slight hardness at the edges, it had stayed pliable and pale green.

What does it matter? I wanted to say. Turning a whole fleet of horses into courtyard ornaments wouldn't have filled the hollowness created by Merlin's taunting, his blocking the path to Arthur's right hand.

"You never told me *why* I can't tell Merlin of my skills," I said abruptly.

Ninianne recoiled. "Isn't it enough to believe me?"

"Not when I suffer the consequences," I said. "He's keeping me from gaining the means to help Arthur and the realm. Besides, he's always known I'm a healer—he probably already suspects."

"You cannot tell him. Trust me on this."

"How can I?" I exclaimed. "You told me *not* to trust you, and never explained that either. Perhaps you don't *want* me to show him because you're fearful Merlin's favour will change if he sees everything I'm capable of."

Ninianne shot up from her chair, face blazing like a wronged goddess. "Is that what you think of me? That I strive to keep Merlin from you out of a petty sense of ownership, rather than for your own protection?"

"I cannot possibly know," I snapped back. "You've never told me a damned thing about you, or what you're thinking. Every day, I see you scowl then simper at him. I watch you shudder with disdain then whisper in his ear and disappear into his tower. You've lived with Merlin for decades, learning his ways, participating in his schemes. Why would I assume you care anything for my protection?"

"And you know everything, of course," she said. "You have no *earthly concept* of what my life here has been like. What I have given, what I've lost, to gain the knowledge I have. Decisions I was too young to understand. Sacrifices I didn't know I would have to make until there was no choice."

Her voice was low again but tremulous, unsure. She pressed her fingers to her lips and sank back into her seat beside mine, next to

the chair she had brought for me after years of preserving her solitude. A thin whistle of doubt cut through my anger.

"Ninianne . . ." I began, but she shook her head.

There was a heavy pause, then she made a sudden sweeping movement with the edge of her skirts, shifting aside layers of soft violet to
reveal her long, gleaming leg.

"To understand," she said, "you must look."

I dropped my eyes to where her hand held back her robe, revealing a band of symbols in dark-blue ink, curving around her upper
thigh in a dance of lines and whorls.

"Who did that?" I asked.

"I did," she replied. "I tattooed these marks, and the same on my
other thigh. They are part of a protective charm that I taught myself,
out of necessity."

She smoothed her robe back into place with uncertain hands.
"When I met Merlin, I was a girl—not a child, but not far enough
from it to know better. I wanted to learn, wished for all the knowledge there was, both to understand my own power and to master
what existed outside. I came here because Merlin promised to teach
me everything I had long dreamed of. But it was not all that *he*
would want."

"Ninianne," I said quietly. "You don't have to tell me this."

She cut me off with a halting hand. "Merlin is fascinated by natural-
born power," she went on. "He has none himself. Nothing to be
ashamed of, but everything he can do, he had to study and learn. It
is difficult, all-consuming. When he sees innate ability, he becomes
fixated upon the potential, the one who possesses it. I understand
this impulse for knowledge and so do you. Whatever you feel about
him, in that way the three of us are the same. As scholars, we have all
felt that pull of obsession. But it has consequences."

I felt a quick, vicarious dread. "What did he do to you?"

"Nothing," she insisted. "But I was too innocent, blind to everything but my great need for knowledge, my wish to impress my fascinating teacher. By the time I realized how Merlin loved me beyond reason, it was already too late." Her gaze strayed to the window, at the enclosing trees beyond. "At first, he accepted that I was still a girl, but that only meant there was a time in his mind when I would be one no longer. Inevitably, he thought I would give myself over to him, at the very least in gratitude for his teaching."

She looked back at me, her eyes Greek fire. "You will ask why I stayed, next."

"No," I said. "I know why. You had nowhere to go."

A deep exhale deflated her formidable figure. "Yes. My home was gone by then, destroyed by war. More to my fault, I had no desire to give up my studies. As the years went by, I learned to live with Merlin's obsession, but I knew the time would come when his wants would overwhelm his reason, his claims of love and respect. I had to protect myself."

"So you tattooed a charm into your own flesh to keep him from possessing you," I said. "Is it permanent?"

"Yes. It means I can never know physical intimacy, nor act upon any desire I might feel for another. I chose knowledge over love because I had no choice."

All at once, it made a sad, terrible sense why she insisted love was a weakness. "Does Merlin know?" I asked.

"Of that I cannot be sure. Regardless, he kept teaching me, and I kept accepting his teaching. It began, after a while, to feel like a sort of power. He probably knows and has been trying to find a counter-charm all these years, not realizing that it's deep fairy magic, old as the rivers and hills, and completely irreversible."

"It sounds more of a curse than a charm," I said.

"Charms, curses—there are not truly such things. There are only questions, and the intent with which one answers them."

"I have always felt the same way about physic," I agreed. "Cure and poison can often come from the same source. But if you are so learned and in command of your powers, why do you stay *now?*"

Her face took on a cast of serenity. "King Arthur. At his first breath, I felt his possibilities more deeply than anything I had ever experienced. So I stay with Merlin, where I can take part in the pursuit of a better world. People talk, of course—they say that I will be Merlin's ruin because of my hunger for knowledge. Future poets will claim I bewitched him, that I teased and tortured a heartsick man for his wisdom until his brilliance was no more. But if I can help your brother fulfil his greatness, what I have sacrificed will mean something, in the end."

"You don't have to renounce everything of yourself for another," I said. "And there are other forms of love than desire. To eschew them all is denying yourself so much possibility."

I circled a palm over my rounded belly and a flutter rose up to meet me, a tiny answering limb, bringing the joyous thrill that this utterly singular sensation always did.

Ninianne's gaze followed my hand around my abdomen. "All forms of love are weakness in some way, and I have no need for any. Even you are more pragmatic than you admit. I tell you this not so you will lament my fate, but protect yourself as well as you can."

"Are you saying I must guard my body in the same way?"

"You cannot," she replied. "You have known love and acted bodily upon it. This charm is not strong enough to counteract the experience of true passion."

She was right; one glance at Accolon and my desire felt like it could burn down the world. "What, then?" I asked.

"It's as I have told you," she said. "Keep the secret of your power from Merlin. Do you understand me, Morgan? It is the only way to stay free."

27

I HALF THOUGHT Ninianne would avoid me after her confession, so it was strange to see her in the classroom the next day, hovering at the far end. She looked equally surprised to see me.

"Merlin summoned me," I explained. "I awoke to a note under my door."

"I doubt he intended it," she said. "He has been up for several nights with the stars. He's in no fit state to . . ."

A scuffling bang cut her off as the tower door swung open and the sorcerer flew in, hair wild, and shrouded in a tattered, shapeless black robe. It was Camelot's Merlin—the mysterious mage of trailing hems and endless secrets—only lacking the control of his public image. His movements were jerking, erratic, a slash of febrile colour high on his cheeks. He halted at the sight of Ninianne's unflinching light, clutching his frayed collar to his chest, black eyes burning like coals.

"I'm not late, and what's it to either of you?" he said fractiously. "You do not know this work, the efforts I make in service of this kingdom. The discoveries of Fate that would remain unknown if I chose the life of ease that others do."

"You hear no words of admonition here." Ninianne's voice was calm, pitched to soothe. "What did the night's work bring? Have you eaten, or will you take a drink?"

Merlin ignored her and started towards me, but she laid a hand on his arm. I watched his gaze catch on hers, his demeanour stilling into enraptured pause.

"You have not slept," she said. "Instead of teaching today—"

"No, my dear," he interrupted. "I'm not in need of anything but to begin today's lesson." He smiled, his voice once again his own. "Will you stay, my faithful Ninianne?"

She hesitated, then joined me in sitting, her eyes never leaving the sorcerer. Instead of taking up his usual pacing, Merlin pulled out a chair and sat down between us. Unease shivered through me; for all our hours spent, it was the first time he had ever taken a seat in my presence.

"Where were we, Lady Morgan?" he said. "Ah yes, I gave you time to think upon your strengths, possible affinities. To help us in our shared quest for your education."

His smile widened, tongue lightly touching his lips, as if my revelation was imminent and would taste delicious.

"All I remember is you sending me away," I said. "And denying me what my brother wished me to learn."

Merlin's onyx eyes hooked into mine for a moment, giving rise to a sharp twist in my head. I rubbed my temples and felt thorns, but didn't dare heal it away.

"Something wrong, my lady?" he asked.

"I am perfectly well," I snapped.

"Lady Morgan might need to rest," Ninianne said. "Given her condition."

"She says she is well," he replied. "And quite the Stoic with discomfort, it seems. A lot can be told about a person by the way they respond to pain. How much they fear it, or how much physical suffering it takes to make one commit a drastic act."

"Is this the lesson?" I said with an air of boredom.

"Perhaps it should be." Merlin reached into the pocket of his robe and drew out a knife with a large, curving blade and a rampant golden dragon for a handle; a relic from Uther Pendragon's time, no doubt.

"No two people feel pain the same way," he continued. "I'd imagine, Lady Morgan, that every individual's body responds to injury and healing differently as well?"

I shrugged. "That's the first, most basic rule of diagnostics."

"Of course. Forgive my slowness—physic is not my strength, where it has been yours. I have often wondered if the pain felt by an individual affects the amount of healing they must receive."

He placed the knife on the table and gave it an idle spin. It whirred on the dark wood, steel catching the low light. Ninianne shifted, clasping her hands together on the tabletop, her gaze on the dying autumn leaves outside.

I hesitated. "That depends on the injury."

"Ah. So if I did this . . ." The sorcerer pressed his forefinger against the knife tip until a small bead of blood welled up. "We can assume, because the injury is small, that the amount of pain will also be small."

"It's not always so simple," I replied. "But one might begin with this assumption."

"I see." Merlin sent the knife spinning harder, and it juddered sideways. "The pain would become a concern if the affliction was greater. Which would you, or a physician, think of first—the severity of the injury, or the pain of the injured?"

"There is danger in pain too," I said. "One cannot just—"

"Which is it, Lady Morgan?" he insisted. "The suffering flesh, or the person it belongs to? What provokes you to the greatest action? Or shall we test it?"

His hand slammed down on the spinning knife. With his other, he grabbed Ninianne's wrist from where it lay on the table, dragged it forth, and plunged the blade into her gleaming flesh.

Her scream was a sound more fearful and uncontrolled than any I'd imagined she could make. She sprung up in horror, trying to pull away, but Merlin used her resistance, dragging the blade through her arm towards her wrist, tearing through the delicate network of veins and down to the bone.

Dark-red beads wept over her forearm; blood the same colour as mine, that flowed the same, and would kill her if she lost it too fast. Water fairy she may be, but she could die from serious physical harm.

"Stop!" I cried.

Merlin sat back, knife dropping from his bloodied hands. "Make haste, Lady Morgan. Before she bleeds all over the table."

I flew out of my chair and grabbed Ninianne's arm. She was rigid with shock, her breaths hard and uneven. I put my hands on either side of the gaping cut, trying to keep my grip as the blood kept pouring, warm and sticky. Flesh was much harder to align neatly than skin, and she was already shuddering uncontrollably. I had never imagined she would feel pain this way, sudden and terrible and human like the rest of us.

"Breathe," I said, fingers slipping in her blood. "Air in, air out. Close your eyes."

Ninianne managed to steady her breaths and control her shaking, allowing me to line up the vessels and tendons. When all was ready, I reached for the warm golden force and her eyes snapped open.

Don't, she insisted wordlessly, but I pretended it hadn't reached me.

I focused on her suffering first, chasing the pain away before concentrating on knitting her flesh together, her veins, her skin. I felt her resistance dissipate as the euphoria of healing took hold, blood receding back into flesh, laceration fusing with ease, leaving only a thin red line on her skin and a horrifying memory.

"All right?" I whispered.

She nodded, still breathing hard, eyes jewel-bright with unspent tears. I placed my bloodied fingers over the scar to heal it away, but her other hand stopped me.

Leave it behind, came the silent command, and I understood. Scars remembered what the mind sought to forget.

"There it is—what she imagined she could hide." Merlin's buzzing voice crawled over my scalp. "Very impressive, Lady Morgan. Astounding, in fact."

He approached us, eyes still tinged with a keen red fire, breaths short but deep, as if he was tussling with some new, unfathomable excitement.

"Go and clean yourself up," he ordered Ninianne.

She let go of my hand and stood square to him, imperious as an empress. "I deserve an explanation."

"Which you will have, of course," the sorcerer said, but his eyes were on my face. "Later. Lady Morgan and I have much to discuss."

"Lady Morgan should not have done that. I did not ask for her help." Ninianne refused to look at me, and her sudden ingratitude stung. "What interests you in such an ostentatious trick? It has no bearing on your work for King Arthur."

The haughtiness in her voice made the sting a burn. She didn't like that I had defied her, but what choice did I have? I stared at her, seeking some sign of alliance, but she kept her eyes fixed on Merlin, light seething from her pores.

"Not everything of interest relates directly to our work," Merlin said. "As a lover of knowledge, the wonder of this should not elude you."

"I see no wonder here," she said pettishly, and for the first time it seemed what I had once accused her of could be true: that Merlin's amazement and his subsequent dismissal had stoked some sharp, unexpected envy within her.

"All the better, then, that you leave us," the sorcerer said.

She looked at me, but her eyes avoided mine. "I'm sure Lady Morgan would prefer—"

"As Merlin says," I cut in, "this is between him and me."

I felt her surprise on the air. Pulling her carriage proud, Ninianne left without giving either of us another glance, room darkening in her wake.

I crossed my blood-streaked arms and faced the sorcerer. "So now you know, for what it's worth."

Merlin smirked. "It's worth a great deal, to have the truth."

"What a way to get it," I snapped. "Debasing yourself, harming another. What if your suspicions had been wrong?"

"But they were not wrong, were they? You would never have told me otherwise."

"You disgust me." I turned away, unable to look at his self-satisfied face. "What do you care, anyway? Healing and physic don't interest you."

"It's *you* I find fascinating, Lady Morgan," Merlin said in my ear. He had moved closer without me realizing, his touch surprisingly hot as he took up my wrist, gazing at the darkening crimson stains. "Her blood on your skin . . . it calls to me. All this time I thought you remarkable, but there was so much more."

I recoiled but my back met the table. He drew my hand towards his mouth; what he thought to do with it I did not know, but I pulled away, repulsed.

"Then harness my potential," I said through a hard jaw. "Show me what you are doing for Arthur."

Merlin eased back, smoothing over his demeanour. "Why would I consider that when you have disparaged so much of what I have tried to teach you?"

His return to inscrutability didn't fool me. Gathering my mettle, I put my fingertips to his shoulder and brushed a feather from his robe. His eyes followed my hand, Ninianne's blood singing from my skin.

"Because you know I have the ability to surprise you, and there are still marvels to uncover," I said. "That *is* what you want, isn't it—to share in my power? As I should share in yours, if we are both willing to bend."

"I barely bend for kings, Lady Morgan," he drawled. "Why would I do so for you?"

"Because Arthur demands it. Do what my brother wants and show me what I need to run this realm."

His gaze snapped to me, sharp as a spider bite. "Know this, my lady—I have been at King Arthur's side since long before he drew the sword from the stone, felt a crown on his head, or knew of his ambitious, fire-breathing sister. *Nothing* will change the fact that I am the one at his right hand."

His arrogance stuck in my craw, affording me one last opportunity to step back from whatever danger I was running towards. But if I did not face this beast jaws first, it could never be slain.

"Then there is nothing to fear," I said. "Teach me, Merlin. Cease to hold back and *use* me."

The sorcerer gave me one last look of scrutiny, then his mouth curved into a catlike grin. "We begin tomorrow, Lady Morgan. I will bend and so will you."

28

MERLIN SAID TO be with him at dawn, so I arrived in the hour before that, when night still clung to the sky. The door to his tower stood ajar, three flights of stone steps leading to the large room that he kept as his study.

The sorcerer's inner sanctum was suitably overwhelming, every wall, surface and shelf crowded with star charts, manuscripts, strange implements and jars containing goodness knew what. It was well lit by sconces and large candle stands, ghostly twilight filtering through a jumble of windows. An incongruous oriel bloomed from a back corner, glazed with a curved pane and bearing a sizeable bird perch. A bowl of raw meat sat next to it, but there was no other sign that anything feathered had ever lived there. Opposite, a small stone stairway spiralled its way up to a locked doorway, presumably leading to the tower top where Merlin watched the stars.

I was unsurprised to find Merlin already there, seated behind an enormous chunk of desk carved from the muscular grooves of a tree trunk, its outer edges still covered in bark. Drawn by its strangeness, I approached and touched the pale, polished top, fingers tracing the half rings that spoke of great age.

"It's as ancient as it looks, and was once twice as big," Merlin commented. "Cut from a storm-struck ash that stood on this very spot in the time of the old gods."

He stood abruptly; I jolted back despite myself and he gave a derisive chuckle. "I didn't expect you so early."

I forced myself to hold his gaze. "I am eager to learn."

"Good. For if your dedication truly is to this work, then there is much to learn and little time. Perhaps not enough time."

"I'm a very quick study when properly taught."

"We shall see." He cast his eyes about the room. "Now, where to begin?"

"We begin with Arthur," I said.

"What I do for King Arthur is prophecy, tracking and interpreting the stars. You have no interest in such things."

"I'm not talking about squinting at the heavens," I said. "You may keep your obsession with that. When I first came here, you were late because you confirmed to Arthur a prophecy that was troubling him greatly. You have foreseen his death."

Merlin turned sharp black eyes on me. "Why do you say that?"

"I told you, I am a quick learner. And I know Arthur, both as my brother and as a King. Nothing else would unsettle him so much."

The sorcerer said nothing for a long moment, aligning his hands and lifting them until his fingertips rested under his chin.

"Very well," he said eventually. "I have foreseen his death. Many times now. No matter how I look for it—in the skies, in the stones I cast . . ." He gestured at a large sphere of purple quartz on a stand, its interior swirling with smoke. "In the clouds of the Fates. Even on the lines of his palms, the same message comes. King Arthur will die, not yet but too soon. And if he does, Britain will fall."

"So he didn't take it well."

"Would you?" Merlin retorted. "He is a young man, hopeful, brimming with plans and ideals, goodness he has upheld in the hopes God would realign the stars for him. But there is nothing to be done."

"Yet you *are* doing something," I said. "It's been too cloudy for stars for three weeks, but you've been working yourself almost into madness. Why?"

The sorcerer swept away from the desk, turning to the deep window recess at his back. Outside, the sky was lightening to a weak, mousey grey, obscured by the enormous oak tree within the moat.

"Arthur has told you to change his fate, hasn't he?" I pressed. "You're looking for a way to prevent his death."

"It isn't possible," he said tersely. "Ninianne even asked the water and it sang the same lament. A fate written into the fabric of existence with such certainty cannot be denied, despite kings demanding it be otherwise."

I was no great believer in the inconstant, shape-shifting art of prophecy, especially not Merlin's manipulations, but the idea of my brother's untimely death struck my heart. I looked down at the desk: the open manuscripts; scattered pages; a shallow bowl filled with ash and the remnants of bird bones—another attempt to wheedle out a different answer to Fate's death warrant. A piece of parchment caught my eye: a list written in the sorcerer's spidery scrawl, headed *Objects of Resurrection*. Every item was struck out apart from one, circled so many times in red ink it had blotted like blood.

"What's the Shroud of Tithonus?" I asked.

In one dramatic movement Merlin swung around and charged towards the desk, gathering scrolls and pages with a sweeping arm. "It's nothing. An idea, a useless notion."

But the revelation had already come to me. "Of course, the language of prophecy," I said. "Telling the truth in one way but lying in another. You said that *if* Arthur dies, Britain will fall. His fate cannot be prevented, but it can be changed in result. The solution to Arthur's death is resurrection."

Merlin straightened and regarded me with a seriousness he had never before bestowed. "Very good, Lady Morgan. You *are* a quick study. Not that there is any gain in you knowing. Resurrection in its purest form is death magic—an art dark and ancient, one I have never been taught. Its tenets are apocryphal at best, scarcely written down. A skill lost to the ages, if it ever existed at all."

"Even still, you are trying," I pointed out. "Burning bones, attempting to commune with otherworldly spirits, seeking objects purported to bring the dead to life. There must be something in it."

"I am more than trying. It is *everything* to me. To bring the greatest High King ever known back from death, to save Britain a second time—it would carve my name into this land for eternity."

"It is fortunate, then," I said, "that you now have me to try with you."

Merlin laughed, rasping until he coughed. "Admirable ambition, Lady Morgan, but if I cannot see my way through these shadows, why should you?"

In one way, it wasn't an invalid question, given our disparity in years and hours spent learning, but he seemed to have forgotten I possessed skills he did not. What was resurrection, if not healing in its purest form?

"Because maybe *I* am a different kind of light," I said. "In any case, to deny me is to deny Arthur's wishes, and you won't want me riding back to Camelot with your resistance on my tongue."

The sorcerer eyed me with interest. "Your determination impresses me, Lady Morgan. It's a pleasure to watch you think. An even greater one, I'm sure, to see you work."

With a flick of his wrist, a chair scraped across the floor, stopping beside his desk. I scowled and stayed standing; flattery from him afforded me nothing but a creeping sensation under my skin.

"What's the Shroud of Tithonus?" I asked again.

Merlin sighed and retook his seat. "A garment of great and wondrous enchantment. You know the Greek myth of Tithonus. The lover of the goddess of dawn, a man made immortal."

"Doomed to age for all time, until he became a particularly musical cicada," I supplied. "An immortal would have no need for a shroud."

"Not many magical objects had the owners their names claim. The creature he became renews itself, breaking free of the carapace of death. The Shroud of Tithonus symbolizes the shed skin of a man returning to life again and again."

"Resurrection," I concluded.

He inclined his head. A slight pressure twinged as the child within turned over and settled its spine against my back, so I took the seat that had flown to my side. "I assume that you have this Shroud?"

"I do," he replied in unexpected honesty. "It was given to me many years ago, though I did not know its true significance until recently. Discovering my possession lent a feeling of providence to my endeavours."

"Yet you are still failing," I said. "You cannot use it."

Merlin's brow pinched. "The right formula must be found first. The Shroud has enough enchantment for one use, one resurrection, and then it will be gone forever. Dust."

"Where is it?"

"Hidden," he said curtly. "Where it will stay."

Sighing, I rose. "Then I might as well go. Either I'm part of this, or not."

I had half turned away when the sorcerer pounced up and grasped my arm, pulling himself into my orbit. "You push me too far, Lady Morgan."

His face was so close to mine I had repulsive visions of him either kissing me or biting my neck, but I didn't let myself flinch.

"Show me the Shroud," I said.

Just as suddenly, he let go and vanished up the spiral stair, where I did not pursue him. Instead, I gathered myself, walking along the bookshelves with their vertical stacks of manuscripts and various scrolls, imagining the knowledge contained within. A volume of anatomy sat open on a worktable and I leafed through it, past the skeleton, a man's tangled gut and then a diagram of the human heart. A chime of recognition rang like a bell in a far-off room: the memory of a notion; a swift scribble in blue ink; of Accolon, reclining in a windowsill and smiling at me in that way of his.

"Here, upon your insistence."

The sorcerer reappeared, interrupting my thoughts. He placed a polished ebony box on his desk and reached inside with extreme care, extracting a rectangle of folded fabric the colour of old bones. I approached with interest.

"Hold out your hands," he commanded.

For a moment I assumed he had brought a fake and felt foiled because I wouldn't know any better. Then the unbleached cloth touched my skin, and a silver-white force hurtled through my body like an exploding star, filling my blood with an unstoppable, diamond-bright vitality. The child inside me awoke, kicking hard as a wild pony. I rocked backwards and sucked in a gasp.

Merlin snatched the Shroud back at once. "What is it?"

I steadied myself against the window seat, vision glittering with light. "The Shroud is real," I heard myself say. "But it's not enough."

Merlin stared at me, kneading the fabric with his fingertips, and I was reminded of Arthur holding Excalibur's scabbard. The sorcerer could no more sense the Shroud's blaze of power than my brother could feel the scabbard's life-song.

"Do not get ahead of yourself," he said officiously. "This Shroud is the end of a process, not the beginning. You do not know more than me."

He returned the Shroud of Tithonus to the box, its absence tugging at me as the lid closed. "For all your boldness, I assume the word *necromancy* still makes your heart shiver, like a child hearing tales of

All Hallows'. To master this art, what you will learn, by most sane minds, is considered to be the stuff of nightmares."

He flourished his hand, sealing the Shroud behind an unspoken locking charm. A swift, protective anger bristled down my back, like a she-wolf kept from her cubs.

"Spare me your concern, Merlin," I said. "I've wanted to unravel the veil between life and death since I was a girl of fourteen. My heart can withstand more than you can imagine."

I remembered it then, as he sneered and took the box away; my attention lost in a memory and the warm peace of Camelot's library, reading a phrase captured in a fleeting moment.

Every life, in its entirety, can be found written upon the heart. So it can be read there in death, and lived again.

29

FOR ALL HIS great dramatics, the work I must do to grasp the horrors of necromancy and the rest of the Forbidden Arts mainly involved reading. Merlin guided my course, piling my workbench with volume after volume of writings, often scribed and bound by his own hand. Some I had read before and some I hadn't, the most interesting those that were strictly prohibited, like the black book I had discovered in St. Brigid's that was subsequently burned.

So I read, intensely, endlessly, until the words blurred and the diagrams became meaningless shapes, and I had to rise and walk about just to recognize language again. Never in my life would I have said there was too much reading before the sorcerer's tasks, but if the key to saving Arthur was within, then I would push beyond my fatigue and find it.

Merlin lingered at my edges, his quill scratching, or fussing with various implements, occasionally drawing me away for something that amused him—whispering to his purple quartz to show me the smoky shapes the spirits sent, or demonstrating how he cast bird bones to bolster his prophecies.

The purpose of the wooden perch by the window also became clear. Late one afternoon, as I read a scroll on blood rituals with grim fascination, there was a muffled thud and an orange-eyed owl alighted there, dropping a dead starling on the sill beneath. The owl gulped at the sorcerer's fresh meat, then flew back into the woods.

"You have a trained owl?" I exclaimed.

Merlin scooped the starling from the bowl and examined it. "Of course not. A waste of my time, training one creature so I can wander the woods with it, hoping it catches something relevant. Instead, preying birds know they can find easy meat here, if they leave their kill behind."

He carried the corpse up the stairs, presumably placing it in a great bird graveyard somewhere, its bones awaiting the privilege of divination. Thereafter, various owls and hawks continued to bring gifts of finches, thrushes and even a dead duck—along with a few voles which Merlin discarded with distaste—and their swooping arrivals ceased to be particularly diverting.

So I persisted and read script in increasing frustration, while he read bones and ashes. But as the year crept beyond autumn, burnished leaves giving way to creeping frost, the stars came out for longer in cold, clear skies, and Merlin chose to send me from his presence so he could consult with the talkative heavens alone.

"Go and rest," he would say. "You will need your strength in the morning."

"For what?" I argued one day. "It costs me nothing to read other people's words, when I should be exploring the means to write my own."

The sorcerer regarded me with faint scorn. "Why, my lady? What have you discovered that we can explore? An incantation to regrow bone, perhaps? An enchantment that guards the body from sword strikes? A method to persuade a stilled heart to beat again?"

Again, the concept tolled within me. "No," I said petulantly. "But perhaps practising other arts—"

"Other arts were not what you wanted, Lady Morgan," he cut in. "They *bored* you. You wanted to serve King Arthur's interests, and this is the work at hand." The threat of a smile curled at his mouth. "Of course, we could always return to our more general studies. I will show you how to make a hen appear as a rabbit, if you wish."

There was nothing to do but put my back to his taunts and keep reading.

Only in the dark, lying awake in the witching hour as the cold winter moons rose and fell, did I let myself think of Accolon, of the library and our idyllic month in Camelot; of the two hearts now inside my body, and one recurring phrase.

Every life, in its entirety, can be found written upon the heart.

After weeks of these words from the past echoing across my sleepless mind, eventually came the night where I could no longer lie still. If I was awake, I might as well work.

I hoisted my rounded body up the tower stairs, child kicking fitfully against my lower back, and entered Merlin's study. His enchanted hour candle showed three hours after midnight, and I wondered if I would find him there, poring over star charts or nightingale bones. But the sorcerer was nowhere to be seen; even demons needed to sleep, it seemed.

The oriel window stood open, fanged with icicles, though it would soon be the equinox, and spring should have been due. A low glow still battled in the hearth, so I churned the embers and added kindling until it burned high and yellow. My abdomen gave another wrenching twist; I pulled my work chair to the fireplace and let the resurgent warmth soothe the stretching pain in my belly. Alys would have ordered me back to bed, I thought, and it occurred to me that in my fervent state of work, I had barely seen Ninianne for weeks.

I turned to my reading pile: volumes on anatomy; so-called blood magic; forbidden scrolls on necromancy; anything I could find on the heart. Checking that I was alone, I drew out my notes from where I had concealed them between the pages of a large lapidary, knowing

Merlin would never look there because he considered himself an expert on stones.

Halfway through rereading my fledgling theory on the curative properties of various bloods, there was a scuffle at the bird window. Usually, I would have ignored the sorcerer's macabre altar, but something turned my head; whatever had fallen was so large it filled the empty bowl. I rose and went to it, candle shining upon a long patrician beak and reticulated feathers black as night, belonging to a large raven of great beauty.

There was no sign outside of the bird that had left it, only bare branches and a gust of lingering winter. The bestower of this unusual prey had not even paused to take its meat.

I shut the window and carried the raven's half-frozen corpse back to my worktable. It bore no visible marks of violence, and I decided to take the longest flight feathers as quills before Merlin reduced the poor creature's regal darkness to dust.

Splaying out a wing, I felt a tiny judder against my palm, soft as a landing butterfly. I lifted my hand, but the bird remained motionless, the depression of my fingers still imprinted on its breast. I lay my hand over it again and felt the same narrow, coruscating shiver— not a life sign but something else: a trace, a suggestion, a bright whisper of an existence that had once been. Guided by the sensation, I held the dead bird's fragile chest to my ear, reaching past the silence for something unknown.

When it came, it was not in sound but in visions—the soaring view of treetops, a tangled nest of twigs lined with feathers, the sunglint of metal on a horse's bridle—the record of a life once lived, carved across a stilled heart, and the slightest sliver of proof for my unsleeping mind.

My hands worked automatically, sifting through the weeks of notes I had written until a page caught my eye—an experimental combination of new knowledge and words of magic I had been trying to fit together with my strongest method of healing. I reread the page, checking the incantation I had tentatively designed and the order of requirements I felt had the most potential.

A place of rest was first, and my eyes fell upon a fair-sized wooden box of crystal shards on Merlin's desk. I emptied the box, lined the interior with a sprig of yew leaves and a bunch of dried sage, and placed the raven within, wrapped in a small bolt of linen.

Securing the box's lid, I gripped the makeshift grave to my chest and intoned my invented nine-word incantation over and over again. The sphere of my abdomen constricted, making me cry out in interruption, but I clutched the box tighter to my racing heartbeat and restarted my chant. At the third saying, the box gave a violent rattle, fighting my hold as if the very essence of life was contained within. Another spasm gripped my body but I ignored it, wrenching the lid off the box.

The raven burst forth with a scream, wings scything the air. It skimmed across the ceiling beams like an unchained wraith, giving another shriek of protest before landing on the oriel windowsill. I watched transfixed as it tore at the raw meat, armoured feathers gleaming blue-black with the renewed light of life. Upon hearing my gasp, it regarded me with unhurried scrutiny, flesh dangling from its sharp beak. I grinned back, my bones thrilling with awe.

"It's alive."

A wiry hand grabbed my arm. Merlin, too, was smiling in wild rapture.

"The bird was dead, and now . . . My remarkable Morgan, what have you done?" His eyes flickered across my face, a devouring look that I felt like teeth grazing my flesh. "How did you do it, my beautiful, clever one?"

I strained away from the intensity of his gaze, but he held fast to my arm. Then his hand was at my face, cool fingers exploring my cheek. "What did you feel when you held that creature close to your body? What did you give to afford it new life?"

The shock of his touch froze my limbs. My belly gave a jolting twinge. "I—I don't know," I said. "Perhaps we should look at the bird."

"Whatever it is will still be coursing through you." His hand moved to the back of my neck, fingers pushing into my hair. His eyes burned red, estranged from reason. "I must possess all of you in this moment, or risk the essence, the magic, being lost."

Another bolt of pain kicked through my gut, affording me a rush of outrage. "Stop this," I snapped. "I am with child."

"It doesn't matter, don't you see?" His voice was desperate, unmoored, far away from his usual waspish precision. "You have enraptured me—your gifts cry out. We must share this power for the sake of greatness."

He was not himself—or perhaps he was, this hungry, febrile, uncontrolled side of Merlin as much part of him as the bored, all-knowing master sorcerer. He had spent weeks in a state of trance, inhaling vapours, eschewing food and sleep, and watching me work with a growing keenness. It was a state he had cultivated and relished, and no more acceptable than a bandit snatching women from their beds.

His bruising fingers caressed my neck, and my vision filled with red at his presumption. In the window, the raven spread its wings and screeched, echoing my fury. I wrenched the sorcerer's arm away and broke myself free.

"*I* have done this, not you," I said fiercely. "This bird could be the answer, but I will do or say nothing more if you ever *think* of touching me again."

Merlin stepped back and exhaled, eyes still smouldering with want. "Withholding will not serve us. What you have achieved is already done."

"It isn't *enough*," I said. "That is a *bird*, not a *man*. You cannot believe that a mild, imperfect spell that restored a mere raven could resurrect a High King? It would be madness to even claim it."

The sorcerer said nothing, long fingers stroking the collar of his robe. I sensed with unwelcome certainty that he was torn between another lustful lunge or trying to out-argue me, and was alarmed that I had come to know such a creature so well.

"You need me, Merlin," I said. "Arthur's reprieve from death doesn't depend on what I've done, but on what I do next. I can cease to work until I leave, then tell my brother how you threw away his salvation for a selfish obsession. Where will your legacy be then?"

Merlin stared at me, red eyes settling to their usual liquid black. He pointed to his desk, at a fat wood pigeon corpse that a buzzard had brought earlier that evening.

"Do it again," he said.

"Absolutely not." A fist of pain gripped the base of my spine, snatching my breath. "I don't . . . work on your . . . command."

Another crushing spasm encircled my body, so searing I doubled over. I fought it, pushing myself upright and heading for the door, when a bolting horse kick crashed inside me. I felt a warm rush of fluid down my leg, and the last thing I saw was the dizzying staircase beneath me before everything was sucked into black.

30

I AWOKE IN near darkness, a film of damp between my back and what I came to realize was my own bed. All was quiet, the only sounds the low crackle of the fire and the faint scratch of branches against windowpanes. The air was thick with the smell of tallow and sweat.

I didn't remember going to bed, and the drapes were drawn, when I had never slept with them that way. As I attempted to reach for one, the hanging flew away from my hand and I was bathed in a golden light.

"You're awake," said a low, soothing voice. "Good."

I shifted onto my elbows, trying to sit up, but my limbs felt weighted, slow. "Ninianne," I croaked.

"Careful now, moving won't be pleasant."

She slipped her arms under my shoulders and hoisted me up against soft pillows. Her copper hair was like trying to stare into a fire and I had to avert my hazy eyes.

"What happened?" I asked. "The last thing I remember is pain, shooting low through my back and . . ." The thought slipped away as a goblet of water appeared before my lips.

"Drink," Ninianne said.

I gulped greedily at the cold, cleansing liquid. "Not too fast!" she warned, but I couldn't help myself. The water was her enhanced kind, tasting of goodness and clarity, washing away the fog in my head with every nourishing mouthful.

As my mind awoke, so did my body, unleashing a deep, persistent ache beneath stiff linens tied between my legs. I put a hand to my belly and found it swollen, still rounded, but flatter. Empty.

"The child," I said. "I was in labour."

Ninianne took the goblet and refilled it. "Yes. Your waters broke and you fainted. Merlin called for me."

"I don't remember, I . . ." A sudden, sickening ache pressed down on my temples. "God's blood, my head is splitting." I reached for the water again, drinking until the pain subsided. "What was done to me?"

"Merlin cast a sleep enchantment on you before he left us. You were feverish, delirious. Given the danger of panic, it was best to keep you soothed while delivering the child. You've been at rest for three days."

"Three days!" I exclaimed. "But that's no way to labour—it's not safe. No wonder I can't remember."

I shifted again and a twinging throb pulsed through my abdomen, bruises coming to life where I had been kneaded and shoved—marks of a birth I hadn't participated in. I had no recollection and, I realized with a sudden sick dread, no baby in my arms.

"The child," I said. "Did it . . . ?"

"He lives," she said. "A son, large and healthy. Dark-haired."

The rush of relief sent me back against the pillows. I glanced around, seeking a cradle, the flutter of small sleeping breaths on the air. "Where is he? I want to see him."

Ninianne's brow flickered with confusion. "He is already gone."

"Gone? But you said he was alive."

"He is, and thriving," she said. "We thought it best if he was conveyed as swiftly as possible to his home and guardians."

"He *what?*" Panic struck my insides like throwing knives. "Are you saying my son has been taken from me against my will?"

"No, in accordance with your wishes, as agreed in the deal you made with Merlin. As soon as the child was born, it was to be taken away and raised elsewhere."

"I never agreed to anything of the sort! Do you truly *think* I would consent to a thing like that?"

She paused, her light dimming like a cloud across the sun. "But he showed me the chains of your binding. The runes can't lie, they—"

"Damn the *runes!*"

I pushed the coverlet back and stood up, but the aftermath of birth had stolen my balance and I pitched forwards. Ninianne caught hold of my arms. As soon as her skin touched mine, her eyes widened in horror.

"By the goddess," she said. "You're telling the truth."

I leaned into her, pain and exhaustion washing through my body from one ordeal I could not remember, and another that was just beginning.

"Ninianne," I said. "What happened to my child?"

She shook her head in still-dawning shock. "Only Merlin knows."

*

NINIANNE TRIED TO prevent it, but a pack of hell-hounds couldn't have kept me from his door. With quick hands, I healed enough of my pain to allow me steady feet, drank another goblet of her fortifying water, then ran to the demon's lair.

"Where is my son?"

"Lady Morgan, what a pleasant surprise." Merlin didn't look up. He sat behind his huge desk, casting coloured pebbles across a tablet, plotting what would befall the world next. "Do come in."

"Where is my child?" I demanded again. "Ninianne said you took him away. Tell me it isn't true."

Merlin considered the scattered stones, then picked up a raven quill, making a careful note. "Of course it's true, as you well know. You agreed to it back in Camelot, as part of the bargain we made."

Sheer fury and panic had driven me up three flights of stairs but had used up my strength. I leaned against my work chair, willing the resurgent pain in my body away.

"No," I said. "I would never . . ."

I thought fervently back to that day when I had gone to the sorcerer in begrudging desperation. I knew to the bottom of my hammering heart that if he had once mentioned taking my child away, I would have torn him limb from limb where he stood.

"Your child will be the best-guarded secret in the realm. Not a soul in the court will ever know if you do not speak of it. Arthur's glory and that of his Crown will be preserved." Merlin met my gaze, his eyes glittering black. "Was that not what I said? To which you readily consented?"

"There was no mention of you *stealing* my child."

"I did not *steal*; you *gave*," he insisted. "Clearly, you were so eager that you did not stop to think how this would be achieved. I cannot, for example, bewitch an entire nation, or convince its High King to overthrow his own ideals and laws. Nor could the integrity of the Crown remain unharmed if you kept the child with you. The terms could only ever be within the parameters of how the world works. I assumed you knew that."

It came to me then that I could shout and rage until the stars burned from the sky, but I could not argue with the sorcerer's reasoning, because every word of it was true.

"You *tricked* me," I said. "You know I never would have agreed to such a thing."

"Indeed I did *not* know that, my lady," Merlin said. "How could I? You told me nothing of the child's father—whether you were on terms of love, indifference or even violation. I believed the decision you made was entirely rational, given your place by King Arthur's side. Hasn't your ambition long been to assist with his rule and strengthen the Crown's greatness? There seemed more reasons for your choice than counterpoints. Did you really think you could stand beside the High King of All Britain—to sit at his *council table*—with a child of adultery at your breast? The slightest hint of your sins could damage his reputation irrevocably, yet you expected all to stay as it was?"

His logic buzzed in my mind like a nest of wasps. "Arthur and I have a bond," I insisted. "I would have protected him with all I had, but he would never wish to cause me pain, or expect me to make this choice. My child is his nephew, and—"

"An *illegitimate* nephew, and proof undeniable of your adultery." Merlin steepled his fingers under his chin, as if only now realizing I was serious. "If you love your brother, Lady Morgan, why would you risk forcing him to put you on trial, and endure scandal on your behalf? He has already weathered so much for you."

A wave of nausea surged up my gullet, my fury drained by resurgent exhaustion. Merlin made a quick gesture, dragging my chair over from its corner. I didn't resist, sinking into the seat and gripping the arms like they were driftwood.

"I'll leave," I said weakly. "Tell me where you took my son, and I'll go and retrieve him."

"You cannot," Merlin said. "You swore to give me a year, and it is four months from over."

"I'll break our bargain," I said. "You cannot physically keep me here. I'll go and tell Arthur everything you've done."

The sorcerer sighed, rising from his seat and leaning against the desk beside me, pointed face arranged into an approximation of sympathy.

"Let's say I could not keep you here," he said. "Even if I let you go galloping off to King Arthur with these unfounded claims, you will still not find your child. His life is elsewhere now."

I recoiled. "What is his life without me?"

"His life without you is one that fulfils our arrangement. The child will be raised in safety, comfort and happiness with a devoted noble couple, unfairly childless and as fine and adoring a set of parents as you could wish for. Within our agreement, your son will want for nothing, be loved and cherished, live a knightly life of ease and success—far from how it would be with you as a mother. If you seek to break the bargain you made, nothing will change, but you risk disrupting the magical balance, and the contentment he is promised may not be guaranteed."

"No," I said. "He is my son and he belongs with me. I *want him back.*"

Merlin sighed in impatience and returned to his seat. "You want what can never be. I could tell you precisely where I sent the child and it would be of no use. He has been placed under a powerful enchantment—unbreakable even by myself—to conceal him from you for all time. The two of you cannot cross paths."

"Lies," I said. "There will be a counter-spell."

"The word *unbreakable* means exactly that, Lady Morgan," he replied. "Do you not see? You can never regain what you gave away, nor change an impossibility. That part of your life is over, but think of the rest, everything we have done for the realm thus far—miraculous work that could alter the very fabric of the future. Power, influence, King Arthur's respect—there is so much yet to gain. What a waste, to throw it all away."

I pushed myself out of my chair, breaking away from his tone of temptation. "Enough of your attempts at persuasion, Merlin. I'll go to Ninianne—if anyone can break your curse, she can."

The sorcerer sat back, stroking his beard, face unamused.

"If that's what you are hoping, Lady Morgan, then I'm afraid I must bear bad news. It was Ninianne herself who cast the enchantment."

*

NINIANNE WAS GAZING into a cloudy mirror when I staggered into her study. Its surface shimmered like a pool disturbed by a breeze, but I was too tired, too hopeless, to feel the slightest stirring of curiosity.

She turned, her beautiful face hollowed out with guilt. "He told you."

"You have to undo this," I said desperately. "Wherever Merlin has taken my son, go and find him. Bring him back to me."

She was already shaking her head. "I swear on the old gods, Merlin never told me where he was taking him. I can no more lead you there than I can undo the masking enchantment."

I stared at her, seeking the lie in her anguished face. She had lied to me before, but I knew her better now, could feel her fluttering heart through the air, leaping with sadness and regret. If this wasn't the truth, then I had learned nothing.

"The spell is utterly unbreakable?" I asked.

"Yes," she said. "It is a protective charm of great and irreversible power, not unlike . . ." She made a low sweeping gesture indicating her ink-scarred thighs. "Different, without visible mark, but it cannot be undone. Even if I held the child in my arms, it would walk me in circles before I got within a mile of you, or anyone of direct blood."

She went to the marble table and pressed her palms against the surface. "I thought it was what you wanted. If I could take it back . . ."

"Would you?" I said sharply. "Knowing the shadow it would cast on King Arthur's rule, his realm, his great destiny. Would you truly undo it, if you could?"

She looked back at me for a long moment, then ducked her head. "I don't know."

My anger drained to hopelessness. "You are honest, at least."

I followed her to the table, where she had taught me so much, and she faced me, emerald eyes glistening. "I am sorry, Morgan. If there was anything else I could do, I would."

A thought shuddered through my aching body. "There is," I said. "You can teach me protective charms."

She shook her head. "That's not the answer. The ramifications alone . . . Fairy magic changes the mortals who practise it forever. You do not age at the pace you should, leaving those you love behind, and it affords awareness—of others, of your surroundings—that you cannot unknow. The more you use it, the more fairy you become, and more detached from the ways of this world."

"I don't care," I said. "This world has never made much sense to me. If you sincerely regret what you've done, you will help me now."

I took her hand, holding it to my fast but steady heartbeat. "You owe me this, Ninianne. I will live with the guilt of my son's loss for the rest of my life, but I deserve the ability to protect my future. Make me stronger."

Ninianne gazed at me, searching my face, my heartbeat, for doubt, where I knew she would find none. At length, she sighed and took her hand away.

"All right," she said. "I will do it."

31

I TOOK A month's lying-in time, which I was surprised Merlin did not object to. My furious grief for the lost child was an inconvenience to him, no doubt, and would only interfere with our work. Therefore, he kept busy with the stars as the clear skies shook off the frosted grip of a long, dark winter, and dared not breach mine and Ninianne's convenient ruse to be in company.

As promised, Ninianne came to my bedchamber every morning and stayed all day, needing nothing but herself to teach me protective charms—the words, the motions, how to form the silvery threads and weave them into a veil of safety, and imbue the magic with conditions of my choosing.

"To form these threads, calm is essential," she told me. "You must focus on the entire elemental structure within you—the air in your lungs, the fire in your belly, the structure of your bones. The roaring water running through your veins. Within that lies your essence, your truth, the surety that allows you to bring forth protection."

It was difficult at first, for one such as me—my restless, impulsive soul never a thing of balance or quietude. But day upon day, I sought the place she promised was within me, beyond the dragon's lair of my fury, or the chasm of my guilt and hurt; the place where my essence sat like a cool, deep lake, serene and silver-blue.

From there I drew the threads like streams, the bright runnels of protection, forging them into a shining mail that would armour me and those I loved. My charms would fade and have to be remade, and I was not fairy enough to learn the unbreakable, but by the time our month was over, my strength and calm had grown beyond where I thought possible, and I was ready, in one way or another, to return to the world of the sorcerer.

*

MERLIN LEAPT UPON my return with an enthusiasm that was almost reverent. Like a cat bringing gifts, he offered me dead birds of all sizes and states of decay, wanting only to see the effect of the raven repeated. It did not occur to him that to repeat a scientific act was one thing, but what we were seeking was change, a gain in strength, to make beat again a heart that was larger than a coin. I did not seek to enlighten him.

Nor did he know about the heartsong I had felt in the raven, the shimmering sensation of a life once lived which I soon learned was essential. Not every corpse yielded one, and more than time dead or bodily condition, the heartsong was the one definitive sign of whether a stilled heart would answer my incantation. When a bird didn't revive, I pretended I didn't know why.

Largely, I did what the sorcerer asked, in part to distract from my true thinking and because the repetition dulled the sharpness of grief over my stolen child. Every day, I armoured myself with the tranquillity and fortitude I had learned with Ninianne, but it could only last so long before the guilt and futile what-ifs overtook my mind. Only the distraction of work could withstand the assault of memory, the brief, transcendent moments when life conquered death all that kept me from drowning in the flood of my losses.

So I worked, with a fevered, unceasing rhythm, barely stopping to eat or sleep. One day, with a month left until my return to Camelot, I caught sight of my reflection in a night-darkened window and saw myself gaunt and pale as a skull, the same obsessive gleam in my eyes as the sorcerer's. On the run from my anguish and Merlin's greedy attentions, my own quest had devoured me instead.

My famed teacher took pleasure in my efforts, but what he did not know was that, since my return to his study, I had kept two sets of notes to record my work: one true and in a code of my own devising, hidden under a floorboard in my bedchamber, and a set of vague, ineffective scribbles kept on my desk. The heartsong I never wrote down at all; I could not lock my secrets away in magic boxes, but Merlin would never hold the key to my mind.

One hot day near the end of July, a dead goldfinch had appeared on my worktable, its heart calling, but its small body missing an entire wing. I had dismissed it, deeming a return to life unfair for a creature reliant upon its ability to fly. But the longer it lay there, the louder its stained-glass aspect sang out to me, along with an idea in the same key.

"I did not think the finch was of use," Merlin said, when I cast around for the box.

"I'm trying something," I said vaguely.

He returned his attention to fiddling with his favourite gold astrolabe; when alone, I had loosened two of its interlocking cogs so his star readings of two nights previously would have to be rechecked and he would not pay special attention to my experiment.

I layered the box with its usual leaves and placed the bird within. Turning my back to Merlin, I concealed a pin in my palm and checked the manuscript page from which had sprung my new possibility.

Three drops of blood from a worthy rival of death, to restore the flesh of the righteous.

The wording, hidden deep in the index of one of the sorcerer's rare volumes on blood magic, was nebulous, the concept of "worthy" so loaded with opinion one could not begin to assess its meaning. A "rival of death" was equally hazy: it could mean a person who had survived severe illness, a pure-hearted knight who had sworn to live chaste, a fairy like Ninianne whose age was slowed to the point of immortality—and a hundred other possibilities. Or, I reasoned, it could mean a woman of few canonical virtues, but with healing in her soul: me.

Surreptitiously, I pricked my left forefinger with the pin and squeezed three red drops onto the finch's breast, then sealed the box as usual. Right away, the container began to rattle, but I left my hand atop it, intoning the incantation in my head, adjusted to include part of an old blood chant I had once used to save Alys's life.

All movement stopped, and my spirits sank. On occasion, the process had begun and failed, the pressure too great for a decaying heart. Opening the box, I unwrapped the bird, now on its side. It looked dead at first, but at the sudden light its head twitched and it chirped, fluttering up onto the edge of the box with ease and unusual tameness.

I tried not to gasp. Sitting before me like a cluster of jewels was a perfect, two-winged goldfinch.

Slowly, I reached out, and the bird let me cup my palms around it without struggle. I splayed one wing, then the other. Only when I had counted every feather and felt along every bone did I allow myself a shaky exhale of joy.

It caught the sorcerer's ear right away, his black gaze rising to the live bird in my hands. He shut the window with a flick, and at the noise the goldfinch took flight, darting around the room on a pair of beautiful wings.

"My word. Feather and bone," Merlin said. He cut keen eyes back to me. "How was it done?"

"I put ground bloodstone in the box," I lied, pressing my thumb against my pricked forefinger and healing away the mark the needle had made.

*

TWO WEEKS LATER, Merlin left a note under my door in the middle of the night saying to meet him outside the house the following noon. After my triumph with the goldfinch, he had obeyed my request to leave me alone to refine the formula, when in truth, my year was coming to an end, and I wished to keep the sorcerer as far away from my work as possible. I had five days left before I was free.

I stepped out into a glorious day: between the long winter and my various confinements, I had forgotten how good summer felt, air warm and sweet with scents of fruit, moat rushing brightly over the rocks. I half expected to see Ninianne, resplendent in the midday sun, but got no sense of her anywhere, and I realized that in my dark cell of grief and endless work, I had lost count of the days since I last laid eyes on her.

Merlin stood at the foot of the giant oak, its roots waist-height, thick boughs stretching far above the tower top. He wore a narrow-sleeved mulberry coat over breeches and boots, and carried an almost human air of authority.

"This oak is all that survives of the original grove," he said. "Three sacred trees placed by the old gods. The elder on the other side is a descendent, not the first. The ash that once grew where the house stands burned with lightning for seven days, and what was left became my desk. When all three were alive, they formed an intersection of magic that imbued the very earth beneath our feet. It is why I chose this place to live and work."

I shrugged. "Very well. Why are you telling me?"

"Because there is power here, waiting to be exploited."

He stepped aside to reveal a large mound, covered in sackcloth.

"What's that?" I said uneasily.

With a flourish of his hand, the sacking flew back to reveal a pale, twisted form, which I soon recognized as a dead deer—a rare and pure white hart, gone very wrong. Its startling hide was marred with violent red gashes, some so deep I could see the remnants of ravaged organs. A front leg had been torn from the joint, leaving a gory bone socket. The creature's fine, antlered head lolled back, one ice-blue eye open in death, the other missing, leaving an endless staring maw.

"A once glorious creature," Merlin said. "Brought too early to death in a state of violence and maim. In other words, Lady Morgan, a marvel yet to come."

"You intend on resurrecting *this?*" I exclaimed. "It's mangled, half blind, unable to walk. It would be sheer cruelty to make it breathe again."

"Not so," said the sorcerer, "if it's resurrected whole."

I knelt at the white hart's head, examining the gaping eye socket, the deep gash under its throat, the jagged edge where the front leg had been torn free. A pack of something had been let loose on the poor creature, and how Merlin had acquired it was best left to the imagination. "Impossible. There's too much missing, and nothing we've done compares. This creature is . . ."

I stopped, mouth formed around the word *doomed*, as a wavelet of sensation shivered across my palm where it rested on the deer's breast. The creature's heart, sturdy and whole, singing despite everything.

In his impatience, Merlin spoke without noting my pause. "A bird is not a man, you said. We must seek to do more. This beast is large— if the formula works, it means a man's body should not take much more. I bring a challenge that could advance our work almost to its conclusion, yet now you balk? Are you too timid for this, after all?"

I rose, dusting dirt and dried blood from my hands. "I'm saying it will fail. If magic is all about cost, this risks exhausting us in body and mind, when we could be seeking more certain solutions."

My objection was fraudulent, based purely on my concern that any shared new effort could reveal the gaps in my supposed formula. I had less than a week left and intended on guarding my secrets.

Merlin sneered, as if I'd confessed to being afraid of the dark. "Very well, Lady Morgan. If you are so fearful, I must try it alone. Though it is strange you will not attempt to help, at least for King Arthur's sake."

His determination to proceed pinned me like a boar hunter's spear. Merlin would fail, I knew that—he still knew nothing of the heartsong or the use of my blood—but his intention to test the spell by himself might be more risk than I could afford.

I pulled a face, pretending his invocation of Arthur had goaded me. "I'm not afraid, as you well know," I said. "Without me, you wouldn't know how to begin. For my brother's sake, I will do it. Dig a grave and call me when the witching hour comes."

Later, when midnight had long passed, Merlin drove a pair of torches into the ground on either side of the slumbering oak. At length, we hoisted the beleaguered deer into the hole he had made and I had layered with yew branches, herbs and goose down.

"We need something to cover it," I said. "Soil will be too heavy."

The sorcerer smiled enigmatically, and in a sweep of his arms, the torchlight was aflutter, leaves gusting in from the woodland and filling the white hart's grave until it left a neat mound.

Five days passed and the temple of foliage remained undisturbed as expected, the white hart likely rotting within its damp earthen cavern. The sorcerer said little, but spent most of the days at his study window, gazing at the mound under the oak tree, his frustration on the air, crackling through me as satisfaction.

Merlin would never know there was more within my power, but I could not forget. And still the white hart lay dead, its heartsong calling out, waiting for me.

32

AT THE FIFTH day's end, I felt the passing of my year at Merlin's upon the moment of midnight. I didn't realize how the bond of magic had weighed on me until it lifted, the great forged chain dissolving as if it had rested on my chest all this time. I was free to return to Camelot, to my own life, to my future, yet I knew I could not go while the white hart still lay inert in the ground. I had come this far; I had to try.

I stole out to the giant oak as the jaundiced moon dipped behind the trees. First, I had sat a long time on the tower stairs, listening for sounds of life, but there were none. Still, my nerves were strung high; I could not afford to let Merlin see what I was about to do.

There was just enough moonlight to guide my way, my senses alert to every snapped twig and owl cry from the blackened forest. At the leaf mound, I crouched down and reached for my knife, drawing it decisively across my palm.

The pain was an instant, shrieking thing. Gulping the night air for fortitude, I pushed my bleeding hand through the leaves and into the grave, until I felt the white hart's tufted hide. As I lay against the soft, cool ground, palm aching hot and blood-slick, I thought of Alys, years ago, making me promise I would never cut my hand again in pursuit of knowledge.

After a while, I began to feel light-headed, and the deer's sodden hair told me there was little more I could give. Sitting up, I healed my slashed palm under a spectral dawn and hurried back to the house. All was quiet as I stole silently up to my room, where I washed my hands and threw the pinkish water from the window before slipping beneath the sheets, and was asleep before night gave way.

*

ON THE SIXTH day, nothing changed. On the seventh, I awoke to a symphony of birdsong so loud it defied the glass in the windows. As usual, I looked for Ninianne in her study and the garden, but she was nowhere to be found, and it occurred to me that she, too, had been free to leave for the two days since my bonds had dissolved. I imagined her, cloaked in violet, crossing the moat at the exact moment of our liberty, like the sun slipping free of an eclipse, and knew with an overwhelming certainty that she had gone. Still I remained.

The August morning was warm and breezeless, the oak casting a dappled green shade as I sat and watched the mound of leaves, as I had done every day for a week. I had not been there long when a slant of shadow cut across my folded legs: Merlin, calm but wild-haired in trailing nightshade robes, his arcane court sorcerer costume that I hadn't seen for a long time.

"What are you doing?" he asked.

"Enjoying the summer, if it please you." My old insolence rose up like groundwater; I was ready to go home.

He drew a hand down his purposefully untrimmed beard. "Watching this failure gets us nowhere."

"Then it's good I won't be here much longer." I felt vaguely like a child low to the ground, so I rose. Over my shoulder, the pile of leaves rippled.

"Where's Ninianne?" I asked.

"Since the term of your agreement is over, Ninianne has no obligation to stay," he said. "Why?"

"I wanted to bid her farewell before I left." I was also seeking some way of keeping in touch, if her natural evasiveness would allow it, but would never tell him that.

Merlin eyed me with suspicion, but the leaf pile rustled and drew our attention, a sound far stronger than the delicate wind could muster. We approached in unison, a strange anticipation filling the air.

A lightning streak of white burst forth in a chaos of prongs and hooves, sending a spray of foliage skywards. Merlin grabbed my arm as the white hart cleared the hole, landing perfectly on four strong legs. It galloped a few bucking steps before circling back towards the oak tree, gleaming and unscarred, neck bending to chew on the fallen leaves.

"By the stars," Merlin whispered. "It's *whole*."

His tone of fascination sent cold dread over my skin, recalling the last time he had seen one of my "marvels," his hand on my neck and the fervour of obsession overtaking him. I pulled away from his grip and approached the deer.

It was perfect: hide smooth and unmarked as alabaster; no gouges or lacerations; no exposed ribs or peeling flesh. The missing front leg had entirely reformed—every bone, joint and hair—and when the hart raised its head to regard me, it returned my stare of wonder with a pair of clear pale-blue eyes.

Merlin followed, his demeanour strangely contained. He ran a hand across the animal's stiff spine, stroking along the white flank towards its neck, fondly, as if it was a lover's cheek.

I wanted time and space to examine the creature by myself, to understand what I had done, but the deer shied away from the sorcerer, pelting for the rushing moat. The water seemed too wide, too fierce, and for a moment I feared my feat of magic would fall short and drown, but with a great, springing bounce, the white hart cleared the rapids in an elegant arc, landing on the far bank and bounding into the trees without breaking stride.

I watched it go: beautiful, a miracle, a paean to my skill. To heal was incredible enough, but this was the summit of my abilities; a power formidable, its potential divine.

Merlin stepped back, his gaze on the trees alongside mine.

"My greatest work," he murmured, then turned away in a billow of darkness and vanished into the house.

*

WHERE IS HE going? was my first thought. Then: *What did he say?*

When I reached his study, Merlin had fastened a waxed cape about his shoulders, black staff leaning against his chair. A leather saddlebag sat on the desk, a vague throb of life emanating from within. I peered inside and saw the box containing the Shroud of Tithonus.

"Are you going somewhere?" I asked.

"Camelot," he replied. "I must go to the High King."

"Good," I replied. "I'll fetch my travelling cloak."

The sorcerer paused, one hand curling around his staff. "I think it best if I speak to King Arthur first, alone. He hears his prophecies from me, after all, and this wonder that we have discovered—"

"That *I* discovered," I cut in, "making more progress in weeks than you did in years. We will tell Arthur together."

"*I* will tell the King because it is I who looks after his interests and always have."

He swept past me, pausing over my table. With quick hands, he gathered the decoy notes on my desk and rolled them up.

"That's my work," I protested as he shoved it into the saddlebag.

"*Our* work, Lady Morgan. Everything you have done was by my design. It doesn't matter which of us put a crow in a box. What matters is who carves the realm's fate into the stones of the future."

A wave of realization crashed over me. "You're going to tell Arthur it was all you," I said. "You're going to take credit for my efforts and claim it was your triumph."

"It *is* my triumph," he said. "Every relevant piece of knowledge you have, I gave to you, and if you hadn't been here, I would have discovered it in time. Whose victory is it, if not mine?"

"You forget I am free to leave," I snapped. "When I get to Camelot, we will see who Arthur believes."

I charged to the door, but Merlin blocked my way. "Why would you leave now, when you are so close to greatness? For the sake of King Arthur himself, it is your duty to keep going."

"No, Merlin," I said. "Our deal is done. I have a son, a life to lead, people expecting me." The thought of Accolon arrested me, the life I might no longer have with him. "My place at Arthur's right hand is waiting. There's always more work, but I can do it without you."

"Lady Morgan, I don't think you understand." Lifting his staff, the sorcerer flung me sideways and into my chair, an invisible rope slithering around my wrists and torso. "I can't let you go, not yet. Do not worry, I will adequately explain your absence in Camelot."

I struggled uselessly against the magical bindings. "What in all Hell are you doing? You cannot tie me to a chair then leave!"

Merlin laughed. "Such dramatics, my lady. The binds will last only until I cross the moat. Hopefully, you will have calmed down by the time I return."

"Where's Ninianne?" I demanded. "She wouldn't stand for this."

"Ninianne does what I ask, always," he said. "She knows whatever I do is best for Arthur, and she believes in him more than any petty dispute she could have with me. In any case, she's gone, to seek a cave belonging to a pair of fabled lovers." A greedy smile illuminated his face. "I am hoping she has finally been persuaded to consummate our love. We will return together, in a few weeks or so."

"Do not count on finding me here."

"I'd advise against unnecessary risks," Merlin replied. "You will never cross the moat without the bridge, and I'm sure Ninianne has warned you the forest is not passable without me or her. You do not want to face what awaits you out there." He picked up his saddlebag and regarded me with a sympathy that made my blood froth. "Be sensible, my lady. You are safe and comfortable, and there is plenty to do. Your return to Camelot will be soon enough, once I've achieved all I need."

He leaned down and fondled my cheek; I would have bitten him if the thought hadn't disgusted me. Then, without ceremony, he left, staff thudding down the stairs.

I strained up and looked out of the window, watching him glide across the bridge and lower it again into the roiling water. The fetters of magic melted away as Merlin dissipated into the trees, leaving me alone with my fury, the defiance I was born with and a faint, shivering fear.

How long could it be before he discovered the fraud of my notes, or realize that he could not resurrect even a butterfly without me? He would make a fool of himself before Arthur, then return swift and angry, or worse, obsessive and lust-filled, intent on devouring my skills any way he saw fit.

There was no space for pause, or to consider the impossibilities; I had to get out.

33

IT TOOK ME no time at all to prepare to leave. I gathered up my true notes and secreted them in a pocket magically cut from inside the bodice of my travelling garb, then waited a few days for a spate of rain to stop. I would carry my work back to Arthur and tell him privately what Merlin had done, with proof that I was the only one ever capable of helping him.

On the first rainless morning, I dressed to depart, stood at the edge of the ferocious moat and realized I had not the first idea of how to get across. I tried some summoning spells at the bridge area to no avail, then walked every inch of the roaring torrent. I couldn't swim, but even if I could, the water was too ferocious and the rocks too sharp; no single spot was passable without risking death.

Part of me hoped Ninianne would sense my confinement and return, but as time wore on it became clear she was not the answer. She had told me, after all, that I could not trust her. By the fourth morning with no epiphanies, I stood on the moat's edge, feeling only the tightening rope of my limitations. Everything I had learned, and I could not raise one damned bridge to walk across a body of water.

I had half turned away in frustration when a streak of white caught in the corner of my eye, leaping forth on the opposite bank. There stood my white hart, majestic and perfect, the limbs and flesh I had regrown supple with strength. The resurrected deer stepped delicately towards the water, ears pricked, blue eyes calmly meeting my stare of wonder.

I did not need a bridge to set myself free, it seemed to say. *And nor do you.*

There was always something else within my control. No matter how fast and violent the moat, it was water, which I had mastered under Ninianne's eye. The Lady of the Lake herself had taught me how to escape from her watery fortress.

The bone-pale stag watched as I held out my palms, seeking the water's essence. After some cajoling, the torrent stilled, pressure tremendous against my hands, like pushing at the flanks of two stubborn horses. I persevered, doing the water's dance, until the moat began to cleave, revealing a narrow pathway through the riverbed.

Tentatively, I edged down the steep bank and began to cross, my every muscle vibrating. In the middle, I looked through the high glassy wall to the frothing rapids beyond, duelling fiercely with the barricade of calm, but felt only my strength and control. The water would answer my call as long as I needed it.

Reaching the opposite bank, I scrambled up, dropping my connection. The great clear dam gave a creaking rumble, curving like a storm wave, and I watched with satisfaction as the seething river crashed back to its rightful place, foam flecking my boots.

The white hart had gone, not even a bright speck amidst the dense woodland, but it had nowhere to lead me now: Merlin's stronghold, and my confinement, were behind me for good. What lay ahead was Camelot, and my deliverance.

*

I SET OFF through the forest, using the sun's climbing arc to find east. For the first hour, I expected the worst, remembering Ninianne's warning and Merlin's threats about guarding forces, but the trees maintained their pleasant demeanour, leaves green and abundant, gilded pollen scenting the air.

At almost noon, I saw it like the descent of an angel: a line of light through the tree trunks, woodland thinning towards what could only be a road. My feet ached and it was far off, but the sight of liberation pushed me forth.

So driven was I that I hardly noticed the forest darkening, a winterlike dusk falling upon the treetops despite snatches of summer daylight still visible far ahead. I stepped into a clearing and found myself encircled by close-knit trees, branches hanging low and thick with moss. The ground rose and fell in dense, spongy humps, undulating beneath my feet.

Halfway across, my foot sank, ankle catching in a deep loop of tangles. I tried to pull free, but it held me faster, so I reached down and met a river of writhing coldness. A small, arrow-shaped head rose up, bare light pricking beady black eyes and a yawning, fanged mouth. I yelped, snatching my hand away as another head arched up, then another, like a thin, endless Hydra.

The forest floor was a pit of snakes.

Fear shot through my limbs as more reptilian heads lifted, surging towards my feet in a slithering pulse. Trying not to stumble, I struck my fingers against my palm and the flame roared into life.

"Stay back!" I shouted, aiming a blast of fire at the heaving mass. A few serpents recoiled and hissed angrily, their smooth skin seemingly resistant to burning. Other snakes streamed in from all sides, drawn by the waking of their neighbours.

I tried to strike my other palm but nothing happened, conjuring hindered by my panic. I spread the remaining flame in an arc, fighting my way across the uneven floor, as the forest seemed to lower to meet me. Large, limbless bodies hung from branches, long-fanged and dripping venom.

One head lunged at me with terrible speed, and I screamed, swerving back into a tree trunk and careering to the ground. Cool bodies slithered across me, twining around my legs and arms, small heads butting at my cloak and boots, seeking skin to bite. I pushed myself up, searing the advancing snakes off my body, then burned the ground in a ring around me until they retreated in their entirety.

Stillness fell upon the darkened glen. Flame still lit, I sought signs of life on the ground or in the branches. Nothing, only a glint of light in the corner of my eye, the edge of the clearing mere feet away. A few more steps and I would be out of Merlin's hellish trap.

A thick rope-like force shot around my ankle, dragging me back to the ground. A muscular body the width of a small tree trunk wound its way around my legs and torso with cool, efficient strength, pulling me away from the light. I jabbed at its sinuous silver-grey scales with the flame, but it didn't flinch, the fire in my hand guttering as the terrible creature encased my arms. At my every gasp for air, it squeezed harder.

With awful slowness, the pale-grey head of an enormous snake rose up before me, onyx eyes like the darkest abyss. It gazed at me, obviously enchanted, and in the midst of my suffocation I half imagined it might speak. Was it even there, I thought, or one of the sorcerer's tricks of the mind?

Then the snake squeezed again, I felt several ribs crack, the pain more potent than anything I had ever felt, and I knew for certain it was real, a predatory animal thinking only of hunger and its own survival. The serpent drew its head back, massive jaw unlatching to reveal a mouth black as Hell's gateway. It gave me one last look, then hurtled at my face; there was nothing left but to close my eyes.

A whistling *thwack* sliced through the air, juddering the snake's coils. The creature gave out a wrathful hiss, unravelling so fast I thudded hard onto the forest floor, my torso screaming. Through blurred vision, I watched the beast striking at a new shadow across the glen. I gulped for air and tried to heal myself, but couldn't muster any concentration beyond the agony of my splintered ribs.

Twenty feet away, the snake rose vertically, advancing at what I now saw was a person holding a sword. Weaving its powerful neck, the creature snapped its jaws, fast and deadly from every direction. The figure elbowed the gaping mouth aside but swung the sword into thin air, and the monster swooped, throwing itself around its opponent's sword arm, rendering the blade immovable. Locked in a stalemate, the snake's tail began to curl slowly around its foe's feet, seeking a different kind of death.

The swordsman was tiring, unable to elude the advancing coils while holding off the snake's head. I tried to stand upright but collapsed under the pain of my ribs. As I gripped my side, my fingers brushed the smooth bone of my father's falcon-handled knife and I managed to draw it, the sight of the keen steel bringing a rush of defiance. Pooling all of my strength, I crawled to the creature's muscled grey side and plunged my blade in up to the hilt.

The snake reared back, baring fangs, but the swordsman's freed arm was faster. His sword swung like lightning, slicing through the creature's lunging neck. The silver-grey head flew off, spurting blood, and landed at my feet, black mouth gaping in a dying shudder. I had just enough time to note the darkness lifting off the trees before I collapsed onto the forest floor.

In an instant, I was scooped against a hard-breathing chest. Bone-cold and my body screaming, I clung on, concentrating on my breaths to stave off the shivers of shock. A firm hand cradled my head as the swordsman leaned over me in concern. I pulled closer to his warmth and the hot scent of his neck sang right through my blood.

"Accolon," I croaked. "Is it you?"

"Morgan, thank God," he said. "Were you bitten?"

"No, but . . ." I stared at him, his stormy eyes and exquisite face, hair damp from exertion. Perhaps I had died after all. "*How* are you here?"

"I've been riding the roads to find you. I heard a scream and ran into the forest." He put a hand to my cheek, regarding me with wonder. "That it was you—the unlikelihood . . . It's a miracle."

My body arched into his embrace, but my broken ribs made me cry out, bringing the sharp clarity of guilt. We couldn't be here, in this wild stroke of providence, with Accolon looking at me with such deep, desperate love. He didn't know what I'd done to him.

"*Sacredieu*, you *are* hurt." He shifted his arms in preparation to pick me up. "Hold on to me."

"No. I can stand."

I dragged my feet underneath me, grasping at a tree root, pushing away from his support. But I was damaged beyond determination; everything felt bruised, lungs snatching for breath beneath my jagged ribs. I took one wobbly step and pitched into a half faint.

Accolon caught me before I hit the ground. "It's not fair," I protested. "You can't . . ."

"I know," he said soothingly. "You don't need my rescue and never have. But please, Morgan, for now—just let me make you safe."

I couldn't bear the hope contained in his words, his belief there was a "now" and therefore an "after" for us, while my poisonous mistakes waited to lay waste to everything.

"I have to tell you . . ." I began, but I didn't have the words or the breath, so I let him sweep me up and carry me through the cool, green wood as my consciousness drifted, with my cheek against the steady rhythm of his still-unbroken heart.

34

MY RECOLLECTION OF the road was hazy, mind drawn inwards by the need to focus on each delicate breath. Eventually, the sound of bickering opened my eyes.

"Careful!" snapped a female voice.

"I'm not going to drop her," I heard Accolon say, as his warmth left me, my body unfurling onto a soft surface with a spike of pain. "Are you sure we shouldn't find help?"

"She doesn't need anyone but me." The reply was lilted, full of disdain.

"Alys?" I said.

"Morgan, *cariad*." A hand cupped my face and she hove into view. "You're safe and I'm going to make you better."

"Were you in the forest?"

"I was waiting on the road. I wanted to go in, but *he* wouldn't let me." She threw a severe look at Accolon, standing anxiously beside her.

"He was right not to," I managed, shifting up to look around.

Stabs of agony tore through my side, sudden and white-hot, snatching air from my chest. I cried out, but it was more breath than I could spare. Rib shards piercing a lung, I thought abstractedly, before the world darkened and pain replaced thought.

"Leave us," Alys commanded, over a deep French murmur of protest. *"Now."*

A door thudded shut against the violent sound of rending fabric and the struggle for my next breath. Before panic could take hold, a weight fell on my chest and an immediate warmth descended across my body, pain washing away like sand marks under the tide. I wondered at it briefly, before relief overcame me and I fell into a deep, grateful sleep.

*

I JOLTED AWAKE as if from a dream, and for a horrifying moment I thought I was back at Merlin's. Fear rushed in, recalling the last time I had woken from such profound unconsciousness: a child, torn from my body and carried away; my life's path forking in an instant; the new, deep scars that would never stop aching.

But I was not in the sorcerer's prison, but rather on a different bed, in a low-lit room I didn't recognize. The sky outside showed full night through long windows, flecks of stars just visible. Without thinking, I sat up, and discovered there wasn't any pain. My body felt strange but pleasant, almost lively, humming with a definitive vitality.

A narrow object slipped from my chest and I caught it, blue-and-white leather giving a direct shot of pleasure: Excalibur's scabbard, its power singing through my veins. I felt quickly around my ribs and found no breaks or bruising, breath easily filling my lungs, as if I had never encountered Merlin's monstrous snake at all.

"Morgan!" Alys rose from a fireside chair and hurried over, shadows encircling her eyes. "How do you feel?"

"Completely healed," I said. "Remade anew, almost."

"Thank goodness." She sank down on the bed. "I didn't know if the scabbard would work or how to monitor your condition. I've just been waiting in hope."

I studied the scabbard with fascination. "My lung was punctured, my ribs crushed—I would never have mustered enough strength to cure myself. Neither of us could have healed me like this."

"My God," she said tremulously. "But for the scabbard . . ."

"But for *you*, who brought it along." I pulled her into an embrace and held her there, savouring her presence. Over her shoulder, I discerned that I sat in a large bed of pale oak, devoid of hangings, within a long, uninhabited chamber. Sheeted furniture hulked in the shadows. "Where are we?"

Alys let me go, fiddling with her hands, and held something out to me: my father's ring with its trio of sapphires. "Fair Guard. At long last."

"My mother's manor?"

"*Your* manor," Alys said. "I showed the chamberlain the ring and he let us in directly. His name's Sir Ceredig. It's a small household, but they've all been so kind."

I slipped the ring back on and rose, stepping cautiously into the room, as if discovering a place from deepest myth.

"So you're back in your homeland, Alys of Llancarfan. With the Welsh."

She smiled modestly. "I'd like to think it helped with the welcome."

"What of Camelot?" I asked. "Is Yvain there?"

"He's due back in just over three weeks," she said. "The nurses' reports have been coming to me, via the King. They say he's healthy and cheerful, constantly chattering away."

I paused and looked back at her. "And Urien?"

"By all accounts, a kind and diligent father. More attentive than most kings, and he and Yvain get on famously." She scowled. "Even monsters have other faces, it seems."

I said nothing, weathering an ache of regret.

"Morgan," Alys said. "Where . . . ?"

"There's no new child," I replied. "He lived, and is safe, but not with me."

Her eyes widened and I had to turn away. In brief, difficult words, I explained enough of what had occurred for her understanding, but not all she would later have to learn. At length, she rose and put her arms around me, until she was sure I could stand alone.

"I would have died," I said, "if you hadn't found me."

"Not me," she replied. "Sir Accolon found you."

I couldn't let myself think of him just then. "How *did* you find me? Why?"

"We went to the inn, as you arranged. Tressa stayed behind in the service of Lady Clarisse, in case something went awry. Which it did—you never came."

In the midst of my grief over the lost child, surviving Merlin's obsession and my fervent descent into mastering death magic, I had barely remembered the plans I made, or the letter I wrote for Accolon before I left with Ninianne. My escape plot had developed no further than crossing the moat and chasing the sorcerer to Camelot.

"Sir Accolon wanted to ride out immediately," Alys continued. "He was sure something was wrong. I convinced him to wait in case of delay or wrong dates, but discovered he'd been going out to search in secret. He's an entire fool, given I was the only one who knew *where* to look. The next day I caught him and said we might as well do things correctly. That's when we found you."

The idea of their reluctant companionship raised a bleak amusement. "Is he here?"

"Of course. I kept him out while you were healing, but the last I saw, he was curled up in the hallway outside." She sighed with a sad inevitability. "He doesn't know you were pregnant, nor anything more than the letter said, but he understandably has many questions."

If Alys thought Accolon deserved consideration, then there was no delaying it. "Will you send him in?" I said. "Then try to get some rest."

She held me briefly again, then left the room. I rewrapped the scabbard in my torn cloak and stowed it under the bed, then retrieved the work notes from the stitched pouch in my bodice. No matter what battles I had lost, or what Merlin was busy claiming at Camelot, I still held enough proof of my dedication to Arthur to win the war.

There was a soft knock and the door creaked open. "Morgan?"

At the sight of me, Accolon snatched a breath and rushed over, but hesitated from touching me. "*Mon coeur*, are you all right?"

I nodded. "My injuries are healed and I slept a long while. Has Alys gone to bed?"

"She muttered something as she passed," he said. "Lady Alys is still not my greatest admirer. She brooked no interference when caring for you."

We shared a rueful smile, eyes meeting, and the moment rounded into a firelit pause. A warmth took up within me, as if I were only now realizsing it was Accolon who stood there, after an absence of more than a year.

With simultaneous haste, we reached for one another, kissing hungrily, his hands gripping me close. My arms went around his neck, trying to hold on to him, to keep time and reality standing still.

"God, I missed you," he said between kisses. "Every day, every hour we were apart. When I got back to Camelot and you weren't there . . . when you didn't come to the inn . . . I don't know what I thought."

His concern turned my blood cold, but I couldn't make myself let go. He deserved the truth, but I wanted to keep kissing him, to take him to bed and trap us there until only our love remained, crystallized in an endless present. I couldn't bear for this to be our last tender moment before I tore our world to shreds.

Eventually, he drew back. "What happened? Why were you in the forest?"

I couldn't answer, or bear his anxious, questioning frown, so I slipped from his arms and went to the fire, leaving his confusion palpable in the air.

"Morgan, please," he said. "What aren't you telling me?"

I sighed into the flames, an endless, echoing sound. "I told you I wasn't what was best for you, Accolon. I tried to warn us both. Everything I do turns to dust or disaster. You deserve a better life, much more than I can offer."

"*Mon coeur*, what is all this?" He followed me to the hearth, turning me to him. "None of it's true, but even if it was—a life with you is all I wish for."

"We can't have it, don't you see? You don't know what this past year has wrought upon us. You don't know what I've done."

"So tell me, and I'll understand," he said. "I love you, that's all there is. Nothing you've done could drive me from your side, ever again."

He embraced me and I allowed it, leaning against his warm strength as my bones grew colder. I buried my face into his shoulder, feeling his hand stroking my hair, the rocking motion of his arms, bearing me up, loving me—he thought—without condition.

"It's all right," he said in low, reassuring tones. "Whatever happened, we're together now. I will keep you safe."

I could let it be, I thought, forget all of my qualms and keep him with me. Accolon wouldn't know I had ruined his life, his future, if I just kept him here like this and never told him what he had lost.

But as the thought came, so followed the guilt, slithering around my body like the giant snake. To conceal the existence of the child— his child, ours—for my own selfish needs was as careless and brutal an act as letting the loss happen in the first place.

You gave away his son, I told myself. *He would never forgive you, and you should not forgive yourself.*

"No, Accolon. That's not all there is."

I broke away from his body, setting him free.

"You had a son," I said. "We did. A child I was unknowingly carrying when you left Camelot. I delivered him in the spring, intending to greet you with him upon your return. But after he was born, he was taken and sent to be raised elsewhere, where he can never be found. We had a child and he's lost forever, because of me."

I saw it reach him like a sudden chill—the realization I was deadly serious, and he could never have conceived of something so bleak. "Morgan, what are you saying? We had a child that you gave away on purpose?"

"No!" I cried. "To keep the pregnancy secret, I made a deal to go to Merlin's and submit to his teaching, on the promise that no one in court would find out, and Arthur's reputation would not be sullied. Merlin bound us by magic oath, and I thought I had solved it all. But the deal was a trick, and when I awoke after the birth, the baby was gone, he . . ."

I buckled, falling to my knees and gasping for breath, panicked with the horror of speaking such awfulness aloud. Instinctively, Accolon swooped to soften my descent, murmuring in comfort. "It's all right. I'm here. Breathe slowly. I'm here."

He knelt beside me on the floor, leading me in steady breaths until I had recovered.

"I'm sorry," I said. "I'm so sorry."

He thudded down onto his side and stared at me with raw, stunned eyes. "Where did he go? The child."

"I don't know. The restrictions of the oath meant I could never hear of it. I was asleep when they took him . . . I never even gave him a name or saw his face."

I choked back a sob, my head in my hands. Accolon put his arms about my shoulders.

"Morgan, you didn't do this," he said. "The child was taken from you without your agreement. It's not your fault."

"It is, don't you see? I *did* agree, even if unwittingly. I should have known there was something amiss, been ahead of it. I'm supposed to be cleverer than this." I made myself look at him, his beautiful, haunted face. "Our *child*, Accolon. How could I have let this happen?"

I expected him to recoil, to realize he was too forgiving, too loving, had soothed where he should have been excoriating me. Instead, he brought a shuddering hand up to my cheek.

"What can I do?" he said desperately. "Tell me what you want. I'll find the sorcerer and cut him to pieces if you ask me to."

"No, it won't help. You wouldn't get close. They'd kill you."

"Then I'll get the child," he said. "I'll find our son and bring him back. If you cannot, perhaps I can. Anything, Morgan—just tell me what to do."

His pleading suggestion that he should find the child hit me with unexpected horror. It was impossible, but the fact that the idea occurred to him brought a dread realization that I couldn't ignore. I lowered his hand from my face.

"What you should do is go," I said. "Back to Camelot."

"Very well, then we will."

Slowly, I shook my head. "Not me, only you. I'll stay here until Yvain returns to the city. I can give you three weeks."

The trio of worry lines reappeared. "*Give* me? For what?"

"To think about your life and future. Alone—without me. You need time to fully understand what I did and decide what it should mean. For your own sake, you must go."

I pulled away from him and rose, but he followed at speed.

"*Mon coeur*, look at me," he said. "You can't send me away. Not now, when we are both hurting. We can talk about this, find a way to survive it together."

"It won't work, don't you understand?" I insisted. "The more we talk, the closer we get, the more you love me and want to tear down the world for that feeling. For you to see clearly, we need to be apart."

"Morgan, don't do this," Accolon said. "I can see in your eyes it's not what you want. I love you, and you love me. Do not choose this for us."

To behold him in that moment was unbearable. His body began to shake, and I was reminded of the day of our first meeting, when I had risked everything to pull him from Tintagel's savage blue riptide and soothed his shuddering shock. This time, letting him swim himself to shore would be his salvation.

"I do love you," I said. "That's why I told you the truth, so it can set you free. If you love me, you'll respect my decision and let me do this for you."

"Morgan, no . . ."

"If you *truly love me*, Accolon, you will leave."

Eras felt like they passed as he stared at me, waiting for some flicker of change, of hope. I could give him none. At length, he ducked his head, swallowing hard.

"*Maudit*," he said, and left the room.

When the door closed, I ran to it, one hand poised to pull it open and the other above my head, holding it shut.

Let him go, let him go, let him go, I told myself, until I was sure he was too far away to hear me call for him.

*

HE LEFT AT first light, Alys told me the next day, and though I answered that it was good and what I intended, my heart still stung with the surprise that he had gone so easily.

35

FAIR GUARD WAS an apt name for my mother's manor. The land encompassed a beautiful, deep-sided valley covered in trees, rivers and streams running through her hills and meadows like silver ribbons. The main house was well-proportioned and interesting, built in pale-bluish stone around courtyard gardens, winding hallways and smaller chambers flanking several large, high-raftered rooms. The house's western side culminated in a high, round tower, balconied and turreted with a slate roof, overlooked by an enormous beech tree; on the easternmost end, a natural spring rose up, silver-bright and trickling.

From the house's main door, a cropped green sloped down to a wide river spanned by an old stone bridge, crossing to a long, flat meadow bordered by silver birches. In the opposite direction, a walk along the riverbank curved towards a generous stableyard built in a neat square. At the back of the house, an orchard grove ran deeper into the valley to a village of whitewashed, thatched buildings, including a mill, a brewhouse and several farmhouses.

Locally, Alys told me, the valley and manor were known as *Ynys-y-Pia*—Isle of the Magpies—for the varied and encompassing waterways and the beech tree's long-standing residents. One day, I took the twisting staircase all the way to the top of the turreted tower and stepped onto its half-circle balcony, to be greeted by the tree's leafy upper boughs and a large, sleek magpie, observing me in front of a domed, spiky nest. Another came, flying the short distance to the balcony's edge and greeting me with a curious, chattering caw.

Keen to be more ally than intruder, I took to bringing up bowls of grain and berries and scattering the mix along the balustrade, and they soon approved of me, occasionally hopping indoors whenever Alys and I returned to the turret.

"You shouldn't encourage them," she scolded. "It'll be an aviary before long."

"They were here before I was," I replied.

The small household also welcomed us heartily, as amiable as Alys claimed, Sir Ceredig the chamberlain explaining every facet as if he had awaited us for years. He met my mother, he said, when she and my father stayed in the manor on their way from their wedding to Tintagel. Along with everything else, the idea that my parents had once looked upon Fair Guard in happiness afforded me a sudden sense of belonging that I hadn't expected.

"These lands have been lacking a mistress; I've always said it," Sir Ceredig told us in Alys's musical Welsh. "It's a house that needs a beating heart."

*

THE FIRST THING I did was write to Arthur, marking my letter for the King's eyes only. I told him the truth—that I was no longer at Merlin's but could be expected back in Camelot in three weeks, and had much of importance to tell him. I also made the heartfelt, non-negotiable request that Merlin should not be in the castle when I returned, insisting that it was essential to our bond as brother and sister.

Not far outside Fair Guard's boundary, a small chapel stood at the most prominent entrance to the valley, and I had told Arthur to send his reply there, stopping short of explaining exactly where I was.

After sending my missive via the huntsman and a horse messenger, Alys and I had nothing to do but wait, so we filled our time acquainting ourselves with the workings of the manor.

"Everything your lady mother told you was true," she said on our second day. "There's a very good living here, with more than enough in the vault to increase the household and make improvements."

We were in the turret, where I had climbed to the upper gallery to examine the empty shelves that encircled the walls. The room would make an ideal study, but below my book-ready landing, it currently contained only two spindly chairs at a long table, where Alys sat beside a pile of leatherbound household ledgers. I had quickly bored of the columns and numbers, but the full administrative history of Fair Guard had engrossed her for hours.

"Did you know there are several other sizeable houses on the lands?" she said as I came down the narrow wooden stair. "Sir Ceredig said they've long fallen into disrepair, but what an interesting endeavour restoration could be. That is, if we're planning on returning. For now, it seems we are safe and comfortable here."

Comfortable, yes, but safety depended on who was seeking you, and the Devil knew who might be looking for me. I considered our situation from the balcony doorway, taking in the river meadow, copper-blushed under the falling sun, the trees and hills marking the valley's edges.

"In those ledgers," I asked, "is there a complete rendering of the manor's boundaries?"

Alys drew a volume from the pile. "Here—this one's a book of dedicated maps."

I took a seat beside her and went to work, studying every treeline, valley bluff and waterway until my eyes were seared with the contours of the land. For the next seven days, I rose early, walking the manor's edges in the burnished light of late summer, casting Ninianne's silvery threads into the air and weaving them into a shimmering veil until the entirety of my realm was shrouded in protection.

The charm was of the fairies, tricky, clever and irrefutable. My inexperience meant it would need renewing often, but the threads were effective and their purpose clear—only those with good intentions in their hearts could walk through the magic and reach us. Those who were malicious, threatening or ill-willed would be sent in circles until they gave up or went mad.

Fair Guard had no curtain walls, no moat, no guards clad in armour, and perhaps we weren't staying long, but while we were here, it was my fortress, made unbreachable by my own hands.

*

ARTHUR'S REPLY CAME late but just in time, saying he would send a small escort to the chapel to accompany my journey to Camelot. I borrowed a horse from Fair Guard's stables, assuring the household that I would return it, along with a pledge to come back myself. Now that I had found this place of peace and acceptance, I was loath to give it up.

Alys and I set out under a cloudy, opalescent morning, riding past the spring and away from the turreted house that already felt more like mine than I ever imagined it could. As we had said our goodbyes, the household seemed genuinely regretful to see us leave, and it was impossible not to feel the same wrench.

"It sounds strange, but I already miss Fair Guard," Alys said as we wove through the softly lit woodland, scents of ivy and sweet bark alive in the air. "It felt so *right* there."

"I know," I agreed. "Like a home. Our home."

"Will we come back?" she asked.

"Yes, one day. But first, Camelot."

We had taken a shortcut—a scenic forest route that eventually crossed the magical boundary in the middle of a clearing. We pushed our horses past the protective charms and into a thick grove of hawthorn trees, branches blurred pink with the early-autumn berries, to where we would get our first glimpse of the chapel and the road.

A few yards inside the tree line, I halted.

"What is it?" Alys said.

"Men," I said. "In red and white."

"Surely that's our escort?"

I put a finger to my lips to quiet her and slipped from the saddle. A group of armed men stood dismounted at the side of the chapel, horses at their backs and wearing Arthur's livery. They were indeed royal guards, arranged in a neat crescent, but an odd wind had blown over my skin at the sight of them, a discomfort in their collective demeanour that I could not parse.

I moved sideways through the trees so I could look at their faces, and realized what had struck me as unusual: they were utterly silent, a company devoid of idle talk, laughter or even impatience, every pair of eyes fixed on the middle distance. The outermost guard twitched a hand up, drawing his cloak to his throat with a shiver, but there was no wind, the day already warm under the clouds.

Then I saw it, carpeting the ground, what the guards could feel but not see: a thin mist rolling white across their boots, trailing off towards the dark hems of a familiar figure.

"Alys," I said, backing away as slowly as I could. "Get inside the veil."

"Why? What's wrong?"

"Now!" I commanded.

I dashed across and slapped her horse on the rump, sending it cantering with a snort towards the web of protection. Grabbing my own reins, I hoisted myself back into the saddle and followed Alys's path to safety with my stirrups flapping. When I reached the charm boundary, I shouted for her to keep riding, and we didn't stop until we reached Fair Guard's rising spring.

"Morgan, what in all Heaven . . . ?" Alys said breathlessly, as a few of the household emerged with curious looks. "What did you see?"

"The one face I told my brother I could never look upon again," I said. "Arthur didn't send an escort to bring me back to Camelot. He sent Merlin."

36

I ORDERED ALYS back to the house and spent hours riding the boundary, casting new silver threads inside the original veil until there was a shimmering secondary wall. By the time I had finished, it was late afternoon and the sky had darkened, heavy clouds hanging slate blue over the rooftops, flecks of rain slanting in on the wind. I ascended the turret stairs, limbs sodden with fatigue and blood twitching with the remnants of fairy magic.

Alys awaited me in the tower study. She wasn't the pacing kind like I was, but the ledgers and quills on her table had been painstakingly aligned, and every surface had been dusted clean. The air was stuffy, so I opened the balcony door and dropped into a chair with my outdoor cloak still on. Within moments, the two magpies flew in, perching on the mantelpiece to shelter from the impending rain. It was testament to Alys's distraction that she didn't think to complain.

"You were gone a long time," she said. "I was worried."

"I wanted to make sure of every last thread," I replied. "Now that it's done, there's time to breathe and think."

"Does this mean Merlin knows where you are?"

"He probably knew as soon as I sent the letter to Arthur, maybe before. Who knows what information he holds from years of scheming and spying."

"He can't reach you, can he?"

I shook my head. "Ninianne's protective charms do not lie. The fact that he's not here bears that out. I sent the huntsman to check the chapel from a distance—he said the Camelot guards were trying to enter the valley and kept walking in circles. What the household must think of all this."

"Thus far, they seem unconcerned," Alys replied. "I told Sir Ceredig we'd be staying a while longer, and everyone is very pleased."

"For how long, when they realize I'm besieging myself away from the High King and his pet wizard?"

Alys sat down, propping her chin on her fist. "Do you really think King Arthur sent Merlin against your wishes?"

I sighed. "I don't know. Unless Merlin saw the letter somehow, or tricked Arthur into letting him go. I couldn't even tell if the guards knew he was there. Perhaps he's finally discovered that the notes he stole are fraudulent, and he can't do what I can. The only certainty is that Merlin knows I've escaped and wants me back in his clutches, and I cannot leave here until I've thought of a way around him."

"What about Tressa?" Alys's voice took on a plaintive note. "She's still at Camelot."

"She'll be fine under the care of Lady Clarisse. Given our delay, I'm glad she'll be present to receive Yvain." I leaned forwards and scrubbed my face with weary hands. "Oh God, he'll be arriving soon and I'm not there. Why has Arthur done this? What should I do now? I need time to *think*."

I pushed impatiently up from the chair, eliciting an irritable caw from one of the magpies. It flew out of the balcony door, pied wings stark against the cloud-darkened sky. A faint hiss took up as the rain began to fall, hitting stone and glass without respite.

"Looks like the downpour that was promised," Alys said. "Let's hope it's not as severe as everyone expects."

The weather had been largely wet going on a fortnight by then, the streams swollen and fit to burst, the river coursing high along the front of the house, and now this torrent, so loud and immediate it felt like my troubles had caused it somehow.

"Even Cornwall never had relentless wet weather like this," I said, watching the river below plunge and crash. "Though you should be used to it. I thought the Cymri were raised by the rain?"

"We are, but this is unusual," Alys replied. "Sir Ceredig says when the wells get as high as they are now, trouble is on the way."

As if summoned, the knight appeared at the top of the tower steps, red-faced and stiff in the knees. "My ladies, thank goodness. You're already in the tower. The river is rising and may flood the lower floors."

"The river hasn't burst its banks," I said. "As long as this rain stops by nightfall, surely it should stay contained?"

Sir Ceredig shook his grey head. "It's the force of the water, my lady. Several trees have been dragged downstream with grasses and mud, causing a dam near the stables. It's too dangerous to clear the blockage, and the banks by the house look likely to break, causing the streams in the north valley to flood in turn. It's happened before, and a few years ago a kitchen lad drowned. Please, stay here in safety."

"What about the rest?" I asked. "The village on the stream plain? The people and their livestock, the gardens and houses?"

"There's a high barn, my lady. They will know how to keep safe." Despite his assurance, he looked wretched. "As for the rest, nothing can be done about the weather. If the water comes, it comes."

"No," I said, striding to the door. "If the water comes, then it will answer to me."

Alys and Sir Ceredig in tow, I ran down the stairs and into the entrance hall. "Call as many stablelads and kitchen boys as you can," I said. "Tell them to grab rakes, broom handles, anything long, and go to the riverbank where the dam is."

Sir Ceredig began to protest, but Alys halted him. "We won't let anyone come to harm," she said, and he bowed and rushed off.

Pulling up my hood, I splashed across the waterlogged green and onto the old stone bridge. The river roared underneath, smashing into the arches and sending up wavelets of spray. Before long, the bridge would be overcome, perhaps washing away altogether. In the distance, a huddle of youths ran along the bank carrying various poles, Sir Ceredig tramping after with Alys.

Rain slashing into my hood, I faced the careering river and extended my arms. There was so much water, I barely had to reach for its essence. The element's force hit me like a joust charge, but I absorbed its momentum, holding the river beneath the bridge until the bed had drained to a trickle. Though more plentiful, the unadulterated water was easier to control than Merlin's enchanted moat, and once steadied, I found I was able to walk down the bank with the river at my fingertips, without fearing I would lose my grip.

Several lads stood in the dry gully, dragging out branches and mud, and pushing the tangle of tree trunks from where they had wedged. Alys and Sir Ceredig stood by, calling out directions and encouragement. As the last trunk broke free and they climbed to shore, I let the water go, easing its passage between the banks. The rain kept battering down, but the cleared riverbed was free-flowing now, and more than deep enough for the banks to hold.

Sir Ceredig hurried over, dripping wet and stammering in astonishment. "Lady Morgan, you . . . The house, the land . . . Everyone is saved."

"I hope so," I said. "I will answer any questions you have, but for now, please, take your brave lads inside. Make sure they are well dried and have a warm meal and potent drink. If any take chill, Lady Alys and I will treat them."

The old knight nodded dazedly, beckoning to the row of equally stunned boys, and we all jogged back into the house.

"We need to get out of these wet clothes," I said to Alys, but she had stopped, her gaze fixed on something outside the doorway. "What is it?"

"Someone's there," she said.

I squinted into the rain-filled dusk. She was right; in the distance, a pair of hooded riders were approaching at speed, horses spraying up water and mud. As we watched, the rider on the smaller horse pulled to a halt and dismounted, running towards us.

"What in God's name?" I began, but Alys was already gone, unheeding of the rain, her focus on the cloaked figure. The stranger's hood flew back, revealing a mass of curling, tow-coloured hair.

"Tressa!" Alys cried, and they threw themselves into an embrace, laughing, crying, kissing, as if their absence had been that of ten years. "My love, where did you . . . Oh, you're drenched. Quickly, come inside."

They ran back into the entrance hall, dripping and breathless, and Tressa embraced me in turn. "Thank God you're all safe," she said. "We were so worried."

"Everything's fine," I said. "Who is *we?*"

Only then did I remember the second rider, a heartbeat before he strode in. He pushed his hood down, water pouring off him like some errant river god brought to land.

"Accolon," I said, and his eyes met mine with the intensity that called out to the depths of me.

"He brought me from Camelot," Tressa said. "Most likely saved my life."

Alys dropped her hands from Tressa's shoulders. "He what?"

Accolon offered her a tired smile, scraping slick hair off his forehead. "I thought you might want Tressa back."

"But I never told you . . ." She trailed off, staring at him for a long, uncertain moment. Then all at once, Alys ran to Accolon and threw her arms about his neck, so fast he almost didn't catch her.

"Thank you," she said into his shoulder, as I watched her forgive him at last.

My emotions were churning harder than the floodwater I had held. "How are you here?" I asked Tressa. "You're supposed to be in Camelot with Yvain."

Her face drained. "Oh God," she said. "I wish I didn't have to bear this news."

"What news?"

"Yvain never came back. The High King sent him to live permanently in Gore."

"*Gore?*" I exclaimed, but her expression wavered in a way that gave me pause, then turned the fire in my bones to ice. "But . . . that's not why you're here, is it?"

Entire worlds seemed to implode in the time it took her to speak. "No, my lady. There's something else."

Reaching into her belt purse, Tressa drew out a crushed scroll and handed it to me, her face lined with a bleakness I'd never seen. I unrolled the damp parchment and saw the blood-red dragon seal.

"What is this?" I said.

"A Royal Decree," she replied. "It's been issued to all corners of the kingdom. King Arthur has declared you an Enemy of the Crown."

37

BY THE TIME the hearth was lit in Fair Guard's half-furnished reception room and Tressa was drying in front of the fire, I had already read the Royal Decree a hundred times.

Corruption brought forth by dangerous knowledge and unfettered ambition.

A fury and despair greater than I have ever known, caused by a sister who encouraged my love and trust.

She of half my blood, whom I once thought loyal, seduced by demons and terrible powers.

Absconding from capture, and refusal to answer such accusations by trial of godly justice, speaking damnably of guilt.

Lady Morgan, Queen of Gore, is declared traitoress to the Crown of All Britain until she returns to court to address her crimes before the High King.

Incendiary phrases, truths twisted into lies; words I would never forget if I lived a thousand years. And then, the final, searing conclusion: *Yvain, my nephew, is given over to the protection of his loving father, lest any association with his mother bring shame on his noble head. If Lady Morgan seeks her son without surrendering to the High King's justice, his punishment will be as hers: a life spent in banishment and ruin, dishonoured in the eyes of the Crown and Almighty God.*

"Arthur cannot mean this," I said. "He *sent* me to learn from Merlin and now I am *corrupt?* Ambitious how? My supposed powers are so dark and terrible I must stand trial?"

I read it again, as if the words might miraculously change. Eventually, I threw the blotted notice onto a table and made myself walk away. "What I do not understand is *why*."

Alys picked up the wine jug, dark liquid splashing onto the table from her juddering hands. Tressa strode across and took it from her, steadily pouring three goblets. I refused my cup and returned to the firelight.

"I think, my love," Alys murmured to Tressa, "that you should tell it from the beginning."

Tressa nodded and took up her wine, sitting wearily in one of the fireside chairs.

"It began a week ago," she said. "Lady Clarisse told me she'd heard rumours that King Arthur had ordered King Urien to keep Yvain in Gore. She seemed perturbed, as I was, but didn't know much, and I couldn't do anything but wait. I had no news of you, except a cryptic message under my door saying 'Safe and well. Here soon.' Which I now know was Sir Accolon's doing."

At the sound of his name, I looked for him, but remembered he had politely withdrawn, saying Tressa should tell her own story. At the time I was glad, unmade as I was by the sight of him, but now I felt faintly bereft.

Tressa took a long draft of her wine and continued. "Then, a few days ago, madness. Four knights burst into your chambers and started throwing open every cabinet, upending the mattresses, pulling down tapestries. I asked what they were looking for, but they ordered me to sit and hold my tongue. I asked to see Lady Clarisse or Sir Kay, but they ignored me and kept tearing through the place like wolves."

"The sword," I said quietly. "They were looking for Excalibur."

"Yes," she said. "After a while, one of them heard the hollow back of the alcove cupboard, ripped it out, and to my great surprise found a sword."

"I should have told you before I left," Alys said. "But I was sworn to secrecy, I . . ."

Tressa shook her head. "My not knowing was better. When they emerged brandishing the blade in that jewel-covered scabbard, they saw at once that my shock was genuine. It saved me."

"From what?" I asked.

"From suspicion that I had anything to do with whatever was going on," she said. "After that, a trio of different knights came, Sir Accolon among them. The other two questioned me—asking where Lady Morgan was, did I know anywhere you might go. I said I only knew what I'd been told when you left, but they didn't want to believe me. They explained that the High King wished it impressed upon me the importance of speaking God's truth, and I had until the next morning to find the words to help the realm."

"What did Accolon do?" I asked.

"Oh, *he* didn't speak, only stood in attendance." Tressa gave a dark laugh. "By St. Petroc, I was *furious*. For the first time, I felt as Alys did about him. I wanted to slap his faithless face."

Alys looked mildly abashed, whether from her memory of hating him or because she had embraced him in the entrance hall, I could not tell.

"I was also afraid," she continued. "Because I had almost directly been told that King Arthur thought me a liar. Then the knights said I wasn't to attempt leaving the castle, and ordered me to tidy up the mess."

"The temerity of them," I said sourly.

"They were fools," she agreed. "And so was I, for thinking the worst of Sir Accolon. When they left, he stayed behind and said I needed to get out of Camelot. He had it all planned—he told me to pack everything and send it to the barracks, where he would arrange delivery to an inn under his name. On the first bell after midnight, he helped me climb over the terrace and took us through a postern gate to horses at the city's edge."

"Mother of God," Alys said. "To think I was appalled with his using the terrace in pursuit of a lover's tryst."

"He did all that and no one suspected?" I said faintly.

"Sir Accolon is a man of canny wits," Tressa replied. "He told the King he had business in Gaul, and his cousin some other tale. We stopped last night at the inn to await the trunks. Everything is there, my lady, safe and waiting—our clothing and things, our work and manuscript, your *Ars Physica*. But when we heard news of the Royal Decree this afternoon, Sir Accolon insisted we ride immediately to ensure you were both safe."

I went and picked up my cup of wine after all, sipping it before one of the windows. Full dark had fallen fast, a sharp crescent of moon hooked between lingering rainclouds. Silence encompassed us, until Tressa cleared her throat.

"On the way, I asked him things," she said. "About the baby. Sir Accolon told me it wasn't his place to say, but I was so anxious he explained enough. I'm so sorry, Lady Morgan."

I met her sad eyes with my own. "So am I," I said.

We fell silent again, and I paced back to the hearth. With my eyes closed, the low roar of the fire sounded almost like the sea.

At length, Alys picked up the Royal Decree. "Is this really King Arthur's doing?"

"It must be, given he put his seal to it," I said. "Whether he came to those conclusions by himself is another matter. Anything Merlin tells him, he has been raised to believe. Maybe now that I'm not there, the sorcerer has too tight a grip on his thoughts.

But to send Yvain away and threaten his future? How could he *do* such a thing?"

Fury gripped tight in my chest. I threw my cup into the hearth, wine flaring in the flames. "I could go to Gore, don't they know that? I could ascend any battlement, unlock any door, send an entire castle to sleep or lay them all to bloody waste. I could carry my son out and bring him . . . back . . ."

My voice broke on the final words. Alys came to me, holding my shuddering body, but I broke free on a fresh gale of rage.

"I have to go back to Camelot," I said. "They cannot get away with this."

Tressa shook her head vehemently. "No, my lady. You can't, not yet. Things aren't right there—you'd be walking into a bear trap."

"She's right," Alys said. "It's too dangerous."

"I'm not afraid of the court," I said fiercely.

"I know," she said. "But they're not why you're still in Fair Guard. You're here because you looked through the trees this morning and commanded me to run back like our lives depended on it."

My glare was all wrath, but she held me steady in her amber gaze. "Morgan, *cariad*, you know I'm on your side, but when you saw Merlin today, your instinct was to turn and flee. You wouldn't have done so if there wasn't a good reason."

A leaded exhaustion settled in my bones. It was awful and futile and horribly true; Merlin was searching for me, the Royal Decree proof that Arthur was deeply under his influence. As long as he was in my brother's ear, I could not risk going to Camelot, or anywhere outside the boundaries I could protect. Instinct told me I would not escape the sorcerer's clutches a third time.

"What now?" I said. "I can't just do nothing."

"Surviving is not nothing," Alys said. "For now, you wait, think, and stay alive."

38

THE MORNING AFTER the Royal Decree, I was still awake after sending a reluctant Alys and Tressa to bed, knowing I would never sleep myself. Overnight, the rain had cleared to a still, bright dawn, and I had observed every moment alone, pacing the reception room, thinking on all I had done and what I must do now. As early as possible, I called for Sir Ceredig and entrusted him with a message, then began the long walk to my chosen meeting place.

I had discovered it while weaving my protective charms, far beyond the house, up a curving path through the dense woodland that sheltered Fair Guard. At the path's end, a crescent of weeping willows sprung from a grassy shore, overlooking a vast lake cut from the valley's steep sides, its surface sheened silver, sapphire blue at its depths.

Accolon found me under the largest willow tree at the lake's edge, its weeping summer branches thick enough to shield us from the world. A parting at the front revealed the water's gleaming expanse, green tendrils trailing atop the water.

"It's good to see you at last." His voice was tender, undemanding.

"I needed time to think," I replied. "Did you sleep well?"

"Not without you."

When I didn't respond, he gazed out across the lake and exhaled. "*Sacredieu*. This is incredible."

"*Llyn Glas*, they call it," I said. "Blue Lake, for the colour of its depths."

"It's beautiful." In his faraway eyes, I read his memories: of his own lake in Gaul, where he had swum and played as a child, and unearthed the bright treasure of the Gaulish coin I wore around my neck. "Is it yours?" he asked.

"It belongs to Fair Guard."

Ours, I wanted to say, but the thought was riven with flaws.

"You came back," I said.

He smiled, water-light rippling over his face. "One might say I never truly left. Wherever I go, my heart stays with you."

The moment hung there, and I let it dissipate. "Thank you for bringing Tressa back. You've earned Alys's forgiveness, which is no small feat."

"It's a relief to be restored in Lady Alys's favour. Reuniting her and Tressa was one of my greatest honours. Though I'm sorry their joy had to come under such circumstances." He cast his eyes from the lake to me. "What will you do now?"

I wanted to say I was fixing things, that my life was in hand, but I had never known how to hide myself from him.

"I don't know," I confessed. "Last night, I wanted to ride back to Camelot, but Alys and Tressa insisted I'd be walking into a trap of Merlin's making. Yet how can I *not* go? This is my life, my reputation, my . . ."

My son, I was about to say. Accolon regarded me gently, as if he had heard the words I couldn't speak.

"If you want to go back to Camelot, know that I will take you," he said. "If they force you on trial, I'll stand as your champion and fell any knight they put in front of me. Say the word, and we will ride."

"No," I said. "You're safe, unsuspected. I won't drag you into this. Regardless, how can I trust Arthur's justice? Look where my faith in him got me. Look what it cost *us*."

My voice hitched, and Accolon drew me swiftly into his arms. Aside from our one embrace a few weeks ago, ruined by my guilt, I hadn't been held by him in such a long time, and I had forgotten how good it could feel, his grace bearing me up until I believed I wasn't sinking.

The thought made me pull away. I went to the water's edge, taking in the lake's glassy lustre. "Alys and Tressa are right," I said. "I can't go back yet. But you can. We're all safe here."

Accolon followed me, shading his brow against the reflected sun. "This time, you won't get rid of me so easily. I'm staying here with you."

I sighed. "You don't have to do that."

"I only *left* because you said I must," he replied. "I want to be here, and you want me here. I know it without doubt, for one good reason."

"Which is?"

"Because you told me the truth."

Momentarily, it arrested me. "I gave you the truth to set you free," I said. "So you could live your own life."

Accolon shook his head. "I know you, Morgan. If this was over, you would have sent me away without telling me of our child and carried the pain alone. I realized it not an hour after I left. You told me because you want our life together and couldn't bear for it to be based on a lie."

As soon as he said the words, I knew he was right. How was it that he knew every part of me?

I yearned to face him, but kept my eyes on the water. "I want you here, of course I do," I said. "But you are sworn to a King to whom you owe service. We can never be seen in public. To live like this is to cut yourself off from every success, the life you once had."

"Details, all," he said. "I have the spoils of success to last us a lifetime, plenty of service accumulated from my year's quest. And who else needs to know of our love? If secrecy doesn't matter to you, nor does it to me."

"There are other, worse things," I said. "I lost your son, Accolon. How will you look at me and not be reminded?"

He turned to me then, his face calm, and more serious than I had ever seen it.

"Morgan," he said, "hear me now, if you never do again. *It wasn't your fault.* I grieve what happened, of course, and maybe it will be hard to live without something I almost but never had. That I do not know. But I *do* know it's impossible for me to live without you."

His absolution weighed heavy on my head. "It will haunt us, Accolon. What if we can speak of nothing else, think of nothing else? Worse still, what if we forget?"

"If it haunts us, we face the phantoms together," he said. "If we wish to speak on it, we can—or not, and decide every day anew. We will never forget, but what matters is this pain is both of ours. We can share its weight, and on days when you cannot, I will carry it for you. You were right that this truth can free us—we can let it exist, feel its sadness, and choose to live beyond. Together."

He lifted my chin and made me look at him. "But unless you chase me off this land, I'm still not leaving."

His confidence brought a warmth to my abdomen, but I resisted succumbing to the feeling.

"Accolon, think on this," I said. "You've always wished for a family, a legacy, a loving, happy place in the world. We cannot marry, and the thought of motherhood while my two sons exist without me . . . it's impossible. I cannot be your wife, bear you children or give you the home you want."

He regarded me intently for an endless, aching moment, and fear sprung up at the thought I had convinced him.

"*L'enfer,*" he said at last. "Will you never listen to me?"

He smiled in mock exasperation, and the charm of it caught in my chest, relief and surprise giving way to a teary, unexpected laugh.

Accolon's face softened. "None of it matters, don't you see? I love *you*. I don't want for anything else." His eyes held mine, stormy, emphatic. "Morgan—you are my home."

The thought of not holding him felt like sheer death, so I reached up and drew him in. Our mouths met with such hunger it shot through my body like a comet.

"If I keep you here, it is ruin," I told him, but he only rolled his eyes.

"*Alors*, ruin it is," he said. "Just tell me to stay."

So I did, and he agreed, holding me close as water on skin beside the still, sapphire depths of our lake.

Stay, I told him, again and again. *Stay with me.*

39

THE ENTIRE HOUSEHOLD took to Accolon swiftly, as most did, and he took to his circumstances with the easy grace that he brought to all things. He arranged for our belongings to be sent from the inn and enlisted a proxy to manage his affairs in Gaul; he learned the name, occupation and familial links of every soul in Fair Guard; he walked the manor's environs for weeks, taking an interest in the stables, the kennels, the land, and gaining the trust of those who maintained them, until they turned to him for every concern.

When a hunting hound had a large litter and one pup was small and weak, Accolon brought her home and raised her by hand, taking his long walks with the brachet under his arm, until she was strong enough to trot by his side. At every mealtime, he lifted his cup and gave thanks to the household, referring to himself and me in terms of "we" and "us" with a naturalness that spoke of a marriage long made. He called the place *Belle Garde* and seemed to let his past life, his fame and success, slip into the wind without a wisp of regret. He shaved his beard off and grew his hair down past his collar again.

We made our bedchamber where I had first lain down with the scabbard on my chest, a long, spacious room with tall windows looking out on forested hills and sky. On the air, the rush and trickle of the river, spring and streams played a constant, tranquil harmony.

"This is the place," we had agreed, looking up at the rafters we would have painted with songbirds; opening an interior door to a fragrant courtyard garden; regarding the enormous oak bed, soon to be draped with sky-blue hangings, made for two entwined souls who never wished to sleep apart.

There, at first, I held Accolon too hard, too greedily, nerves still afire with the fear of loss. I lay awake as he fell asleep, and awoke before him every morning, heart racing with the belief I would find him gone. It seemed impossible that I could open my eyes and see him facing me, his dark lashes twitching in a dream; or stir in our sleepers' embrace, his lips hot on the back of my neck, and not think of impending bells, or fear discovery.

We ate and drank together, danced close at long last, and took endless walks through Fair Guard, my trepidation gradually assuaged by his tender, easy presence, until my eyes closed and opened believing he would be there whenever I looked for him.

The only thing that neither Accolon nor anyone else could do was free me from the vault of wrongs I could not make right, the key to which was still trapped within the walls of Camelot.

*

SOON, AUTUMN CAME, and so quickly life seemed to move beyond me. The household settled under Alys and Tressa's efficient management: rooms were opened and painted; furniture found and rearranged; the gardens detangled and prepared for spring planting. Tressa took charge of the orchard and had beehives built for our own honey, while Accolon organized the stables, talking at length about horseflesh and bloodlines, and joining the huntsman on his quests for game to feed us.

At first, they asked my opinion on plans and improvements, forging ahead when I told them they should do as they saw fit. All I could do for them was keep the valley safe, so for that reason I emerged from my bedchamber and rode Fair Guard's boundaries, casting Ninianne's silver threads between the trees. Otherwise, I was standing at the edge of a future that others saw clearly, but I could not fathom beyond the burning hollow inside me, filled with the embers of a past not extinguished.

"Where shall I put the *Ars Physica*?" Alys asked me one day, bending over a trunk in the turret room.

I had kept the round tower as my own, unable to escape the idea that the balconied room was a study, with its good light and the upper gallery's encircling shelves. In the absence of my final decision, Alys had made the long table that was already there her desk, and had better chairs brought up, with the intention we would sit for hours amongst ink and parchment, as we had in times past.

"Leave it in the trunk, for now," I said.

"Won't you need it for our work?" she asked.

"How can I work when there is so much left undone?" I replied. "I cannot sit with books and pretend my troubles in Camelot have disappeared."

It was only partly the cause: the Royal Decree and its unanswered accusations still smouldered in my mind, but every time I thought of sitting down to study or write, I found the impulse gone. I had so much learning from my time at Merlin's to put to paper before I forgot, but when I tried to cast my mind back, my lungs constricted with an airless fear, as if crushed again by the sorcerer's nightmarish snake.

Alys closed the trunk. "What will you do?"

I shrugged. "I won't stop you, dear heart. Begin the herbal you've always wanted to write. Let Tressa practise illuminating manuscripts. Use your time and don't wait for me."

"This time is yours too," she argued. "The freedom to read and work is what you always wanted."

But I wasn't free, and they could not see it. She and Tressa tried on other days, in other valiant ways, to draw me into a discussion of our future work, and I couldn't seem to tell them the truth: that what I once trusted to teach me how to fix things was no help to me anymore. My faith in knowledge had gone.

"Maybe tomorrow," I would say, and the same the next day, and the day after that, until they understood the time would never arrive and ceased asking.

*

OFTENTIMES, IT WAS as if I was outside of a room, looking in. From the doorway of my existence, I could see others settling, living, going about their days; I could listen to their talk and jests, and in turn they could see me. I was visible at the edges, and heard if I spoke, so it was easy for most to believe I was there in the same way as they were, even if my mind was far along the distant road, besieging a great golden castle.

As Alys and Tressa managed the household—viewing ledgers, planning improvements and mapping the rhythms of the day—I thought of Camelot and Sir Kay's organizational fervour, of Lady Clarisse and the women, imagining what was said of me. As Accolon stood on my balcony and declared the river meadow the perfect shape for a tiltyard, and I urged him to build one, I thought only of the Royal Court riding north after Harvest, and whether Merlin would follow Arthur or return to his lair.

As the household sat down to dinner with idle chatter and companionable laughter, talking of the new tiltyard's progress and how Accolon meant to use it, I thought back to Arthur's Pentecost tournament, wondering if everything that had befallen me had begun there, or longer ago.

"Jousting season is upon us," the huntsman said to Accolon one evening. "*Your* season, so it is said."

Accolon smiled modestly. "*Oui*, once upon a time."

"The stables thought you might enter a few, given some of the fine horseflesh you've got. Or are you afraid of men with younger bones?"

"Bold talk for one who only faces fleeing deer from horseback," Accolon rejoined, and the table laughed. "I'd like to think I can still knock any man from his horse," he added. "But we'll never know."

"I suppose the famous Sir Accolon of Gaul couldn't just go and joust," Tressa said. "Unless you wanted to be swooped upon with recognition."

"Ah, but there are ways," he replied. "You can enter into the lists with an alias and never remove your helm. Knights of great prowess often compete anonymously to experience the joy of the joust without expectation. I used to consider it."

Alys raised an eyebrow. "Are you calling *yourself* a knight of great prowess?"

Another laugh rippled along the table, and I sensed eyes on my face: Accolon, catching me hovering on the conversation's periphery. Alys's gaze shifted, becoming watchful, and I knew then she must have done battle with her very nature and told him of my time in the turret, the malaise of purpose I never let him see.

I spoke before he could. "Why don't you do it? Joust—return to what you love."

"I could ask you the same question," he said.

I didn't respond. Accolon put his hand on mine, turning it over so we were palm to palm.

"Morgan, far be it from me to tell you how to feel. But back when you spoke of this place, it was with such passion, such ambition. There were things you wanted, work you wished to do. It still matters to you."

"What of it?" I said. "Something can matter yet cease to be."

His brow creased and it made me ache. "Do you not miss it?"

"Do *you* miss your life?" I said. "Do you want to go back to competing, chasing the thrill of victory?"

"No," he said. "You are my life now—this is. It's not who I am anymore."

"Then why can it not be so for me?"

"It isn't the same," he replied. "I school the horses and ride my tiltyard every day. Whatever has happened, *mon coeur*, you did not come here to stare at an empty table."

He could be more forthright with me than anyone, and his words did not go unthought of, if not taken quite the way he intended. The next day, I entered the turret room and found Alys and Tressa working at the table as usual. They looked up at me as if expecting a scolding, but I managed a smile.

"Give me some parchment," I said. "I've thought of something I can do."

Tressa's face brightened, and she handed me a sheaf of hers. Alys's expression remained grave.

"What are you doing?" she asked.

"I'm writing to Arthur," I said. "I must act somehow. If I cannot go to Camelot, it doesn't mean I should allow my brother to forget me."

Alys reached out, as if to stay my hand, then thought better of it. "To what end?"

"Because this isn't fair," I said. "I am owed more than what he's given me."

What good is it? they wanted to say. But either they trusted me or knew saying so was futile, because they handed me a quill and poured my ink, and watched as I made my outrage my work.

I wrote Arthur copious pages every week: words of fury, words of pain, all of my questions, doubts and grief. Memories of times we had spent, our past lives, and the hours talking over Crown and realm; every moment of our bond, committed to ink.

Hours I spent, exonerating myself from the Royal Decree and its claims, explaining to my brother why it couldn't be true, that I knew it was Merlin in his ear. The decree may have carried his seal, I told him, but I was certain the words were not his. I urged him to assure me he had not meant to commit the damnation of my character to parchment, nor mark it in blood-red wax with the beastly royal mark of Uther Pendragon.

From my quill, words upon words, telling my brother what I could not show him. In return, he sent an icy regal silence.

Not that my mind wished to hear it, nor did my hand want to stop. What else could I do, after all? Any resurgent notion of riding off to see Arthur was cut short by the thought of the sorcerer, keeping guard. As the months wore on, I no longer knew where the court would be, where Arthur now preferred to spend Eastertide, or if he was still in the habit of being in Camelot for Guinevere to go a-Maying. Perhaps that was why he had not written back: he was in Carduel, Caerleon, or hunting his forests around London, and hadn't yet seen anything I'd sent.

But as autumn's red-gold procession dimmed into frosted winter, slowly lightening towards the spring equinox, I knew Arthur would not have stayed away from his beloved golden city for so long, that under Sir Kay's diligent eye his correspondence would not have sat unread, and I swore to give up, as I had many times before.

Yet when I sat alone in my echoing turret, faced with my frustration—when I thought of my mistakes, my failures, of the lost child I never named, and of Yvain with his mother's face fading from his mind—still I wrote my letters, with the silent, useless fury of unfulfilled purpose and vanishing hope, and still my brother sent no reply.

40

"I THINK THE household would like a Midsummer's Eve feast," Alys said, some time after our first May Day. "Sir Ceredig told me it was once the custom, which was forgotten without a lord or lady. Some are wondering whether you'll revive it."

I gave no answer, having nothing to say. We were in my turret, but I was languishing as usual, circling the room as Alys sorted through some plant cuttings Accolon had brought her from his last hunt. He had earned her forgiveness with Tressa's return, but still worked to build a friendship beyond their compulsory common ground, often bringing her some sprig or cluster of unusual flowers for her studies, and transforming her mere tolerance into a mildly grudging fondness.

At her right hand sat the household ledgers, which she had spent the morning checking, ready for Tressa's neat scribing pen. How she kept all of these things balanced, I did not know, when my mind still felt like a fogged road without end.

It had been a fortnight since the messenger delivered my last letter to Camelot, and though after nine months Arthur's lack of reply shouldn't have come as a surprise, his silence pricked me with fresh failure each day. In addition, Yvain would have his fourth birthday in a few weeks, and my head was full of him, waking from a dream the night before where we no longer recognized one another. Even if he did remember my face, I wondered whether what was said of me would turn his child's heart hard.

"What do you think?" Alys nudged me with her quill as I passed, breaking my reverie.

"About what?"

She sighed wearily. "About Midsummer's Eve. I think it would be nice for the household."

I waved a vague hand and walked on. "Then you know my answer."

"Yes," she muttered. "The answer is always the same. *If it suits you, Alys, do as you wish. I cannot think of that now. I have letters to write. Nothing else matters.*"

Her words drew me to a halt. "I beg your pardon?"

My voice held a slight edge, but Alys stood and faced me, unbowed and unrepentant.

"Morgan," she said. "This is no way to live."

It was spoken with such clarity I couldn't even ask what she meant. I knew.

Cautiously, she approached, taking hold of my elbows. "I have long given up on trying to return you to our studies, but Fair Guard, this household, it awaits *you*. It needs you to participate."

"Fair Guard is perfectly fine," I said. "If the household needs a mistress or master, it has you and Tressa. It has Accolon. I am of no use to them, or anyone."

"That's not true," she said. "Regardless, you need to start caring, for your own sake."

I pulled away from her grip. "I *do* care. It's all I've been doing. I care that the life I was promised has vanished, and Camelot's accusations have gone unanswered. I care that a child I never met was snatched from me. I care that Yvain is in Gore, out of my reach, and you've all forgotten about him."

"I did not forget him," she said gravely. "I never could. That's not what this is about."

"Then what *is* it about, Alys?" I demanded. "What do you want from me?"

She considered me for a tremulous moment, fingers agitating her braid.

"Three questions," she said. "Answer them, for my sake, then I will keep my counsel for good."

Anyone else and I would have walked out of the room, but it was Alys; I loved her far more than my pride.

I crossed my arms and looked away. "Three questions," I agreed.

"Do you want to go to Gore?" she said. "To get Yvain, set Castle Chariot alight. You know we'll ride north with you tomorrow."

I sighed, turning back to her. "I know you would, but it's impossible. Even if I snatched Yvain back, then I am taking his freedom, his place in the world. Whatever I do, he will grow up to resent me, but I cannot ruin my child's life. As my son, he has no future."

Her second question came with a deep intake of breath. "And your other son—yours and Sir Accolon's. Is there any hope of finding him, at all, in this world? Do you believe it's possible?"

To answer felt like a spear to my gut. "No," I admitted. "I know Ninianne, I know the power of the fairy magic she cast. Her own regret was real. Neither I nor Accolon will ever see our child, in any lifetime."

Alys nodded, a glimmer of tears on her eyelashes.

"There's a third," I said quietly.

She dabbed her eyes with her sleeve. "Camelot."

I didn't need the question. "I'm not going back there."

Until I said it, I had no concept it was what I had decided, but the words felt startling and awful and true all at once.

Alys exhaled. "Are you sure?"

"Yes," I said, more certain as the thought took hold. "I cannot walk back into that poisonous court and face trial for wrongs that in truth have been *done* to me, nor risk our lives on the chance Arthur made a mistake. Letter after letter I've sent and nothing. Either Merlin influences him still, or . . ."

I couldn't say it, or let myself believe it—that Arthur had participated in my downfall, whether he wished it or not. Nine months he'd had to recant, to act, to break free of whatever fog Merlin had trapped him in, but he hadn't made a single move.

"I can never go back," I concluded.

Tentatively, Alys took up my hands. "If all that's true, *cariad*, then maybe it's time to . . . accept that it's over."

"*What?*"

I broke away from her, limbs burning with fresh anger, though I knew there was nothing but love in her words. I circled the room again, but as I paced, I realized the onset of fury hadn't felt fortifying for a long time. It was useless, this exhausting fire, wasteful, a potent but empty sensation that was no longer part of my power.

"This cannot be," I said. "Merlin, Urien, Guinevere, Camelot—how have they managed to defeat me?"

"Morgan," Alys began, but I shook my head.

"Is this how I lose, Alys? I haven't conceded a chess game since I was a child and *this* is the checkmate I must accept?"

With an impatient intake of breath, she swung away and marched off to the small trunk that I wouldn't unpack. Kneeling down, she opened the lid and pulled something free, then returned to me, arm outstretched.

"Here," she said firmly.

In her hand was a narrow rectangular object, wrapped in grey muslin. I blinked as though it were a mirage, then took it from her, hearing the faint rattle within of thirty-two expertly carved pieces.

"The chess set?" I said in wonder. "How . . . ?"

"I know you told me to burn it after Sir Accolon left Tintagel. God knows I wanted to turn every trace of him into ashes, but somehow I just couldn't."

I unravelled the muslin, and the checkered surface appeared, shining as it used to in the chapel candlelight. A vision sprung up of Accolon and me, talking, laughing, playing, our eyes holding long enough to last an eternity. We were so young, so naive, back then, but the memory was cool and happy, a balm to my fractious heat.

"The one place I could always win," I murmured.

Alys didn't respond, and when I looked up her eyes gave nothing away. "Why did you give this to me now?" I asked.

"Because *that* is a chess game, Morgan." She pointed at the black-and-white box, then opened her arms in an encompassing gesture. "*This*, where we stand here and now, is life. It's joyous and awful and complicated, sometimes painful, but it's real and true. Often, it doesn't make sense—there isn't always a move you can make to fix things, or a logical way out of a trap. But there's always light to be found, if you would just turn halfway from the darkness."

I stared at her, wishing I could argue; I had never liked being wrong and wasn't used to it, but Alys was brave, and honest, and more right than I had been for a very long time.

"You have fought through failure, adversity and pain," she said. "Those who have wronged you, curse them all to Hell, but the way they win is if they stop you from choosing your future." She took up my hands, holding them fast within hers. "*Cariad*, if nothing else—do not forget that this is your one and only life."

Instead of admitting to her deep, irrefutable wisdom, I drew away and went out onto the balcony. What greeted me there was Fair Guard, with its beauty, its pull of belonging that in my distraction I had forgotten to feel; a place I loved that loved me in return.

Here, there were no battlements, no bells and no overcomplicated, arbitrary rules. It was a home, a better way of life for all of us.

But to embrace this meant accepting that my life in Camelot, and everything that went with it, was over, and forfeiting a battle for the first time since I was born. Or I could push on with the fight for my place in the great golden city, where the opponents were unclear, the spoils tainted by conditions, and the chances of victory near impossible.

The choice was a simple one. Either I went to war, or I had to find peace.

*

I DON'T KNOW how long I stood on the balcony, but when I returned to the study, Tressa was sitting beside Alys at the long table, scribing diligently. They looked up as I came in, innocent, unquestioning, as if I hadn't stormed outside with my life on a forked road.

"We'll need proper desks at the earliest opportunity," I said. "This study is barely a room. After that, we must fill the shelves."

The slightest smile flickered between them. "Very well," Alys said. "Then what?"

She was testing me, but I was ready. "We make plans for Midsummer's Eve. After that, there are many improvements to consider. This valley, these people who have welcomed us here, they deserve as good a home as I can give them, to share in my skills and all I have. I can at least try to be of use."

Alys and Tressa grinned in unison. "And after that?"

I smiled and went to the small trunk, pushing open the lid.

"Our manuscript," I said. "I think it's high time we finished it, don't you?"

*

ON THE FIRST warm day, Accolon and I went up to the lake.

In our arms we cradled two small sacks, each bearing a slim sapling from Alys's nursery garden. Last autumn, they had been seeds, and in a few years they would be apple trees, but for now they were more than that—a symbol, a tribute, a way to remember.

On a sunlit slope above the water, we planted each tree in memory of two sons—one shared and unnamed, and another I had nursed and raised, but equally far away now.

There were no words, no gestures great enough to restore what was lost, but that was not the purpose. My defiant soul had to learn that a desire for contentment in the face of loss was no sin, no matter how vast the failure. For the sake of everything else I loved, I must find a way to acceptance, and life.

Thereafter, Accolon and I spread blankets and sat under the willow tree, talking endlessly and making love beneath the swaying green fronds. He spent hours in and out of the lake, swimming and diving, while I lay drowsy in the warmth, watching his swift arms cutting through the silver-blue water.

"When I die," he said, as we lay side by side, limbs entwined, "bury me here, under this weeping willow tree."

I curled closer to him, trailing a hand across the sleek bones of his face. "That will never be," I said. "For I will defy it, with all the power I possess. How else would I survive?"

Accolon regarded me for a long moment, his storm-dark eyes sparking in the oscillating light. He took my hand and raised us up, leading me to the water's edge. When we reached it, he didn't stop, lake water invigorating across my feet.

"What are you doing?" I said. "I can't swim."

"Not yet. You don't fear the water, do you?"

"No," I replied.

"And you trust me?"

"Of course. But—"

"Then you will learn, and we can swim together."

The thought was all that buoyed me as I let him guide me into the depths, first bearing me up on his palms as I flailed and sank, until I calmed enough to listen to his advice. As the hours flew by, the water that ran in my veins bolstered my strength, and I went deeper and farther than I ever thought I would go. Finally, under the sunset, Accolon and I swam together from the middle of the lake, reaching the shallows breathless and exhilarated.

"There," he said. "You can no longer remember a time when staying afloat felt impossible. You trusted me, then yourself, and now survival feels innate."

"How did you know?" I said.

He gave a rueful smile. "Because *someone* saved me from drowning once, and thereafter, I never took the feeling for granted."

I kissed him in the water, then went ashore to the willow and wrapped a blanket about my shoulders. Accolon swam another slow circle, emerging from the lake like a cascade and lying down soaking wet beside me, his handsome head slung back in repose. I studied his face in the blue-gold light, his aspect of relaxation sending heat up my spine. I could tell by the curl of his mouth he knew I was watching him, but he kept his eyes closed.

"You should go to the next tournament," I said. "Anonymously, but go."

"No, *mon coeur*. It's not my life any longer. I am so happy. I don't need anything more than I already have."

"I watch you running drills, hitting the quintain, practising the charge all day long. I see the light in your eyes when you come in from the tilt meadow. You don't need it, but you love it."

He opened his eyes, brow arching.

"Morgan," he said, as if it was a complete sentence.

"Answer me this," I countered. "If our lives were lived in the open, would you be going? In absolute truth."

He sighed. "Yes. In a different predicament, I—"

"Then you must go," I cut in. "This is not a predicament anymore. It is a life, the one we have chosen. Go and be safe and careful, and when you win, you'll send your victory up in my name and it will mean something better than before, because you're coming home to me. Yes?"

His answer was to take me in his arms, drawing us down beneath the willow tree until night had fallen and new dawn gilded the horizon, and neither of us had noticed.

If the outside world came looking, it would not find me.

41

FOR SEVERAL WEEKS, Accolon rode out to tournaments within a few days' travel, guarding his anonymity closely, and collecting victories under a helm he didn't remove until he had accepted his prize and galloped away from the jousting arena. When he came home, his reports of various escapades and the intrigue surrounding the nameless knight sweeping the southwest tilt fields brought laughter to Fair Guard's dinner table.

One afternoon, I was idly reading on the turret balcony when one of the magpies gave an alerting caw and I saw Accolon returning, still ahorse and halfway up the riverbank. It took me the entire journey down the stairs and out onto the front green to realize he had not ridden alone.

"Morgan, *viens ici*," he called. "I've brought someone to see you."

He dismounted near the spring, allowing his chestnut stallion to drink. Behind, a stout brown cob carried a lanky figure, face lit up under a nest of red curls.

"Robin!" I exclaimed.

"Lady Morgan, it's you!" Robin said, attempting to bow and dismount at the same time. "I hardly believed it when Sir Accolon told me."

I embraced his slight frame, all limbs and points where it was finding height faster than breadth. "Goodness, you've grown! How old are you now?"

"Fourteen," he said quickly.

Accolon regarded him with a wry amusement. "Maybe in a year. Not quite thirteen, this one, and too young to be riding the roads alone."

Robin blushed and made no protest.

"Where did you find him?" I asked.

"No, *mon coeur*—he found *me*," Accolon said. "Apparently, he was hovering around the tournament, then appeared at the riverside tree where I had stopped to disarm. He came upon me so quietly he's fortunate he didn't end up thrown in the water."

I laughed at the image of their mutual discovery, the roving free-lance ways Accolon had easily returned to. He was a knight-errant at heart and always would be.

"He *won*," Robin said. "I didn't know who it was, but I watched and thought, *If only I had the chance to serve such a knight*. When he rode off with no squire, I thought it was Providence. When I saw it was Sir Accolon, I was certain it was a holy miracle."

"You see the difficulties of my position," Accolon said archly. "How is it possible to refuse one who regards you as a gift from God Himself?"

"How indeed?" I replied. "So you're no longer at Camelot, Robin?"

"No, my lady, since this Eastertide past. My father fell ill and died last winter."

"I'm very sorry. That must have been hard."

He nodded sadly. "The physic said it was expected, but I often thought of you, Lady Morgan, afterwards. That maybe you could have helped him, like you helped me."

The sentiment caught on my heartstrings, memories of my own father's sudden, preventable death playing their long-echoing chord. Robin's mother, I knew, had died when he was so young he had no memory of her. "I would have done all I could. I deeply regret your loss."

Accolon put a hand on the boy's shoulder. "I said Robin could stay with us at *Belle Garde*. I will train him to be a fine squire. If Lady Morgan agrees."

They both offered beseeching looks, making me laugh. "Only after I take our new guest to see Lady Alys, and he submits to a hot meal and a long rest. You look like you haven't slept in a three-month."

"She is the mistress here, so I would heed her," Accolon told him. "I'll see to the horses."

He took the reins from the beaming boy and left us to make our way inside.

"What happened in Camelot?" I asked him. "They didn't force you to leave?"

"No, my lady," Robin said. "They took Papa's quarters and put me in the bunks with the other stablelads. I didn't mind that, but things had . . . changed."

"In the castle?" I asked.

He shook his head, looking around Fair Guard's entrance hall. Accolon's dog heard us, bounding across in expectation of her master. Upon seeing it was me, she feigned her usual ignorance, but her curled hound tail wagged curiously at the newcomer. Robin bent down and rewarded her with a scratch behind her silky ears.

"More the people," he said. "It was as if King Arthur was always the sun, but a cloud had suddenly come. Then, just before I decided to leave, *it* happened, and night fell."

I frowned; we heard little news of Camelot, aside from stories of an ever-increasing number of knights on quests. "*What* happened?"

"I didn't see it, but everyone knew right away. King Arthur and the court were at the evening meal when, in the middle of the thanks-giving prayer, the entire room fell to darkness. The ladies screamed and knights rushed to arm themselves—some thought it was a raid, or the Devil himself. They said a gust of air swept through the room like a restless spirit."

My heart gave an anticipatory jolt. Profound darkness in Camelot's Great Hall could mean only one thing. "The wall of candles."

Robin nodded. "Went out all at once, along with the rest of the light. After that, the bells of St. Stephen's started ringing in lament, and they told us to ready a state of mourning in solidarity with the High King."

"You don't mean . . ." I dared not utter the words.

"Yes, my lady. Merlin the Wise is dead."

*

HOW HAD I *not known*?

The strangest thing was I hadn't sensed it. To be bound by magic was no small matter, and though our disastrous deal was immutable beyond death, the fact that I didn't feel Merlin drawing his final breath was almost as great a surprise as the news he had died at all. What I did feel was relief, and the darkest rush of triumph, for which I carried no shame. In this, I had defeated him.

His influence hadn't breached Fair Guard's world. Not one word from souls on the road or passing through the valley mentioned a cave, or entrapment, or the death Merlin had foreseen that would reverberate throughout the kingdom. In time, the sorcerer would be recorded in the chronicles not as a man with a hunger for knowledge, demonic heritage and an unquenchable desire to control, but Britain's agent of royal glory, without whom its High Kings would never be the same.

Where was Ninianne, I wondered; were the rumours true that she was involved? Did she still serve Arthur, as she swore she always would? What of the house in the forest, the moat, the snakes; the stacks of manuscripts, scrolls and pages? What of the mysteries Merlin kept locked in his tower: records of his prophecies and the country's greatest secrets; the miraculous Shroud of Tithonus, Arthur's deliverance from death?

What of Arthur, trapped in the web of lies the sorcerer had wrapped around him? Camelot had not been the same, by Robin's word, the light of the Crown darkened since its High King had thrown in his lot with Merlin's avaricious hunt for glory, leaving him isolated and untrusting.

There was so much he did not know, lost beneath the sorcerer's insidious lies. Arthur no doubt believed he had lost his route to resurrection, when in truth, it was me who could have been his salvation. Too late now, any regret he might have had; I had chosen my future and was free of it all.

Then it came, one morning in early autumn, as if summoned by the sheer subversive force of my wanting to be left alone: a note left at the chapel, marked private, my name written in a hand rarely seen but I knew intimately, from the memory of letters sent between new siblings discovering their mutual affinity, before I ran to live within his golden walls.

Morgan, it said. *Meet with me. Choose anywhere, but come. Your brother, King Arthur.*

To any promise, no matter how boldly sworn, there is always an exception. The outside world I would not let find me, unless it was him, my brother. Only Arthur could undo what had been done.

42

I TOLD HIM to come alone to the small chapel on the edge of Fair Guard's valley, leaving instructions within of where to find me. When I arrived at the edge of the hawthorn grove, a horse already stood outside the church door, so I waited, then watched him emerge.

He wore a concealing hood, but his bearing I would have known anywhere. King Arthur of All Britain, modestly clad in plain grey, but known to the earth, the air, the light all around him, every regal step a declaration of ownership. The land he walked upon was mine, but the entire world was his domain.

I sank back into the trees and let him come to me.

When he entered the small, circular clearing, I was standing in the centre, behind the protective charms, though he could not see the veil's silvery sheen as I could. I didn't fear my brother would harm me; nor would I be proven a fool.

Arthur pushed his hood down, striding across a carpet of white hawthorn blossom. He wore no crown, but rested a hand upon his sword hilt, and I recognized the sun-gold grip of Excalibur, glowing in the woodland shade. Its scabbard was the jewel-covered counterfeit, the true miracle still safe in my tower at Fair Guard.

He stopped before the veil and fixed me with our mother's grey gaze, standing steady as a marble statue. He looked like my brother and a King, and felt like neither.

"Sister," he said evenly, and the sound of his voice suddenly rendered him real. I had sat for hours, arguing with him in my mind, until it felt like we had confronted our differences many times, when in truth, my brother and I had not laid eyes on one another since the godforsaken day I left for Merlin's.

"Arthur," I greeted him. "It's . . . it's . . ."

Was it *good* to see him? Interesting? Daunting? After all that had happened, where were either of us to begin?

"I know," he said, in lieu of my finishing. "It's odd to meet this way, and not how I wanted it to be. I had hoped to see you sooner."

"I wrote to you every week for months," I said. "You never replied."

He inclined his head in acknowledgement. "We found ourselves in a strange situation. At the time, I did not know how to respond."

"No doubt Merlin read my letters and deemed it better not to," I said. "I suppose his death is the only reason you are here now. Tell me, how *did* the sorcerer meet his end?"

Arthur drew a heavy breath. "He was lured to a cave and entombed there, by the lady he was in love with. She had been learning magic from him for years and betrayed his trust. He could not break her spell in order to set himself free."

The confirmation that Ninianne was the author of Merlin's death was simultaneously astonishing and unsurprising. "I suppose I should be grateful that I'm not taking the blame," I said. "Still, I'm not sorry to hear he's dead."

Arthur recoiled, face creasing into a look of genuine hurt, fleetingly younger than he had ever looked. "Is that why you came here, to mock Merlin's death to my face?" His voice shook, and I thought he might burst into tears. "It took almost a *year* for him to die in that cave. My men searched, even found him, and still I could not set him free. God knows what torture he endured before his candles went out, and you revel in it?"

My brother's anguish struck my heart as it always had, but nothing could make me regret the sorcerer's demise.

"I came because you asked me to," I said. "Why, after so much time and silence, did you summon me?"

He sighed, his hand reaching up to his temple as usual, rubbing the edge of a crown that wasn't there. "I don't know, Morgan. Would you believe me if I said I suddenly felt compelled?"

"I might. I wouldn't be surprised if at the moment the life candles went dark, a great many things became clearer in your mind."

His eyes flashed with anger, but I saw him take hold of it; he was trying. "Whatever the cause, I just wanted to look upon my sister again, who I once knew so well. A great deal has happened, but I thought if we were to meet, I could see if . . ."

He trailed off, glancing away.

"To see if I was all you had accused me of being?" I said sharply. "What have you decided, now I'm here? In fact, forget it. Instead, tell me how Merlin convinced you to tear us asunder. Explain to me *why*."

"Must we speak of this now?" he said. "There is so much to discuss, and I didn't ask you here to trawl through the past."

"You gave my *son* away, Arthur." My voice rattled, the words still raw. "You handed Yvain to his father and told the entire world I was corrupt, a traitoress. The *past* you wish to ignore changed the course of my whole life, and I deserve to know what happened. Why did you issue the Royal Decree?"

My brother stood silent, stubborn as we both could be, but my defiance was older and more hardened than his. I stepped back, about to walk away, when he reached out, his hand slipping through the protective charms without resistance. He didn't touch me, but I paused.

"Merlin came to me a few days after you were due back," he said. "At first, he spoke well of you—how you were quick to learn and he had harboured great hopes for your future. Until, after a while, you became . . ."

"Corrupted," I replied.

Arthur nodded gravely. "He said that in the last few months, your work had progressed rapidly, but your interests had taken on a darker bent. He worried perhaps he had pushed you too hard, or shown you concepts so difficult your interpretation crossed the boundaries of what is acceptable to God. Eventually, he confessed that if he had known what his teachings would unleash within you, he would have left well enough alone."

"Oh, of course," I said. "The great Merlin can practise these concepts and be lauded for doing so, but *my* mind could not cope without turning to corruption? You know me, Arthur. How could you believe such a thing?"

His cheeks flushed. "My only thought was to be concerned. Merlin said you stayed up all hours into the night, working with a fervour he had never seen. That you ate and slept little, as if there was an urgent matter you could not let rest."

I heard my own behaviour spoken back to me, memories of my pale, gaunt reflection, when work and thoughts of usefulness were the only things driving me beyond the howl of my grief.

I had a child, I wanted to say; *he was taken away against my will. It was work or burn to the ground.*

But the confession wouldn't come, chained to my tongue by the godforsaken deal I had made, or because it was too late regardless.

"Merlin's words are twisted," I said. "He encouraged everything, told me my work was good for the realm."

Arthur nodded. "He said he tried to steer you onto a lighter path, but you became obsessed over my rule, the realm, my future. Then, when he saw the prophecy, he had no choice but to act. He had to inform me."

My thoughts juddered to a halt. "What prophecy?"

"I suppose he felt it safer not to tell you," Arthur said. "The stars said that a great betrayal would bring about my end, the destruction of the kingdom, and to be wary of those close to me. After what he had seen, Merlin calculated that no one else could be the betrayer but you, and brought me the news."

"And naturally, you believed it."

"All I felt was utter shock," he replied. "I told him to bring you back to Camelot so I could judge for myself, but you had absconded."

So a foggy prophecy of Merlin's had brought about my downfall, not his wish to claim credit for my work. Maybe the cunning goat had believed it, or he saw himself made obsolete. Either way, my escape had played into his scheming hands.

"Then you assumed my guilt," I said. "Never mind that this *prophecy* is an outright falsehood."

Arthur shook his head vehemently. "Merlin wouldn't lie to me. Nothing he's ever told me has been untrue."

Too late had I realized the sorcerer's unbreakable effect on Arthur, the way he had captured his young mind. This fantastical, avuncular wise man had guided him since his earliest years, and made him a King—what uncertain youth *wouldn't* believe Merlin's voice to be the ultimate gospel?

"You've said yourself that Merlin's insight wasn't perfect," I said. "What about my loyalty? All the time we spent together?" I pointed to the sword at his hip. "I didn't speak a word about Excalibur, which would have been the quickest way to betray you."

Arthur glanced down at the sword in doubt, returning his hand to its sun-shot hilt.

"Merlin manipulated you," I continued. "They were his words on the Royal Decree, and he made you believe them. I understand why you held faith in him, but what about your faith in me?"

My brother's shoulders had dropped as our conversation wore on, but he drew them back now, almost imperceptibly, regaining the tall, cool poise of a king.

"Morgan," he said, "if you think Merlin spun me a tale and I simply believed it, then you are gravely mistaken. He was my chosen adviser, not my master. I have a mind and eyes of my own. Writing the Royal Decree against you was the hardest thing I have ever done, but they were my words."

I didn't believe him, but saw that it would take more for my brother to condemn his dear, dead sorcerer. "Then you admit sending Yvain away was *your* doing?" I said.

"You gave me little choice," he said. "He had been with King Urien, safe and well, and you were nowhere to be found. I could not argue to bring him to Camelot when he had a loving father who wanted to keep him in his homeland."

His admission was worse than a thousand Royal Decrees. "My son was the one promise you made me, and now he forever belongs to Gore," I said. "I am your *sister*, Arthur. We had a bond that was strong and good. It should never have been so easy for other forces to come between us."

Arthur sighed; it wasn't without regret but still felt like a knife wound.

"It's not so simple, Morgan, as you well know," he said. "There were many things that contributed to my concern for you. Before you left for Merlin's you were unsettled, increasingly impatient with the ways of court. Guinevere expressed serious misgivings after the way you began treating her. I couldn't ignore a prophecy and all I had observed just because you were my sister. Those are the very times a High King *must* be impartial. I would send my own wife to trial to uphold the integrity I have promised this realm."

I made a sound of disbelief, but he didn't waver. "You told me that I should be different from Uther Pendragon. This is one way I have tried. And why I did not come here to churn up the past."

"Why *did* you come here?" I asked.

"Because the future is all that matters." Like a sudden sunbeam, his face softened, and he held out peaceable hands. "You're right that our bond has always been strong, Morgan, and we were so close to our zenith. We can find our way there again."

His beseeching tone moved me despite myself. "What are you saying?"

"Come back to Camelot," he said. "We could be what we once were. Brother and sister. High King and adviser. You and me."

This I had not expected, but I could always read him up close. He had never known how to lie to me and wasn't lying now. Tentatively, I stepped outside the protective veil.

"How can you say that, after all that's happened?" I asked. "You said that you meant everything on the Royal Decree, that Merlin wouldn't lie. If you believe I am capable of those things, why would you wish for my return?"

"It is . . . complicated," Arthur said. "To his mind, I think Merlin was telling the truth. He didn't *lie*, but he doesn't know you as I do. Therefore, perhaps his interpretation of the prophecy was not with full clarity. You still learned from him, knowledge I asked you to seek, and maybe, with endeavour, that could be a boon, not a curse. For the sake of the closeness we once had, I feel it is our duty to try."

He offered his hand and I took it, as if preparing to swear an oath. He put the other on my shoulder, as he used to do, casting his silver-grey gaze upon me, and it was as if we had never been apart at all.

"Morgan," he said. "I need you. I need your wisdom, your skills, now more than ever. There will be forgiveness if you agree to take the first steps towards earning it."

My spirits lifted, then stilled. "*Earning* forgiveness?"

"Yes, of course," Arthur said. "I believe it's possible, with some effort, and the concessions you would make. There would still have to be a legal process of sorts, but if you repent wholly, then I can make the argument that I am showing you mercy."

I pulled my hand out of his. "*Mercy? For what?*"

"Come now, you've been no saint," he said. "It is necessary for you to face judgment for the sake of the court. I am the King—I cannot be perceived to be wrong. If I simply welcomed you back to Camelot without your utmost repentance, I would make myself look weak at best. It would sully Merlin's memory as my adviser, and the great service he did to my Crown. The realm, my authority, would never recover."

I stepped back in silent horror, dropping his hand from my shoulder. He regarded me with a puzzled brow. "Sister, I am showing you considerable favour. What were you expecting?"

Somewhere within my outrage, I found my voice. "Far more than throwing myself upon the blade of justice for the sake of Merlin's reputation," I exclaimed. "First of all, I would expect the Royal Decree to be publicly renounced. Thereafter, I would expect not only my life at Camelot back, but what I was promised—a fair arrangement for my son, a seat on your council, time away from court to live freely. Nothing less than complete exoneration is due to me."

"I don't think you understand," Arthur said. "What you speak of is impossible. Remember, yours is the reputation that needs to be saved, mine the regard to earn back. It is for *me* to forgive *you*."

I bristled. "I've done nothing wrong."

"Then prove yourself. Return to Camelot and do public penance. Show the world you are loyal and uncorrupted, earn my trust, and I will see where we stand."

"You'll see?" I exclaimed. "You should trust me because I am loyal and always have been. Never can I accept these terms."

He bridled, his tone sharpening. "If you do not, I will have no choice but to believe in your guilt, that Merlin's every word and his prophecy are true. This is not a negotiation—it is an olive branch. Be careful not to snap it in half."

"Believe what you wish," I shot back. "You always have, in truth. Everything has always been entirely on your terms, no matter how much you preach fairness."

"Morgan, this is not a game," Arthur warned. "If you refuse me, it is exile."

I nodded, my eyes fixed on his. "Then I choose exile."

My brother recoiled, staring as if he could not believe my temerity.

"My God, what a fool you are," he said. "Do you understand what you have done? Exile is serious, and permanent. It is a death sentence, but with no relief. Camelot, myself, everything you once had will be closed off to you forever. You must never set foot in any court of mine again, nor may you move unchecked through my kingdom."

His tone of authority flashed fire up my neck. "You can keep Camelot. The entire place is fuelled on lies and hypocrisy, and I want none of it. Nor will you tell me what I can and cannot do. If I wished, I could walk into your precious court, lay it to bloody waste and run this country without breaking stride. You'd do well to remember that."

Arthur's eyes turned winter cold. "Merlin was right," he said. "This power he gave you has twisted your soul to darkness. Thank God I trusted him—without his intervention, you would have destroyed this realm."

"Your sorcerer gave me *nothing*. Merlin did not own knowledge, nor control who uses it and how." I moved forwards, pointing at him in furious emphasis. "*I* learned the power I hold, and it's mine. If you believe I am corrupted, maybe take caution. Your deadly prophecy might yet come to pass."

In a rapid flash, Arthur drew Excalibur, blade dazzling with its internal light. "Enough of this. You are an Enemy to the Crown, and will come with me."

Before he could charge, I whipped my hand and sent a spark of friction through the air, cracking against his arm like a bolt of lightning. Arthur stumbled backwards, staring at the scorch on his grey silk, then up at me in incandescent horror.

I stepped back into the silvery protection of my charms. "Put your sword away, *brother*. You have no power here."

I raised my hand again and he recoiled, though Excalibur held firm.

"Morgan, I'm warning you," he said.

"This country deserves better," I replied, and strode out of the hawthorn grove without looking back.

It was four peaceful years before I heard of Camelot again.

43

SINCE WE SETTLED there, Fair Guard had held many a feast day celebration for those who resided within the valley, which, as the household had grown and the repair work on buildings flourished, had become quite a merry crowd. However, no event was so great or anticipated as the feast we had revived to honour Midsummer's Eve.

By our fourth summer solstice, Alys was as good as Sir Kay at planning a revel, and just as strict. She and Tressa had worked us hard for days before, until the grassy square behind the dining hall looked like a fairy glen from an ancient tale. Long tables and benches ran alongside the spring, under arbours hanging with high-scented wild-flowers and berry branches meant for plucking at leisure.

By late afternoon, we were almost ready. I was standing by Alys's designated worktable, tying a series of painted lanterns to a rope and admiring Accolon as he carried out the last bench across his shoulder. He swung it down onto the grass opposite me and smiled, pushing rolled shirt sleeves up his forearms.

"I've been instructed to hang the lanterns," he said. "Once—in Lady Alys's words—you have eventually stopped toying with them."

"She gets stricter every year," I said, slipping into his arms. "Can you believe it's this time again? It's gone so quickly."

He drew me in for a kiss, smelling like beeswax from carrying furniture all afternoon. "Four years since our first Midsummer's

Eve feast," he mused, "and six since we were reunited in Camelot."

It was strange to hear mention of Camelot; we spoke so little of it since my break with Arthur, its existence felt like a faraway concept.

"Which particular reunion?" I said.

His grin was mildly devious. "The true one—our storm. If you don't count all of the furious confrontations, inadvisable deal-making and tournament distractions."

"Sometimes, I think that was part of it," I said wryly. "It feels so long ago, and barely a moment at the same time."

"I, for one," he said, "will always be thankful that my ambitious cousin persuaded me to board that ship across the Channel."

His tone was light, but it reminded me that he wasn't without his private losses. He missed Sir Manassen, I knew—the only family left to him that he cared for—but he had thrown everything over for my sake and never looked back.

"He wasn't wrong," I said. "I have been trouble for you. Do you mind it?"

"Haven't you ever thought," he said softly, "that perhaps I love you more for it?"

I put my hand to his cheek, warmed by the pleasure of looking upon his face. "These past few years," I said, "despite everything—exile, our losses, the rest of it—I have been happy, because you made it so."

"So have I, *mon coeur*." Still smiling, he kissed me with abandon, ignoring the bawdy whistles of others. After a while, we glanced up to see a stern Alys marching towards us. "Speaking of trouble," he said, "I'll be in it deeply if I don't string Lady Alys's lights."

"Make haste," I said. "Or we'll never persuade her to enjoy the evening."

Accolon kissed my palm and jogged to his duties. I watched him climb gracefully atop a bench to put up the lanterns, my heart full of the rare, exquisite feeling where everything seems, for a fleeting moment, as if it cannot be anything other than good.

By some miracle, when the festivities began and dusk fell the sensation lingered, imbuing the celebrations with a pure, irresistible joy. All were happy, every soul well fed on the huntsman's bounty, deep in their cups from Tressa's pyment and honey mead, the music melodic and raucous, the urge to dance unquenchable.

On the cusp of sunset, the entire household took to the green beside the spring to dance through the year's longest moment. Accolon swept me into a close hold, swinging me around and off the ground, as Alys and Tressa dance-stepped towards us, arms about one another, laughing and singing.

At the music's first bridge, Accolon pulled me to his hot chest for a kiss, then pressed his lips to my ear. "More wine," he said. "I'll be back."

He set off through the revellers, slapping backs and laughing as he passed. Alys and Tressa each grabbed one of my arms, and our trio skipped around in a clumsy circle, too tipsy to follow any rhythm.

As I slowed to gather my breath, I caught sight of Accolon at the wine table, a goblet in each hand, head bent to one of the grooms talking animatedly in his ear. Frowning, he put the cups down and they set off towards the house with a haste that fluttered uneasily in my gut. Untangling myself from the dance, I followed their path through the building and to the main doorway, where Accolon stood talking to the huntsman, the groom, and the former guard who now took care of the bird mews.

"Two horses are all we can see," said the falconer. "Mounted, but it's too dim to discern much more."

"*Alors*, go forth," Accolon replied. "I'll be there in a moment."

They filed out onto the front green, leaving him behind. He paused, then strode to the fireplace, above which his horse-hilted longsword hung when he wasn't at tournaments. He lifted the weapon down and girded it to his belt with expert hands.

"Accolon," I called, and he spun around. "What's happening?"

"Riders have been spotted approaching the house. Possibly knights." He pulled the sword half out, checked the edge with his finger, then slid it home.

"It'll be someone straying from the road," I said. "You know no one can get through the protective charms with ill intent."

"It's just strange—everyone we know is here," he said. "But you're right, I know." I glanced down at the sword and he smiled ruefully. "Old battlefield habits."

I put a hand on his elbow to bring him back to the music and joy, but urgent shouts from outside pulled him away. His sword rang with speed as he drew it.

I dashed out behind him onto the daisy-speckled green. Twenty yards away, the men stood in front of a large grey courser and a pack-pony strapped with a lance and armour. There was only one rider after all, his gold spurs glittering in the falconer's torchlight.

"If you would listen to me," the knight said irritably. "I demand to see your lord."

The voice brought an unpleasant prickle of familiarity, but Accolon was already sheathing his sword.

"Manassen!" he exclaimed. "What are you doing here?"

Sir Manassen of Gaul's stern face unfolded into a smile. "Accolon, *Dieu merci!* I thought I'd never find you."

He dismounted and Accolon pulled him into a brotherly embrace. "Sweet Lord, how long has it been?"

"Too long, cousin." Sir Manassen clapped Accolon's back, then beheld him at arm's length. "Still in fine fettle I see."

Accolon laughed and turned to the men standing by. "Gentlemen, this is Sir Manassen of Gaul, my cousin and friend to *Belle Garde*. Please, rejoin the festivities with my gratitude."

With murmurs of welcome, the household members strode back

towards the revels. Sir Manassen looked up at the building and its environs. He still hadn't seen me.

"What is this place? It seems you live quite the life of leisure."

"Pleasures untold, cousin." Accolon put a hand on his shoulder and guided him to where I stood. "You remember Lady Morgan. This is our home."

Those tender words—*our home*—warmed me to generosity of spirit. I stepped forwards, offering up my hand in greeting.

Sir Manassen ignored it. "I should have known," he scoffed.

My hand clenched as I withdrew. "How did you find us, Sir Knight?" I said.

He spoke directly to Accolon. "At the tournament near Caerleon. I saw you ride, saw you win."

Accolon frowned. "But I took all precautions towards anonymity. You've never seen my armour, or the destrier I rode."

"I'd know the way you sit at tilt anywhere, on any horse," he replied. "I withdrew my name from the competition the moment you felled your first challenger."

Of course, I thought. *How did I not see that was a risk?*

"When you left, I followed," Manassen continued. "I lost you when you entered the forest proper, but you carried little, so I knew you couldn't be travelling far. I tried every inn and manor until I arrived here."

"And here you are," I said. "One has to wonder why."

He regarded me blandly. "If I'd known *you* were here, my lady, I'd have found some better way of springing this good man from your ensnarement."

I started forwards, ready to throw him off my land, but Accolon moved first, blocking the space between us.

"Manassen, that's *enough*," he said in a low, serious voice. "Morgan is quite capable of defending herself, but your ill nature is my cross to bear, not hers. So listen well—I am here because it is where I want to be, with the woman I love. I am happy, I am whole, and this is my home for the rest of my life."

"Cousin, I didn't—" Sir Manassen began.

"I'm not seeking your approval, so don't struggle to give it," Accolon cut in. "But I will have your civility. To welcome you as a guest would give me great pleasure, but that depends entirely on Morgan's grace. If you cannot show her the respect she deserves, then I will throw you out of her sight myself."

Sir Manassen stiffened, his only movement the dip and rise of his Adam's apple. He made an awkward bow.

"I apologize, Lady Morgan, for my rudeness, and beg mercy of your honour. Perhaps we could begin again."

I regarded him coolly. His intentions were pure, or he would not have found his way through the protective charms, but something still festered under his hard composure. However, Accolon's joy at seeing him meant that, much as I wanted to, I couldn't banish Sir Manassen back into the night.

"Very well," I said. "I accept your apology and extend our hospitality for as long as you need."

"I am obliged to you, my lady." Sir Manassen offered me a nod of unconvincing deference and turned to gather his horse.

Accolon smiled at me with such unrestrained happiness it almost drowned out the scratching of my unease. "Thank you," he said, taking my face in his hands and kissing me, still tasting of sweet wine. I thought of our two goblets, abandoned on the feast table.

It would be the last we poured out that night. Sir Manassen did not condescend to attend the celebration, nor was he left to rest, and when I woke the next morning after falling exhausted into an empty bed, the warm body against mine was missing and the bedsheets cold, and Accolon hadn't returned to me at all.

44

THEY SPENT THE entire next day together, Accolon showing Sir Manassen around the manor, the stables and kennels, his horses and the bloodlines he was developing there. In the afternoon, they took a pair of young destriers and went to the tilt meadow, running soft charges with Robin keeping score. I watched them from my study balcony, showing off, pulling tricks with the quintain and making one another laugh like they were barely past the age of majority.

I didn't begrudge Accolon time with his cousin, but a tiny, dark part of me never stopped wondering why Sir Manassen had come, and how long he would stay. Loath to lose my Gaul for another evening while they reminisced, I arranged for a private dinner in a small chamber off the main dining hall.

Sir Manassen seemed surprised to have been summoned, his posture tense as we greeted one another. "My thanks for the invitation, Lady Morgan," he said, eyes avoidant.

"I thought you and I should speak, Sir Manassen," I said. "Host to guest."

Accolon followed behind, kissing me on the cheek. "Are you certain this is wise?" he murmured.

"No," I replied. "But we can weather it for one night. I'd like to know more of your cousin, and he should have a clearer view on me."

"As you wish," he said, pulling out my chair with his usual courtesy.

Bread and wine arrived first, and we raised our goblets in thanks for the food and the company. Other than that, we ate the first few courses largely in silence.

After the meat platters had been taken away, I called for the cups to be refilled and lifted mine. "I would personally like to welcome our guest, Sir Manassen, to our home. He has travelled far and wide and finally found us. Though you never explained *why* we have the pleasure of your company, good sir."

Our guest said nothing and drank long of his goblet.

"He wished to see me," Accolon said.

"Undoubtedly," I replied. "But the tournament where he saw you was two months ago. There aren't that many places to look between there and here."

Sir Manassen put his cup down with a thud. "I rode slowly, my lady."

"Morgan," Accolon said, "what are you suggesting?"

"Only that he could have arrived much quicker, so he either went somewhere else, or he was hesitating over some specific purpose that gave him pause."

Accolon made to protest, then looked at his cousin, who sat straight as a pikestaff. "Is she right?" he asked. "Is there a purpose for this visit beyond long absence?"

Sir Manassen held firm for a moment, nostrils flaring in irritation. "Yes," he conceded. "A serious purpose. But I would rather we speak of it alone, as brothers-in-arms should."

Accolon sat back, his expression pained. "Brothers-in-arms would not keep *any* matter concealed until now. Morgan can see where I am blind, it seems."

"Denounce me, if that's how you feel," Sir Manassen said. "This is only for your ears."

"If it's how I *feel*?" Accolon exclaimed. "All night I stayed up talking to you. All day we have been together. You had hours to speak to me alone, and you chose not to. Anything you have to say can be spoken before Morgan—the person I trust most."

Sir Manassen gave a contrite nod, offering me his brief, milk-souring glance of old. "Very well. Your knightly service is severely overdue. Whatever you are doing *here*, whatever *this*"—he gestured at us both—"is, you are still sworn to the High King."

"I'm aware of that," Accolon said quietly.

"Are you?" snapped Manassen. "Because from where I stand, it seems you are breaking your oath."

I took a sharp breath, ready to bite back. Accolon's hand slid over mine, urging restraint.

"Does King Arthur know Accolon is here?" I asked.

"No," Sir Manassen replied. "The court doesn't even know for certain where *you* are, Lady Morgan. They certainly don't know about your *entanglement*. The King would hardly wish for my cousin's return if he did."

"Where does he think I am?" Accolon asked.

"Still in Gaul, on various business. Ever since I realized the story you told *me* when you left was untrue, I've been pretending that I've had contact with you, and searching in the meantime."

Sir Manassen drew a deep breath, and when he released it, his whole body seemed to deflate.

"Accolon, *écoutes*," he said. "I am not here to question your life, but the situation is gaining attention. Your twelve-month quest and King Arthur's favour gained you indulgence in terms of service owed, but that was years ago. Your disappearance has been frequently mentioned at court. It may be that someone else comes looking for you."

"Let them," I retorted. "They'll never find us in a thousand years."

Sir Manassen regarded me as if I were mad—he had found us, after all.

"We're protected here by Morgan's skills," Accolon explained. "You only found us because you bear no ill intent."

"I do not," the knight agreed. "At least that proves it. In any case, the King said he wishes to see you at Camelot in all haste. To know you are well, and to discharge your forty days' service before he rides north in the autumn."

"He told you that himself?" I asked. It didn't sound like Arthur at all—errant knights or matters of petty fealty were generally managed through Sir Ector.

"Yes," Manassen said grimly. "He called me to his Council Room. It wasn't the first time he's asked about Accolon, and he always speaks in very fond terms, but he impressed on me how important it is that our code of honour is followed with fairness and diligence. He was personable enough, though he walked all around the table and never suggested we sit."

That *did* sound like Arthur—courteous and not unfriendly, but in full regal possession of his environment; a demeanour put to subtle but commanding use.

Accolon picked up the wine jug and poured for us all. "What else?" he asked.

"Nothing," Sir Manassen said dismissively. "That is the main thrust of it. I'm sure His Highness just misses your presence."

He took his goblet and his hand shook a little, quickly corrected.

"Cousin," Accolon warned, "do not lie to me again. *What else?*"

Sir Manassen sighed. "The King didn't *make* me find you, but he implied that if I didn't, our place in the Royal Court, the future we spent years securing . . ."

"My absence risks *your* standing in court?" Accolon said. "But you didn't know where I was! You've nothing to do with the choices I have made."

"Don't give it another thought," said his cousin. "You must only consider your own oaths, and my troubles are my own. I did not come here to sing you a sad song."

"Yet sing you did."

My voice cut through the room like a misericorde. I looked at Accolon, already deep in thought; he hadn't heard my words, much less felt their sharpness.

Sir Manassen raised his cup with barbed deference. "I'm sure you would see it that way, my lady, but by your own assertion, I could not have set foot on this property for ill purpose."

That I could not argue with; my charms were strong, constantly improving, and had been well tested over the years by those far less honourable than Accolon's virtuous cousin. But it was not Sir Manassen's sense of honour that concerned me.

*

"YOU WANT TO go, don't you? To Camelot."

I watched him pause from where I sat on the edge of our bed. Accolon shrugged his tunic onto a nearby chair and poured water into a washing bowl. I imagined the chill, tingling sensation as he submerged his hands. He always took it cold—it enlivened the soul, he said.

"No," he replied. "But I may have to."

"You *don't*, can't you see? We are safe here—no one is coming for you."

The water made a hollow sucking sound as he scooped up two palmfuls and splashed it against his face. Grabbing a towel, he dried himself with punishing roughness and turned to face me.

"I swore an oath. When I hear I'm at risk of breaking my code, of course I feel I should go."

"You feel that way because you have been raised to it." I stood up and went towards him. It was a warm night, but my bed robe felt cold against my skin, insufficient, gooseflesh rising under the thin silk. "A King calls and you come running—a reaction drummed into your bones since childhood. The system is designed to make you obey."

"It's more than that," he said. "I was a free lance and chose to kneel to a lord I believed in. I did not take it lightly, and to fail in duty is to fail in—"

"Do not dare say 'honour,'" I said. "The meaning of honour sits far outside the demands of kings. Whatever we are told, they do not get to dictate what is inside a true heart."

The last word caught on my breath and he came to me at once, closing the space between us.

"I know, I know," he said, his hand at my cheek. "And my heart is here, with you. But the honour of fealty is different—it *is* dictated, and has tenets that I swore to. Regardless, you heard Manassen. His future is at risk if I don't go."

I pulled away from his touch. "So you won't listen to me, but you'll take up your cousin's cause when he didn't even ask for help?"

"He never would, and that is precisely when he needs help," Accolon said. "I chose this life of secret exile, not him, and he shouldn't face the consequences. It cannot be true-hearted honour to let a loved one suffer for my actions."

"Even if it puts you in danger? The Royal Court is filled with serpents. There will be pressure, gossip, explanations expected."

"I can handle the court," he said. "No one knows where I've been or with whom. Besides, Manassen would never advise me to walk into a snake pit. All he has done our entire lives is protect me."

"That doesn't mean you owe him this."

Accolon's face fell to seriousness. "He saved my life, Morgan. You and he may never have a meeting of minds, but Manassen has done more for me than I can ever repay. My oath to King Arthur is one thing, but if my cousin needs my help, then he must have it."

I said nothing, doomed to understand him completely while wishing he would fight harder against his good nature, his honour, the love outside that which he held for me alone.

Accolon sighed, putting his arms around my waist. His forehead brushed mine, warm skin and cool damp hair, smelling of fresh water. I let him rest there, watching his eyes close, absorbing his touch.

"Don't go," I said. "Stay with me."

His eyes opened again, midnight in the low light of our chamber. He leaned in to kiss me, and I savoured the sweet heat of his mouth, the flush of desire I never failed to feel. There was much more to say, but it was already too late. He pulled me closer in hunger, and I cleaved to him with a rush that felt like relief. We knew what to do here, in the blur of hands and fabric and skin against skin, where there was only the two of us, safe within the certitude of our love. Here we were eternal, deathless, and all else ceased to be.

But I had made my plea, and he knew he must answer it.

45

ONE HOT, BRIGHT morning, a week after his cousin left us, I woke to find Accolon sitting on the edge of the bed, his head bowed into a shaft of early sunlight. I shifted closer, resting my chin in the valley between his shoulder and neck. He smelled like sleep and sun, but his back was cool, as if he had been up for a long time.

He sighed and said, "I must cut my hair," and I knew he was leaving that day.

I pressed my lips to his skin, shutting my eyes tight against the moment, its inevitability, everything that would come next. No matter his claims of indecision, the long hours we spent up at our lake, torn between desire and argument; no matter how endless we made the nights or how hard we loved, they had only ever been the intervening days between Midsummer's Eve and when Accolon would return to Camelot.

At length, I lifted my head and said, "I'll do it for you."

I fetched a brushing stool and shears, and he sat facing away, sun casting white streaks over his shining hair. I ran my hands through it, luxuriating in its sleek, careless length, spreading it loose above the wing points of his shoulder blades. The first cut made a definitive *thunk*, too loud in the stillness of the room. A cascade of darkness fell softly between my feet, then again, as I cut, cut, cut it all away.

"It's only forty days," Accolon said into my silence. "There will hardly be time for you to miss me."

I was glad he couldn't see how much the thought hurt. "I miss you when you're gone for a day. Then there's forty days next year, and the year after that, and so on forever. You will always owe service."

It quietened him into thoughtfulness, and I moved to his front. He studied my face as I trimmed what was left, the court-appropriate, much-admired knight emerging at my hands, almost as I had seen him again all those years ago when we were at odds, then reunited, but kept apart by everything that he would soon go cantering back to.

"I swore to it, and must do right by my cousin," he said, though he sounded unconvinced. "I will bring you news of court."

"I don't care about the cursed court," I said. "I'm happy with everything we have. With you. My one wish is to never have to think of Camelot ever again."

He took the shears away and pulled me between his knees, threading his fingers through mine, the way he had since we were first together at Tintagel. His touch wove into my blood as yearning. Forty days was far too long.

He tilted his head up, eyes dark and serious. "Know that I would give it up if I could. If there were any way to break free of my oath without repercussions, and ensure Manassen's future, I would renounce my links to the court and not look back."

"Would you?" I said.

"In a heartbeat," he replied. "But we cannot waste our lives on impossibilities."

Wordlessly, I wrapped my arms around him, holding his head to my shuddering body, his strength, his embrace about my waist bearing me up until there was no more time and he had to prise himself away.

"I have to get dressed," he said. "And gather my things, since I know you disdain packing too much to help."

Calmed by his jesting tone, I let him go. He kissed me once, deeply, and rose. I watched him vanish into the dressing room, fear and love fluttering in my chest like birds chased from a tree, and not a thing I could do to prevent the day's razor-sharp moment from arriving.

*

NO HORSE AWAITED him at the main door, but Alys and Tressa did. We were the only ones in the household who knew that this wasn't the same as riding out anonymously to a tournament and returning with prizes and tall tales.

"Where's Robin with your horses?" I asked.

"At the stables," Accolon said. "I thought I'd walk along the riverbank to take the morning air, then ride from there."

I smiled in gratitude; he knew I had never been able to bear watching him ride away with his armour strapped across the saddle, and the thought of where he was going this time made it impossible.

He turned to Tressa. "Be sure to have that apple press fixed for when I return. We'll spend the autumn making cider like they do in *Normandie*."

Tressa nodded with her usual fond stoicism, and he barely had time to kiss both of her cheeks before Alys was there, throwing her arms around his neck like he was her long-lost brother.

"Take this," she said, pressing a small leather satchel into his hands. "There's ointment for cuts or bruises, bath herbs for sore muscles, a few vials of my best tincture for if you take too much wine. But *don't* take too much wine and then ride. And some of that tisane mixture you like. I've labelled them all so . . ."

Tears stole the rest of her words and she swiped at them, flushing ferociously, as if caught in the act of finally liking him.

He regarded her with unconcealed affection. "Lady Alys, who takes better care of me than you? Thank you. I will come back twice as fit because of your great skill."

Alys and Tressa embraced him again, then melted back into the house, leaving Accolon and me standing on the front green, morning sky rising blue and endless behind him.

"It's time, then," I said. "I would walk part of the way with you, but . . ."

"*Non, mon coeur.*" He put his arms around my waist and pulled me close, our bodies merging in perfect unity as always, two halves of one whole. "Stay here. Think of it as me going to the stables like any other morning. Then, when I return, I will walk back up the riverbank and into your arms, and it will feel as if I were never gone at all."

"It won't feel like that, not for a moment," I said. "Please, be safe."

"Don't worry. You know my reputation." He smiled in his slow, charming way and patted his sword. "With this, and Lady Alys's remedies, I am invincible."

Invincible: the word echoed in my mind. Before I knew why, I was exhorting him to wait and flying up the steps to my study, then back down again to greet his puzzled look.

"Take this," I said breathlessly, pushing Excalibur's scabbard into his hands. "Put your sword in it, hang it on your belt, and go nowhere without it. Promise me, Accolon—swear you will keep the scabbard close."

"I promise," he said, gathering my hard-breathing body against his chest. "Anything for you."

"Good." I reached up to kiss him again, tasting the smile on his lips. "I love you. So much—too much. Now go, quickly, before I stop you."

"I love you," he said. "Though it can never be too much. *Au revoir*, Morgan. Until we meet again."

His warmth left me, a fine hand trailing through my loose hair as he went, his smile loving and beautiful and all it could be. I watched him walk along the riverbank with long, graceful strides, his face tilted up to the sun, pure light anointing his striking bones.

When I could see him no longer, I returned to our empty bed-chamber and swept up his shorn hair, clasping a long, ash-dark lock to my heart and sending up a prayer in the name of Sir Accolon of Gaul.

46

THOUGH ACCOLON HAD said I should keep company and not shut myself away with my agitated thoughts, I spent a few days in complete solitude in my study, aside from his dog, uninvited, watching mournfully from the doorway. Every time I returned from downstairs to retrieve the food left for me, she lifted her head from her paws as if he might be behind me, before laying her chin down on the floor again, her grief vaguely accusatory.

"You're not the only one who misses him, you know," I told her stiffly on the fourth day. I could not speak to her as he could, with his easy assumption that she understood. The brachet looked up from under hooded eyes and gave a thin whine. I sighed and clicked my fingers. "Come on. *Avec moi.*"

The hound reluctantly got to her feet, padding at my heels through the echoing house. I walked her along the riverbank as he would, but with an air of awkward politeness between us, like a pair of acquaintances who knew each other only due to their bond with one person. The thought struck as ridiculous; if Accolon ever found out about my lapse into sympathy with his canine companion, I would never hear the end of it.

"Company, that's what you need," I said. "Other animals."

The stableyard was quiet, the lads and grown hounds joining the huntsman in the woods. A few of the brachet's younger descendants were roaming the courtyard, some wrestling, or harassing the stable cat hissing from a high sill, and another pair lying flat out in a patch of sun. The brachet jogged off to greet them, tail waving.

A contented familiar whistle echoed from somewhere within. Seeking it, I promptly bumped into Robin on his way out of the main stalls. A box fell from his hands, scattering various grooming implements.

"Lady Morgan, I'm very sorry," he said. "I didn't expect you."

He stooped, gathering up horse brushes, and I knelt to help him. "I expected you even less," I said. "Shouldn't you be with Sir Accolon?"

Robin frowned with understandable confusion; Accolon had left days ago, after all, and he had probably been as much around the house as anyone. "Er, no, my lady."

"Why not? You're his squire."

He retrieved the last hoof pick and placed the box on a nearby sill, then offered me a kerchief to dust off my hands. "I wanted to go, my lady, but the day before he left, Sir Accolon came to the stables and said he would rather I stay. When I asked why, he said, '*Alors*, who else would I trust to oversee the horses?'"

To hear Accolon's direct words was a momentary comfort. I imagined him speaking them, brisk and easy, never hinting at whatever serious reason he must have had.

"It makes sense he wanted you here as his proxy," I replied.

"I will do my best, my lady. All I want is to make him proud, but when he said I couldn't go with him . . ." Robin ducked his head, sinking down on a hay crate. "My first thought was that there was something wrong. I don't know why—it seemed strange he wished to go alone. I told him I was worried for him—that we all were."

"What did he say?" I asked.

"We were in the stable, next to his chestnut travelling horse," he said, eyes softening with memory. "He put one hand on the horse's nose and the other on my forearm, how he does when I'm supposed to listen. He said, 'Robin, tell the household not to worry about me, or anything at all, because they are under the care of Lady le Fay. When I leave, she will brood alone for a few days, but know she is there and is everything you need.'"

Of course Accolon knew exactly what I would do, despite his advice, and his deep, accepting knowledge of me made me miss him so powerfully for a moment that I couldn't speak.

At length I said, "Lady who?"

Robin stared at me in alarm. "I'm sorry, my lady. I forgot you didn't know. It's just something I . . . we . . ." He took a deep breath, crimson to the roots of his pale-red hair. "Lady le Fay. It's what the household calls you. It's a term of affection, upon my honour."

I laughed. "Then I am grateful. Where does it come from?"

He still looked stricken, so I placed an encouraging hand on his arm, as was Accolon's way. "You can tell me. Please."

He relaxed under my touch and smiled. "When I broke my leg and you healed me, some believed it was God's plan—the horse kick—and there was no right to fix me beyond the will of the Lord. I couldn't have explained what you'd done if I wanted to, but there were whispers, suspicions. A few said you might be a witch. I'm so sorry to even *say* it, my lady."

"Oh, Robin!" I smiled and squeezed his hand. "So what if I am?"

"It shames me to admit it now, but at the time I was afraid. I feel awful because you've always been so kind to me, but back then, I was half-terrified I was cursed."

"It's all right," I said. "You were a child, and there were a lot of whispers about me in Camelot. Still are, I assume."

He hung his head, shaking it at himself. "I should have known better. And when Sir Accolon came to see me, I . . . I told him. All he did was ask me about my leg, and I burst into tears like a baby and confessed that though I was so happy I was fixed and could maybe be a squire one day, perhaps I was doomed to suffer some worse punishment because I had been healed by . . . well, you know."

"A witch," I supplied with a smile.

"Yes," Robin said guiltily. "But right away, before I'd even stopped crying, Sir Accolon asked if he could tell me a secret, and that's when he said it. He told me that you were special, yes, but to think of you more as *une fay*—a woman of great skill, with knowledge vast and well earned, and a part of her that is wondrous. He told me that nothing you did could ever be cursed—it just . . . is. That it's a gift we are lucky you share. He said you were the cleverest person he'd ever met, and deserved the utmost respect, never fear."

Robin sat straighter. "He made it all make sense and gave me back the happiness I first felt when you healed me. You saved my life, and he told me to believe in it."

We sat in silence for a short while, Robin contemplating a time that for him felt so long ago, and for me felt like no time at all. Accolon's absence, the weight that I had been holding off for days with solitude and silence, all at once became tangible, settling across me like a thundercloud. But storms had always been part of our strength.

"And the name?" I asked.

"The next time he saw me," Robin continued, "he asked if I had seen Lady le Fay—so I thought. Later I learned I got his language slightly wrong, but he never corrected me because it was something we shared. After that, it became how Sir Accolon spoke of you. When he brought me to Fair Guard, the household heard it, and they had their own wondrous stories of you—a time with the river they speak of?—and the name stuck."

He blushed even deeper and ran a hand through his curls. "I hope my lady doesn't mind. But it was Sir Accolon who gave it to you, and we all use it in fondness, loyalty and great respect."

My heart felt like it had grown with his every word. "How could I mind such a thing as that?"

He smiled in relief. "It means we know you protect us, that you care about Fair Guard and our happiness. Most of all, it means we believe, as Sir Accolon always has, that you can do anything."

The thought of Accolon's undying faith hit as a sudden, fierce injustice. His forty days had barely begun; how would I last, this year and hereafter, knowing where he was and that he would prefer to be at home? If I could do anything, surely I could fix this? With the scabbard I had kept him safe, but there must be a way to set us both free.

The scabbard. That was the answer—the one thing Arthur wanted that he didn't know he lacked. For its return, he would do anything.

I would follow my Gaul and retrieve Excalibur's missing piece, then make one final deal with my brother: release Accolon from service without prejudice, assure Sir Manassen's place in court, and take the Crown's iron-clad threats off my existence if I swore never to cross his path again.

Swiftly, I rose, Robin following automatically.

"Ready the horses and gather the household," I told him. "It's time for me to return to Camelot."

"Of course, my lady."

We nodded at one another in reassurance, then I moved off in the direction of the house. Pausing, I turned back to see Robin watching me with a face of wonder.

"Morgan le Fay," I said. "It has a certain ring to it."

47

CAMELOT SEEMED TO have grown in stature—its walls more imposing, the cathedral spires crowded and ornate, the castle's towers and turrets reaching even higher into the sky. Its gold sheen was almost blinding, endlessly numerous windows glinting in the high summer sun like shards of fire and ice. Dragons leapt from walls and flagpoles, blood red and sharp-toothed.

I had left Alys, Tressa, Robin and the rest in a sheltered glen a mile beyond the city, new charms strung through the trees like winter spiderwebs. In my absence, the protective veil around Fair Guard would have faded, so I had brought as many of the household as possible for safety's sake. They were primed to keep comfortable but stay alert, given I had no idea how my arrival in court would be received.

The castle's Entrance Hall was a towering, circular atrium lined with stained glass, coloured sunlight cascading down onto another enormous dragon, tiled into the polished floor. Unusually, the hall was almost empty, containing only red-and-white liveried guards. I recognized none of them and fortunately it was mutual; within moments, a young man holding a polished pikestaff had informed me that the court was assembled in the Throne Room, and accompanied me there without qualm.

The huge gold-studded doors to the Throne Room stood open, framing a wall of well-dressed courtiers: wide-shouldered knights devoid of weapons but girded with wealth; silk-clad lords and clergy; ladies trussed and embroidered, murmuring in low, conspiratorial tones. The guard gave my name to a herald before marching back off to his sleepy patrol, and I wondered if he would ever know whom he had let slip through his idle net.

"The court presents Lady Morgan!" the herald announced.

My name sounded strange, even though I had requested it spoken that way, half-formed and somehow insufficient. Still, it had its effect. Every head in the room swivelled to behold my presence, especially those who had heard of me only in retrospect, with all the dark and terrible glory that had been stitched to my reputation. I raised a hand and pushed my hood down, causing several ladies to gasp.

"It's *her*," someone whispered.

"She has returned," said another.

"Lady Morgan, come forth to the throne!" a different herald called from the front of the room.

The crowd parted before me like bare skin under a blade. A reverent silence had fallen, but it was not long before the whispers took up, hissing through the air behind bejewelled hands. I caught it in snatches: the quick recounting of my past and pedigree; my marriage and the scandals therein; a long list of my suspected sins and crimes. Strings of lovers were hinted at, but to my relief, no one mentioned Accolon.

"You know, she is very learned," said one. "That's almost certainly what has led to this trouble."

"Her skills became corrupted. Lord only knows the darkness she contains."

In a way, it thrilled me: their fear, their awe, my dubious legend on wagging tongues, the worry that I held power dreadful enough to upend their entire world, when in fact their world was determined to destroy me. Let them talk, let them believe it; I would forge my own path over their gossiping bones.

"King Arthur loved his sister once," said another. "Until her unnatural ambitions led to betrayal. If he knew she was here now . . ."

I looked around, seeking the end of the sentence, but dead silence returned. In one startling movement, every person turned to the front of the room, like a church congregation awaiting God Himself, and I realized I had reached the dais. Stepping forwards, I took a deep breath, lifted my eyes, and braced myself to see my brother again.

A vast throne greeted my sight, gilded, dragon-carved and empty. Camelot was without its King.

A hundred questions sang out simultaneously—Where was he? Had he left upon hearing my name? Was this a trick?—when a flash of light on jewels caught in my consciousness.

The dais was far from unoccupied. Beside Arthur's forbidding chair, in the second, smaller throne, sat Queen Guinevere. She was swathed in gold brocade, except for the white ermine trim of her mantle, a dainty crown encircling her yellow hair; a queenly embodiment of the throne itself.

"Lady Morgan, Queen of Gore," she said. "How unexpected to see you at court. I do not have all day. Come forth."

I stalked closer to the dais. Sir Kay stood just behind her, his face so studiously expressionless it looked painful. He glanced at me, allowing a slight quirk in one corner of his mouth, then returned his gaze to the middle distance.

Guinevere shifted in her seat, pale-green eyes tracking my movements. Her chin tilted in anticipation of my deference and a surge of ire ran up the back of my neck. I regarded her haughtily and watched her realize I wouldn't be bowing or kneeling or anything of the sort. Her regal appraisal became a hard stare.

"What brings you before my throne?" she demanded.

"I've come to see my brother. I require an audience with him at once."

"That will not be possible," Guinevere replied. "The High King isn't holding court today. As you can see, I am sitting as Regent."

"Then I will speak with him in private," I said. "Tell him to expect me in his Great Chamber. He will not deny me."

Her laugh scattered across the room like broken glass. "Oh, Lady Morgan, what a way to attend a Royal Court! Giving orders, no courtesy about you, and all alone with no retinue. I heard you had fallen on hard times, but have you no pride?"

I couldn't tell if her mocking was strategic or personally indulgent, but it was all the same to me. "My lady must save her concern," I said blithely. "I have not known hardship, and my retinue is far from here. I would hardly condescend to have them set foot in a castle where the Regent herself is unwelcoming."

"That's a shame," Guinevere said. "If they are loyal subjects, they should not fear their High Queen, even if you do."

It was my turn to laugh. "*Fear you?* No, my lady. I don't fear anyone." I looked around the Throne Room, surveying the stricken crowd. "You've all heard of me, after all. I can feel it on the air—your discussions of my powers, the fervent speculation, the nightmares you've woken from thinking about what I can do. And it's mostly true—I could make you all grow pigs' tails, weave a gown that would poison the wearer in three heartbeats, or reduce this entire court to ashes with a flick of my wrist."

I flourished my arms wide, relishing the collective intake of breath. "Tell me, my lady Queen, what could I *possibly* have to fear from you?"

Guinevere flinched, and satisfaction flared in my blood like a sunset across water. Her youthful gleam had faded, hidden beneath the cloud I had brought, while I felt like the rain within, vital and relentless.

I assumed a more conciliatory look. "Of course, there'll be no need for my lingering here, provided I get what I came for—an audience with King Arthur."

"I told you, Lady Morgan, it's not possible." Guinevere sat straighter, emerald rings quivering as she gripped the arms of her throne. "My lord husband is on a hunting trip, unable to be summoned. He is expected back imminently, but I do not know when."

I glanced at Sir Kay, who gave an almost imperceptible nod. "Very well," I replied. "Then I'll wait."

The Queen huffed. "How? I'm sure you wouldn't condescend to stay here."

"I'll stomach it in the short term," I said.

I had no desire to reside in Camelot under Guinevere's authority; nor could I afford to be anywhere else until Arthur's return. I must be there the moment he arrived, so he could not seek to ignore or avoid me.

"There's no room," Guinevere said. "In truth, Lady Morgan, you may as well leave now. Given your past behaviour, it is highly unlikely the King will consent to seeing you, or consider it anything but an insult."

"My lady Queen?" Sir Kay said. "I beg your pardon, but I would advise that Your Highness should not *assume* what my lord King Arthur will consent to regarding this situation. Lady Morgan is his sister, with whom he once held a deep closeness. Isn't waiting for his word the most just and godly way to proceed?"

The Queen looked sourly up at the Seneschal. "Perhaps," she said. "Though I thought there was no room for—"

"There's no lack of suitable chambers, my lady," Sir Kay cut in. "Let me bear concern for the arrangements. We wouldn't want to cast a shadow over Camelot's hospitality, or the Crown's willingness to extend it. The High King would expect all protocols followed, as I'm sure Your Highness agrees."

Guinevere eyed the room and her subjects, still silent, in awe, but observing with a keen edge now. Even a High Queen long established— indeed *especially* her, still childless, never universally popular—faced scrutiny in the glare of her husband's reflected light.

"If that is your advice, Lord Seneschal, then I will heed you," she said tartly. "I hope for your sake my husband shares the same view when he returns."

"I commend my lady to God." Kay bowed and descended the dais without a hint of self-reproach, though by the time he reached me he had turned distinctly green at the gills.

"Come on," he hissed. "Before one of you unleashes all Hell."

He ushered me firmly from the room, whispers flying again in earnest as we passed. For Kay's sake, I resisted the temptation to demand they speak it to my face.

"Your former chambers are occupied," he said. "I'll put you in the East Gallery. It's pleasant, and far away from the Queen, which is safest."

"For *her*," I said, and he gave me a scolding look. I sighed in concession as we turned into a long gallery hung with tapestries of Troy in flames. "Thank you, Kay. I don't know why you did that, but I'm grateful."

"I don't know why I did it either," he said drily. "Maybe because of the look my lady mother gave me, or perhaps I don't believe you'd come here if it wasn't for something important. I hope I won't pay for my blind faith when Arthur returns. In the meantime, I'm trusting you not to cause trouble, Lady Morgan. My good name is at stake."

"Oh, you have a good name these days, Sir Kay?" I jested. "I had one, once."

"My God, then we are all doomed." Kay glanced at me sidelong. "It hasn't been the same here, you know. Since you left."

"For better or worse?"

"That, my lady, you will have to ask King Arthur himself. But if you want my opinion—and few people do—I believe it'll serve the two of you well to speak honestly. Though knowing how stubborn you both can be . . ."

Leaving the thought unfinished, he stopped to open a door, revealing a neat bedchamber with grapevines painted on the walls. "I'll assign a page for anything you may need. I don't advise wandering the castle, given your inauspicious reputation, but the Queen may well ask you to dine in the Great Hall this evening."

"Surely *not*," I exclaimed.

"I'd lay coin to it. After my little show in the Throne Room, she'll be at pains to demonstrate her queenly hospitality. And to perturb you, of course. But for God's sake, if she does, do not refuse. Go to your seat, eat your meal and do not utter so much as a squeak of unrest. If you want Arthur to meet with you, then you cannot give him a single cause not to."

I rolled my eyes, vexed at the thought that even I must now treat Arthur's formidable moods as one would a frightened horse.

Kay raised his eyebrows. "Don't look that way. This is Camelot—you know how things have to be."

"Is Arthur really on a hunting trip?" I asked.

"Yes, an informal jaunt. He rode out with Sir Accolon alone, though there was vague talk that others could join them. Our brother was in need of peace, and Sir Accolon puts him at ease. It's been over a week now. Longer than expected, but I'm sure they found some adventure and will be back soon."

"Good," I said, pleased that Accolon had recovered Arthur's favour, and because Kay had inadvertently answered a question I didn't know how to ask. "Thank you again, Kay. Truly."

He nodded, somewhat abashed, and bade me farewell. As he predicted, two bells later, a chamber girl knocked on my door with a forest-green gown in my size, saying that Queen Guinevere had invited me to dine in the Great Hall, and Her Royal Highness would not *for anything* take no for an answer.

48

"LADY MORGAN, A thousand welcomes."

Guinevere's warm tone was completely at odds with the frigid watchfulness in her eyes. She took hold of my elbows, planting a kiss on my cheek so dry and cold it would have made Judas seem sincere. A cluster of her women watched from the ladies' table, and I wondered what would happen if I pulled her into an embrace and called her "sister."

Sir Kay hovered nearby, observing our exchange. Behind him, Merlin's life candles still stood on their stands in a spiky wall, but darkened now, their wicks dead as the demon himself. There was less triumph in it than I had hoped for; the damage the sorcerer had wrought could never be undone.

Kay's eyes flashed in encouragement, so I smiled at the Queen, polite, accepting. "I am *honoured* by Your Highness's invitation."

My voice was not without edge, but Guinevere didn't seem to notice. She gestured to a chair at the end of High Table. "Please, do sit. There are a few faces I'm sure you'll be interested to see."

She glided off and I frowned at her retreating golden back. Despite Sir Kay's correct prediction, her taking such great pains to acknowledge me publicly was still strange. There was no need for her to try this hard, given we despised one another.

I sat in my allotted seat and surveyed the room. Sir Manassen was nowhere to be seen, but I didn't much care; he was the least of my plans. A wine page filled my goblet and I picked it up; the gold sides were engraved with images of Julius Ceasar, defying his wife's pleas to stay at home on the Ides of March, part of a set sent to Arthur by the Pope himself. I recalled the day my brother received them, our private meeting where he worried aloud that the gift was a bad omen, a warning of his fate.

I put the cup down without drinking and pushed it away.

"Temperance indeed? That isn't like you."

The voice was male, familiar, and accompanied by a looming shadow, huge across the table. Hatred flared deep within me, vicious and unforgotten. If I didn't look up, then it couldn't be true.

"What, no warm greeting?" he said.

In the end, the Devil's temptation proved too great. I raised my eyes to look upon King Urien of Gore.

He was still a magnificent brute, still undeniably handsome, frame broad and powerful and swathed in green-and-gold silk. His hair was glossy and teased as usual, chestnut beard tightly clipped along a hard jawline resisting the ravages of age. Not much had changed in him, but for the pointed white scars along the left side of his face, in the shape of the flames I had burned him with. Proof of my loathing, my vengeance, and the fact I had escaped him.

As I gazed upon my work, the scars shifted and my estranged husband smiled.

"My darling wife," Urien said smoothly, and sat down in the chair beside me as if we had never been apart.

I caught the clove scent of his beard oil and shock shot through my gut at his sudden proximity. *Why had no one thought to tell me he was here?*

Catching hold of my breath, I looked along High Table. The Queen sat among her favoured ladies, delicately peeling the shell from a boiled robin's egg. Sir Kay had been busy pointing pages in various directions, but now stood stock-still, arrested by the sight of me and my husband side by side. I stared at him in question, and he shook his head; not a single happening occurred in Camelot's household without his knowledge, but this had eluded him.

Urien reached for his goblet and raised it towards the thrones, drawing Guinevere's gaze. She nodded with only slight acceptance, but the subtle smile of triumph on her face was absolute. This was a punishment, a courtly test; a game I hadn't come to play but could not afford to lose.

I snatched up my cup and took a long drink.

Urien chuckled. "That's the Queen of Gore I know."

"Your Queen of Gore doesn't exist," I retorted. "Maybe she never did."

"Oh, you did, my Queen, much as you may try to forget." He reclined comfortably in his chair, tilting his body towards mine, his expensive scent once again filling my airways. "You were there in all your hunger, every time I wanted you. You pulled me close, you lay down for me, you cried out my name."

"And yet," I said, "never once was I thinking of you."

His self-satisfied smile dropped several notches, which pleased me, even if my assertion wasn't altogether true.

"If you say so, my lady," he said. "Regardless, I am still the only man who can lay claim to you. Do not forget that."

Suddenly, his hand pinned mine to the table, his fingers pushing between my knuckles. An ordinary marital gesture to the rest of the world, but his forceful presumption made my blood froth.

"You will tread carefully or know the consequences," I said, sending a flash of fire along the inside of my fingers. "Do not forget *that*."

Urien pulled away, cradling his scorched hand. "I should have known I would not find you changed. Though seeing you has lent an interest to proceedings. I find it an unexpected pleasure to look upon you again."

"I cannot say the same," I said in a bored voice. "Why are you here, Urien? Camelot is hardly where you belong."

He picked his goblet up and took a casual swig. "That's where you're wrong, my sweet. Since your departure I have frequented Camelot more and more, and the High King and I share a far greater regard than when your poison stood between us. Indeed, after your fall from grace, I believe he finally understood what I endured."

"So you say. Regardless, there's no justification for springing yourself on me like this. We have no reason to speak."

"That's not quite true, is it?" he said. "We are married, after all."

I snorted. "There's nothing that means less in this world than the lie that is our marriage."

I picked up my goblet and found it empty. Urien snapped his fingers for the wine page, placing my cup on the tray alongside his. The gesture of husbandly authority chafed, his every move shouting of possession, testing my promise to refrain from trouble.

He handed me my refilled cup. "So *you* say, my darling wife, but there are still ties that bind us. One I'm sure you would not deny."

He flourished a large hand into the softly lit depths of the Great Hall, towards a small table tucked beside a pillar. Keen-eyed women, kerchiefs ready at their belts, occupied most of the seats—nursemaids, sat amongst their young charges. Behind the pillar, a pair of boys were surreptitiously duelling with two long-handled spoons.

I recognized him immediately, and my heart took a freefall with nowhere to land.

"Yvain," I whispered, like a benediction.

He was both the child I had nursed, laughed with and held while he went to sleep, and also different—tall and long-limbed, his movements rangy and confident. I had marked his eighth birthday at his apple tree beside the lake; old enough now for cup-bearing, his own master-at-arms and the start of his knightly education.

His face still held the ghost of sweet babyhood, but had grown leaner, defined, the bones of his father prominent, but made finer by echoes of my mother, and therefore his High King uncle. His head of curls had softened into waves and been cut back, but retained the dark-gold shade from the day he was born. I could not see if his eyes were still mine.

"Yes, there he is. Our son." Urien's voice was brisk, but I could feel his focus on the side of my face. "What do you think of him?"

I knew it was manipulation, for some purpose I was not yet aware of, but I could not look away from my son, his newness and familiarity, the wondrous surprise of his movements and his radiant, playful joy.

"He's beautiful," I said.

"Impressive, isn't he?" he replied. "Strong, healthy and handsome. Charming beyond his years. The High King quite agrees. King Arthur has been a very diligent uncle, overseeing his education, speaking of his intention to make Yvain a great knight of Camelot. He has often praised the way Yvain is being brought up—with a constant, loving parent who has his best interests at heart."

I knew that wounding me was his intention, but still felt it in my abdomen like a poison arrow. "I should speak to him," I said. "I'm his mother. He needs to know I'm here."

I started up from my chair; Urien grabbed my wrist like a striking cat.

"Sit *down*," he ordered. "Good God, woman, what are you thinking? You cannot simply appear and declare you're his long-lost mother. He's a child—he will be upset, confused, overwhelmed. Do you wish to frighten your own son?"

His peacock eyes flashed with genuine concern, and somewhere in the annals of memory, I recalled Alys telling me that Urien was an undeniably good and careful father. *Even monsters have other faces,* she had said, and his protectiveness now, along with the sight of my thriving, happy son, did not contradict the claim.

"Of course I don't," I snapped. "So this is why you came here tonight—to taunt me with my son. That is the King of Gore *I* know."

He released my arm and sat back. "In truth, it was more of a test. To see if your reaction proved you worthy of Yvain even learning who you are. As it stands . . ."

"Do *not* tell me how it *stands*."

I shot up, not caring whether the meal was over, if Sir Kay was viewing me with concern, or if Guinevere was taking note of every move I made. It was all utterly meaningless until Arthur returned. "I know you, Urien. You were never going to let me do more than look at him."

"Don't be so sure," he replied. "I am a fair and reasonable man. If *you* tread carefully, and learn to behave in an appropriate manner, who can say—there may yet be an arrangement to be made between us."

Resisting the urge to cover him in wine, I took another longing glance at the children's table, hoping for one more glimpse of my son before I left. Yvain was seated with his back to me, still jostling his vanquished companion, his perfect profile barely visible in the shadows.

"And if I *don't* behave?" I asked.

Urien made a quick hooking gesture with his hand, and the nursemaids jumped up, ushering their charges out of the Great Hall, secreting Yvain away where I could not reach him.

"Do as you wish, my lady," he said. "Just remember which one of us holds the power."

49

I SLEPT LITTLE, disturbed by visions of Yvain and restless for news of Arthur, so I rose early and crossed the quiet Entrance Hall to the only place where I might not be unwelcome: the Seneschal's Great Chamber.

Sir Kay glanced up from behind his desk and gestured to a chair. I declined and he nodded, letting me pace around the room. Eventually, his quill ceased scratching and he cleared his throat.

"About last night," he said. "I'm sorry I was not able to warn you. I knew King Urien and your son were due. Your former rooms were being retained for them, which is why I didn't lodge you there, but they were unexpectedly early. Apparently, the Queen knew they had arrived and no one saw fit to inform me."

"I didn't think you'd kept it from me," I replied. "Guinevere obviously wanted my surprise to be pure."

Kay rubbed his chin, as he always did when reaching for diplomacy. "I assume King Urien went directly to the Queen because he had news of Arthur, and in the shortness of time before dinner she forgot to mention it."

"Safest to explain it thus," I said grimly. "How did Urien have news of Arthur?"

"He was on the hunting trip," Kay replied.

My entire body hollowed. "What?"

"He heard of the excursion on his way to court, sent Yvain to a liegeman's manor nearby, and joined them." Kay paused, looking thoughtful. "The news he brought was rather strange—he said their party got separated, so he collected Yvain and rode back to Camelot. Don't worry, Lady Morgan. I'm sure Arthur's return is—"

It was the last I heard; I was already charging out of the Seneschal's chamber and up a side stair. When I reached the familiar door, I burst in with the wrath of the Furies running through my blood.

"Where is he?" I screamed.

"Sweet Christ!" Urien reared up in shock. "What in all Hell are you doing here?"

I could not recall the answer, too consumed with white-hot fury, until I realized he was shielding something. A small, dark-gold head peered out from behind my husband's towering frame, his deep-blue eyes a mirror image.

Yvain.

He was even more beautiful close up, staring at me from under a creased brow that sang so much of my father it hit me in the chest. I moved towards him, arms outstretched, and my son shrank back, cowering once more behind his huge guardian.

Urien held out a warning hand. "Don't speak to him. Not a single word."

I couldn't if I tried, my entire purpose forgotten at the sight of my child. I stood mute as Urien knelt to his level, speaking with a gentleness I had never heard.

"Yvain, go and tell the nurse to arrange your riding habit," he said calmly. "It's a fine day—we will ride out and I'll show you the tilt field. Stay in your bedchamber until I come for you, yes?"

Yvain nodded, wary eyes flicking to me. Urien squeezed his shoulder. "Good boy," he said, planting a kiss on the top of his head. "I won't be long."

He ushered our son to the interior door and pulled it firmly shut, waiting several beats before rounding on me.

"God's blood, woman," he growled. "You have no right to come barrelling in here like a damned banshee. I ought to call for the guards."

The spell of my peace broke immediately. I charged towards him, spitting rage. "You won't get past me to summon anyone. Not until you answer my questions."

Urien's tremendous frame stopped me halfway. He gave me a long, seething look, which I met with equal intensity, and he spun away in exasperation. When he turned back, he had smoothed over his demeanour, and my battle-hungry body felt it as disappointment.

"You shouldn't alarm the child," he said sanctimoniously. "It's not a favourable impression for a mother to make. Not that he will ever know you as such, so far."

He took a turn about the room, and I tracked his movements carefully. The chamber had little changed: walls still sky blue and much the same furniture, including the rug where Yvain had taken his first steps, though Alys's loom was gone, along with Tressa's writing desk. The terrace door stood open, the scent of honeysuckle drifting in, sweet and evocative.

Urien noted my observation. "I hear these were once your chambers, yet Yvain had no familiarity with them. He doesn't remember his time with you at all."

He was keeping his distance, but had no real concept of how much danger he was in. My limbs itched to spring at him and scratch his tanned flesh to shreds, but to have me escorted away flailing and spitting was his aim, and I would not indulge him.

"You were on the hunting trip with Arthur," I said evenly. "My anger was because you didn't see fit to mention it last evening. I'm worried for him."

Urien gave me a probing look. "Your brother. I see. *He* is your concern. Why? I'd warrant he won't be happy to see you."

"You know nothing of our circumstances."

"I know more than you think, dear wife. In courtly terms, only your status as my Queen is currently preventing you from being locked in a dungeon."

"Lies, same as always," I said. "Even so, I'd rather be locked up in a dungeon than have my name uttered in the same breath as yours."

Urien's blue-green eyes flashed; I had gored him. "Locked up with your Gaul, no doubt," he snapped. "To await the adultery stake."

I tried not to stiffen. "What *can* you mean?"

"You know full well," he replied. "Your illicit Frenchman, so charming and adept. The 'he' you are truly looking for."

It had to be a trick. True, they had been in company, but Accolon was clever, careful. He would never expose us. "I have no earthly idea what you're talking about."

"Oh, spare me, woman," Urien said. "Your estranged brother isn't why you stormed in here spitting feathers like a harpy. Can you be sure your gallant knight never spoke a word to prove you were his conquest? Do you know nothing of men?"

I was sure Accolon had nothing whatsoever to prove, but to engage with Urien now was a dangerous game, the veil between anger and violence thinning by the moment.

"I've had enough of this." With the greatest restraint I had ever shown in my life, I put my back to him and headed for the door.

"A free lance, my Queen—really?" he called after me. "How quaint—like a washerwoman's favourite ballad. You know, I feel rather sorry for him. Your pauper paramour is so protective of you, and you immediately deny his existence. Brushed off like the streak of dirt he is—Sir Accolon of Gaul, your lover, your fool."

His laugh grated across my nerves. I charged back and thrust a finger in his face.

"You strike his name from your tongue and keep it that way. Sir Accolon of Gaul is a better knight, a better lover and a better man than you can *contemplate* being. You are not fit to breathe the same air as he. There—is that confession enough for you?"

Urien's face darkened with blood. His hand rose, straining to grab my neck and shake me into submission. And the blackest, bitterest parts of me wanted him to, so I could steeple my fingers against his chest and pull the breath out of his lungs until they collapsed.

Instead, he stepped back, rubbing a hand over his jaw.

"Don't bother confessing to what I already know," he sneered. "He is not so subtle, your arrogant bedfellow. Any word I tried to speak of you, he was there with some clever observation or argument to weaken my point. He almost had your credulous brother reconsidering his view on you, but it soon dawned on me where his eagerness was coming from. I can spot a man bewitched by bodily pleasure from a mile away."

"I swear to God, if you've brought your spurious accusations to Arthur—"

"I would never demean myself to speak of it," Urien interrupted. "Besides, the High King has been unsettled since his sorcerer's death. Suspicion dogs him, and he fears treachery at every turn. A private reminder in King Arthur's ear of your self-exile, and an explanation of the violence you perpetrated upon my face, and your lover leaping to your defence took on the cast of conspiracy. It was unfortunate our party got separated, or I would have offered to deal with the Frenchman myself."

"God's teeth, now I know you're lying!" I said. "On your *very best day*, you could not defeat Accolon in a battle of swords *or* bare hands. He would beat you bloody."

Urien's lip curled with disdain; I had speared him again, his endless vanities. "That's not what I meant. I am a *King*. I hardly need to condescend to a swordfight with an expensively dressed stablehand."

"Enough talk," I snapped. "Tell me where they are before I truly lose my temper. You remember how that can feel."

He covered a shudder with a look of contempt. "Despite your unnatural threats, I cannot. It's true that I lost them. A few nights ago, we were invited onto a luxurious boat, where there were women, drugged wine. All I remember is waking alone in the forest. I heard on my ride back that a duel would take place between two fine knights, so perhaps there's something in that."

"Drugged wine? Strange women on boats? Mysterious duels? A wild and unlikely tale. Tell the *truth*."

"Believe what you wish," Urien said. "What occurred in the forest is the least of your problems. When King Arthur finds you here, you will either have to account for what he may consider as traitorous, or burn at the adultery stake for the marital treason you have admitted to me. Unless . . ."

I regarded my husband closely, his hands loose at his sides, face calm now, unflustered. He did not believe he was lying, and my knowledge of Arthur's fraught mistrust, combined with our last confrontation and his formidable fury, made Urien's claim ring terribly true. Scabbard or not, Accolon and I would never gain our freedom if my brother believed I was acting against him.

"Unless *what?*" I said.

Urien smiled, a slow, fox-like expression of old. "I can prevent all of this, my lady Queen. Save your life."

"What the Devil do you mean?"

"Don't toy with me," he said. "You know what I mean. Return to Gore, our marriage, my bed. I will make no adultery complaint, and will smooth your way with the High King."

Of all the possibilities on God's earth, Urien's reply wasn't one I would have predicted in a thousand years. Shocked, I began to laugh, high-pitched and uncontrollable.

"Have you abandoned your senses?" I exclaimed. "We *have* no marriage, aside from in law. The last time we saw one another in Gore, you threatened to kill me and I swore I would kill you first."

Urien chuckled along with me, as if it were an amusing part of our familial history, rather than a set of violent, intrusive memories. It was the most we had ever laughed together in our entire union.

"This makes no sense," I said. "Why would you even suggest such a thing?"

His face fell abruptly to seriousness. "Because somehow, dear wife, I am still compelled by you. Never have I desired a woman as much as you, and God forgive me, that has not changed."

"No," I replied. "You just want to win. To retake possession of me and regain mastery over the woman who dared leave you."

"That's not what drives me," he said, but I had watched his demeanour change as I spoke, his shifting shoulders and heightened colour, eyes glazing as he imagined my words played out and wanting it all the more.

"I've confessed to loving another man," I said. "That I've been an adulteress for him *constantly* and you fail to compare in every way, yet you still want me as your wife?"

"You *are* my wife," Urien said. "Nothing but death can change that. All I want is for you to act as such. Is it so wrong?"

I suppressed the urge to start laughing again. "It isn't just wrong; it's twisted. Do those scars on your face mean nothing to you?"

Perhaps they didn't, I thought; my burning his face had done little to mar his good looks. His peers would have lauded his bravery and I doubted women had ceased to fall into his bed as a result. Why then did he want this?

As if hearing my thoughts, Urien said, "Do you really want to know what convinced me?"

"I'd be fascinated," I said drily.

"The night on the boat, in my sleep," he murmured, "I had a dream that I awoke in your bed, with you beside me. We were warm, unclothed, entwined, the crown of Gore around your head. I had never felt more satisfied. And when I returned to Camelot, you were here, as alluring as I had ever seen you. I thought surely it must be Fate."

In one lunge, he had hold of my waist and pulled me against him, one hand caressing my cheek. I froze, paralyzed by the sudden, rough intimacy of it.

"See," he said. "Even now you hesitate to resist."

His presumption melted my inaction. I shoved him hard and tore my body away.

"Dear God," I said. "You call a lascivious dream you had in a drugged haze *Fate?* You *despise* me, Urien. Not as much as I despise you, but still it is true. The only fate awaiting me in Gore is death at your hands."

"Kill King Arthur's sister? That would be foolhardy by anyone's standards. I'm sure you do not fear harm from me, given what you . . . can do." He gestured at my hands, the cords of his neck tensing. "In practical terms, you know I've always wanted you back, to restore Gore's image of unity, have more children. Returning to a godly path would certainly reinstate you in your brother's good graces. What's more, there's the true reward—you will regain a son."

Images of Yvain flew into my head: at the previous night's banquet, playful and confident; his stricken face when I had first charged in; the deep blue eyes that were mine but did not know me. His trusting nod to his father, which I felt within like a great empty craving.

"Yvain will have his mother back," Urien said. "You'll watch him grow into the great knight he will become."

I turned away so he would not see the pain the thought had conjured. "This is nothing but a devil's trick."

"I agree it's a generous offer," he said. "But it's a true one, with little reason to refuse. Going to bed with me never taxed you in the past. Obedience might take a little practice, but I am willing to be somewhat patient."

I said nothing, which he took as the advent of victory.

"Well, what say you?" he pressed.

Slowly, I rounded on my once husband, relishing the shadow of fear that passed over his face. "Do you honestly *think* that after everything you've done, I would *ever* lower myself to be near you, sit next to your vainglorious throne, or God forbid let you crawl into my bed? *I would rather die.*"

Urien hardened, jaw muscle twitching beneath his beard. "Don't be hasty, my lady, given death is genuinely on the table. When King Arthur returns and I add adultery to your list of betrayals, my offer may not sound so unsavoury."

Before I could respond, a cacophony of bells began to ring, a discordant set of notes clanging persistently, meaning one thing: the High King was back. I spun on my heel and headed for the door.

"Where are you going?" he demanded. "We aren't finished."

"We are, Urien," I said. "In every way. I learned long ago that you cannot bestow or take away my future. That power lies with me."

50

CAMELOT'S GRAND ENTRANCE Hall was already crowded when I got there, bodies pouring into the circular atrium from every compass point. White sunbeams sliced through the air, cutting across the swelling congregation, already vibrating with gossip and speculative gestures. I walked the crowd's edges towards the main entrance; if Arthur was about to march through the doorway, I wanted to be the first thing he saw.

The sound of my name held me back.

"I've been looking for you." Sir Kay's expression was taut, worried. "You left my chamber so abruptly. What's going on?"

"I could ask you the same question," I said above the still-clanging bells. "Is Arthur coming?"

Kay glanced around the room like a guard dog on the alert. "I don't know. I was called to the Queen soon after you ran out. She has concerns, based on things she's been told. I've been ordered to treat the situation as one of grave seriousness."

"Serious how?" I asked.

Before he could answer, a distinct hush fell in the atrium, crowd turning in a wave to the back of the hall, where Camelot's broad main staircase curved grandly down. On the central stair platform, overlooking her courtiers, stood Queen Guinevere, a dozen of her women gathered behind. She studied the room slowly, her beauty drawn grave.

Kay's hand fidgeted at his belt, and I realized that he was wearing a sword. "What is all this?" I demanded.

His eyes met mine, all guilt. "The Queen has ordered the castle locked down until she receives news of the High King's arrival. She . . . ah . . . ordered that you, in particular, should be contained."

"What!" I exclaimed, though the bells drowned me out. "One day I'm her guest and the next her prisoner? Queen or not, she invited me to stay under Camelot's hospitality, and I have done no wrong. Whatever Arthur and I have to resolve, it has nothing to do with her. I'll tell her exactly why she dare not 'contain' me."

I charged forwards and Kay grabbed my elbow. He let go immediately and held up his hands in apology, but it was enough to give my temper pause. "Lady Morgan, listen. It would have been guards, but I said I would find you myself. Please, do not do this."

His face was beseeching, urging me to hear that he was only trying to help—me, himself, the entire situation. But what good was this godforsaken trip if I could not retrieve the scabbard from Accolon, or if Arthur had time to fortress himself away from me?

Kay and I were still locked in a stare of unmade decisions when a murmur took up within the crowd.

"It's a litter," someone nearby said. "A horse bier with four knights."

"Is it the King?" said another.

"They're bringing it forth."

Suddenly, the cacophony of bells stopped, leaving a quiet so profound that the entire room fell to silence.

"Make way for the bier!" came a shout.

The crowd rippled back and outwards, like a river cleaved by a boat prow. Sir Kay glanced at the Queen, still standing atop the stairway. Her tall body was rigid, eyes fixed on the movement near the door, as the air filled with a panicked buzz.

"All right!" Kay bellowed above the rising commotion. I watched him dive through the mass of bodies, shoving his way to the door. "Move back, make a path!"

Accustomed to obeying the Seneschal's organizational orders, the court began to shift, making a wide opening down the centre of the hall. Loud, regimented footsteps emanated from the doorway and four half-helmed knights appeared, inching towards the wide circle in the centre of the Entrance Hall. I could only see their heads and shoulders, but their strained, controlled posture spoke of carrying a heavy load.

"It's a bier draped with the King's standard," I heard someone say. "You don't think . . . ?"

There was a great thudding boom as the unseen bier was placed on the floor, reverberating like thunder around the atrium.

"Queen Guinevere, and my lords, ladies and gentlemen of Camelot!" declared a crisp, commanding voice. A herald stood in the main doorway, his face solemn as a requiem. "His Royal Highness, Arthur, High King of All Britain, has been in a duel for his life."

The room gasped, punctuated by a few small screams. Up on the stairs, the Queen staggered into the arms of Lady Isabeau. All eyes turned to the draped bier in horror, but the herald's face yielded nothing.

"The King was grievously injured in the swordfight, but is alive and will be well," he said, followed by a collective cry of relief. "His Royal Highness sends a direct message and requires all to listen closely."

He surveyed the room with severity until there was hush, then began.

"To my loyal subjects at Camelot. By the grace of God and Excalibur, I live, after a hard-fought duel for my life, and now lie healing in an abbey under the care of godly nuns. Though I was almost cut down by the Devil's treason, a fair maiden of great magic came to my aid, a pupil of my loyal adviser, Merlin the Wise, whose legacy lives on through her service. By the Lord's righteous will, I proved victorious, and will return to Camelot stronger than ever."

The congregation began to whisper with the same confusion I felt. *Ninianne* was with Arthur? How—and why? And if not Arthur, who was—

"Queen Morgan of Gore, come forth!"

My title of old was so alien to me that I didn't immediately realize who was being called.

"Is she here?" said the herald. Several heads turned, a tentative hand or two rising to reveal my attendance.

"I'm here," I called. "Let *no one else* speak to my presence but me."

I strode forth through the parting crowd, carving a pathway to where the herald stood before the anonymous, knight-guarded bier. It had been placed in the centre of the atrium, atop the great red dragon tiled into the floor. Another long-clawed beast roared across the red-and-white flag that concealed the unfortunate soul beneath.

I stopped at the edge of the circle. "Well?"

"My lady, King Arthur wishes to convey a further message, publicly, to you."

The herald cleared his throat and averted his gaze, holding a hand out towards the bier. Cold bright dread replaced the heat in my veins.

"Lady Morgan, once my loyal sister, now traitor to my Crown," he intoned. "To you, I send Sir Accolon of Gaul, your lover in adultery and unwilling accomplice in your treason, dead, and slain by my own hand. His death pains me deeply, but you gave me no choice. By divine providence and the Lady of the Lake's grace, your treachery has been revealed, the great betrayal prophesied by my loyal adviser, Merlin the Wise. Excalibur's life-preserving scabbard, which I once entrusted to you and thought in my possession, was a counterfeit. The true scabbard you stole out of hatred, and gave to Sir Accolon

with the treasonous purpose of bringing about my death, and usurp-
ing the Crown of All Britain.

"Though noble Sir Accolon was innocent of your crimes, the violence you would have done me, I visited upon your lover in a battle
of swords, as a grave punishment to you. The blame for his bloody
demise lies at your feet. And when I return, you will answer for your
treason before me as your King, then before God in holy judgment.
Let all hear and understand what you have done, Morgan—dark
sorceress, traitor, she that I once called sister. Never will there be a
betrayal so costly as this."

The room held its breath, every pair of eyes boring into my bones,
threads of fear and hatred weaving together until it was palpable as a
hangman's rope. I stood, airless, almost floating, all comprehension
snatched from my mind.

"No," I heard myself say. "Arthur wouldn't kill a knight he loves
and respects, not like this. He would never command you to bring
such a message."

Yet it was his voice within the herald's speech, clear, cold and
formidable, as if Arthur himself stood before me, his steel-grey eyes
cutting into my soul.

"It cannot be. Not Accolon. He . . ." My voice cracked, breaking
under the force of realization until it was a howl. *"Let me see!"*

I charged forwards, trying to claw my way past the bier knights,
but they gripped my arms and held fast.

"Guards!" Guinevere commanded. "Arrest her! She has committed treason to this Crown and fulfilled the prophecy of betrayal the
King was warned of."

I tore away from the knights as armoured guards clattered
forth. I held out my hands and halted them with a wall of air, the
element obeying me so fast it felt innate. The crowd gasped,
shrinking in unison.

"How dare you!" I said. "Bring me this prophecy and the proof of which stars foretold it. Show me where my name is written!"

Guinevere stepped forwards, regal and blazing. "Do not listen to the poison this woman spits. Queen Morgan of Gore is a traitor and an adulteress, and long has been. Her betrayals will be well proven at trial."

"No," I protested. "I loved my brother. I gave my mind, my skills, everything I had to help him and this realm—you all know it to be true. If I could betray him, then so could *any one of you*." I pointed savagely at the Queen. "Merlin's prophecy might speak of *you*, Guinevere. What could destroy Arthur and the realm better than a betrayal perpetrated by his beloved, trusted Queen? Your treachery could be on the wings of Fate yet to come."

Guinevere's face drained to a bloodless outrage. "You blasphemous *witch*. I thank God my lord husband will finally be free of you. You will burn in Hell for what you have wrought upon him."

My spine prickled like the hackles on a wolf. "I will have my revenge, Guinevere. If you make a single misstep in your entire life, I'll be waiting to rain chaos on your wrongs."

"Guards!" she called. "Throw her in the darkest dungeon in chains!"

The knights moved but I remained, glaring at the Queen, pressure building within, the thrill of destruction crackling in my blood. I looked around the room: at the high stained glass encircling the atrium, so easily shattered with the force of the air, to rain vicious shards upon the upturned faces; the tile and stone beneath our feet that would yield to an earthquake. There were no flames in the hearth, but I didn't need them—fire already lived inside me, driven by a rage that could never be doused. I could raze Camelot to the ground and burn the ruins in the work of a moment.

My hands lifted, the entire congregation cowering, and I returned my gaze to Guinevere, savouring her look of pale-green terror as I prepared to shut my eyes and damn the consequences.

An upright, matronly figure stepped out of the Queen's shadow: Lady Clarisse, her wimple trembling slightly. She placed a hand on her daughter-in-law's arm, but her eyes were on mine—wide and worried, like her son's when he had found me. My heart leapt in affection, the urge for devastation slipping away, as the same son's sharp tones cut through the roaring darkness in my skull.

"I have it in hand, Your Highness," Sir Kay said. He waved away the enclosing guards, then took my elbow again. "I will escort Lady Morgan and secure her in her chambers. As a Queen herself, she must be kept in a manner appropriate to her rank."

"Are you sure that's wise, Lord Seneschal?" Guinevere said tersely. "She seems a great risk to us all."

"There won't be any trouble if this is done lawfully, my lady. The High King would not wish for anything less." He turned to me, urging me with his eyes. "Come along, Lady Morgan."

The red roar in my head had not quite subsided. "You as well, Kay?" I hissed. "How many more knives must I endure in my back, when I could kill everyone in this room in a heartbeat?"

I tried to pull away, but his determination outdid me. On the staircase, Lady Clarisse drew the Queen's attention long enough for Kay to whisper in my ear.

"Lady Morgan, I know you. I'm not fool enough to believe you want to kill *everyone* under this roof." He gave me a sardonic half smile, the memory of which, and the time we had spent as friends, formed a bittersweet knot in my throat. "Do this quietly, and trust me."

My eyes flickered to Lady Clarisse's kind face, urging courage, then held my chin high and walked beside the Seneschal as he led me from the room, turning my back on the terrible, silent bier, and the whole gilded, rotten place.

*

WE HAD ALMOST reached the spur of hallway that led to my temporary chamber when a large figure stepped out from the shadows.

"I require a moment with my wife, Lord Seneschal," Urien said, his eyes fixed on me. At Sir Kay's hesitation, he added, "From a *King* to *his Queen*."

Kay's jaw tightened and he reluctantly stepped out of earshot. Urien leaned in and I resisted the instinct to recoil.

"Such a shame for your Gaul," he said in low, quiet mocking. "A tragedy that so valiant a knight must fall for your treasonous sins. I must say, your theft of King Arthur's scabbard was a fine touch to ensure your lover's brutal end."

He shifted closer, his breath hot against the side of my neck. In the blurring shadows his scars had vanished, as if I had never taught him a lesson at all.

"What a mess you're in, my Queen," he went on. "How *will* you solve your predicament?"

I met his eyes, stony and defiant, when in truth I felt hollow as a cavern.

"Are you finished?" I said.

His reply was a soft laugh, ever sure of himself. "One word, my darling wife, and you'll be saved from all this." He raised a hand, trailing rough fingertips down my cheek. "You know how to find your way to my bed. I'll be waiting."

51

NO ONE CAME in to light the candles, so I remained where I had landed, perched on the edge of the bed, as the slanting summer light deepened from gold to a faded bloody hue, before being swallowed by darkness.

My mind played a single refrain:

He is dead, he is dead, he is dead.

Only when night had settled in, and the sounds of the castle had narrowed to the murmuring of guards outside my door, did the voices take up in my head, speaking of danger, safety, betrayal and possibility. My choices were few and some were unclear, but my fight now was to stay alive.

"The guard changes two bells after midnight," Kay had told me before he left. It was all he could do, but it was enough.

By the time the first bell rang, my decision was made, but it took another hour before I got to my feet. The only light in the chamber came from the embers of the small fire and a soft blue glow from the horizon, in the way summer skies never quite surrendered to full dark.

Too much light, and not enough; I wanted to act but not to be seen. When the riddle's answer came, the irony made me laugh aloud.

Merlin's infernal mist.

Conjuring the mist was the easiest it had ever been. I closed my eyes and thought of a winter fog, rising in frozen white clouds, and of my own need for concealment. I had not even opened my eyes before I felt the cool surety in my blood, the drifting coldness billowing around my hems.

By the time the next bell came, the mist shrouded my body like a cape of chill gauze. At the sound of the retreating footsteps of the changing watch, I slipped out of the door and down the corridor, passing the new guards sent to stand over my imprisonment.

One shivered as I glided between them. "Cold night for the time of year," he said.

"Either that or a spirit walks these halls," said the other. I wondered if that was what I had become now: a shade, a phantom haunting my own life.

Urien had eschewed putting guards at the doors to my old chambers, presumably so I would have easy passage to his bed—caution overruled by hopeful lust. My former bedchamber was lit by a row of small candles, though I could feel in the air that not a soul was awake. Like the reception room, it contained the same furniture, though the alcove where I had hidden Excalibur remained torn open, leaving a gaping maw.

The one other difference was a curtain drawn across the dressing room archway, and the fact that an intruder lay in what was once my bed. Mine and Accolon's bed, as I had thought of it during our blissful month alone at Camelot, a reunion beginning a life together that had somehow ended here, like this.

The hangings pulled back with a faint hiss, and my mist fell away. Candlelight spilled over the bed, revealing the large, slumbering form of my once husband. Urien lay on his back, emitting a series of snores, trapped air giving off the sour reek of wine. In the low, flickering light, the marks where I had burned him seemed to twitch and leap.

He had fallen into bed drunk, no doubt after celebrating his way through the evening. Beneath my hand, the fabric began to smoulder, the heat of my rage immediate, licking through my body as flame.

This time, he would die for what he had done to me.

However, setting his bed alight wasn't the way. My son was likely sleeping nearby, and starting a fire risked him, myself and the castle. Camelot perhaps deserved to burn, but not all of its inhabitants, and fire would draw attention, when I had more to do that night. Most of all, it was too quick, too easy—Urien might escape, or not feel a thing.

I let go of the hangings, leaving scorch marks behind. Instead, I grasped my father's falcon-handled knife at my belt and drew it free with care. Earlier, I had sharpened the blade on Tressa's whetstone until the edge sang like a skylark.

I knew exactly what to do: the sharp tip in his inner jugular, and Urien would bleed like a stuck pig, waking as the steel slid beneath his skin. But for once, the knife felt insufficient in my hand, not enough to satisfy the enormity of all I felt. I wanted worse for him, a bigger gesture of my hatred. A bigger blade.

My eyes cast about for the answer, and within moments, I found it, propped by the side of the bed: Urien's sword, gold hilt shining like an answer from God.

To kill a knight, a king, unarmed, with his own sword was no small thing—a death of shame and prostration, an act so grievous it made men shudder; the inglorious end they feared most. It was perfect: Urien should die like a coward in his bed, at the mercy of the woman he had wronged.

I picked up the weapon and held it before me. It was lighter than I expected, with none of the sleek silver heft of Accolon's rearing-horse longsword or the ominous regal weight of Excalibur. A hollow sword for a hollow man. Still, it would serve.

I lay the blade flat across Urien's throat, then placed my other hand on his forehead, preparing to awaken him. If he tried to fight, he would bring about his own death even quicker, and I savoured the exhilaration of physical supremacy that had never before been mine to feel. That men chose steel and force and destruction over subtler, cleverer means made a sudden violent sense.

I turned the sword to its edge.

"Cursed woman, *stop!*"

Two small hands hooked through my elbow, staying my sword arm. I looked down to see Yvain's beautiful face, his deep-blue eyes glaring at me in horror, mouth twisted with what was left of his cry.

The sword slipped from my hands, landing soundlessly on the rug. I sent a quick charm of unwaking into Urien's forehead and swooped over my terrified son.

"Yvain, my love . . ."

I tried to put my arms around him, protect him from what he had already seen, but he shoved me away, face dawning with disdain.

"It's *you*, isn't it?" he said acidly. "You're my *mother*."

"Of course I am, but . . ."

Pushing past me, he grabbed Urien's sword and heaved the blade up, point shaking in the air between us.

"It's a good thing you are my mother," he quavered. "Because if you were not, you would die by this sword. False, wicked creature!"

"Yvain, please. Let me explain." I took a step towards him, arms outstretched, and the fright on his face was more painful than if he had run me through. He dropped the sword and began to shudder uncontrollably, putting his hands over his ears.

"I won't listen. I know you talk to demons and want to twist my mind."

"No, never," I said. "I couldn't harm you. I'm your mother and I love you."

"Liar!" he screamed. "You came here to kill my father in his sleep."

Tears ran down his face, and I watched him hold his breath exactly as he used to at two years old, his happy mind always unable to accept the onset of sadness. "My father is a great man . . . true and valiant. All my life he has loved me . . . unlike you. The Devil . . . has possessed you, like they say. *You* deserve a shameful death, not . . ."

He crumpled to the floor, weeping like the child he was, every sob an arrow to my heart. Instinctively, I bundled him into my arms and carried him away, to the former dressing room whence he had come, now a richly appointed child's bedchamber.

The bright joust-themed tapestry that Alys had woven for Yvain at birth hung at the bedhead, a set of pewter knights in combat on a side table. A boar-head banner in green and gold dangled from the wall, and I realized with a jolt that Urien had sought to make his surroundings feel safe, familiar—that to Yvain, his home was in Gore and always had been.

I set him down on the bed, unresisting of my arms and hiccupping now and then. I trailed my fingers through his dark-gold hair, along his perfect face, and he let me, gazing mournfully into my eyes, too tired to do battle anymore.

"Forgive me," I said.

My plea reignited his anger, and he pushed my hand from his face with a teeth-baring scowl. A bottom front tooth had been recently lost, leaving a small, whistling gap.

"If I were a righteous knight, I would punish you," he said. "But because you are my mother, my soul would be lost like yours. I am the son of a devil, and for that I am eternally shamed."

I hung my head, feeling the wellspring of my own tears, wanting only to hold him fast and say how I had tried to do my best for him, had loved and cherished him as much as I could; how he was torn away from me by his greedy father and self-righteous uncle.

But as I ran through my past, the impulses I had followed, the freedoms I had yearned for, the effect my mistakes had wrought on my son's life, there wasn't any justification I could make. Whether I meant to or not, I had abandoned him, whereas he had lived a happy, gilded life with a loving father and an all-powerful uncle who would pave his path to greatness. Yvain would thrive because he had always belonged to this world, and I never had, never could. I deserved his hatred, and his hatred of me would save him.

I raised my head and met my son's stubborn, furious stare. He looked more like me than he ever had, and even in my deep despair it pleased me. I hoped that Urien saw it too, and was reminded that our glorious child was not sprung from his arrogant rib, but formed and brought forth to life by a woman who could never be erased from him.

"Yvain, my love, listen," I said. "I'm sorry, truly I am. You were right—I was angry at your father, and the Devil overcame me. I didn't know what I was doing."

Tentatively, I put my hand to his face again, and he didn't shy away, emitting a soft, childlike sigh. "But *you* stopped me, and no more will I act in such a way. Think what you wish of me, but you must never, ever feel shame for who you are, or hate yourself for my sake. You are not the son of a devil—you are yourself, and a miracle."

I drew back the bedcovers and eased him onto the mattress. His long legs folded beneath the sheets, and I pulled the coverlet to his chest, holding his deep-blue gaze.

"God brought you into that room to save both your father and me. And you did, with all the grace bestowed upon you. You are noble and decent and brave, and will never do wrong to anyone. Your honour is enough for us both, and for that you should be proud."

I brushed my hand over his eyes, feeling his mind tilt towards sleep.

"I won't tell anyone," he said drowsily. "It would be worse for me if I did. They would think me ignoble. So I won't say about it . . . all right?"

"I know you won't," I said. "Because I will spare you this, for the rest of your life. When you awake, you will not remember what you have seen, or the fear and awfulness you felt. You will only know you are good and true, and that you will succeed despite your mother."

As I spoke, my thumb traced chevrons on his temples, cleansing the memory, the horror, his worry out of his mind, until he fell into a profound rest.

"I love you, and I'm sorry," I said, kissing his untroubled forehead. "Goodbye, my precious eyas."

For a few more breaths, I watched his tranquil, beautiful face as one watches a small god, in awe and despair. When I could no longer bear it, I returned to Urien's bedchamber and plucked my sleep spell from his wine-sweating brow. The King of Gore grunted and stirred onto his back, returned to his usual guiltless rest.

A flare of hatred burned in my gut, Urien's sword catching my eye where Yvain had dropped it. I retrieved the blade from the rug and laid it carefully across my former husband's huge chest. Pressing down with my fingertips, I fixed its weight with my magical will so it would hold him until morning, when Urien would wake to find his throat fortuitously uncut, a sword laid like a threat across his body and his imprisoned wife gone, and wonder for eternity how it all came to pass.

52

I LEFT THE mist at the cathedral door. I didn't care if I was seen anymore, whether by a sleepless deacon or patrolling guards. The entire knightly presence of the court could charge into St. Stephen's with their blades drawn sharp and it would not have mattered. It was finished, over; let them come.

But first, I had to see him.

The nave was lined with candles, densely lit rows of iron stands giving way to small tapers at my ankles, glittering along the elaborate tiles. All else was dark, every high window struck blind, the intricate arches, narrow-carved like rib cages, vanishing into shadow as if reaching directly into the night sky. There would be no more dawns, or so it felt.

At the transept crossing, the lights curved into a supernova up the steps of a central platform where the priest usually stood at Mass. There, a thick slab of white marble lay atop a heavy stand, stark and unadorned, the flickering firelight bright enough that my eyes resisted its glare. The image was so dazzling that I didn't see the figure lying motionless until I was halfway up the altar steps.

I stopped and recoiled, as if not expecting what I was there to see. A long body lay across the marble, shining like winter dawn, clad neck to foot in polished silver mail, a tunic of white silk overlaying the steel. I moved closer and a slash of red appeared—a pointed crimson tail, curling beneath rampant claws and snarling teeth: Arthur's roaring dragon, like Uther's before him, but rendered in the colour of blood.

A wave of anguish rocked me sideways. This was not a dream, or a game, or a mistake; they had dressed the one slain in the livery of the man who had murdered him.

I rested my palms on the cold marble and made myself look.

They say the fallen at peace seem to be sleeping, waiting for God in serene repose. That it is a comfort in grief to look upon one who has transcended life to be reborn in Heaven. But all I could see, as I cast my eyes upon the man I loved, was death.

Accolon's beauty was unexpected, glorious and terrible as an angel's, and equally impossible. I knew every part of the face before me, every angle, every sculptural plane and curve, yet what made him was gone, extinguished; alien without the spirit that conjured joy and laughter and love every time I had looked at him. His closed, dark-lashed eyes spoke not of sleep but of absence, his top lip counterfeit in its upturned curl.

Below, his hands were pale, elegant fingers threaded across the rearing horse grip of his sword, staid and motionless as they had never been. Grasping the sword hilt, I pulled the blade free, throwing it to the floor with an echoing crash, and raised a trembling hand to his face. His ash-dark hair was cool as I pushed it off his brow, the skin I brushed sheer cold.

On the surface, it was him—Accolon, my Gaul—tranquil and at rest, but beneath, only emptiness, an abyss into which his essence had fallen, leaving him profoundly and violently gone.

An incense-scented draft gusted over the candles, dancing light across his skin, and for a moment my mind brought him to life: Accolon smiling at me from across a room; holding my eyes in the midst of talk; his youthful face long ago, deep in thought, hands fluttering beneath his golden coin, drawing me deeper into my fascination. But the flames settled and the image receded, and we were no longer there—young and hopeful in Tintagel, just beginning, or together at the lakeside in Fair Guard, older and scarcely wiser in the intensity of our love—but here, on different sides of the earthly veil, at the end.

Accolon was dead; it hung in the air like the stars themselves spoke of it.

"No," I whispered, my fingers still entwined in his silky hair. "This cannot be, it can't, it can't."

Urgent now, I ran my hand down his cold face, across the sleek bones, willing him to shift or smile or lean towards my touch as he had done so many times. Nothing happened, and it pierced me despite knowing it could not, every small realization a sliver of glass in my heart, until it was made entirely of shards.

But I could not stop. I leaned over him, running my healing hands along his neck, his shoulders, the top of his arms, desperately seeking a twitch of muscle, a shiver of breath underneath the cold steel holding him to the marble slab. My fingers searched his chest, gripping the silk, trying to sense a fault, a rupture, anything I could heal. I wanted to reach into his stillness and fill it with my skill's golden warmth, repair what had been broken, undo what they had done.

"Please," I heard myself say. "There must be something. I can fix this, I can."

There was nothing, not a trace of him that would yield to me.

After all we had been through, this couldn't be the end, a senseless death based on punishment and distrust and a series of terrible untruths. For all I had tried to keep us safe, I had still been the ruin of Accolon, had let the world bring about his destruction when I should have made him go, far away from me—or if not, kept him close and never let him leave at all.

"No, Accolon," I said, trying to hold on to myself as my body, my mind, my entire being began to shatter. "You can't leave me. Not . . . like . . . this."

My words turned to weeping—brutal, wracking sobs that sucked the air from my body. I sank down onto Accolon's chest, pressing my face so hard against his sternum that I could feel the steel rings of the mail hauberk against my cheek through the tunic's thick silk.

"Stay with me," I cried, and it was all I could say. *Stay with me*, over and over.

My noisy flood of grief rang through the cathedral, echoing up into the bonelike arches, a chorus distorted with rage and devastation. Eventually, I forced myself to stand up, staring down at his lifeless form, blood roaring with hurt, seeing stars.

What would I do now? I couldn't leave him here, among his murderers; those who claimed our love was treasonous, fraudulent, a convenient tryst between a manipulative, vengeful harlot and a bewitched but honourable knight. No one who wished to bury Accolon in Camelot was fit to stand beside his tomb.

Suddenly, his voice was in my head, deep and contented: an idle conversation amidst dusty sunlight and the scent of books, as our love unfolded anew.

When knights die in faraway lands, it is always the heart they ask to be sent home. They say the soul is contained within.

And up at our lake, enrobed in our happiness:

When I die, bury me here, under this weeping willow tree.

I could not have Accolon whole, but I could do as he wished and take what mattered: his knighthood and his heart. I would lay him to rest beside our lake, under the willow tree's swaying leaves, and curl up with him there, until we were both stardust.

Outside in the distance, a cockerel crowed, and I looked up at the east transept's towering window to see the first hint of rising dawn etched across multicoloured glass. Soon the castle would awaken, and someone would send for me and find my chamber empty. It had to be now.

First, I took his golden spurs, worn at his heels since Tintagel. Aside from me, knighthood was all Accolon had ever wanted; this part of him, they did not get to keep. When the spurs were unfixed and safe at my belt, I contemplated the rest.

Silk, steel mail, a cage of ribs; it would take more than a knife. My affinity was found within the noble art of healing, but all light had its darkness. All restoration must first begin with destruction. With concentration, and the dread knowledge I had consumed over hours in Merlin's study, I could rend and carve and lay waste as well as any knight or king. My hands were my longsword, my mind the heavy armoured shoulders necessary to force and break.

For Accolon, I would tear asunder the body I had gazed upon and lain with and loved, and not flinch from my purpose. For Accolon, I would walk out of Camelot's cathedral changed, with blood on my skin and his soul in my hands. One way or another, I would bring him home.

I steepled my fingertips against his chest. Fabric parted, mail parted, and I saw what had been done: the marks of Arthur's violence across Accolon's torso—bruises, deep slashes, a thousand killing blows that had poured forth his blood. There had been no mercy in the battle, no singular lethal strike, and for this I acknowledged a terrible gratitude, for the heart had been spared, his alabaster chest unmarked where it resided, yet stark as an X on a treasure map.

Skin and bone split under my severing thumb. I reached inside, gently, firmly, seeking the anatomy I knew, the careful cuts I still had to make. A body many days past death will not bleed in any usual way, but the heart was slick and solid in my hands, surprising in its heaviness.

It came forth sudden and whole, like a babe from the womb, and I beheld it for a moment, still and glistening like a garnet in the blaze of candles, its shining surface strangely blank, as if I had expected to see my name carved in the curving muscle. I took my kerchief—the square of Parisian blue silk he had once given me wrapped around the chess set—and laid his heart upon it, tying the ends in a careful knot.

Once done, I put my hands on either side of the cavity in his chest and eased it shut, feeling bones and flesh knit back together with my steady breaths. On his skin, I left a neat red line—a final mark upon his body, a signature for all to see—then gathered up my lover's gentle heart in one hand and his silver longsword in the other, and placed a farewell kiss on Sir Accolon of Gaul's curved-bow lip.

The laceration in the mail and silk remained open, framing my careful work. The eyes and minds who looked upon this aftermath wouldn't know for certain what I had done or why, but they would wonder, and speculate, and fear what was possible at my hands.

And they should fear me, the power I possessed, and the bright, ravenous rage that now fuelled my every breath. From that moment onwards, even I did not know what I was capable of.

53

I LEFT THE cathedral as if on wings, through courtyards and under archways, blurred instinct leading somewhere. It wasn't until I reached the lower stables, peaceful and tinged with pale-blue dawn, that I knew where my grief had brought me.

Accolon's travelling horse whinnied when he saw me from his stall. His two other mounts I assumed lost to the hunting trip, but my Gaul had left his favourite to rest—a fleet, handsome stallion with a flame-bright chestnut coat, who he had let me name Phénix.

I tacked the horse, slid Accolon's sword into the saddle scabbard and mounted up in the courtyard. The guards at the stable gate were barely alert at that hour, and I trotted past them with my hood up, not so fast as to be noticeable, but before they spotted I was a woman absconding on a horse of knightly quality.

At the city gates, I looked back; no one was in pursuit, nor were any alarum bells ringing for my escape. Camelot stood mute, golden and forbidding in the sharpening light. I wondered if I would ever see it again, and found I felt nothing. Arthur was the reason it was once my sanctuary, not the great stone-and-glass edifice he had built. It was empty now and always would be, both of the High King I believed in, and the brother I had loved.

Accolon's heavy heart was still cradled in the crook of my arm; I hooked it onto the saddlebow and rode into the forest where I had left the household. We had two hours or so before my escape would be discovered, and we needed to be far away by then.

"Morgan!" Alys exclaimed as I rode through the glade's protective threads. "Thank God, you're back."

She and Tressa sat drinking from steaming cups beside a healthy fire. They jumped up as I dismounted, embracing me in turn.

"I—I thought you'd be asleep," I said.

"Some are," Tressa said. "But some of us couldn't."

I glanced around the quick camp they had made: sheets stretched between trees where the household slept; a long, low branch as hitching post for the dozing horses; the pot of herb tea brewing over the fire. All, and nothing, was normal.

"We heard a commotion on the road yesterday afternoon," Alys said. "Ringing bells, slow hoofbeats, chants of lament. What's happened?"

The enormity of the question made me dizzy. But I had taken my moment's weakness in St. Stephen's with Accolon; for him, and the sake of the household, I must hold myself steady.

"We have to leave," I said. "Now, quickly. I'll explain on the road, but—"

"That's Sir Accolon's horse," said an uncertain voice, and I turned to see Robin emerging from between the other tethered mounts. "Phénix. He brought him to Camelot."

His eyes grew wider with every step. By the time he reached me, he looked like a child. "Where's . . . Sir Accolon?"

There were a dozen things I could have said, but I was dumbstruck in the face of Robin's innocence, his growing worry that I could not quell. The moments that followed would change him—as I was when Sir Bretel crashed to his knees and told us my father had been killed—his life forever coloured by what came hereafter. If I could, I would have torn myself apart to prevent him ever knowing, but I could not change what was true. Our life as we knew it was already over.

"Morgan?" Alys's voice cut into my silence.

I looked back at her and felt the hollowness behind my own eyes. She brought a hand up to her mouth.

"Oh God," she said. "Oh God, no. It can't be. He isn't . . ."

Tressa's cup fell from her hands, and I watched it descend in slow motion, its soundless bounce onto the forest floor. She grabbed Alys's arm and held up a warding hand, as if to stop me uttering the final words.

"He's dead," I said. "Accolon is dead."

The horrifying truth of it cut through the air, vicious and permanent. My women ran to me, but I had already fallen, bracing against the dirt in prostration, my lungs tearing with screams I could not hear above the roar of my blood.

Accolon's horse reared up in fear, and I willed its hooves to crash down upon my head, but Robin had the reins, drawing the frightened animal aside, and there were arms about me, clutching my body, cradling my head, absorbing my cries. Warm tears seeped into my skin—theirs, ours—bringing me back to myself, a reminder that this grief would not be mine alone.

Eventually, I looked up and saw the rest of the household gathering, solemn and unsure, waiting to hear what came next. They needed me now, as much I needed them.

Gripping Alys's and Tressa's hands, I stood up, breathing deep of the forest air. "It's true. Sir Accolon is dead and lies in the cathedral of St. Stephen's. Slain in a duel by King Arthur himself."

It wounded even more deeply when spoken aloud. A collective gasp rippled around the glade.

"My own brother killed Sir Accolon," I continued. "Not for any wrong he did, but as punishment to me, for a treason the King believes I have committed. He isn't at Camelot, but we must leave here immediately, before he returns. I swear I can keep you safe in

Fair Guard, but trouble may yet come. Speak now, and I will free you of your association with me, and any danger therein."

I looked around the crescent of melancholy faces. A few tears ran down cheeks, some heads in hands. They had loved Accolon more than they did me, not because I did not have their loyalty, but because he made himself so easy to love. Perhaps it was for him, their good-humoured, honourable champion, they had stayed all along.

"It is no small thing to be at odds with the High King," I said. "I swear on Sir Accolon's immortal soul I will understand."

Robin, still holding the becalmed horse, stepped forwards. "I'm for Lady le Fay and I'm staying," he said. "Whatever comes."

To my astonishment, every head in the household began to nod. "For Lady le Fay," they said in succession, until the wind lifted the chorus into the treetops and the horses began to stir. I couldn't have spoken even if I had the words.

"Then we ride for Fair Guard," Robin declared, and the crowd hurried off, gathering belongings, packing saddlebags. He turned to me, suddenly more man than boy, and held out Phénix's reins. "He's a good horse, my lady. You should ride him home."

A rush of gratitude and loss crashed over me as he turned away. I put my hands on the saddle and leaned against it, trying not to look at the ominous silk bundle. My eyes landed on Accolon's sword.

"Robin, wait." Gently, I drew out the blade, offering it up to him across my palms. "Accolon would have wanted you to have this. He loved you, and you made him proud."

Robin took the sword into his hands as if it were glass, gazing at the silver horse hilt. "I loved *him*," he said. "He was like a—"

A sob cut him short, and I couldn't bear to supply the words, or watch the tears streaming silently down his haunted young face.

"I know," was all I could say. "He knew."

*

WE WERE SEVERAL hours beyond Camelot, riding mainly in a shocked, devastated silence, when a crossroads came into view. So far, we had thankfully not encountered another soul, but ahead of us a pale horse cantered out of a small, tree-enclosed track, its rider wearing a cloak of bright violet. The sight struck me with instant recognition.

I gasped. "It's *her*."

"Who?" Alys said, but I was already gone, pushing my horse in pursuit.

"Ninianne!" I called, and she halted, hooded head swinging around. "I need to speak with you."

I had not seen her for half a decade, and as ever, she looked no older. Her emerald eyes glittered with hardness, but her expression was hunted, a look of shock I had little seen. I had caught her unawares and she did not like it.

Ninianne glanced briefly behind her, whence she had come. "This doesn't concern you, Morgan," she said in her deep, resonant voice. "You must accept what has happened and move beyond."

Anger flared in my bones. "My brother killed the man I loved as punishment for my so-called treason and it doesn't *concern* me? You were there—I deserve to know what happened."

She pushed her hood down, copper hair blinding in the sun. "You know what you did. Everything else is far beyond your understanding."

My gathering wrath ignited into a wildfire. It was as if we had never been at Merlin's together at all, had never spent those hours in study, or sharing our lives as women surviving the world of men. She had delivered my lost son and taught me the charms to protect my existence, yet that meant nothing to her fairy heart?

"After all we've been through," I said, "you accuse me of treason *and* insult my intelligence?"

With a wordless look of scorn, she dug her heels into her horse and galloped off the road, veering into the trees. Accolon's horse quivered in anticipation, eager for the chase, but for the sake of the stunned household, I curbed my impulses and trotted back to Alys.

"It's Ninianne," I explained. "I must follow her, find out what she knows."

"What was she doing at a nunnery?" Alys asked. I frowned and she pointed towards the neat, tree-lined track. "There's an abbey down that road, with a good infirmary. I considered going there before I chose St. Brigid's."

I stared at her, then off into the forest where Ninianne had vanished. I could still hear the faint thud of hoofbeats on the breeze.

"It's a trick," I said. "Her insults, her evasion. She *wants* me to follow her."

"Why?" Alys said.

"To direct me away from where she's been." My heart took up a stuttering rhythm, like the beating of a broken wing. "Arthur's there. His message said he was healing at an abbey. Ninianne must have stayed until his guards arrived from Camelot."

"Then you should away from here and quickly," Alys said. I gave her a significant look and she paled. "Oh no, Morgan. You can't be thinking of confronting him, not now."

"The worst has already happened, Alys. There's nothing else they can do to me. Take the household home, dear heart. I'll catch up with you."

"*Cariad*, no," she protested. "He has armed men now. You'd be mad to attempt going anywhere near him."

I smiled, for the first time in what felt like an age. "I am destined to be the madwoman for eternity, but I will fear no man on this earth. I deserve satisfaction—we all do. *Accolon* does. And I will have it. This isn't over by a very long way."

54

THEY WOULD NOT put a king in with others, but it was easy to tell where Arthur's chambers were. I left my horse concealed some way down the track, used the mist to enter the abbey, and the armoured men placed at intervals led me to a cloistered courtyard, where four knights were stationed at one door. A town crier declaring the High King was inside would not have been more obvious.

I could not open the door myself without risking discovery, but all these men required was the familiar image of a woman they thought benign. When I glided past them under a shimmering veil of enchantment, they saw a nun's habit and scrubbed face, a rosary hanging from my belt instead of my falcon-handled knife. In my empty hands they saw a bowl of poultice and strips of linen, the scents of vinegar and thyme conjured in their confident, unassuming minds.

"Sister," the biggest knight said reverentially, pushing the door wide. Once it was closed, I drew down the wooden bar, locking us in.

The room was rich, perhaps not grand enough for a king, but well-furnished and luxuriously draped—bishop's chambers or some such, kept for when important men condescended to visit. A wide window ran along the facing wall, admitting a rectangle of light across a canopied bed, its hangings left open.

I don't know what I expected, but it was not to find Arthur asleep. I had seen him amid many losses of control: bursts of youthful joy; fury, hot and cold; anxiousness when some plan went awry, or when Merlin left his mind cloudy and fractious. I had seen him crushed by pain, when his vicious headaches took his strength and only the healing power of my hands could restore him.

But I had never seen him asleep, and powerless, as he was now.

I approached the bed, and it occurred to me that it was the third time I had edged towards a man lying prostrate in as many days, for vastly differing reasons. Arthur lay on his side, knees and elbows drawn tight, curled defensively in on himself. His sleep was deep but uneasy, brow furrowed, jaw set in a tense, teeth-grinding line. His bed shirt showed the stiff outline of bandages strapped around his torso, beads of blood blooming through: Accolon's brave, futile attempts at survival, from their wretched game of kill or be killed.

I swayed forwards, steadying myself against the bedpost. How in all Hell had it come to this?

On the road, I thought I wanted answers, with notions of revenge in its wake, but now I felt only the overwhelming need to look my once-beloved brother in the eye and see who he had become without me.

Arthur stirred as if sensing my presence, hunched body loosening. As he unfurled, the lemon-pale light cast a sudden glare, glancing off a long, narrow object in the bed beside him. Clutched in Arthur's fist, bright and deadly, was Excalibur.

Next to his sleeping body, the sword was awake, glittering like malevolent stars. Beneath its dazzle, dark-red streaks danced along its perfect edge, singing of violence. At the sword's point, a ruby of blood had dried like a perfect teardrop.

Accolon's blood.

The blood of the man I loved, that Arthur had fought to shed, as a savage, unjust punishment to his own *dear sister*.

Bitter fury caught like claws in my chest, crying out for me to answer the blood upon Arthur's blade by spilling yet more—his own, the parts of his essence that were Uther Pendragon's, all the men in their righteousness and brutality, stretching back into the shadows of time.

Standing in Urien's chamber, I had spared his life for my son's sake, but Arthur had no such saviour. My brother always insisted everything he did was by his own command, the burden of responsibility solely upon his crowned head. So be it.

I raised a hand over his body, hovering like a question. Arthur shifted again in sleep, a prism of dawn illuminating the bones of his face. In the sudden change of light, I saw only my mother's calm, pensive goodness, what was left of her in him echoing through.

And with it came a memory: of a love between brother and sister that had transcended blood ties from the first; of two formidable souls finding their reflection, and the tragedy of it shattering; an immense loss I would grieve with the rest. As I stood before Arthur now, with all the power I ever needed, I knew I could not harm him.

I lowered my hand and retreated, crumpling onto a long bench at the foot of the bed, onto a pile of rich garments. A scale of pleasure ran up my body, building quickly into a melody. I glanced down, drawing back a red mantle, and another starburst of goodness rushed into my head. A column of blue-and-white leather lay beneath my fingers, last seen in Accolon's fine hands.

Excalibur's scabbard, pristine and singing with life.

I grasped it to my chest, shivering with the vitality it brought. Every muscle strain and shred of tiredness evaporated, the rigid ache in my skull vanishing to leave a diamond clarity. Even the physical emptiness of my grief felt fainter, faraway.

Yet I held the incredible object, and Arthur did not. He could have been healed and returned to Camelot already if he had slept with the scabbard in his arms, and instead he chose to cradle the sword. Accolon had died, and I had been denounced as treasonous for the scabbard's theft, when Arthur didn't even appreciate its miraculous purpose. He certainly didn't deserve to possess it now.

I, on the other hand—the fairy, the witch, the traitor sorceress with healing in her blood—who else could make greater use of its potential? Arthur could keep his life, his blade, his bloodshed and the ways of men, but the death-defying scabbard I would take. He would learn its worth because it was gone.

I was halfway past the bed and preparing to once again assume the guise of a nun when a cloudy voice rose from the pillows.

"Who's there?" Arthur rose onto his elbows, squinting. Upon seeing it was me, his eyes snapped wide. He pushed himself upright, snatching Excalibur across his lap.

"Morgan!" he said. "What are you doing here?"

I took him in, drawn and colourless, flinching against the stiff bandages, but otherwise broad and fit, grown into his formidableness, stronger than he'd ever looked. The injuries Accolon had inflicted would have felled any other man, quickly and without question, but not King Arthur. *He is made of stubborn fortitude*, Kay had said.

"I was at Camelot when Accolon's bier arrived," I replied. "What do you *think* I'm doing here?"

"Now, Morgan, be calm. There are men outside waiting for my shout."

"Yes," I said. "They let me in. You can thank your sorcerer for that talent. Call for them, if you wish. They will die."

His sword wrist twitched, lifting Excalibur. "What do you want from me?"

"I've been asking myself that since I arrived here. To kill you, I first thought."

"How *dare* you," Arthur growled.

I waved his kingly offence away with my free hand; he hadn't yet noticed that I held the scabbard with the other.

"I could have killed you many times by now. But maybe I was drawn here for a greater purpose. Perhaps we are destined to confront one another, and everything that led to this moment."

"What could there possibly be to say? You know what you did, and the vengeance I was forced to enact." He raised his sword higher, but saw the blood and lowered it again with a sigh. "Sir Accolon was a good man, an honourable knight. I regret that he had to die. But I am High King—I had to act."

"To punish me. The sister who you supposedly loved, who you once professed to trust above all others."

"Yes," he said. "The sister who once swore she loved *me*, and was loyal, and put *me* above all else."

"I *did* love you," I said fiercely. "I *was* loyal. There was no greater faith in my life than that which I held in you."

"Yet you ran the first moment you tasted power, and never came back," Arthur said. "I asked you to return to Camelot, obey my tenets—ideals you once told me you admired—and you refused. You chose betrayal and dishonour again and again."

"What *you* did—the Royal Decree, calling me corrupt, believing every terrible thing Merlin told you—it wasn't based on any code of honour. You gave away my son and wanted me put on trial to save face. Which *noble tenet* was that?"

The repetition of our argument in the forest brought only an overwhelming weariness, so I walked away, towards the window. Arthur moved with me, shifting his legs out of the bed and sighing so deeply it sounded like a groan.

"If there were wrongs to put right, Morgan, why did you choose exile over explanation?" he said. "Why did you hide yourself away and guard your borders with all the might that sorcery could provide?"

His eyes on mine were like the press of cool steel. I still held the scabbard in my arms, but he hadn't looked at it. I thought back to the hawthorn grove, when everything had seemed so clear, but now I found my reasoning elusive. I had never believed right and wrong were straightforward; any cure could also kill with a change of intention. Why *had* I thought mine and Arthur's complications were so easy to understand and act upon?

I sank onto the windowsill, anger giving way to a bone-deep sadness. "I don't know," I said.

Arthur's shoulders dropped, fingers uncurling from Excalibur's hilt. "Don't think I didn't feel it, Morgan—your absence, the great hurt between us, my uncertainty in your guilt when alone in the dark. I missed you every day. I wanted reconciliation, but you never afforded us the chance."

To hear him tell it so plaintively was to feel it as the truth— Arthur's truth, different from mine but no less lived and felt. I gazed across at this man, this King, my brother, his eyes shining silver with grief. His argument was convincing and logical, and blisteringly, devastatingly wrong.

"There must have been another way," I said. "You didn't have to believe Merlin or deny me my son. Accolon didn't deserve to die. It didn't need to end like this."

Arthur rose, leaving Excalibur behind on the bed, its light muted. He picked up a bed robe and slipped it on, wincing with the effort. My sisterly heart flinched at his suffering, and I wondered if looking upon the wounds Accolon had made, to chase away the pain of his last desperate acts and absolve them, might begin to heal more than a hurting body.

"Morgan," my brother said. "What's to become of us?"

"I wish I knew," I said. "If I've learned anything, it's that with loss, with mistakes, there is often a way forward, even if there is no way back." A warm tear curved down my cheek, stinging my lips with salt. "Accolon showed me that."

Arthur nodded with genuine sadness. "I am sorry for his loss and will always regret what had to be done—you must believe that. For his sake, might there be a way forward for you and me? Some peace we can find?"

"You must first ask yourself what you believe I truly am," I said. "Am I a traitoress, a woman of too much ambition, a sorceress of powers that frighten you? Or your sister, a woman whose wit and knowledge you admired, with a love you were once sure of, who merely wanted some freedom of her own? How would you feel, Arthur, if the answer falls somewhere in between?"

"Above all, you are my sister," he replied. "Perhaps I should seek to understand you better."

He said it slowly, thoughtfully, but with a strange ease, as if I had asked him to admit he had broken an object of minor value, rather than set alight every belief he had held for the past half decade.

Arthur raised earnest eyes to mine, his gaze flicking to the scabbard as he did. It was the first time he had allowed himself to look at it, which would not have felt so significant if he hadn't cut his eyes away just as quick. I felt a sudden sinking sensation.

"How so?" I asked regardless.

"What if I said I would do anything to regain what we lost? Would you accept my word?" He gestured to a nearby table, upon which was a wine tray. "Would you share a drink with me, Morgan, to affirm that we will try?"

I nodded, sadness tumbling through my body like a storm cloud. Arthur lifted the jug to pour, and I turned to the window, unlatching one of the panes and pushing it open, savouring the kicking gust of breeze, scents of burgeoning apples and morning sky.

"The first time we met, you poured me wine," I said. "Do you remember? I was surprised a High King would think of such a thing on his coronation day, much less after the shock of learning his true heritage. But I soon came to learn you were a different kind of man, and could be a different kind of king. After years of despondency, you afforded me hope."

Arthur smiled in memory, his face youthful again, not far from the boy-king of that day. "You will have it again, Morgan. *We* will. I swear it."

He placed the jug down and limped closer. His eyes cut to the scabbard, gleaming like a sliver blade. "Take this wine and we will drink to a future of hope." He offered up the goblet and held out his other hand. "Here, give me the scabbard, and I will resheathe Excalibur as a symbol of future peace."

Any remaining hope I held died. Though I had suspected his intentions when he first ignored the scabbard, confirmation of his ruse landed like a sword strike. Arthur had learned how to lie to me.

"You still believe it, don't you?" I said. "The prophecy, my betrayal, that I hate you and want your Crown for myself. You believe every word Merlin told you, and anyone else who wanted us torn apart. It will be written into history and cannot be undone."

He paused, then decided to spare me the insult of more pretence. "Sister," he said dangerously. "Give me the scabbard and I will have mercy."

I laughed, though it seared in my throat. "Oh, Arthur, there is no mercy in you. I know that now. And in turn, nor can there be any in me."

With a conjuring flick of my hand, I captured the wine in his goblet and threw it in his face. Arthur cried out in anger, swiping the bloody liquid from his eyes and diving at the bed for his sword. In the time it took him to grasp Excalibur, I had leapt onto the windowsill and pushed the pane fully open, holding a hand out towards him in threat.

Arthur stopped, half-furious, half-fearful. His recognition of my terrible potential shimmered through me like the darkest power.

"The scabbard is mine," he snapped. "I suppose that's why you are really here. To steal it back and take my sword too, so you can wrench my Crown from me."

"Is that all you care about?" I exclaimed. "Your sword, your power and what others have against you? You're my brother, Arthur. We loved and respected one another. I stood before you in my grief and humanity, despite the damage I could have wrought, and that is all you can say? *I never wanted your Crown.* My God, what use would it be!"

Nothing stirred in his cold eyes aside from his fury and mistrust, forged by Merlin's lies and Guinevere's hatred and honed over so many years of suspicion and belief in treasonous conspiracies.

I brandished the scabbard at him. "This is the only thing I want. The scabbard is a symbol of healing and restoration—all you have done is invoke death and destruction in its name. You are not worthy of its possession, and I am taking it. As you did with Yvain and Accolon, I will ensure you never see it again."

"Guards!" he called. Iron footsteps rang outside. The barred door rattled, then a thud of armour on wood when it didn't open.

"I would have gone to the ends of the earth with you, Arthur," I said. "I would have used every ounce of my power for your good. What a future could have been made between us, if you trusted your clever sister. Now all you will get from me is chaos."

Another crash came from the door, the first splinters flying across the room. Arthur turned towards the noise and I took my opportunity, ducking out of the window.

At my movement, he swung back, eyes and sword blazing. "In the name of the Crown of All Britain I command you to stop!" he roared.

"Oh please," I scoffed. "What could that possibly mean to me anymore?"

I jumped down, landing safely on my feet in a bed of asphodels. "All empires fall, brother, and so too will yours."

55

I RAN TO my waiting horse, the scabbard gripped tight under my arm and the shouts of men far behind me, amidst the roar of thunder in my blood.

By the grace of his fine nature and keen training, Accolon's horse was swift and willing as I dove at a gallop into the forest. Sounds of pursuit echoed from behind us; for Arthur, the abbey knights had armed and mounted themselves with terrifying speed. Their horses were fresh but larger, less responsive, accustomed to a sedate Camelot life. Not a soul saw us cut into the trees, my mount putting distance between me and royal punishment with sure-footed bravery.

Birds scattered shrieking from the bushes, but the horse held firm, sensitive to my urging hands. A fallen tree trunk loomed across our path and there was no time to slow, but Phénix pulled his legs up and flew over, like the mythical bird he was named for, rising from ashes.

We made several misleading serpentines, throwing our tracks into disarray, then I slowed our pace to a walk and listened to the air. No deep shouts, no gaining hoofbeats, no rustle of leaves from creeping capture: I had evaded Arthur's men for now.

I rode the horse into the stream and let his head down to drink, surveying where we stood. Golden sunlight filtered through the trees where the forest began to thin, giving way to open skies and meadow grass dense with wildflowers.

We pushed towards the light, stream sloshing under the horse's hooves. I let my awareness attune to its sparkling song, following its trail until the high chimes faded behind something far greater, a music low and deep, and a sensation of an all-encompassing calm. Drawn to the forest's edge, we found ourselves on the prow of a meadow valley encircled by trees, swaths of green sloping down to the edge of a huge lake.

It was almost perfectly round, and shone dark as night even under the bright-blue sky, speaking of infinite depths. These impossible places existed, Ninianne had told me: the faraway lake where she was born and spent her true youth, until death came for her loved ones and Merlin came for her; and another, hidden in a charm-veiled forest, where she had given Excalibur to Arthur in a cascade of mist. Lakes so endless no man could reach the bottom; secret fairy abysses, forbidding and sublime.

This was one of them, I was sure; a deep, ancient presence I hadn't been seeking but seemed to find me, an irresistible natural force drawing me out of the trees into a still and soundless peace. No one would find me here, the water assured me as I approached its bulrush edges; I was safe and could take my time.

I dismounted and took my boots off, pacing forth until I felt the lake's crystal stillness lap across my toes. The water was chill but revitalizing, and I was reminded of the healing Cornish spring I had once found with Accolon, how we had run in separately and emerged together.

I looked down at the scabbard, still looped around my wrist, and held it to my chest, its power reaching through my skin, making my entire body quiver with light. Every ill I felt—the aches of hard riding, the jaw-clenching headache of fear, the burning poison of despair and horror churning in my gut since hearing of Accolon's death—dissipated until there was only a quiet but soaring euphoria, as if I could sprout wings from my shoulder blades and fly away on the wind.

Was this how Accolon had felt when he wore the scabbard? Did he know why he felt transcendent as he rode, free of care or human pains, so assured he would solve everything and ride back to me in triumph? Or did he just believe himself happy and whole as he left Fair Guard, riding on a trail of light, not knowing that death sat mounted beside him?

Did the scabbard's great power calm him as the king he loved and respected pushed hard to cleave him in two? Did he wonder why he did not bleed? And when the scabbard was taken from him and all the agony and exhaustion descended at once—did he know then that it was a senseless waste, and wish he had not left me, only to die at the hands of the man to whom he had sworn to keep his oath? At what dreadful, devastating moment had Accolon realized he was never coming home?

A hot, furious tear ran down my face, marking the scabbard's blue leather like ink, and another, joining the lake with my anger, my hopelessness, my grief. With great effort, I prised the miraculous object from my body and held it at arm's length, trying to shake free of its coursing brilliance, its power, my covetous desire to secrete it away and use it for my own selfish ends forever.

Yet with great magic came an inevitable cost. With the scabbard in my possession there would always be a bargain to be made, a way back into Camelot and Arthur's glittering web. I was stubborn as the tides, but days would come when I would feel weak, tempted; when the seductions of stability, familial recognition and cheap power would feel easier than the life of loss I was now facing. Never again did I want to consider the possibility of return. I had chosen exile, and there I would stay.

What's more, if I kept the scabbard for myself, then was I any better than the men who waged war and stole and killed in their endless quest to live forever? Even Arthur's virtues had succumbed to its fantastical gifts, so desperate was he to win his duel with death. No one had questioned if this wondrous object *should* be owned by any one man, or if such supreme authority could be rightfully bestowed upon a single chosen soul. To carry immortality at your hip was too much power for any individual to possess.

I knew, as the lake had known from the first moment, what I must do.

I moved forwards, bare feet sinking into the yielding ground. My skirts rapidly soaked up beyond the knees, but they didn't float or drag me down, the water's embrace holding me steady. Trailing my free hand along the tranquil surface, I closed my eyes, asking the lake to show me its depth, its endlessness, to speak its ability to carry the secrets of time and keep them close.

To my request, swift and certain, came the answer: what I gave to the lake, she would keep for all eternity, for no mortal hand to ever touch again.

Waist deep, I stopped and pulled the scabbard from my wrist, savouring its thrill of prowess for the last time. Then, in the sight of the lake, the trees, the skies, everything, I held it aloft.

"No one should have this!" I declared. "Not man, not knight, not king, nor I. The scabbard belongs to the lake, and there it will remain."

Around me, the water began to shift, rippling outwards in steady circles until it was blood-warm against my legs. The whirlpool split wide, waiting patiently as I drew my arm back and threw the scabbard with all the force it had imbued in my body. It sailed through the air like an arrow, falling point-down into the swirling chasm, blue-and-white leather vanishing forever, lost to me and all others who did not deserve it.

Immediately, the water stilled and turned cool, but I kept my hand beneath the surface, feeling the lake seeping into the enchanted hide, pulling the scabbard into its fathomless caress, where its wonders and dangers would be kept safe.

I looked up and screamed—to the heavens, to Merlin, to the brother I once knew. "It's GONE. Do you hear me? GONE FOR ALL TIME."

A flock of crows took flight from the treetops, sky filling with hard rasps and black feathers. Guided by their darkness, I emerged from the lake's embrace, water raining from my sleeves, my skirts and the ends of my hair: a deluge in the shape of a woman.

56

I REACHED THE household sooner than expected, catching up to them on a curving pass hemmed in on one side by yet more dense woodland, and the sloping ridge of a small hill on the other.

"Thank God," Alys said. "We thought we'd lost you. Are you all right?"

"I'm fine." I beckoned to Robin. "Tell everyone we need to ride faster, and leave the road as soon as possible. There's a stone bridge not far from here—remember? If we cut off the road there and follow the river, it'll take us towards Fair Guard in concealment."

"Morgan, why?" Alys said.

"Go," I urged Robin. "Tell them, now."

He nodded and rode off, but Alys's scrutiny held firm. "What happened in the abbey? Did you find King Arthur?"

"Yes," I replied. "I'll explain later. First, I must get you and the household to safety. Push forth your horse. I mean it."

But it was too late. A rumble sounded above us, growing louder like approaching thunder. A row of horses ground to a halt atop the slope, mounted with knights, their steel-clad chests crawling with red dragons.

A figure rode out in front on a huge white warhorse, gold-armoured, fair head encircled with a sunlit crown. Against the blue horizon he shone like a burning star.

"Arthur," I uttered in disbelief.

Asleep in the abbey he had not seemed anywhere near well enough to ride forth in urgent pursuit, but such was the power of his self-righteous rage. He drew Excalibur and pointed the blazing sword directly at me.

"Quick," I shouted, as his men took off down the hill. "Into the woods."

We rode as fast as we could into the forest, until we reached a clearing within a circle of hazel trees.

"More riders, my lady," Robin called from the outer edge. "Fully armed. They're looking for us."

"Then let's go the other way," Alys said.

"We can't," I replied. "Arthur's band are coming from the opposite direction. We're surrounded."

I looked at her and Tressa in sheer hopelessness, but they were keeping their calm, as though it was only a matter of clever thinking and we would be out of the trap. But we were caught; Arthur was raised hunting in the forest, and had won as many battles by ambush as he had on open battlefield. And we were no army.

"Go," I told them. "It's me Arthur wants. Take the household back to Fair Guard. He won't pursue you."

Alys shook her head, reaching out to take my hand. "After all these years, don't you know better than that? I have never willingly left your side and I'm not about to start."

"Me neither," Tressa said, taking Alys's hand and joining us in a trio, as we had always been. "I'm not going."

"Nor I," came an earnest young voice: Robin, pulling his leggy hunter alongside Phénix. "It is the knightly thing."

He sounded so much like Accolon that I was momentarily struck dumb, too choked with emotion to order him away. In the midst of my pause, more voices came, defying my request, our household forming a circle, drawing swords and knives, professing their loyalty and refusing to leave.

"You must go," I insisted. "If it looks like you are loyal to me, if you try to fight, nothing will halt Arthur's men. We couldn't withstand them unless we were made of . . ."

I trailed off, mind whirring, looking around at my assembled people, their solemn aspects motionless, like statues. Several shouts came from the trees, along with the crunch of branches, making our hounds bark. Arthur and his men were all but upon us.

"Robin, take Alys's hand," I commanded. "Everyone, shift your horses. Join hands with the person beside you and close your eyes."

Alys gave me a questioning look. I nodded with as much assurance as I could muster, and she shut her eyes with the rest. As the household linked hands between their horses, I went into the centre of the circle and put my palms to the ground. I felt the essence of earth beneath me, mingled with the life force of the entire household, an unbroken channel waiting for my opening request.

"I need you all to keep completely still." I dropped my voice, intoning rather than talking, soothing, persuasive. "Imagine yourselves rooted to the forest floor, part of the land, becoming harder and quieter. Feel the essence of the earth itself rising into your bones, until they can withstand all the chaos of the world. You are ancient, immutable. You are stone."

I felt our disparate breaths lengthen, syncopate, and become one collective rhythm. My eyes remained open, but the forest began to fade into a green-and-brown blur, the only sound in my ears the steady thrum of the circle's singular heartbeat. I drew a long breath and retreated into my mind, asking my questions of the earth: how we could become more like it; if the element would bestow its favour and make us strong.

I imagined my insides hardening, petrifying, and sent the force down my arms into my hands, willing it through the channel between us all. Once the connection took hold, I stood upright with the earth's elemental force running through my body, pushed forth by my own sheer will.

A faraway commotion sounded, and I knew the searching knights were close, but I had ceased to care. My skin became a carapace, every hardened tendon a trickle of power that I gathered within me and sent out in waves, as the people I knew became grey and ragged. Their features stiffened, disappearing into rock, until we were nothing but a circle of stones, the remnants of an ancient ceremony, a monument to Mother Nature herself.

Whether I could bring us back or we would remain a forest curiosity, I could not be sure, but as the knights broke the treeline and entered the clearing it didn't matter. They couldn't touch us, couldn't harm us, could hack and slash at us with their swords for centuries and never make a mark. We were of the earth itself, no longer of their world.

Through my serene grey vision, I saw Arthur ride up, incandescent in every way.

"Where did they go?" he demanded. "We had them penned in. They could not have slipped away so easily."

"I—I don't know, my lord," stammered his knight-captain. "We thought we had them trapped in the clearing, but when we got here, only this stone circle remained. Perhaps they found some other way."

"Impossible," Arthur said. He dismounted, stalking between two grey lumpen horses and into the centre, where I stood. "I saw them with my own eyes, I . . ."

He stopped dead in front of me and stared, his eyes searching my face.

"No," he whispered. "Can it be?"

I glared back at him in defiance, unmoving but willing him to know what I had done. In my mind, I sent out a silent scream, and my brother recoiled, staggering backwards.

"What is it, sire?" said the knight.

Arthur looked at him, shaken, as if he had forgotten there were others present. "N-nothing," he said, pulling himself to full height and putting his hands on his hips to conceal the fact they were trembling.

"We'll find them, my lord," said the knight. "I'll send the men out in star formation, scour the whole—"

"No need," Arthur cut him off. "Something strange has happened here this day. These are the traitors we were seeking."

The knights regarded their King with concern. "Th-the stones, sire?" asked one.

Arthur pointed at me. "This here is my sister Morgan, who absconded from the abbey. Traitoress, my would-be usurper and Enemy to the Crown. Can you not see her features set beneath the stone?"

"I cannot say, Your Highness. Certainly it looks like it could be a woman's form."

"I am sure of it," he said. "As sure as I am that she will be no more trouble to the realm."

In swift strides, he left the circle, hoisting himself astride his horse. His men assembled before him and didn't see his slight wince, though I did.

"Mark this day," Arthur declared. "God has bestowed a blessing upon us, and a punishment upon those who stray from the path of goodness. After she committed treason and tried to evade justice, the Lord Almighty has struck my traitorous sister down, turning herself and her followers to stone. Here they will stay for eternity, locked within the prison of their own wrongs. We should thank Him for the glory He has bestowed upon my Crown. Amen!"

"Amen!" repeated the knights. "Praise be to God!"

If my limbs could have shaken in fury then they would have, but even imagining the sensation risked breaking my stone armour. Of course Arthur would see my astonishing feat of magic and assume it was a gift from the Almighty. To his mind, every wonder of the world must pertain somehow to him, proving his power, his rightness in everything and his glory under Heaven. He would never know that the miracle was mine.

After the knights bowed their heads and Arthur led them in a lengthy prayer, they trotted away, leaving us sinners to our stonelike punishment and the Devil.

In my state of fiery indignance, breaking the stone spell was easy. I let every emotion flow through me: the rage, hurt and sorrow; gratitude for our safety; the love for those who stood beside me in loyalty, until the stone facade cracked and shattered, returning my body to me in all its strength and weakness.

Before me, Alys, Tressa, Robin and the others reverted to flesh and blood, stretching their limbs and glancing around as if the world didn't look quite the same. The horses stomped experimentally, tossing their heads, ready to be cantering again. Alys and Tressa checked on the dazed household, offering water and comfort. I went to my horse and ensured Accolon's heart was restored, then rested my head briefly against Phénix's neck, tiredness seeping into my bones.

Alys appeared at my side. "Are you all right? You look grey as . . ."

"Stone?" I said with a wan smile. "I will be. But for now, it's over."

She considered me, a philosophical look in her golden-brown eyes. "Is it ever over, truly, with you?"

I laughed, sudden and involuntary, and a rush of love ran through me that she had managed to invoke levity in us. It was always her greatest gift.

"What of you and King Arthur hereafter?" she asked.

I shook my head. "I don't know. Let's go home."

Yet in truth, I knew where my brother and I stood, with the same certainty that I knew the lake would keep the scabbard in its depths for eternity. I did not know when it had begun, or where it would end, only that I would come for Arthur when he least expected me.

All that was left to me was war.

57

WE WERE NOT far from Fair Guard's boundary when the sun began to sink behind the treetops and the light took on a soft, copperish haze. At the edge of my senses, I felt the shimmer of the manor's ancient spirit: the high valleys, deep woodland and rich green meadows; the rising spring and rivers running like silver; *Llyn Glas*, our blue lake and the willow tree, calling me home.

Just before the final bend, we were interrupted by the sight of two men at the forest's edge, horses tied nearby. One stood fully armoured with a drawn sword, the other kneeling bare-chested and blindfolded, hands bound in front of him. His gold spurs trembled in the fading sun.

Alys leaned towards me. "What do you suppose that's about?"

"What it's *not*," I said wearily, "is any of our business. Men, yet again, addressing their problems with swords, according to rules they made up. I am so very tired of it."

I indicated for the household to ride on. We needed to get back to Fair Guard, withdraw from this world for a good while.

"Is someone there?" called a man's voice. "Wait, please!"

My limbs stiffened, and Accolon's horse stopped in response. I looked back to see the kneeling knight's sightless face upraised. He had been badly beaten: lips split, nose bleeding, a laceration at his hairline already angry with infection. My concern for his injuries was instinctive, but I pushed my sympathy away.

"This man holds me illegally and without cause," he went on. "He has beaten and imprisoned me, and—"

"Without cause!" roared the other, cuffing his captive hard on the side of the head. "I'd advise my ladies to keep riding. This is a personal matter—not for delicate eyes."

His authoritative tone prickled at the back of my neck. "And yet, sir," I said coolly, "you insist upon playing out your private business on a public road."

The prisoner struggled with his bonds, unaware that he knelt beside a gaping, stone-rimmed hole, overgrown with grass—a well, long abandoned. "I am a knight of King Arthur and cannot be treated this way," he declared. "I demand you get word to Camelot."

His voice had taken on its usual self-righteous tone, bringing a torrent of unwelcome memories. If not for this man, Accolon would still be alive at Fair Guard, and I would be there with him, rather than returning with my life obliterated and a near-impossible future ahead of me.

Once again, I made to turn my back upon his doom, when Alys rode up and gasped. *"Iesu mawr!* It's Sir Manassen."

"In the flesh," I said grimly.

At the sound of his name, Sir Manassen stopped struggling. I dismounted and walked over to him, tearing the blindfold off. He hissed in pain from his tenderized face, squinting up at me through a pair of swollen, purple-black eyes. He had been beaten for several days.

"Lady Morgan, *Dieu merci*," he said. "Tell this brute who you are, that I have standing . . . I . . ."

I ignored him and addressed his captor directly. "What has he done?"

"I'm not sure it's for a lady's ears," said the armed man, then gave a resigned shrug. "He's been living in sin with my own wife while I was away. Caught them sleeping side by side. So I tied him up and took him prisoner."

"And beat him bloody for a week?" Alys piped up.

"As is my right," he said tersely. "She was given to me in marriage, not him."

"You vicious cur," Manassen spat. "He treats his wife worse than he has treated me—beats her for the slightest hitch in his mood, keeps her locked away, complains at her every word. Her life with you is a prison."

"Is this true?" I asked.

The man regarded me with offence. "That, too, is my right as a husband. My wife's purpose is to obey me, warm my bed and keep loyalty with only myself and God. How will she learn if I don't punish her?" He gave Manassen a shove. "In any case, there's no excuse for him to defile her."

"I *didn't*," Manassen protested. "She and I met a long time ago, before him. We . . . love one another."

A brittle laugh escaped me. "You *love her?* Sir Manassen, paragon of moral virtue, is caught sleeping with another man's wife, and love is your excuse? The same *ensnarement* you so disapprove of?"

Manassen offered his ferocious look of old. "I did not do this to amuse you, my lady. But if you don't help me, this man of violent appetites will run me through with my own sword and throw me down that well to drown or bleed to death."

"Or be devoured by noxious vermin," remarked his captor.

"You won't dare, blackguard," Manassen snapped. "This woman knows me and will not let me be executed without justice."

The man regarded me with new caution. "Is that true, my lady? You are friend to this knight?"

I glanced down at Sir Manassen's bloody, stubborn face, his kneeling pose saintly in the evening's pink-gold light. Around this time, Accolon would be pouring the first goblet of wine in our chamber, drinking to our health and lacing up my gown with clever fingers, before we joined the household to eat outside. Later, perhaps we would play boules or hear some music, Accolon leading the melody with his lute; then, if the moon was high, he and I might take the long walk up to our lake, to lie under the willow tree, and stay there until dawn.

But Accolon was dead, and I was going back to Fair Guard to sleep alone, all because Sir Manassen rode through our veil of protection and guilted my Gaul into leaving. Whatever Accolon had claimed about knightly oaths, it was for love of his cousin that he had ultimately given his life.

"No," I said. "This knight is no friend of mine."

"Morgan . . ." Alys murmured, as I started towards my horse, but my fury, my hurt, was too great to heed her.

"Lady Morgan, wait!" Manassen called. He struggled to his feet, limping in pursuit. "If you will not help me, then fetch my cousin. You may despise me, but his love has never wavered. Send Accolon to my aid."

His name spoken aloud, and the innocence with which Manassen invoked it, hit my gut like a broadsword. A faint groan came from Tressa, waiting some yards away.

"My God," I said. "You don't know."

"Know what?" he asked.

"Accolon is dead."

"*Dead?*" Sir Manassen collapsed back onto his knees, gasping for breath like I had kicked him in the ribs. "How?"

"Slain by King Arthur himself." The words caught in my throat, raw and terrible. "All because *you* told him to go to Camelot, *you* told him that *your* future was in jeopardy if he didn't save you. We were happy—couldn't you see that? We were *safe*. Yet for your own selfish ends you sent him into the jaws of a dragon."

I pulled my hand back in a half fist to strike him, and Manassen didn't flinch, so willing to take the blow that I dropped it again. He shivered, bare chest rising in gooseflesh.

"I was supposed to be there, to meet him. But I went to her first." He gestured to where his beloved's cuckolded husband stood stunned into silence. "I thought if I was a little late, Accolon would understand."

"He *would* have understood," I said bitterly. "He wouldn't have judged you, scolded you, or dismissed your feelings as weakness. If you had told him the truth, he would have waited to ride out and would still be alive. And *I* would have been in time to settle things with King Arthur—Accolon's freedom, my own, your future. Everything."

Sir Manassen stared at me with pure agony, tears cutting a bloody track down his cheeks.

The man with the sword cleared his throat. "My lady," he said gruffly. "This crime involves my marital property. If you intend to intervene—"

"She will not intervene," Manassen cut in, voice clear as a Matins bell. "Nor should she. I have failed and will take my wrongs to a fool's grave."

Hoisting himself to his feet, he paced to the edge of the well and regarded me steadily. "Accolon was the best knight—the best man—I have ever known, and he loved you. What you had was true and beautiful, and I should have let him be. For what it's worth, Lady Morgan, I'm sorry."

I couldn't speak, so he turned stoically to his executioner. "I'm ready. Do your worst."

"*You* don't get to decide that," growled the man. "But let's get this over with, then I can go home and deal with my wife. If she isn't solicitous enough of my forgiveness, perhaps you'll have *her* company in the well."

"You can rot in Hell," Sir Manassen said through gritted teeth.

The cuckold pushed the swordpoint against his exposed belly. "This is nothing for a woman to see, my lady."

I thought of Accolon's heart in my hands, what it took to snatch his soul away from Camelot. "I've seen and done much worse," I said tiredly. "But you will release this knight into my custody. He is indeed sworn to King Arthur, so you must make your trial petition to the Royal Court."

The man snorted. "What authority do you have to speak for the King?"

"Absolutely none," I replied. "I speak only for myself. You will hand this knight over to me regardless."

"Nay, you are too late. He dies here, now."

I caught a zephyr of wind in my palm, feeling its lively summer force dancing through my fingers. At my request it gathered into a gust, and I sent it forth, whipping the man's sword out of his hand and pushing him onto his back.

"Or, if you prefer," I said, "I can take him by force."

The prone man spat an oath, swiping at my skirts as I passed, but I was already incanting, filling the channelled wind with the power of paralysis. He thudded back against the grass, face fixed in outrage.

Manassen twisted sideways, almost toppling into the well. I caught his arm and dragged him clear, then took out my father's knife and cut the grimy bonds from his wrists. "There," I said. "You're free. Now put your clothes on."

He was halfway through pulling on his boots when he let out an anguished groan, lamenting loudly in French. Accolon's regional curses landed like a spear in my chest.

"Stop it," I snapped. "Get up, and remember that you are alive."

To my surprise, he did, falling silent and lacing his second boot.

"My apologies, Lady Morgan," he said, heaving himself up, "but we both know you should have let him kill me. I'm not worthy of your rescue, or your grace, and will never be able to atone for what has been lost."

A swell of emotion rose in my throat, half sob, half laugh. "Mother of God, you sound just like him."

His brow pinched in question.

"Accolon," I said. "When we first knew one another, all he used to say was he wasn't worthy—of me, of knighthood, of success. It was never true, but to hear it wasn't enough. He had to learn, and he did, because of you." A tear escaped and I let it fall, though my voice held steady. "You found him, saved his life and taught him that he was worthy. He knew how to be happy because of what *you* did, and so we were. Do not let it go to waste."

"But what is left for me?" he said. "To die a noble death in penance—"

"Letting yourself die is too easy," I cut in. "To honour the ones we love, or avenge them, we must survive."

He paused, seeming to consider it; another surprise. "Perhaps you are right, Lady Morgan."

"I know that."

I beckoned to Alys and Tressa, who dismounted and brought across bandages and their saddlebag of remedies. "We will heal what we can on the surface, but the rest you must learn from. Take that wisdom and fix things. Or break them. You choose."

Manassen pointed at his former tormentor. "And him?"

"Him I leave to you. I was never going to let him return to punish his wife. Is it true, what you said?"

"That he is a brute and a scourge upon her? Yes."

"No," I said gently. "Is it true that you love one another?"

He managed one of his typical sharp looks, made less severe by his puffy purple eyes. "I would not lie about such a thing."

"Then you have somewhere to go. At the very least you can carry her the news."

Alys and Tressa began examining his injuries, applying salves and testing bones, finding nothing more serious than cuts and bruises. Once he was bandaged and ready, I picked up his sword and handed it to him, releasing the paralysis cast over his captor.

He ducked his head. "Thank you, Lady Morgan, for saving me. Even if I will never know why."

"I'm not saving you," I said. "I'm giving you the chance to save yourself. It's what Accolon would have wanted."

*

WE HAD NOT ridden much farther when fast hoofbeats sounded behind me and I heard my name called.

"Lady Morgan, *attendez!*"

I slowed as Sir Manassen pulled up alongside Phénix, but did not stop.

"Why?" I said. "I'd like to reach Fair Guard sometime on this endless day."

"This will not take long. Please."

His bruised face bore some semblance of his former seriousness, and I knew what had restored his calm; I had seen him avenge himself on his beloved's husband, executing him swiftly in the manner of a knight. Would that I could so easily find peace.

I sighed and let him hand me down from the saddle. Immediately as I touched the ground, Sir Manassen—dirty, bloody and the most unknightly he had ever been—planted his sword at my feet and knelt before me.

"Lady Morgan, I wish to swear fealty to you. For saving my life, and for the love you bore my cousin."

"What madness is this?" I said, ushering him up. "You are sworn to King Arthur."

"So I will stay, in official terms," he said. "King or not, I cannot keep faith with the man who killed Accolon out of spite. How could I bear such dishonour? I know in my heart where my loyalties lie, and that is with you."

"Don't do this now," I said. "Think on it. Ride to your lady. Marry her, if she will have you."

"I will," he agreed. "But on this I will not change my mind. If *you* will have me, then I will serve you. Sword and spurs."

I opened my mouth, but words were hard to find. I was so tired, with so much to do; some of Fair Guard still didn't know that their beloved knight-errant would never walk our halls or ride his meadow tiltyard ever again. I could barely contemplate any of it.

Sir Manassen rested a hand on his bloody planted sword. "A reckoning must be had, my lady. I see it in your eyes that you will be the one to bring it. Let me help you. Let me *swear* to you."

Slowly, he knelt before me again and looked up, his steel-brown eyes grave and certain, as ferociously determined as we would both have to be.

I reached out and placed my hand on his head. "I accept your loyalty, Sir Manassen of Gaul, as a knight of my household."

He rose and plucked his sword out of the ground, sheathing it with a sigh, as if free of a great weight. "Thank you, Lady Morgan. It means a great deal."

"Why?" I asked.

For the first time in our lives, Sir Manassen of Gaul smiled at me. "It is what Accolon would have wanted."

58

FOR A WHILE I thought I might die.

When Fair Guard's hawthorn-lined entryway came into view; when we passed the stables full of Accolon's beloved horses; when Alys, Tressa, Robin and I walked together along the river towards the house and beheld the turret and the birch tree, all looking the same but irrevocably changed now, every window full of shadow and silence. When I saw the edges of his tiltyard, tinted by the deep-blue dusk, I felt I had reached my end in so many ways.

Without Accolon, I would always be adrift; no matter what I did, the current of my grief would drag my broken, unresisting soul beneath the riptide until I was nothing but a shipwreck, disintegrating in the dark depths.

But as the sun rose and set through the decaying summer, a crisp and painfully beautiful autumn and the wintry death of the year; as the mourning household honoured their champion knight by returning to laughter and music and the day's familiar rhythms, still I lived. Suffering was not exquisite, my hours spent both tormented and nourished by memories in a dizzying whirl, but my passion and despair were nevertheless a reminder that Accolon would want me to keep on. He had taught me how to swim, how to survive, after all.

His heart I had kept in the blue kerchief, turned back into stone so it would not decay as my heartbreak weathered me. To lay him to rest under our willow tree was his wish, and every day I took the silk bundle from the silver box in my study and imagined making the long walk up to the lake, returning the heart to delicate flesh and committing him to the earth. And every day, I could not bear to let him go.

Then, near the end of March, I awoke to a bright, lively morning that I soon realized was the day of my birth, and the equinox. When I went to the turret and drew out the silver box, I knew, as sure as the darkness could be felt in perfect balance with the light, that the time was right.

I had not been to our lake since my last time with Accolon, in the hazy summer days before he left for Camelot, when we swam and laughed despite ourselves, and loved beneath the willow tree in a desperate defiance of his leaving. In his honour, the lake had remained unchanged in its beauty, morning light dancing off its surface like a shower of stars.

It took no time at all to ask the earth to shift and make a hole at the foot of the willow trunk, large enough for a solitary heart. Once it was done, I knelt and unfolded the Parisian blue silk, taking the solid weight into my hands. My second enchantment had made the stone smooth and pale, lightly streaked with veins, more a marble sculpture than the rough grey rocks I had made of us in the forest.

I held the heart to my chest with a tenderness so deep, my transformation of the stone back into cool, sleek muscle came with a sudden bolt of resistance to what I must do next. Instead of placing it in the ground, I curved my body around the renewed heart, as if hoping it would join with my own and reside there for all eternity.

Then I felt it: a light tingling through the bones of my hands and up through my limbs, manifesting as pinpricks of light inside my mind, like a spray of dew shaken from a leaf. A faint, high sound rang beneath my skin, vague and ethereal, chiming far away.

I had known this feeling before, in the presence of birds hours, days and weeks dead, and in a wild white hart, torn to shreds in violent death, until it lived again. A flutter, a silvery essence, a choral note; a melody darting through Accolon's heart, singing of a life once lived, and something else: potential.

The impossibility of his heartsong rocked through my being. In Camelot's cathedral, I had embraced him, laid my head on him, put my hands to his chest to split mail and bone and heard nothing. But it had been years since I had sought the sensation, or remembered such a thing existed. Even if I had, in St. Stephen's, amidst the stunned, blood-roaring fury of my despair, I could not have heard such a subtle whisper without hours of calm. I could only weep and disbelieve, and take of him what I could before they came to take me.

Now I had peace and time to listen, the defiant stillness of Accolon's lake a silent sanctuary to hear the truth—the undying traces of his existence, the threads of life running through his heart like a cloud's silver lining. Accolon was dead, but he was not yet gone, and the thought sparked in my core, fiery with hope.

Mon coeur, Accolon had always called me—*my heart*, the red-chambered centre of the soul, upon which all life was written. His blood and bones and skin were not what made him, and all could be formed again, if my mind and skills could be pushed beyond miracles.

Everything I needed, I could find, and the rest I held within me, fuelled by the twin powers of rage and love, which would be enough: to save Accolon, save myself, and bring us back to one another.

*

BY NOON, THE day was a glorious one, the sky a lively blue and scudded with wisps of cloud, a clear, pale sun just warm enough to counter the fresh breeze. The air smelled of water and greenery, of blossom about to bud—of spring, and new life.

I had spent the rest of the morning in my study, rereading my secret notes from Merlin's and the remembered knowledge I had recorded since: lists of formulae; healing theory and techniques; ancient words on the hidden qualities of the body; forbidden ideas on how to speak the language of death, and in doing so, defy it.

By the time Alys found me, I was out on the balcony, Accolon's heart in my hands, stone again in its box, observing the view from on high. The home I had chosen stretched out before me, its forests and fields ready to burst into colour once more. Across the fast-running river, the jousting meadow lay lush and overgrown, in need of care but not forgotten.

"I must have the tiltyard cut back," I said, as she stood beside me. "Restore the boundaries and the quintain, so Robin can train on it again. It should be put to good use."

"I agree," she said. "I'll make arrangements." She paused for a long moment, then released an audible breath. "I thought you were up at the lake."

"I was."

She glanced at the silver box. "Oh, Morgan, it's all right that you couldn't bear it. There will be other days."

I kept my eyes on the tiltyard. "It's not what you think, this time. The lake gave me what I needed. The water, this day, the harmony between light and dark—my future became clear. I dug the hole, unfroze the heart, was ready to do what is expected, and then I heard it—the truth, the purpose of all of this. Right away, I knew what needed to be done."

I opened the box and drew the marble heart out of its blue silk, cupped in my two hands. "I'm not meant to let him go, Alys. I have the skills, the power, the ability to learn. I'm going to bring Accolon back."

Alys stood very still, gazing at me with a serene, half-smiling acceptance that was entirely her, but I had not expected.

"Heart theory and healing," she said. "Knowledge and magic. It has been within you all along."

I nodded calmly, though my own heart soared at her instant understanding. "But it will take much more than me to be certain of success. More books, more time, more study. I can hone this power, master it enough to make the whole world tremble, but to recreate a person from just a heart, I need something else, more powerful than anything I could create in a lifetime. An object that makes the healing power of Excalibur's scabbard look like battle-field stitching. To return Accolon to me whole, I need the Shroud of Tithonus."

"How will you get it?" Alys asked.

"I don't know for certain where it is," I said. "But there is only one place to start looking. I must go to Merlin's."

*

WHEN WE RETURNED to the study, Tressa was there, sitting at the scribe's desk and rifling through a pot of quills. Alys went to her side and kissed her, taking up the chosen ink bottle and pouring it into her inkwell.

Sir Manassen entered, bowing at the knee, providing a vague amusement that I hadn't felt for a long time. I ushered him up and let him kiss my hand, then moved to the new chair behind my desk, a tall and heavy seat, pale beech wood carved with a hundred different birds. A pair of chiselled peregrines stood sentry on either side of the chair back, and as I sat, two live magpies flew in and alighted between them with casual belonging.

I laughed at Sir Manassen's look of surprise. "Lady Alys says I shouldn't encourage them," I explained.

"But they are far too clever to listen to reason," Alys said wryly.

Sir Manassen inclined his head, almost smiling. "It seems somewhat apt."

"How have you been?" I asked him. "Did you recover comfortably from your misadventure by the well?"

"I did, my lady. The salves that Lady Alys sent were very helpful. My now wife is pleased to have me at full strength, and sends her thanks."

"Are you happy now, the two of you?" I said.

"We are, my lady. Married life suits me very well."

His face softened in a way I had never seen, and his obvious contentment struck bittersweet in my chest, a chord of joy and grief that I could not afford to feel just then, when there was so much to be done.

"Good," I said briskly. "I must meet her soon. We will dine."

"That would please us both," Sir Manassen said. "But first, I have received official notification of the Royal Court's return to Camelot for Eastertide, and I am expected to attend. It is time."

I sighed, resting my palms on the desk in front of me and regarding him directly. "Are you certain you want to do this? You have sworn me no official oath. I can still release you from your promise and restore your fealty to King Arthur. No one will know."

Sir Manassen's face returned to its stonelike determination. "Lady Morgan, the oath I took to you was the most serious of my life. The debt of gratitude and honour I owe to you is eternal, and I will spend my remaining years serving its cause. Not only for Accolon, but because when you should have walked away, you saved my life."

"I am grateful for your faith, Sir Manassen," I said. "But you are a forthright and honourable man, and what we are about to embark upon pushes many boundaries. There will be subterfuge, spying, pretence. What you bring to me, I will use for ill purpose. I can still accept your loyalty and not ask you to do this."

"My lady," he said sternly. "It is a boon no one in Camelot knows I serve you. My loyalty is my own business, as it was King Arthur's business to kill my honourable cousin for no better reason than to punish his own sister. I cannot keep faith with such a man. I wished to join his court because his way was meant to be better—based on justice and fairness, not vengeance and executive power. Everything Camelot stands for is a lie."

"The greatest lie," I said. "A gleaming Crown, a glorious reign, a glittering castle rotten from within. If I can, I intend to expose that lie, and bring Arthur's great golden edifice crashing down. I am no longer part of their world, and in exile I am set free. I will become exactly what Camelot says I am, and rain chaos upon their heads."

The knight gave a solemn nod. "Then command me, my lady. What you wish will be done."

"Very well, Sir Manassen." I stood up from the chair, magpies ruffling their feathers behind me. "You will carry a message to court, under the auspices of protecting your King, which I will write and sign as proof, and you will speak aloud. I have been too quiet for far too long. Let Arthur and Camelot hear my voice."

I looked at Tressa, already waiting with parchment before her, quill poised.

"Where I will start is with the truth," I said, and she began writing. "I am an adulteress, a woman of ambition and cunning, and a sorceress in possession of great knowledge and exceptional powers. I have both given and taken, fixed and broken, wronged and been wronged, and never in my life have I stopped fighting for the freedom that is rightfully mine. For all this, I am not sorry. I have been a despairing girl, a reluctant queen, a firebrand wife, a sister in need, a thwarted mother, an unrepentant lover, and have chosen defiance against this realm and its attempts to cage me. But I am not a traitoress, neither to King Arthur nor the Crown of All Britain.

"I loved a good man, Sir Accolon of Gaul, who was valiant, honourable and true, and did not deserve his death at King Arthur's hand.

Such an act was selfish, cruel and unjust, and a scourge of shame against the High King. I am not guilty of treason, but I will have vengeance upon those who brought about my ruin, and in doing so caused the death of the man I loved better than this entire godforsaken world.

"For all of this, I will work to destroy the castle of lies and artifice that Camelot represents. Every gossiping hypocrisy of the court, I will expose it; every foot Queen Guinevere puts wrong, I will shine upon her an unforgiving light. And for my self-righteous, murderous brother, I will save my closest scrutiny—every ideal, every rule he spouts forth that he secretly ignores when it does not serve his purpose, he will feel my sharp gaze and hear my voice in his inconstant mind, calling him the deceiver he is. The loyal sister who once loved him is now a Fury reborn. King Arthur will feel my wrath and remember me, and know what it is to have Morgan as an enemy."

I closed my eyes and let out a long breath, and it was as if the whole room, the building, the land beyond within the silver-threaded veil of my protection, exhaled with me.

"Is it finished?" Tressa asked.

"Yes," I said. "And it has just begun. All I must do is sign it."

Alys received the paper from Tressa's desk and brought it to my waiting hand.

I reached across my desk and picked up a shining, blue-black quill, a gift one of the magpies had left me in the final, aching days of last summer, as they shed their feathers and were remade. Steeping the nib in ink, I read the letter, then marked it with three words, encompassing my sense of self, my enduring presence, all that I had become.

I lifted the paper and blew on the ink, taking one last glance at what I had done. It looked and felt entirely right.

Sir Manassen took the parchment from me with an undaunted bow. "Any concluding words, my lady?"

"Yes," I said. "Tell them, I am, and will remain, Morgan le Fay."

ACKNOWLEDGEMENTS

As always, my first and deepest thanks go to my agent, Marina de Pass, for being such a fantastic advocate for my work and writing career, and for helping me navigate my debut year while writing the "Difficult Second Book." Your support, faith and advice give me strength whenever things start to feel impossible.

Many thanks are also due to my editors for their enthusiasm, advice and continuing belief in my work: Jenny Parrott and Imogen Papworth, for their diligence and care in helping me shape this book into what I knew it could be, and Amanda Ferreira, for being my champion across the Atlantic.

I owe a huge debt of gratitude to the publishing teams who work so hard to get books out into the world in all their forms. Special thanks to Matilda Warner for being the best publicist an author could hope for, and the rest of the brilliant Magpie team: Lucy Cooper, Mary Hawkins, Paul Nash, Laura McFarlane, Francesca Dawes, Julian Ball, Ben Summers, Hayley Warnham, Anne Bihan, Beth Marshall Brown and Mark Rusher. Extended thanks to everyone at Oneworld Publications for always being so welcoming, and to Juliet Mabey for baking me such a fantastic cake. Thanks to Nicola Wall and the production team at Audible for bringing Morgan to life so beautifully in audio. Thanks also to Anais Loewen-Young, Erin Bonner, Bruce Mason and everyone at Penguin Random House Canada for getting

Morgan into the hands of her North American readers. I am also indebted to Francine Brody for her keen eye and skill for detail. My life as an author could not happen without you all.

One of the most wonderful things about becoming an author has been the opportunity to meet so many book lovers and fellow writers, both online and in person. A massive thank you to all of the authors, bookshops, booksellers, bloggers, reviewers and readers for supporting my debut novel and the continuing enthusiasm for my future books. You are all stars, and I've loved being part of such a vibrant, friendly and dedicated community.

A particular thank you is again due to my critique partner and friend, Jess Lawrence, for the chats, accountability and generally keeping me going as I faced the challenge of my second book. You will never know how many times your wit, patience and kindness were my sanity.

Many thanks to my family for reading my books with excitement and enthusiasm, without me even having to force you into it. And to Carly especially, for wanting to collect every version. Cousin, I am honoured.

Finally, I owe more gratitude than I can express to my son Milo and my husband Jason, who make everything possible. Your presence, pride and unconditional love have been my fuel, and this book could not have been written without you. Thank you.

SOPHIE KEETCH has a BA in English Literature from Cardiff University, which included the study of Arthurian legend. Her debut trilogy is a feminist retelling of the story of sorceress Morgan Le Fay. The first book, *Morgan Is My Name*, was a #1 Audible bestseller and one of *Paste Magazine's* Best Books of 2023. The audiobook, narrated by Oscar-nominated actress Vanessa Kirby, was a *Times* Audiobook of the Week.

Sophie is Welsh and lives with her husband and son in South Wales.